THE CAPTIVE RISING

Book Three In The Captive Series

LK MAGILL

First Hale Press

The Captive Rising/ LK Magill – 1st ed.

Ebook ISBN 978-1-950928-08-8

Paperback ISBN 978-1-950928-09-5

Hardcover ISBN 978-1-950928-10-1

DEDICATION

To my tribe... and the One above.

ACKNOWLEDGMENTS

You may have noticed that the writing style in this book differs (just a bit) from the first two in the series. And the reason for that is simple… as a writer I have grown.

Between completing The Captive Missing and starting The Captive Rising, I wrote another 3.75 novels (yes… there's an unfinished novel lurking around my computer… and no, you don't know anything about that one, wink wink).

So that being said, I hope you really enjoy The Captive Rising. This is Gabe and Bee's story with some appearances by Val, Jason and Charlie (because they just couldn't be denied).

Beta readers, beta readers, beta readers… you guys are awesome. Sara Mae and Emily - I truly appreciate your input and willingness to take time out of your busy schedules to read/discuss with me.

Author Lindsay Bergman! Girl, our writer's retreat was amazing. I love being able to share our creative journey even though we write in such different genres. You rock. (When can we escape again?)

CHAPTER 1

Gabe

His palms were sweating now, the line along his brow, too. But it wasn't hot in the SUV. Nope. It was his nerves. His fucking nerves clutched at him, they wouldn't let go.

Swallowing, Gabe widened his eyes. He used to be better at this.

Outside the SUV's window, rain coated the highway. He could hear the drops falling, echoing against the metal roof, splattering across the hood and doors. It was a downpour. If the temperature in New York dipped just a few more degrees, then they might even get a flurry of snow.

Music from the speakers pumped with the violent under-tones of a rap song. The Cambric driver bobbed his head in time with the beat, murmuring the slurred words quickly under his breath. An oversized guard was sitting shotgun and with a huff of disgust, he leaned up to the radio and switched the station.

"Hey man, what the hell?" The driver's hand shot out to change it back.

"I don't get paid enough to listen to that shit," the guard growled.

"Quiet," Shane spat. One word from him had both of the men falling silent.

Gabe's chest tightened. The asshole himself was seated in the back, right beside Gabe. He was wearing a gray suit and a lavender tie.

Stealing a quick glance at the prick, Gabe's teeth ground together inside of his head. They hadn't seen one another in years. Shane's face sported a short beard now. It was blonde, the color of his thinning hair. Even with those blue eyes of his locked on his cell phone, he still managed to look smug.

Evil piece of shit. *What did you do with Val? Where the hell is she?*

The questions pounded around like a drum beat inside Gabe's head. He was still reeling from the shock of it all. Their exchange at the courthouse had not gone as planned. Not even close.

Squeezing his eyes shut, Gabe reached up reflexively to loosen his own tie. It suddenly felt too tight around his neck so he tugged at the navy-blue knot with one finger.

Inhaling deeply, he paused before letting loose a shaky breath. The meeting today kept flashing through his mind. He couldn't wipe it away.

Jason had been tense, his shoulders tight beneath his black suit jacket. Gabe had been walking next to him, also wearing black, the color of mourning. It had seemed fitting that they both chose it.

"You sure you want to do this?" Jason tugged at Gabe's

elbow, pulling him to a stop in the crowded hallway of the courthouse.

All around them, other people had continued to cruise by. Lawyers, plaintiffs, defendants, court clerks, janitors, secretaries, everyone. Jason's voice had dropped to a whisper, his arctic blue eyes zeroing in on Gabe.

Sucking in a breath, Gabe glanced down at the guy's hand. He was fidgeting with that silver wedding band of his. The ring Val had given to him. Gabe nodded his head as if to reassure himself that he was doing the right thing, then he glanced away.

"Yeah," he said quietly. "I'm sure."

"We can try to find another way…" Jason's voice wavered.

"No," Gabe cut him off. "This is the only sure way, and you know it."

Giving his head a quick shake now, Gabe opened his eyes. *The only sure way.* Hah. Neither of them had known how wrong they could possibly be.

"Don't get undressed yet, lover boy," Shane interrupted Gabe's thoughts as he glanced at the gold Rolex on his wrist. "We're almost there."

Gabe's insides flipped then, and he fought the flash of rage that surged through him at the sound of Shane's voice. Shit, he wanted to ruin the prick. He wanted to slam the guy's head against the window glass over and over until it shattered.

Shane had gone back on his end of the deal. He was supposed to give Val back. He was supposed to set Val free and stop fighting the court case over Jace. In exchange for those two things, Gabe had agreed to turn himself back over to Cambric.

The Agency would own him once more, but his conscience would be clear.

No more listening to Jace cry for his mommy at night. No more killing a bottle of Gin with Jason just to get the guy to stop asking about Cambric. He'd wanted to know about the breeding program, and Ben, and what you had to do to pass training.

Shit. Gabe just didn't have the heart to tell him, so he'd agreed to the deal. Easy right? Nope, like all things with Cambric, there was a catch.

Shane lost Val. She disappeared. The asshole had announced that tidy little fact the moment Jason and Gabe had settled into the meeting room at the courthouse.

Val was missing.

And to top it all off… if Gabe had changed his mind and decided *not* to turn himself in, then Cambric would keep pursuing Jace. Not only would they continue to fight the court case, but they'd also produce evidence that this illegal backroom deal was proposed by Jason himself. Which of course, was true.

And that wasn't even the sucker punch. Ready for it? Agent John *I'm A Complete Asshole* Finn was there to confirm it.

He *knew*.

Shane had contacted the FBI Agent the week before and had him do an internal investigation, which turned up (surprise, surprise) nothing. Finn knew that Cambric no longer had Val, and he hadn't told them.

And sure, Finn had tried to talk Gabe out of turning himself in, but he hadn't explained *why*. He'd kept his mouth shut. He'd betrayed them. Not for the first time, Gabe reminded himself, and released a slow breath through his nostrils.

Grumbling under his breath, the Cambric driver checked his blind spot before changing lanes. The SUV rocked with the abrupt movement as Gabe focused his attention out the rear window. Darkness was falling all around them now, as the rain continued to pelt down.

Clearing his throat, Shane stared pointedly at the side of Gabe's head. Gabe could feel the implication. Shane's order had yet to be obeyed.

Jaw ticking, Gabe worked to tighten his tie once more. Securing it as instructed, he smoothed his slick palms down the front of his jacket before returning them demurely to his sides.

He couldn't hit Shane.

He couldn't hit a free man, no matter how badly he craved it. It was against the law, not to mention he was a little outnumbered. Three to one to be exact.

Nope. Gabe would have to content himself with the knowledge that Jason had wrecked that smug face a few months ago. He would have to learn once more to live in dreams that danced inside his own head.

As the driver merged off the freeway, water splashed up from puddles that were steadily forming in low spots on the asphalt. Muddy rain coated the passenger side window for a moment before sliding slowly away.

Gabe blinked at the maze of roads and humanity rolling by. This wasn't the way to Cambric. They should still be driving north.

"Where are we?" The question jumped from his mouth

before he even thought about it. Four years as a free man would do that to you.

Shane's quick bark of laughter filled the small space. There was no way he would be answering to a captive. Involuntarily, Gabe's hands clenched themselves into fists. He had to work hard to release them.

All this time, Gabe had assumed he would be returning to The Agency's property in upstate. He figured he would be readmitted through intake, the way Val had been. And he figured he was pretty well prepared for that now, since it was the one thing Gabe had wanted out of Agent Finn... prior to his betrayal and all that.

Where was intake located? What had he seen them do to Val? Who had been there?

Of all the places Gabe had been inside Cambric, intake had never been one of them. It was an unknown that he'd wanted to learn about in an attempt to mentally prepare for it. The worst thing a male D2 could show at Cambric was fear.

But it had been a battle to get the information from Agent Finn. Gabe recalled their heated conversation. Jason was pissed, having been locked out of the room. It was just the two of them then, only Finn and Gabe. That's when the former had tried like hell to talk Gabe out of turning himself in.

Trust me, he'd said. *Don't go back in. Please, don't do it.*

Looking back now, Gabe wondered how long Agent Finn had known the truth. Those bastards at Cambric didn't have Val. She was dead and buried somewhere, or worse, alive and in the possession of some rich psycho.

Gabe tried to wipe the dread from his thoughts. He tried like hell not to feel like his sacrifice was for nothing. After all, they still had the court case. Cambric folded just like they were supposed to and the Judge had ruled in Jace's favor.

Val's boy was now forever free, and other captives would someday be able to use his case to gain their freedom, too. At least Gabe hoped so.

Rocking to the left, Gabe's shoulder tapped against the passenger window as the SUV took a sharp right turn and then another left before merging onto a narrow two lane highway. Forest surrounded them, swallowing up the view on either side of the road. It was pitch black outside now, and the rain continued to pour down.

Occasionally, headlights approached them from the oncoming lane. Gabe held his eyes open as long as he could before he was forced to blink or look away. He liked the pain. He wanted to hurt.

He wanted to *do* something, to have some sort of control. Hell, he was half-tempted to slam his own head against the window glass right now.

Val was probably dead, or being hurt. And it was all his fault. His. Fault.

If he'd just gone back to Cambric to begin with, none of this would have happened. Jace would still have his mommy. Jason would still have his wife. And Bee...

God, the thought of her made Gabe's heart want to explode.

What would she do when she found out her best friend was missing? As if Gabe leaving her like that hadn't been bad enough, now she wouldn't have Val either.

If he closed his eyes, he could still see Bee standing on their dock in the Maldives, her tear-stained cheeks, her red-rimmed eyes. The baby-blue dress she'd been wearing had picked up in the breeze, whipping around her tanned thighs as he'd turned the boat motor over and driven away.

Shit.

Gabe's eyes shot open now, and he bit hard on the inside of his cheek. So, what prevented him from head-butting the glass until he blacked out? Well, the answer was pretty simple really. It was hope. The most dangerous, toxic and addictive drug that any captive could possess.

Hope that Val was alive. Hope that the answers of what had happened to her lay somewhere inside of Cambric. Somewhere that Gabe was sure he would eventually end up.

It might take him months, maybe even years, but he would find out the truth. He would keep himself in check, if for nothing other than that.

The SUV slowed. An enormous razor-wire fence shot up before them and behind it stretched a collection of brick and concrete buildings that towered under metal light poles. *What is this place?*

Gabe's mouth hung open slightly. The sweat on his brow dried up. Suddenly, he was parched. His breath came out hot and dry.

Pulling to a stop alongside a guard shack, the SUV shifted into park. A thin man in a rainproof trench coat walked forward before leaning down to lay his wrists just inside the open driver side window. Water dripped from his dark cap. The gold emblem that decorated its peaked front was familiar.

He was law enforcement of some sort, Gabe realized. He was a prison guard.

Gabe's lungs shriveled in his chest. He began to wheeze. Why the hell were they at a prison? Were they going to kill him? Torture him?

If he hadn't already sweated every drop of moisture out of his body, Gabe felt certain he would've pissed himself.

"It's well after visiting hours," the guard remarked.

"We hoped an exception could be made." The driver handed over a thick envelope. Rain pattered on the pavement.

Making slow work of opening the envelope, the guard thumbed through the stack of neat greenish bills. Gabe could almost smell the new mint off the money. He had felt the crispness of cash run against his fingers in his free life, so much cash. But what had his success bought him in the end? He still hadn't been able to avoid the inevitability of this path.

The guard said nothing. Tucking the soggy white envelope into his coat pocket, he simply backed away.

Up ahead, the imposing chainlink gate rolled slowly to the right and the SUV navigated through it. Darkened buildings fanned out all around them. Gabe squeezed his eyes shut, leaning back into the leather of the carseat.

He couldn't breathe. He couldn't breathe.

His heart was screaming at him, thumping harder and harder. His fingers gripped impulsively at the seatbelt where it crossed his lap. His brain was swimming. Don't pass out. Don't… pass…

His head must have lolled to one side because the punch from Shane came hard against the center of his chest. Gabe coughed, then choked in air. His lungs began to work again and he fought the swirling feeling that caused darkness to flicker in his mind.

"Don't faint on me, you delicate piece of shit," Shane spat out the words, before shoving a selection of tiny pills into Gabe's palm.

Raising his eyebrows in surprise, Gabe blinked down at

the familiar drugs. Red to get you high and blue for... well, to get you hard.

What the...?

Cold, sick, overwhelming dread tipped itself into Gabe's bloodstream and moved fast to overtake him. They weren't going to leave him here as a prisoner. They weren't going to put a bullet in his head and bury him out back.

This was a client trip.

Holy shit. They wanted him to fuck someone at this prison.

"We don't have all night, lover boy." Shane forced an open water bottle into Gabe's other hand. "She doesn't like to wait. You know that."

"*She?*" Gabe's whisper caught on his lips as his hands began to shake.

"Yeah, she." Shane smiled wryly, enjoying every second of this sort of torture. "You're owner, Sharon. You know, the one you stabbed in the back... she misses you."

CHAPTER 2

Bee

Ugh. Why'd he have to be so hot?

Bee nibbled at the pencil she held carefully between her lips and glanced down at her tiny square of a desk. It's not like his good looks were anything new, but at least when they'd been kids together she hadn't noticed. Now though...

Gabe sauntered up the narrow aisle in their shared classroom with that perfect smile fixed on that handsome face of his before choosing the empty seat directly behind her. Again.

Val gave him an easy wave and Charlie slapped at his shoulder, but Bee only swallowed and tried not to let the stiffness she felt show in her shoulders.

All of the female eyes in their classroom had tracked his progress and she could feel their disappointment ripple at his choice of seats. And that was a lot of disappointment considering there were seventeen girls and only two guys. Gabe and Charlie. That was it.

This permanent placement opportunity had seemed like a Godsend right before those two had walked through the classroom door three weeks ago. It was hard enough submitting to her D2 training without Hot and Hotter observing every little detail.

Bee hated performing. She hated pretending.

But if she could graduate with permanent placement status, then she would only be required to fake it with one client. Just one. Not twenty-one. Or a hundred and one. None of whom she got to pick out. None of whom she got to choose. It irked her somewhere deep down in her soul, the submission.

"Hey," Gabe whispered the word so close to her, that Bee could feel his breath on the back of her neck. It sent goosebumps to run down her arms and tingle up her spine.

Sucking in a breath, she gave her head a little shake. Nope. She was not going down like this. No way. No one ruffled her.

No one.

Not even the Greek god with the golden hair and dancing brown eyes currently sitting behind her.

"I know you can hear me," Gabe's whispering continued and Bee felt a gentle tugging on the ends of her long chestnut hair.

Whipping around in her seat to face him, Bee glared as his fingers released the tendril he'd been twirling. At her angry stare, Gabe's smile only widened.

"What do you want?" Bee hissed. Their instructor would be walking in at any moment.

"I want you to stop ignoring me." Gabe drummed his now empty fingers on his own desk. "You act like we didn't grow up together. It's rude."

"You think I'm rude?" Bee was incredulous as Val cleared her throat and Charlie ducked his head. They were listening.

"Yeah." Gabe had the nerve to bite at that sexy bottom lip of his before leaning casually back in his seat. "You are rude, Bee Bee."

"Don't." Bee sucked in a breath before resuming. "Call me that."

"No?" Gabe's eyebrows raised now and he huffed a quick laugh. "You liked it just fine when we were seven."

"Well if you hadn't noticed, we aren't seven anymore," Bee spat. "And you may think that you're Cambric's gift to women, but not everyone here agrees, Gabriel. So stop trying to get me in trouble and keep those hands to yourself."

Gabe's eyes flashed at the use of his full name. He hated it just as much as she hated his nickname for her. She could hardly remember a time on that playground when he wasn't teasing her or pulling her hair. Come to think of it, there wasn't much difference now, was there?

Whirling back around in her seat, Bee had just enough time to clear her expression and draw in a breath. In the next moment, Ms. King strode into class on those three inch pointy heels of hers. If she'd caught Bee speaking out of turn again, it would have spelled trouble.

Not that Bee wasn't used to being in trouble. She was actually pretty freaking great at it. Seemed like her own big mouth was forever spewing out unacceptable opinions. Which inevitably were against Agency rhetoric and therefore punished.

The other girls rarely experienced that problem. The smart mouth. The sassy talk. Val absolutely never talked back, and so when Bee spoke out of turn or hesitated to complete a task, her non-conformity stuck out all the more. After all, she and her sister looked just alike.

But Bee was working on it. She'd promised herself when she'd been given this opportunity to be permanent placement that she'd be perfectly behaved. Well... better behaved at least. Yeah, way better.

"Oh, I've noticed," Gabe mumbled.

Lifting her chin, Bee sat up straighter in her seat and crossed one *slender leg over the other beneath her desk. Nope, she thought, she was not responding.*

All the while, Ms. King was facing away from them, scratching an endless stream of words across the smooth black chalkboard. She was old school. Blackboard, erasers, chalk, pencils, lined paper, cursive hand-writing, corporal punishment. Yep, Ms. King was very, very old school.

Shifting around in her seat, Bee bobbed her right leg before uncrossing it, then re-crossing it. She stared at the sway of Ms. King's silver-blonde hair. Then she studied the boring words on the boring board before closing her eyes.

Why? Why did she care? She was always the girl that took the bait. Always.

"Noticed what?" Bee whispered finally, ducking her head so that no one could see her lips moving.

Gabe's desk creaked. He was leaning towards her. She could practically feel the energy from his body pressing closer to hers.

"I've noticed that we aren't seven anymore," Gabe murmured. "And the thing is, Bee Bee... I think that you've noticed, too."

Opening her eyes in her darkened hotel room, Bee blinked blearily at her demanding phone. The freaking thing kept ringing, and ringing, and ringing. Sucking in a ragged breath, she swiped it off the nightstand next to her King-sized bed, and sent it crashing to the floor.

Damn, she thought. How is it possible that that delicate little box hadn't shattered already?

Rolling out of the expensive sheets, she stumbled over on unsteady legs and dropped to her knees on the plush carpet. Yep. Her phone just kept right on howling, not a crack in it.

Val's name and number filled the screen. Bee huffed a breath. She'd finally gotten a cell phone, after everything that had gone down, and now Bee's *former* friend would not stop calling.

Well, too little too late.

Angrily, Bee fumbled for the tiny side button, holding it down until the entire phone switched off. Then shoving up to her feet, she swayed slightly as the blood rushed from her head. She was still drunk. *Crap.*

Stumbling forward, Bee caught herself on the edge of the mattress and sat heavily. Her eyes came to rest on the half empty bottle of Vodka where her phone had been only moments before. Good thing she hadn't knocked that particular item off the nightstand. Wasted Vodka was not an option these days.

It was necessary to her, the alcohol was, as necessary as breathing. Because those memories of Gabe? God, they just kept coming didn't they? Bee. Saw. Him. Everywhere.

She saw him at Cambric, back in the day. Val and Charlie, too. When they were all so young. Too young and too dumb and too naive in so many ways.

But what did it all matter now? Gabe was gone. He'd given himself back to The Agency of his own free will... with *lots* of help from Jason, the entitled jerk.

And sure, Bee knew Gabe's reasons. He had screamed them at her over and over in the Maldives, but she'd just screamed right back. Then the screaming had turned to begging, then the begging to crying, then the crying to kissing, until finally there was nothing left to say.

So it was done. Gabe went back to Cambric and Val was free.

Not that Bee didn't still love her best friend, she did. And it wasn't that she didn't want Jace to have his mommy back. It was just... *why* couldn't they have waited until the court case was resolved? Was it so wrong for Bee to want Gabe to be free, too?

But Gabe had refused to listen to reason, and Jason right along with him. They couldn't trust the process, they said. They couldn't trust that the judge would find in their favor. They *had* to manipulate the system. They *had* to make their little backroom deals.

So now there was nothing left to do. It was over. Gabe and Bee were over.

Except, the memories were just so damn haunting. Even now, Gabe's face would not leave her alone. Those golden curls? That pearly white smile? And the sound of his voice? She could *hear* him inside of her head. Teasing. Taunting.

Bee's chest squeezed tighter and tighter. It hurt. God, it just hurt so bad.

She couldn't handle it. She couldn't handle living in their home or sleeping in their bed or being anywhere near the ocean, in fact. And that's why she'd left the Maldives. To escape Gabe. Because even though his body was gone forever, Bee saw him everywhere.

And every time Val called, Bee saw Gabe.

And every time Jason called, Bee saw Gabe.

And every time her mom reached out, or her dad passed her money, or the press called for an interview... Bee. Saw. Gabe.

It was just like back at Cambric, with the walls closing in and a client prep meeting on her calendar. There was only one way to endure. There was only one way to get that release, that escape. And since Bee absolutely refused to get hooked back on the pills, she'd opted for the next best thing. Alcohol.

With a shrug, Bee wrapped her perfectly manicured nails around the long neck of the Vodka bottle and brought it to her lips. No need to twist off the cap, it was already long gone.

CHAPTER 3

Gabe

Inhaling, Gabe took in the all too familiar scent of a sterile cement room. When he went to roll over, he let loose a low groan. He hurt. Every muscle in his body was aching.

Flopping onto his back, he raised his hands to the bridge of his nose and winced at the contact. He had two blacks eyes, he could feel it. That's what happens when your face meets the pavement, more than once.

"You look like shit." The male voice sounded strange, like it was coming through a speaker.

Carefully, Gabe peeled one eye open and discovered that he could, in fact, still see. That's when reality hit him. He was lying on a thin mattress in the corner of a narrow gray room. No blanket, no pillow, no nothing.

He was back at Cambric. In Isolation.

"I'm surprised they got your face," the voice again. "That was a big no no once upon a time."

"Charlie," Gabe exhaled the word as he stared through the single glass partition that separated their rooms.

"Hey, Gabe." Charlie quirked a small smile. "I think I'm finally prettier than you."

"Unlikely," Gabe grunted.

Struggling to sit up, he was forced to stop and place his head between his knees. The room was spinning. He was on a carousel ride, and he could not get off.

Lips parting, Gabe worked to slow down his breathing. Nice and easy. He didn't want to pass out again.

The last thing that he really recalled was the parking lot of Sharon's prison. He'd been sitting in the backseat of that SUV, with the rain pounding down all around them and Shane shoving meds in his mouth.

And suddenly… he'd snapped. A lifetime of fear and training and submitting had gone up in smoke. He just couldn't do it. Not anymore. Gabe couldn't fucking swallow one more second of captive life. Figuratively and literally.

He'd spit the pills out in Shane's face, then he'd gone down swinging. Four years on the outside had taken their toll and there was no way in hell that he was marching into that prison to service Sharon Baine. Not willingly.

What happened next was a blur. His fist connected with Shane's throat. It felt gooooood. He could still hear the slight gurgling sound in his head. He liked it.

But by then the driver had gotten out and ripped open the rear door. The Cambric guard that had been riding shotgun was quickly climbing back between the seats.

Then someone was yanking at Gabe's legs and he was being drug out of the SUV. He didn't see who it was because he was busy scrambling and clawing to get back to Shane. He wanted to hit him some more. So much more.

But then Gabe's face smacked down on the asphalt of the parking lot and he was seeing stars. The rest came in brief waves.

The driver stomping the shit out of him. Gabe rolling over and taking the asshole to the ground. The other guard calling for help.

Handcuffs. Fists. A baton.

An injection.

"What brings you back here, Gabey?" Charlie was talking. "Last I heard, you were in paradise… an untouchable one."

Raising his head, Gabe propped his elbows on his bent knees and looked at his old friend. Charlie was thin, so very thin, and his short blonde hair was dirty. Those hazel eyes of his had a slightly glazed appearance and his skin was scary pale.

He wasn't healthy. Shit, even more than that, he looked sick. Like… the cancers almost got you, kinda sick.

"You alright?" Gabe's brow furrowed, wondering.

"I'm fine." Charlie pressed his palms against the glass and leaned forward, bracing his weight.

"Then why're you here?"

"I asked you first." Charlie quirked another smile.

Same cool, unaffected asshole, like always. The familiar banter relieved Gabe, if only for a moment.

"It's complicated," Gabe offered finally. "But in a word… Val. I came to trade for Val."

"Ah." Charlie ducked his head as a pained look came over his face. "A bit late for that, huh?"

Gabe's eyes narrowed. His throat felt suddenly tight. Too late? Yeah, understatement of the century.

Swallowing hard he asked, "You know anything about it?"

With a shrug, Charlie raised his head and stared blatantly into a camera positioned in the upper corner of his cell. Those were new, Gabe thought. It was surrounded by a thick plexiglass box and the little red light on the thing was glowing steadily.

Pushing carefully to his feet, Gabe limped over to the glass partition and leaned his forehead against it. Charlie came in close on the opposite side and between the two of them, they were able to block their faces from the camera. If they whispered like this, then they could probably talk for just a little while before drawing notice.

"She was taken months ago," Charlie said, his voice raw. "Shane dressed her up like a slutty secretary before he took her away. No captive has seen her since, but two guards swore up and down they returned her to Isolation that same night. She was scanned in, but never scanned out."

"Shit." Gabe sucked in a breath. "How do you know all this?"

"I saw him take her. When they didn't bring her back to me, I sort of lost it," Charlie admitted, running a trembling hand back through his unkempt hair. "I stopped eating and I've been down here ever since. I overheard a few of the guards talking about it, but everyone thinks the same thing."

"What's that?"

"She either never came back from that client," Charlie reasoned. "Or a guard took her, maybe killed her. I don't know. It's been happening a lot lately."

"What are you talking about?"

"The missing." Charlie sucked in a breath and glanced around. "Ever since you got out, captives have been going missing, a few gone each month, for years."

"Shit," Gabe exhaled the word. "What happens to them?"

"I don't know." Charlie shrugged again, but then cleared his throat. "They're probably dead, Gabe. They were all problem captives, even Val."

"Don't say that."

"It's true," Charlie's voice cracked and he squeezed his eyes shut. "And it was my fault. I made her into a problem. It was me."

"What are you talking about?" Gabe repeated.

"Just..." Charlie pushed away from the glass and shook his head. "Just do what they tell you to, okay? Just play by the rules."

"Charlie," Gabe bit out his friend's name but the other man was already turning away. "What're you talking about? Charlie."

But he wasn't responding. Charlie kept his back to Gabe and swayed a little on his feet. The sharp angles of his shoulders could be seen poking through the gray shirt of his uniform. He was starving. Shit, hadn't he just said he'd stopped eating?

"Chuck," Gabe tried again. "When's the last time you ate something?"

With a beep, the door to Charlie's room opened. Automatically, Gabe took a step back. A male nurse pushed into the space, rolling a tray of equipment in front of him. The array of items on the tray were way too familiar, causing Gabe's gut to drop. Not good. Not good at all.

Behind the nurse, came not one, but two Cambric guards. Gabe frowned. Charlie didn't even bother to glance over.

"Time to eat," the nurse announced. "You ready to do this the easy way?"

"No," the word Charlie spoke was quiet.

Gabe's heart began pattering in his chest. Tapping a hand against the glass, he tried to get their attention. Come on Chuckie boy, he thought. You don't want this.

"He'll eat," Gabe offered quickly, but the nurse only rolled his eyes and motioned with one hand.

In an instant, the guards were on him.

Charlie looked so weak and unsteady, but even so, he fought back, or tried to. He pivoted on his heel and took a swing, but the shot went wide. All his fist caught was air.

Then one of the guards was wrapping Charlie's body tight with his strong arms and taking him to the ground. Then the second one crashed down after him.

In a blink, the three men were on the floor, struggling. Gabe cringed, then slapped his palm on the glass harder. He could hear Charlie grunting, then gurgling.

Walking calmly up to the pile, the male nurse held up a single syringe and flicked his finger against it. He was bored. This was just another day to him. Gabe bit down hard on his lip and inhaled sharply through his nose. They were going to suffocate him, or break a bone.

"Stop!" Gabe shouted finally.

The nurse ignored him and continued to wait for an opening. Kneeling down quickly, he saw what he'd been looking for and gripped a thin arm. Depressing the needle in less than a second, the nurse stood back.

Gabe held his breath. Counted.

By the time he got to five, the struggling stopped altogether. Charlie's legs went completely limp. One of his hands hit the floor, his palm spreading out loosely. Then the guards were pushing up off of him. They'd barely even broken a sweat.

That's when the feeding tube came out, along with an IV bag.

Turning away, Gabe closed his eyes. Blowing out a ragged breath, he leaned his back against the glass partition and slowly slid to the ground. When he was sitting flat on the hard concrete, he pressed his palms to the cold ground.

Keeping his eyes shut, Gabe tipped his face up to the ceiling and fought the cinching tightness in his own chest. Welcome home, he thought. Welcome fucking home.

CHAPTER 4

Val

VAL HELD THE SLEEK SILVER CELL PHONE UP TO HER EAR AND listened to the familiar ringing. Each chime was drawn out, extended in her mind as she visualized the turmoil at the other end of the line. Finally, like it had countless times before, the ringing ceased and an empty automated voice gave instructions on how to leave a message.

Squeezing her eyes closed against the flood of guilt, Val hung up and sucked in a harsh breath.

"She answer?" Jason asked, hovering just on the outskirts of their room.

"No." Val rose from her perch on the end of their massive bed and threw a glance over her shoulder at their sleeping son.

Jace's arms were outstretched, his legs, too. He looked like a scrawny starfish taking up every inch of space possible.

"She just needs more time," Jason reasoned.

"It's been months." Val paced over to the wide windows of

Summer House and looked out into the darkness. "She's never going to forgive me."

Walking towards her, Jason loosened his maroon tie and shrugged out of his suit jacket. "This isn't your fault," he said before coming up behind her and stopping short.

Tentatively, his hands reached out to trace along her bare arms. She was wearing one of his t-shirts, it was soft and smelled like him. It made her feel better, even when Jason's words did not.

Keeping her lips pressed together, Val didn't respond. She and Jason had already had this argument. They'd talked in circles over and over about who was to blame for Gabe being back at Cambric. Jason had said it was Gabe's idea, one that he'd then willingly gone along with.

But that didn't make any difference to Val. She knew who was really responsible. She knew who was actually to blame.

And it was her.

A body for a body. A life for a life.

Gabe had gone back, so that Val could come out. Simple as that… and Bee knew it, too.

So when Bee refused her calls, Val knew why. Every single day, when Val looked down at her hands, she saw Gabe's blood all over them. Literally. And when she looked at herself in the mirror, a woman stained red with the punishment of other captives stared back at her.

Because it was more than just Gabe.

It was Charlie, too.

And it was Amber and even Mandy. It was Ben, who'd risked himself for her, and it was all of the other captives at Cambric, the ones she couldn't set free.

Because the second Val had stepped foot off of the Militia's compound in the Blue Ridge Mountains, it was all over.

A reporter had snapped a photo of Jason returning to Texas with Val at his side. It made the evening news and the entire nation had seen it, including Shane and by extension, Cambric Agency.

When they realized that Val was alive and in the possession of her husband, the entire facility went on permanent lockdown. Val had escaped and they didn't know how she'd done it.

The next day, all of Cambric's guards had been fired along with all of the support staff. The Agency's security protocol changed, then increased. Their hiring process become detailed, lengthy and full proof.

So the years of covert work that Ava's underground had spent infiltrating Cambric and sneaking captives out, were all wiped away in the blink of an eye. The underground would never get back into The Agency. Ever. They'd never again rescue captives from inside those brick walls, just like Ava had warned her.

A shudder ran up Val's spine at the thought, causing Jason's hands to retract. He was afraid it was his touch that repulsed her, he'd said so before. But it wasn't her husband that made her feel sick to her stomach, it was herself.

Opening her mouth to speak, Val started to explain herself for the hundredth time, but then she stopped short. No matter what she said to him, Jason refused to believe her.

"I'm sorry," he mumbled. "I forgot."

"You can touch me." Val turned quickly to face him. The hem of his shirt brushed against the tops of her thighs, causing his eyes to drift down to her bare legs.

"Not without making your skin crawl," he whispered, frowning.

"That's not true," Val protested, and deliberately she reached for him.

"It is," he countered, watching as her hand came to rest on his chest.

Then, as if to prove it to both of them, Jason stepped in close and ran the tips of his fingers down the side of her cheek. Val kept a calm, accepting expression on her face. This was okay. They would be okay.

Scrutinizing her for a moment, Jason's arctic eyes narrowed.

"Don't use that face," he whispered before stepping back to run a hand roughly through his own hair. "Please, don't ever fake it with me."

"I'm not, I just…" Val dropped her hand before mumbling, "I don't know how else to be anymore."

Jason sucked in a breath and drug both of his hands down his face.

"I hate what they did to you," he said against his palms.

"I know." Val hugged herself, though it wasn't cool in their bedroom.

Dropping his hands, Jason closed the distance between them and pulled her body into his. Wrapping his arms around her waist, he laid his chin on top of her head and released a frustrated breath.

"It might help if you talked about it," he went on. "You're safe with me Val, I swear it. They can't get to you, or Jace."

Closing her eyes, Val absorbed his scent. She inhaled the smell of his cologne after a long day of work before sneaking her hands up the front of his chest. Gripping his cream-colored dress shirt in both hands she shook her head once.

No. She didn't want to tell him. She didn't want him to know.

Clearing his throat, Jason's arms fell from around her body and he backed away. He was frustrated, disappointed, upset. This tension between them lingered now, it just wouldn't go away.

Watching him in silence, Val worried her lip between her teeth as her husband worked with jerky fingers to unbutton his shirt. He'd come in late from the office again today, and it had her wondering.

Jason had made promises now. Promises that involved giving up his businesses, giving up his work. And over the past several months, since leaving the Militia compound, he'd assured her that he was moving forward with the plan.

But still, she wondered if he would be able to give up Riggs Oil. That company, in particular, was like a beloved mistress to him. It pained him to separate himself, even though he denied it to her face.

Shadows danced along the far wall. The flames from their bedroom fireplace were flickering.

Listening to the crackling of the burning wood, Val sighed. It was nearing the end of February in Texas and it was bitterly cold at night. For a moment, she flashed back to late winter in New York. Gabe was there at Cambric now, and he was probably very, very cold. Squeezing her eyes shut, she shivered.

"I think we need to speak to someone," Jason bit out. Shrugging his shirt off his shoulders, he tossed it carelessly over a pale-green armchair. "A therapist, or a counselor."

"A Senator's wife cannot appear unstable," Val repeated the

words Jason's mother had so generously given her not two weeks before.

"I haven't announced my intention to run yet," Jason countered.

Val's stomach sank. "Are you backing out?"

"No." Jason paused, his eyes darting over her face. "I never stopped working to free you, and I won't stop for Gabe, either."

Nodding her head, Val looked away. They had to get Gabe out. They had to.

"Hey." Jason cleared his throat and crept closer. "I think you'd feel better if you just talked about it. You can tell me, or a therapist, about what happened to you in there. Won't you even consider it? I'm not going to judge you, or be mad. I promise, okay?"

Val bobbed her head and managed to avoid his gaze. Jason ducked his head lower, trying to glance into her face. He wanted every detail from her. He'd asked before. If it was up to Jason, he'd have a complete accounting of each second they'd been apart.

But how could she possibly tell him?

She'd have to explain the client videos, the submissions, Shane, the breeding program, Charlie, the starvation. How could Val give Jason what he wanted, without reliving the whole sordid nightmare? Didn't he understand what he was asking?

She already spent every single day forcing those memories from her mind. She spent each night fighting against sleep just to prevent the dreams from coming.

Swallowing now, her pulse skittered and jumped. God, she could really use one of those little white pills. The longing for

Cambric's meds had her gut twisting and her face scrunching up. Were they drugging Gabe? Was he okay?

"Are you asking me to tell you, or are you ordering me?" Val crossed her arms over her body and tipped her chin up to meet his gaze.

"Val," Jason began, his eyes bright with some emotion she couldn't quite name. "I am not your owner anymore, I am your husband. This is a two way street. I don't command you to do things, I want you to do things. In the end, it's your choice whether you do them or not."

"Alright," Val answered.

She pressed her lips together.

His brow furrowed.

In the stillness, Jason had his answer. No answer at all.

With a sigh, he stalked away and closed himself in their adjoining bathroom.

Val exhaled.

"Mama?" Jace's small voice broke the quiet of the darkened room.

"Right here, baby," Val responded.

Making her way to the bed, she climbed in beside her son and scooted close to him under the covers. He sighed quietly, nuzzling into her as she wrapped her arms around his spindly body. Running her hand absently over his back, she listened to the way his breathing evened out. He was wearing a pair of super hero pajamas now. They were his new favorite thing.

Val's heart swelled. Jace's presence beside her was her only refuge.

Ever since her son's plane had landed on Texas soil, Val hadn't let him out of her sight. During the day, she drifted from room to room, following him. At night, she tucked him into their bed and watched him sleep.

Jason had yet to protest, but she felt his concern growing. He'd mentioned a private school, a personal bodyguard, but none of that had happened yet. Val didn't know what she'd do when the time came for Jace to return to a normal life. Just thinking about it had panic swirling in her veins.

In the bathroom, she listened as the water from the shower poured down. She could hear it spray and patter as Jason washed himself. After a while, the faucet twisted off and she heard the click of the glass door opening, then closing.

In her mind, Val could picture the fluffy white towel Jason would wrap around his waist. She could see the damp glisten of his dark hair, and smell the soap on his slick skin. Then the bathroom door was swinging open and a brief swath of light from behind her appeared, then switched off.

Angling her head up, Val let her eyes adjust to the moonlight seeping in through the windows of their room. She watched her husband's figure move through the dark, step into a pair of pajama pants and slide into bed.

Laying his head on his pillow, Jason blinked at her over the body of their sleeping son, nestled contentedly between them. Val blinked back.

After a beat, Jason reached across Jace's body and took Val's hand in his own. His fingers laced themselves in hers. His thumb drew lazy circles on her palm.

"I love you," he whispered. "You don't have to be afraid anymore, okay? I promise, Jace is safe. *You* are safe. They can't touch you. I swear I will *never* let anyone touch you ever again."

"I love you, too," Val replied, and felt her heart beating hard.

"I'm sorry," he continued. He just couldn't stop saying those words to her. *I'm sorry. I'm sorry.* "I'll make it better. I promise."

Giving her hand a squeeze, Jason stared into her eyes a moment before letting his gaze roam over her face. It was like he was memorizing her, soaking her in. She did her best not to look away.

After another few minutes, his eyes fluttered closed and his fingers went limp in her hand. Her husband's breathing became even and quiet, mirroring that of their son.

Sucking in a deep breath, Val retracted her hand and tilted her head toward the ceiling.

Sleep was a luxury that she just couldn't afford.

Because as soon as Val closed her eyes, Cambric was all around her, smothering her with its too cold cement rooms and solid slamming doors. Charlie was still there, hungry. And now Gabe was, too.

The nightmares were waiting to sink their claws deep, so Val held onto wakefulness as long as she could.

CHAPTER 5

Bee

Brushing the back of her hand over her forehead, Bee exhaled a breath and glanced around. She was standing in a little makeshift kitchen, one of eight others crammed into the oversized room. Behind her, Val was quietly studying the selection of recipes that were detailed on small lined cards spread out on the white tile counter.

"Blueberry muffins?" Val asked aloud.

Her voice lifted with the question. She was unsure, although that was nothing new. Val was unsure about pretty much everything. Unless she was specifically told what to do, Bee's best friend and probable sister would freeze up.

Not Bee, though. Her own heart strained at the idea of a choice, even one as tiny as which recipe to make for the class test.

"Let me see," Bee whispered.

Crossing the small space in two strides, Bee propped her elbows on the counter and bumped Val's hip with her own. Val gave her a quick smile and angled her head in close so that their hair twisted and mixed together as they read.

"These are boring," Bee complained. "What if we took some of the strawberries from this recipe and substituted them in for the muffins?"

"Bee..." Val's voice dropped low in warning.

"Oh, come on," Bee chided, her heart was leaping now, thumping in her chest with excitement. "It's not that big of a change and it's not like the rich geezer who gets to have sex with us will care in real life."

"But..."

"Val," Bee whispered, reaching to squeeze her best friend's hand in her own. "This is what fun feels like. Come on, live a little."

"If this is what fun feels like..." Val straightened and placed a hand over her flat stomach. "Then I don't like it. It makes me want to throw up."

"Relax." Bee dismissed her friend's worry with a bright smile. "They have three Agency guards taste testing... we can't lose."

Ducking her head, Val silently agreed, like she always did. Bee smiled in triumph then, and together they began gathering the materials they would need.

All around them, the rest of their class murmured and prepped and cooked in the other small kitchens. Ovens were opened and shut, bowls were set on counters, spoons stirred and eggs were cracked. Mostly, the recipes all involved baking.

Over the past month, Ms. King had demonstrated each option and they'd all been given time to practice. Even Gabe and Charlie were required to participate. They were working in the kitchen just beside Bee and Val now.

Moving to open one tall wooden cabinet, Bee took down the measuring cups and large bag of flour and set them on the counter.

Next came the salt, measuring spoons, and a bowl. Val walked over with the eggs and then turned back to the sink to wash the strawberries. Bee hummed quietly under her breath.

"Hey, what'd you choose?" Gabe's voice drifted into her space like the most delicious cologne.

Ugh, Bee thought, resisting the temptation to inhale deeply.

"Muffins," she supplied finally, and then continued to ignore him. Don't look up at that crooked grin. Don't do it.

"Ah," Gabe huffed as he set his own bowl down. They had to share the long counter that ran between their two kitchens. "You guys don't stand a chance."

"Is that right?" Bee looked up.

Dusting her hands together, she finally gave Gabe her full attention. He grinned broadly.

"That's right," he said.

"You see those guards over there?" Bee gestured to the three hulking figures sitting lazily at a long table at the far end of the room. "They salivate just looking at me... whatever you idiots are making, I promise that you won't win."

"Cookies, Bee Bee." Gabe's eyes twinkled as hers narrowed. "No man can resist chocolate chip cookies. The only way you're winning is if they get to taste you. And we both know that's frowned upon here."

Bee's mouth dropped even as her cheeks heated. A dull ache bloomed and spread itself between her hips. Did he really just...? Taste her.

The words flashed in her head and although she wanted to be pissed, a few choice images came to mind. Gabe. Her. Tasting. Yeah. That ache way down low turned itself into a demanding pulse. Damn him.

With a frown, Bee huffed an indignant breath. Gabe chuckled quietly and ducked his head. Why? Why was he so hot?

Beside her, Val placed the clean strawberries carefully on the counter along with a cutting board and knife.

"How small do I need to cut these?" She asked, and had Gabe's spine snapping straight.

There was no recipe for strawberry muffins. It was simply not an option. He knew it. She knew it.

Beaming, Bee watched as Gabe's eyes darted over the bright red fruit before coming up to rest warily on Bee's face. For a moment, she just let him look. That's right. Look who's going to win now.

"I'll cut them," Bee announced finally.

Nodding, Val drifted away.

"What the hell are you doing?" Gabe hissed.

His teeth ground together, as his eyes flashed. Guess those precious chocolate chip cookies of his were all but forgotten.

"Winning," Bee countered, before plucking at the first berry and slicing it confidently in half.

"You can't be serious," he demanded.

Quickly, Gabe's hand snaked out and covered hers, preventing Bee from cutting the halves into smaller pieces. At his contact, butterflies released in her belly. Quickly, they morphed into tingles that spread out all over her skin, racing up her arms, and down her spine.

In shock, Bee looked up into Gabe's face. What the...?

Gabe's brow furrowed and he squeezed her hand once... hard. He was absolutely not smiling.

"Why aren't you following the recipe?" He asked carefully. "You looking to get hurt?"

"It's not a big deal..."

"That's bullshit and you know it," he growled. "Why do you always do this? Just follow the damn rules, Bee Bee."

"Gabriel," Bee hissed, her eyes dropping from his angry face to his hand. "You're still touching me."

Following her gaze, Gabe's eyes drifted down to settle between them. Beneath the wrap of his palm, her hand was trembling. Maybe on the outside she could still act tough, nonchalant, indifferent. But on the inside, he had her flying.

Suddenly, she wondered if he could tell. Then she wondered why. Why did his touch make her feel this way?

Slowly, Gabe's grip on her gentled. He let his thumb brush along her wrist. Back and forth. Back and forth.

Popping her eyes back up to his, Bee held her breath. Gabe was staring at her now. One beat. Then two.

Breaking contact, Gabe stepped back as if he'd been burnt and whirled away. In silence, she watched him stalk to the other side of his own tiny kitchen and brace both of his arms against the sink. His head was tipped down, his shoulders tight beneath the gray fabric of his uniform.

Charlie stepped up beside his friend then, and they murmured quietly for a second. Glancing over his shoulder at Bee, Charlie raised his eyebrows in question. *What did you do? He seemed to ask.*

Swallowing hard, Bee looked down.

Deliberately, she resumed her chopping.

Smirking bitterly, Bee squeezed her eyes shut and held back the flood of unwanted memories. Gabe at Cambric, the first time he'd touched her. He'd been so pissed at her that day with the stupid muffins. Back then, it hadn't even occurred to Bee why it bothered him. She didn't get why he cared.

And sure enough, she'd presented those strawberry muffins for their class test and just as predicted all three guards had devoured them. Because despite everything, Bee really could cook. But then, just like Val had known and Gabe had known, Bee was in for a world of hurt.

Rule breaker.

Choice maker.

Agency rhetoric be damned.

And Bee had taken the brunt of it, after all, it had been her idea. So thankfully, Val didn't have to suffer that time around. And although Gabe had stood up like an idiot and claimed he'd been the one to tell Bee to do it, no one had believed him.

Ms. King was a lot of things, but she was not stupid.

So Bee had spent the next month eating nothing but strawberry muffins. Water and strawberry muffins. Morning. Noon. And night.

If Bee ever tasted a strawberry again, she would most definitely throw it up.

Staring into the bathroom mirror now, Bee steadily applied eyeliner. On the sink, her phone continued to vibrate. Glancing down at it, she released a sigh. Mommy Dearest was definitely trying to plan an intervention, no doubt.

And it wasn't a surprise, they'd played this game before. Back when Bee was first released from Cambric and reunited with her birth parents, she'd been hooked on pills. At that time, it hadn't really been a choice. Gabe had been sold and gone for over a year and Val right along with him.

Left alone at The Agency, Bee had serviced a multitude of monthly clients first, then, when she'd failed at that, came the parties. Lots of men. Lots of parties.

Bee'd needed the drugs to keep working and Cambric

had been happy to provide them. Only, the more she'd tasted that certain sort of chemical release, the more she'd needed. High was the only way to live, or the only way to survive.

But the Durand family would not tolerate an addict as their sole heir. Nope. And getting her clean had not been easy.

Val was MIA at that point and Gabe was under Federal protection. Bee was alone in the world, or at least she'd felt that way. Even though her parents had been desperate to support her, and Jason had tried to help as well.

So really the only difference now was that Bee's current state was by choice. Val and Jason weren't here right now in this very hotel bathroom because Bee chose not to take their calls. Gabe wasn't here because he chose to leave her. Choices. She'd always said she'd wanted them.

Sucking in a breath, Bee twisted the lid of her eyeliner back into place and tossed it into her cosmetics bag. Expensive clothing, some with the tags still on, hung from the shower door. There were more clothes in the hotel suite's closet and still more draped over the couch. She'd been shopping… again.

Retail therapy. It was a real thing.

Her nails were freshly done, her hair cut into a sleek bob and colored to perfection. As a rich bitch, Bee found that as long as you paid everyone around you to make your outside look good, most people didn't care if your inside was a mess. People that didn't really know you, anyway.

So even though Val was worried, and Bee's mother kept calling, Bee was able to keep drawing money from her trust fund. Daddy came for weekly inspections of the outside package and made a choice of his own. The choice not to notice the alcohol on his daughter's breath or her slightly slurred speech.

He was the one and only person that she had to impress. Daddy held the purse strings and therefore the alcohol buying strings and so for him, Bee always picked up her phone.

In fact, he was who she was going to meet for lunch in half an hour. Mommy Dearest of course would be there too, begging him to send Bee to rehab. But this was a game they'd played before as well, and thankfully now Bee understood the rules.

Though she hated rules, as well... a rule.

"Daddy?" Bee picked up the phone this time and pressed it to her ear. "Yeah, I'm leaving in ten."

CHAPTER 6

Jason

"WHEN'S THE LAST TIME YOU SLEPT JOHNNY?" JASON LEANED back in the stiff chair in Agent Finn's office and surveyed the man himself. His short black hair looked mussed and there were bags under those dark eyes of his. "The guilt finally getting to you?"

"Why are you here?" Finn's brows drew together even as he tried to stifle a yawn.

"You're a mess." Jason gestured over the wooden desk that separated them. "Your suit's all wrinkled and… is that puke?"

"Huh?" Finn glanced down at his button up shirt and swiped a hand absently at a whitish stain. "Just spit up."

"Spit up?" Jason's eyebrows shot to his hairline as a million tiny puzzle pieces started to click into place. "Like, from a baby?"

"Look." Finn narrowed his eyes. "Why exactly are you here again?"

"You owe me," Jason snapped. *You owe Gabe, you lying, with-holding piece of shit.*

Tapping his fingers on the arm of his chair, he watched the FBI Agent he'd known for over a decade squirm. That's right, squirm. The shoe was finally on the other foot and Jason couldn't deny that it felt good.

Did he plan to press his advantage? Hell yes, he did. Jason planned to exploit every single avenue that he possibly could to get what he wanted, and Finn was only the beginning.

But Jason had to admit, this particular exploitation tasted pretty sweet. And not just because Finn had sat idly by in that courthouse and let Gabe turn himself over to those monsters. Although that would be reason enough to leverage the shit out of the guy. Nope, it was also because Jason would never forget the night Finn had ambushed him and taken Val.

Did the son-of-a-bitch get her out in the end? Yeah, but the damage that occurred in between was still there. Yes, Jace was legally free, and yes, Jason had Val back... physically at least. But his wife was far from back mentally. Someone needed to pay for that. A lot of someones.

"You think I owe you?"

"I know you owe me." Jason smiled. The biggest, fattest, fakest smile he could.

"I don't have time for this," Finn countered. "I'm not babysitting your court case anymore so my boss has me neck deep in missing persons again. There's no reason for you to be here."

"Isn't there?" Jason sank deeper into the uncomfortable chair and glanced around.

The place was just like before. Blank white walls in the shape of a box with a single window that looked out onto the street. Finn kept his desk neat and empty, save for a single computer monitor and an old style black telephone.

There was a time the office had been lined with white boards containing the faces of missing children. One of them had been Veronica Durand and it had changed everything about Jason's life. Everything.

"Can we talk?" Jason asked, his eyes traveling back to rest on Finn's tired face. "Like freely?"

With a sigh, Finn reached beneath his desk and the click of a button could be heard. Standing abruptly, the agent stalked to the door and flipped the lock. Jason didn't bother turning to watch.

He let Finn stand at his back and stare down at him a moment. They'd worked together for too long for Jason to get nervous. Finn couldn't get to him. At this point, he wasn't sure anyone could.

"I'm not your contact," Finn spoke quietly before crossing back to his desk and settling down in his chair. "Why are you here? I'm tired of asking the same question."

"Actually…" Jason inhaled a breath and leveled Finn with a long look. "You are my contact."

"What?"

"Clay Montgomery," Jason cut in. "Man that guy has a lot of pull. Am I right?"

"Jason," Finn warned.

"You see…" Jason leaned forward in his chair. "He had my wife, Johnny. He had her for *months* and no one knew it. Well, except for you, of course."

Finn's mouth snapped shut and his jaw ticked. That's right, Jason thought, you let me sell an innocent man back to satan, and all the while my wife was safe and sound.

Giving his head a little shake, Jason went on. "The Militia got her out of Cambric when I couldn't, and you want to know what the real kicker is? The Agency didn't even know they'd done it."

"What's your point?"

"Well, no one does anything for free right?" Jason's pulse picked up. "And Clay has a sister. Maybe you know her? Ava Moore is her name. Val told me she was pregnant… like *really* pregnant, but that would've been a few months ago. She's probably had her baby by now."

Agent Finn's eyes darkened but he didn't speak. Jason smiled.

"My wife may not be willing to tell me how many times she was raped in that fucking hell you dropped her in-"

"Jason."

"But she *has* told me all about her time with the Militia." Jason's eyes glittered as the color drained from Finn's face. "So my point is… you owe me, among other things. And seeing as how Clay Montgomery wants all these things from me, I managed a few stipulations of my own."

"How is she?" Finn asked quietly.

"Excuse me?"

"Val," Finn continued. "Is she getting help?"

"You don't talk about my wife." Jason raised a finger in warning. "And if you ever happen to see her, you keep your mouth shut. I don't forgive you, and she doesn't need to assuage your guilty conscience by listening to your half-assed apologies."

"You got my messages then?"

"I deleted your messages," Jason spat. "And that's not what this is about."

"Then what is this about?" Finn swallowed thickly before blowing out a breath.

"I'm running for Congress."

"I saw your announcement last week." Finn dipped his head.

"So, a reputable politician like me can't be seen in talks with a shady organization like the Militia, can I?"

"Probably not," Finn's voice was low, measured.

"But no one would think twice about me staying in contact with an old friend," Jason offered. "One who I worked closely with in the past... say on an FBI investigation."

"Alright." Finn huffed a breath. "I'll verify it with Clay, but it seems strange he wouldn't have mentioned it already."

"You do that," Jason agreed. "And I asked him to let me be the one to tell you. I have to say, I like surprise on you, buddy. It's a great emotion. Kind of like... surprise, I've known all along your wife was safe and yet I let you sell an innocent man to a company full of monsters."

"I tried to talk you both out of it," Finn managed.

"Oh yeah... *Please, trust me. Just don't do it*," Jason mocked.

"Listen asshole." Finn spread one palm flat on his desk and leaned forward, his first real sign any of this was getting through. "You two should have fucking trusted me. That part's on you."

"Huh." Jason pursed his lips and looked away.

Yeah, that part *was* a bit of a hard sell. Especially when Jason agreed 100%. Gabe had been sold, lock, stock and barrel, by no one other than Jason. He'd had to get his wife back. He'd been desperate.

So yeah, there was no way out of that one, save to undo

what he'd done. Which is why Jason had sold his soul to Clay Montgomery.

"So I'm your contact then," Finn broke the silence finally. "What do you want me tell them?"

"That I'm sticking to the timeline," Jason offered and shifted around in his seat to check the pocket of his jacket. It was there. "I've hired a campaign manager, I've given up all of my companies."

"Alright," Finn was measured. "Is that it?"

"As far as Clay goes? Yeah, that's it."

"Okay."

"But there's one other thing." Jason slipped his hand into his jacket pocket. "And it's off the record."

"You don't want me to tell Clay?"

"I don't want you to tell anyone."

"You trust me to do that?" Finn lifted an eyebrow in question, sarcasm leaking from every word.

"Like I said." Jason took the pair of plastic baggies from his pocket and set them carefully on the desk. "You owe me."

"What's that?"

"Those are DNA samples," Jason explained. "They're labeled."

Reaching across the desk, Finn's eyes dropped from Jason's face to the baggies. In silence, he read the names written across each one, and frowned. When he tipped back in his chair, his expression was guarded, but curious.

"I ran those already," he countered. "Twice."

"No." Jason shook his head. "You ran Val's DNA against Lillian Durand. Veronica was taken so young that you guys didn't have a good sample."

"And they didn't match," Finn reminded him.

"So run these," Jason insisted.

"Why?"

"Call it a hunch. I've lived with Val and Bee for long enough. I just need to be sure."

"Jason."

"You owe me, FBI Agent slash Constitutional Militia contact, Johnathan Finn," Jason cut in.

"I don't owe you shit." Finn ducked his head before wrapping his large hands around the bags and drawing them closer across the desk. "But I do owe Val... and Bee. Off the record then?"

"Off the record," Jason agreed. "And Finn?"

"Yeah?"

"You only bring those results to me, understand? I don't need anyone else taking advantage of my girls."

Bobbing his head soberly, Finn's jaw ticked a moment before he murmured under his breath. "If I get a chance to kill him, I want you to know that I'm taking that shot."

"If I have it my way," Jason whispered. "That chance is all mine."

Brushing at his suit, Jason stood abruptly and buttoned his jacket. They both knew who the *him* was. The dead man's name didn't need to be said aloud.

Finn stood then too, and offered his hand for a shake. It hovered there between them, over Finn's empty desk. Jason's jaw clenched and he had to fight his impulse to spit on the ground instead.

But after hesitating for several seconds, Jason eventually extended his own hand and clasped Finn's. It didn't mean he forgave the guy. But in this world, a promise didn't hold very much weight without it.

CHAPTER 7

Gabe

Leaning back against the wall, Gabe kept his arms crossed loosely over his chest and waited. Training Room 106 was just across the hall and although he shouldn't be, Gabe couldn't seem to stop staring at its locked white door.

Bee was in there. Again. And for some reason the idea had him churning.

Shifting uncomfortably, Gabe swiped the back of his hand beneath his nose with a sniff before forcing himself to glance away. The long hallway was lit with fluorescent lights and echoed with the constant foot traffic of hundreds of captives. Cambric kept a pretty steady schedule when it came to training, prep and classes and the oversight needed at this stage was usually thin.

Which is why Gabe could afford to linger here. He'd just spent the night down in breeding, for the millionth time it seemed, and so he had the rest of the day free.

So why was he hanging around here when he could be sleeping or hitting the gym?

With a huff of breath, Gabe's eyes traveled back to that particular door and held. Bee Bee. There was just... something about her.

Patting at the pocket of his pressed gray slacks, Gabe assured himself his little surprise was still there. He only hoped that Bee gave him the chance to give it to her. She was always brushing him off, or looking at him like he was some kind of jerk.

Couldn't she see how charming he was? It seemed like every other female around couldn't resist him. But not her. She didn't even want to be friends.

Which is the only thing Gabe needed from her really. He wasn't out to ruin her or anything. He knew the rules about permanent placement females, it was just... for some strange reason, he craved her approval. He had to have it.

The beep of the door across the way had Gabe straightening. Between the flow of bodies walking this way and that down the hall, he kept his eyes fixed on Training Room 106. There was his Bee Bee finally coming out. Her long brown hair was slightly mussed and those wide emerald green eyes seemed glazed over.

Gabe's gut dropped. Pushing off the wall, he made to move towards her. Then came that asshole Ben, walking out of the room just behind Bee. He had his wide palm on her lower back and he bent his mouth down close to Bee's ear, whispering something.

Instinctively, Gabe's hands curled themselves into fists and his jaw ticked with tension. If he could have anything in this fucked up little world it would be ten minutes alone in a room with Ben.

Just before Gabe got to them though, Ben moved off, leaving Bee blinking quietly a moment as the door at her back swung shut.

"Hey," Gabe spoke to her as he came to a stop at her side. "You okay?"

For a second, Bee didn't answer. She stared down at the floor before lifting her eyes to Gabe.

"What?" She asked, as if she'd only just now noticed he was there.

"Are you alright?" Gabe repeated himself and frowned.

"Yeah." Bee gave her head a little shake before squaring her shoulders and collecting herself. "I'm fine."

Before Gabe could speak another word, she was pushing past him to walk off down the hall. The click, click, click of her black heels sounded in his ears.

His breath released in a giant whoosh. Just like that, she moved away from him. It was like he didn't even exist.

Rolling his shoulders, Gabe gritted his teeth and picked up his feet to catch up. When he came up next to her, she glanced at him in surprise then looked quickly away. Gabe flashed her a big smile and stared at the side of her face. Her perfect, beautiful face with those pouty pink lips that were featured in more than one of his personal fantasies.

"I got you something," Gabe whispered.

When Bee looked his way and narrowed her eyes, Gabe felt his chest swell in triumph. That got her attention.

"What are you talking about?" Bee asked, but she just kept right on walking.

Snagging her by the elbow, Gabe drew her into a side hallway where they were thankfully alone. The room at the far end was rarely used.

"Here, check this out." Reaching into his pocket, Gabe pulled out a small yellow bag and handed it over.

Blinking up at him, Bee's brow furrowed and one hand propped itself on her hip. There was that sassy, know-it-all from class. Gabe grinned.

"What is that?" Bee asked, refusing to take the bag.

"They're called potato chips," Gabe supplied, knowing the cafeteria didn't serve such items. There was no way Bee had ever tasted one. "You can eat them."

"Where'd you get them?" She questioned, still hesitant.

By the way she licked at her lips though, Gabe knew he had her. Hell, hadn't he just watched her eat nothing but strawberry muffins for an entire month?

"You'll love them." Gabe ripped open the bag and held it out to her. "Trust me."

"I can't afford any more trouble." Bee's eyes popped up to his and, for the first time, Gabe noted the vulnerability there.

His heart kicked at him, and for a moment he felt the need to pull her in against his chest. But that wouldn't do. He couldn't have this woman like he'd had so many others.

"I didn't steal them," Gabe assured her. "You won't get in trouble."

With a quick nod, Bee snatched at the bag and brought it close to her face. Dipping her nose down, she inhaled deeply. Gabe breathed in right along with her. Then in the next moment she was shoving her hand in the bag and pushing the crispy yellow chips into her mouth.

Groaning, her eyes flitted up to his briefly before they closed. They were good just like he'd said, and the look on her face combined with the sounds she was making was all the reward Gabe thought he'd ever need.

As she ate quickly, handful after handful, Gabe watched. All captives ate this way when it was something they thought maybe they weren't really supposed to have. Hunched over, possessive. When you grow up with any sort of pleasure being ripped away from you, you learn to take what you can as fast as you can.

To Gabe, there was no shame in the way she ate. The only shame was how much he wanted her to consume him like that. But as long *as that particular desire stayed hidden inside his own head, he figured they were both safe.*

"Thank you," she whispered, swiping the back of her hand over her greasy lips. "I want to save the rest for Val."

"Of course." Gabe dipped his head.

The sisters did everything together. Next time, he'd make sure to bring two bags.

"Listen." Bee folded the edge of the bag down carefully so as not to crush what was left inside. "What sort of payment..."

"Nothing," Gabe cut her off. Captives never gave food like this, not without something to trade.

"But, now I'm in your debt." Bee looked worried, and Gabe simply could not have that. He didn't want her worried because of him.

"Alright," he said. "I'll tell you what I want."

"What?"

"A truce." Gabe smiled. "I want us to be friends."

"Gabey."

"No really." Gabe reached out and plucked up a single strand of her thick hair. "You're always brushing me off, it's bad for my image."

"Your image?" Bee cracked a smile and Gabe felt himself flying. He felt high knowing he put that look on her face.

"That's right," Gabe teased. "So from now on, you've got to talk to me in class like everyone else."

"Is that all?"

"Nope." Gabe shook his head slowly as he released her hair and retracted his hand. "You're going to have to let me eat meals with you, too. People need to see how cool I am."

"You're ridiculous," Bee accused, but she was still smiling. "I sit with Val."

"I know," Gabe countered. "So you'll have to tell her she needs to be my friend, too. We can all hang together."

"All that for a bag of chips?" Bee's eyebrows wiggled at him.

"What can I say?" Gabe's eyes twinkled right back. "They were expensive chips."

Rolling over in bed, Gabe reached his arm out to draw Bee in. He needed just five more minutes of sleep and he wanted it to be with her back pressed against his chest. He loved the curve of her waist and the swell of her hips beneath his palm. Not to mention that the smell of her sweet skin was even better than the ocean breeze.

So it wasn't until his hand came up empty that he opened his eyes, and remembered.

Bee wasn't taking up space next to him in their king-sized bed in the Maldives.

Or rather, Gabe wasn't there… with her.

And he never would be again.

With a long sigh, Gabe squeezed his eyes shut and flopped miserably onto his back. The mattress beneath him now was thin and even if his body wasn't still hurting from the fight, he'd still have been sore.

"Morning sunshine," Charlie's voice sounded through the glass partition, drawing Gabe's eyes up and over.

"How long have I been out?" Gabe asked quietly before pushing up to sitting.

"Don't know." Charlie shrugged, then nodded towards Gabe's door.

Following his old friend's line of sight, Gabe spied the empty food tray he'd set there last night. Or maybe, it had been in the afternoon, seeing as the contents had been a bowl of soup and simple green salad. He'd downed everything in three seconds flat, drained the single iceless glass of water and yet, he'd still been hungry.

"They know they have to feed me, right?" Gabe tried to joke but it fell flat. Truth was, Cambric didn't have to feed him at all, if they didn't want.

"Maybe they don't want *you* to eat as much, but that's all they've been trying to get me to do for months," Charlie reasoned.

"They didn't come for you?" Gabe questioned.

"No." Charlie shook his head. "And the lights never shut off."

"Weird," Gabe commented. "I mean, that would've been weird before I left."

"It's still weird," Charlie assured him. "Something's up."

"Like what?"

"Don't know." Charlie heaved a sigh before sinking slowly down to a crouch.

Gabe eyed him a moment, he was so beyond thin. With a grunt, Gabe got up to stretch and limp lamely over to the glass partition. Rubbing at a sore spot on his chest, he looked down at his mangled suit and white button down shirt

There was blood spray all over his clothes. They hadn't bothered to change him before throwing him in here and he hadn't had the chance to shower. If he was lucky, some of that blood was from the Cambric driver, although most of it was probably from Gabe himself.

Unfortunately, he knew for sure that none of it belonged to Shane. When you punch a guy in the throat, they don't tend to bleed on you.

"You hear that?" Charlie asked, and had Gabe pausing to listen.

"Nah." Gabe shook his head. "I don't hear anything."

"No beeps," Charlie commented, his hazel eyes flicking around absently. "No boots on the floor, no slamming doors."

"No guards," Gabe murmured.

"No guards," Charlie agreed and finally... finally, the guy smiled.

CHAPTER 8

Gabe

THAT SMILE WAS WIPED OFF CHARLIE'S FACE NOT VERY LONG after that. It was hard to tell time with no meals, no one walking by, and the lights always shining. The only thing Gabe could use to gauge the amount of time that had passed was his ever increasing hunger... and thirst. The lack of water was the biggest issue of all.

"I'm sorry." Charlie gestured to his own untouched food tray in the corner of his room. "If I could give that stuff to you, then I would."

Gabe licked his cracked lips and let his eyes travel to the red tray in question. It had been placed in Charlie's room at the same time as Gabe's soup and it contained basically the same items. The only difference was, Gabe had devoured his immediately and Charlie had refused.

His single tall cup of water sat there tauntingly now, along with a bowl of cold soup and a disgustingly soggy salad. There was even a stale bread roll, which looked awesome.

Letting his eyes travel back over to his friend, Gabe's brow furrowed and he let loose an annoyed grunt. Back in the day the man in question had been beyond fit. His shoulders had been broad, his chest chiseled and thighs powerful. Now he was all boney angles and gray sickly skin. The hair on his head even seemed thinner, but maybe that was just perception.

"Why'd you stop eating?" Gabe asked. They were both sitting propped up next to the glass partition. "You mentioned something about Val."

"I told you," Charlie answered, his gaze drifting away. "They didn't bring her back."

"No." Gabe shook his head. "Try again, there's got to be more."

"Doesn't matter."

"It does," Gabe countered. "Give it up."

"What do you want me to say?"

"The truth," Gabe answered easily. "I need to know what happened to her. She's the reason I'm back. Are you sure she's dead?"

"I'm not sure of anything." Charlie shrugged.

"But now you want to die," Gabe supplied. "Why? What happened?"

"Val was taken, because of me. She was refusing to submit, because of me. I'm the reason she's gone. So yeah, I'm pretty sure I don't want to live like this anymore."

"You caught feelings for her." Gabe nodded his head slowly in understanding. "How?"

"We… were in breeding. Together."

"Ah." Gabe blew out a breath. Jason had been freaking out about that, but at the time they hadn't known who she'd been put with and Gabe had refused to give the man any details. He'd figured that it served no purpose other than to help Jason torture himself. "Did you two…?"

"We came close," Charlie admitted. "But that's where everything went bad. I was so sure she was going to get us all released, like last time. I thought she was involved in some kind of investigation. If we could just hold out long enough, you know?"

"You had hope."

"I'm an idiot." Charlie bit his lip hard a moment before going on. "Now she's gone. Dead or… I don't even know."

Pinching the bridge of his nose, Gabe sucked in a breath. Survivor's guilt. It was a real thing and Gabe understood it maybe a little too well. That combined with Charlie's smashed hopes for freedom had the guy in a tailspin.

And it's not like Gabe hadn't been there before himself, he had. In fact, it was very tempting to go right back there now.

But the difference was, Gabe had a score to settle. He had vengeance to exact and he knew if he was calculating enough and patient enough he would get a chance to collect.

Of course, things would be way easier if he had a bit of support, like a childhood friend he could trust.

"Well." Gabe cleared his throat. "Looks like you've got a debt to pay then."

"What?" Charlie's brow furrowed.

"You owe Val, and dead or not, she owes me," Gabe reasoned. "I traded places for her and her kid."

"What are you trying to say?"

"You now owe me," Gabe explained. "In a round about sort of way, but still… it works."

"You're an asshole, Gabey," Charlie scoffed and fell silent.

Gabe let his friend think. He let that captive's brain of his swirl and dwell and calculate. Maybe to a free person, this sort of exchange wouldn't work, or maybe it wouldn't matter. To a captive though, living without money your entire life, this kind of payment system made sense. Not only that, but it was a big deal. Trading and being even was a big deal down here in the empty halls of hell.

"Fuck you," Charlie spat finally. "What do you want?"

"Well it's an awfully big debt," Gabe drawled.

"Just say it."

"First things first." Gabe paused for effect. "I want you to eat."

"Bullsh-"

"Second…" Gabe interrupted. "I want you to get strong again, like before. We've got a lot of work to do, you and I."

"Gabe."

"A debt's a debt, Charlie. The idea is that you don't get to pick the payment."

Grumbling under his breath, Charlie glared at him for a good long minute. But then, pushing weakly away from the glass, he stumbled over to the food tray by his door. With a backwards glance at Gabe, Charlie picked up his water cup and began to drink.

The tightness that had formed itself inside Gabe's chest began to ease.

Over the next hour or so, he watched the guy eat. And despite the jealous protests of his own stomach, the sight flooded Gabe with relief. He'd finally realized what he wanted to do with the rest of his pitiful time here on earth. Now that he was committed, Gabe was actually looking forward to having a little help.

Of course, he also really needed a few Cambric guards to show up with some food and a change of clothes. That, along with an opportunity to earn his way out of Isolation.

But that would come soon, right? It had to. He was hungry and thirsty and now Charlie was willing to eat, too. The guards could see that. They would come soon.

Only, they didn't.

If Gabe had been able to count the days from that moment, then he would've known he and Charlie had already gone without food for two nights. If he'd been able to keep track of the sun and the moon, then he would've counted out an additional seventy-two hours before The Agency's brand new staff finally showed up.

CHAPTER 9

Bee

THE UPSCALE RESTAURANT WAS IN A PRIME LOCATION overlooking a lush green riverwalk in Texas. It wasn't too far from the hotel where Bee was staying and her father had sent his car service to pick her up.

Daddy had a few minor stipulations to her current situation, and Bee did her best to accommodate them. One being that she stay local, so his weekly visits weren't an inconvenience for him, and another being that she not drive.

Neither of these requirements meant much to Bee who now preferred to live her life through a blurry cocktail glass anyway. What did it matter where she stayed as long as it wasn't a shit hole? And as long as her black credit card kept swiping away, the fact that she used a driver to travel didn't matter. If anything, it made getting blasted and still making it to the nail salon easier.

Walking up to the pristine glass doors on her red high heels, Bee brushed at her designer dress before going inside.

Normally, she would be checking her purse for her ever present flask of alcohol, but this particular meeting wasn't the place to bring it.

As the hostess pulled open the door and led her inside, Bee's fingers pulsed subconsciously along her patent leather clutch. Right now, she'd really like to take just a tiny hit, but she knew she couldn't.

"Veronica." Bernard Durand stood up from a table by the window and smiled.

His emerald green eyes, so like his daughter's, flitted quickly over her face. He was checking for sobriety, Bee knew, and the knowledge didn't bother her, not really. Over the past years of getting to know one another, she could honestly say he was a decent person.

Looking up into his face now, she pursed her lips and wondered what it would have been like if she'd never been taken. He was tall and slender, with perfect clothes, straight white teeth and a short crop of thick brown hair.

She'd gotten her looks from him, clearly, as she didn't resemble her mother hardly at all. Speaking of which, Lillian was mysteriously absent.

"Daddy." Bee smiled in response, thankful that this particular meeting appeared to be a one on one session.

Typically her father was much easier on her than her mother. He was indulgent and often overly generous. Maybe he was making up for lost time, or maybe he blamed himself for losing her in the first place. Bee found she didn't really care.

Leaning up, she kissed him once lightly on the cheek before allowing him to help her into her seat. As the two of them got settled, a waiter wandered over with a large bottle of sparkling water and menus.

"I'd like a gin and tonic as well, please," Bee announced as the waiter began scribbling on his little white notepad.

"She'll just have the water," Bernard interrupted. "And I'll have the steak sandwich with the parmesan fries. Veronica, do you want a salad?"

"Um…" Bee glanced down at the menu and bit at her lip. She really wanted that gin and fucking tonic. "Yes, the seared salmon with avocado should be fine. Thank you."

Ducking his head the waiter slipped his pen and paper into his pocket and walked away. Bee followed his figure a moment with her eyes, hoping against hope that the guy would take pity on her and put in that drink order anyway. But alas, he veered towards the kitchen and left the bartender alone.

You don't bite the hand that tips you.

Bee sighed.

"It's just past noon," Bernard reproached. "Too early for a drink."

At least in public, Bee thought, but didn't dare voice that opinion out loud.

"Of course, Daddy," she said. "I don't know what I was thinking."

Her father's brow furrowed a moment and they sat in silence. Out the window, people walked casually by on the sidewalk. It was spring time in Texas and the weather was blessedly mild. Of course, these few weeks of perfection wouldn't last. The humidity would soon strike along with the brutally hot sunshine.

"Your mother has… concerns," Bernard began, causing Bee to look over at him.

"She always has concerns," Bee countered. "Where is she today anyway? I thought from all her texts she'd be here."

"I asked her not to come." Bernard tapped a single finger on the white tablecloth.

Biting her lip, Bee held back the response she wanted to give. Which was: thank you for saving me from two hours of nagging torture. Instead, she simply smiled and traced a finger down the outside of her glass. The waiter had poured the sparkling water for them both and yet, Bee had no desire to drink it.

"We know this is a difficult time for you," Bernard said quietly. "Your mother is worried you've fallen back into old habits."

"Daddy… really?" Bee huffed an indignant laugh.

"You're isolating yourself," he went on, leaning forward. "You have no friends, no social calendar. We'd like you to move home."

"What?" Bee gaped. *No, no way. Not going to happen.*

"Look, counseling wouldn't be such a bad thing would it?" He reasoned. "You've lost someone very close to you and now you refuse to speak to Val or Jason."

"I haven't *lost* anyone," Bee countered. "My boyfriend left me. I'm dealing with it."

"All the more reason for you to come home. It would only be for a few months, until you get back on your feet."

"Is all this because you think I'm using again?" Bee asked. She had to find a way out of this. She could absolutely not move back in with her parents.

"Well…"

"Because I'm not." Bee gave her head a quick shake. "I'll take a drug test if you want."

"It's not just that," he admitted. "Although I think we'll go ahead and have a test done anyway, it would help your mother. But it's also not healthy for you to be so alone, so isolated."

"Okay." Bee sucked in a breath. "But I'm not. I have loads of friends… from before."

Her mind clicked back to that six month stint right after she'd first gotten released from Cambric. Bee had moved in with her parents then, and they'd proceeded to drag her to every country club dinner, outing, and social meeting they had.

Eventually, she'd met up with the other trust fund twenty-somethings in her parent's circle of friends and that's when the real partying had begun.

Clubs. Drinks. Nightlife.

Jason had joined her for awhile, after Val blew him off.

It only stopped when Gabe came bouncing back into her life. He was finally free from Federal protection and had a plan. It was that same pipe dream he'd always had, and at the time she'd gone where he'd wanted without a second thought.

That, in retrospect, had been a mistake. A heartbreaking, soul-sucking mistake. She'd given up everything for him, time and again. In all her miserable little life, while claiming to want choices, Bee had always given hers up in favor of Gabe's.

No more, she thought. Not ever again.

Bee wasn't going to give up her freedom. Not for a man who'd claimed to love her, and certainly not for her parents. So, she'd have to convince her father she was coping.

That left her with the elite social scene. Bee figured she

could play that hand again. If Daddy needed proof that she was okay and had loads of friends, then she could make a few calls. Not a problem. Anything to avoid the round the clock surveillance that moving back in with her mom would bring.

"Give me another week," Bee reasoned, reaching for his hand across the table. "Let me show you I'm not isolating myself and I'll take a drug test. Okay?"

"Well…"

"You remember Camilla Evans, right?" Bee plucked at the first name that sprang to her mind.

"Lionel's daughter?"

"Yes." Bee nodded enthusiastically. "We've got plans tonight."

"Oh, you do?" Bernard's brow furrowed a moment before lifting. "That's great honey. Your mother will be so pleased to know your moving forward with your life. And the Evans family is one of the best."

"That's right." Bee smiled sweetly. "Camy and I go way back."

Bernard Durand and Lionel Evans were both very well connected men. Not only were they both insanely wealthy but they played golf together pretty much every Sunday, or they had four years ago. And little Miss Evans, with all of her sassy red hair and tons of money, had been right up there on the party list. Jason had introduced them one night at a club, and the girls had hit it off.

Snatching at her clutch now, Bee drew out her phone and held it down in her lap. Quickly working her thumbs across the screen, she tapped out an SOS text.

Bee: Camy it's been awhile but I'm back in town. Tell me there's a club we can tear up tonight.

While her Daddy leaned back in his chair and sipped at his water, Bee stole glances at those three little response dots. They blinked and blinked and blinked some more. Then... bingo.

Camy: Little Bee Bee Durand. Long time no talkie.

Gritting her teeth at the nickname, Bee forced a quick smile and tapped a response.

Bee: Yeah I know. I've been MIA, my bad. Hung up on a man, but that's done. Save me.

Camy: Folks got you on the run?

Bee: Is it obvious?

Huffing a laugh, Bee's eyes darted up to her father who smiled tentatively back at her.

Camy: Rumors abound. Never fear though, your wish is my command. Cool if Stacey and Gino come with?

Camilla never went anywhere without her entourage. Bee rolled her eyes before typing.

Bee: Always. When and where?

Camy: Let's do Black Lights. Say around 11?

Bee: Perfect. VIP table is on me.

Or on Daddy, Bee thought ruefully. If only she hadn't donated her settlement money.

Camy: Now you're talking. See you then.

Shoving her phone back in her purse, Bee sighed as the waiter approached with their meal.

If she had her choice she wouldn't be going out on the town tonight. If she had her own money, Bee would be holed up back in her hotel suite with a fresh bottle of Vodka and the promise of oblivion. But alas, that eventuality would have to wait.

CHAPTER 10

Gabe

Riding up in the elevator, Gabe ran his fingers through his still damp hair and exhaled. He'd spent the past three nights down in breeding and for the first time in years, he'd hated every second of it.

Hence the long shower right before he left.

With a quick shake of his head, he glanced up to the corner and eyed the steady red light of a surveillance camera. There was one in every elevator and at the end of each dormitory hall. It was only a matter of time before the cameras started popping up in their bedrooms, but for now Cambric was still too cheap.

In front of him, a bell dinged and the doors slid open. Stepping out, Gabe held his arm beneath the scanner on the nearest wall and listened for its beep.

The hall was dimly lit, with only a few overhead lights shining down. Despite the fact that there were no windows allowed here, The Agency tried to keep to a normal time schedule. They dimmed everything in the evenings and brightened it come morning.

Music thrummed steadily from a few open doors and chatter could be heard drifting down the hall. The trainee floors were always like this. They were pretty much all slammed together here and the whole atmosphere was sort of like a never ending party. The girls training to be monthly, party and hourly D2s were rowdy and fun and the guard staff here was light.

Cambric had a philosophy within their training system. There was always a method to their madness, always. After all, most customers who pay for sex actually want the other person involved to enjoy it, or at least to be able to fake it really well. And what better way to prepare captives to sell sex for a living, other than to make the act into an adventure.

Up to this point each captive here had had their every breath regulated to within an inch of their life. As children and up through completing high school they'd been monitored every second. You couldn't step a toe out of line and not have someone come down on you.

Then all of sudden there was the final selection that placed you into your category. D1s were kept in the tower where they'd all grown up and the D2 trainees were moved next door.

So, for the first time in their lives, D2 captives had the option of listening to music. Not choosing the song mind you, but being able to flip a switch and turn it on and off. Then came the open doors, the lack of a guard escort, the classes and relative freedom. Not real freedom, but the illusion of it.

It was intoxicating in itself. Plus, the working D2s down on the lower levels tended to pass their extra pills up. You could get high if you wanted, and so long as you were functional, Cambric staff looked the other way.

Truthfully, as long as everyone kept to their schedules and submitted to their training, then there wasn't that much to regulate.

Sex between D2s was not a big deal and as long as fights didn't break out (which they rarely did) then everything was cool.

The only exception being the permanent placement females. But there weren't that many of them, and as an extra precaution they were housed one floor up.

Gabe eyed the ceiling above him a moment as he cruised towards the room he shared with Charlie. It was quiet up there but still pretty lax. Gabe had ventured up a time or two, and it's not like anyone cared or really noticed. There was no specific mandate that male captives could not be up there, it's just that all the rooms were occupied by women.

When he shoved open the door to his room, Gabe found Charlie sprawled on his own bed, reading. The guy took studying to a whole new level. He was always scribbling down notes and flipping through pages in the night. Every test the guy took, he aced. Every assignment was days early, and about five pages longer than it needed to be.

Gabe admired the guy but still, he couldn't quite figure out the point. Why try so damn hard? He was just going to end up fucking rich housewives like the rest of them.

"Einstein." Gabe smirked at his friend before flopping down on the neighboring bed. "Do you know what time it is?"

Charlie's eyes flicked up and over before returning to his book. "The middle of the night, I think. Not sure."

"So why aren't you screwing that redhead down the hall?" Gabe drawled. He didn't know why, but he had a hard time letting the studying thing go. "You're wasting your time with those books."

"I already did," Charlie countered. "And you're one to talk."

"What's that supposed to mean?" Gabe frowned.

"A few months ago you would've stopped by two rooms on your

way here." Charlie snapped his book shut and eyed him with a triumphant smile. "At least."

"I was just down in breeding," Gabe countered. "Give me a break."

"It's not the same thing, and we both know it."

"Fuck off, Chuck."

"Don't call me that." Charlie gritted his teeth before moving off the bed to punch Gabe in the arm.

Rolling away from him, Gabe didn't quite escape in time and the sharp impact had him grunting involuntarily. The guy packed a good hit, even when playing around.

"Alright, okay!" Gabe laughed.

Scrambling back, he held up one hand while digging in the pocket of his pants. When he pulled out a little red box of kid's cereal, Charlie snatched it up. It was his favorite, Gabe knew. He'd picked it up along with another bag of chips from breeding. If he did his job down there, the guards occasionally let him walk away with a few precious items.

Holding it in both hands, Charlie eased down to sit on the edge of his mattress. Normally, the guy would already be ripping it open and chugging the contents like water, but this time he sucked in a slow breath instead.

"What?" Gabe asked.

They always traded like this. When one of them was down there, the other would bring a snack back. It was not a big deal. They did it for each other all the time.

"You might want to keep it," Charlie said finally and held the box out between them.

Gabe's brow furrowed but he didn't reach to take it. "Why?"

"I don't know." Charlie sighed, and looked down at the floor a moment. "Just save it, I guess."

"Tell me," Gabe demanded and snatched the box back.

"You shouldn't care." Charlie raised his eyes to Gabe. "You know you shouldn't, I know you shouldn't. But still... it's about Bee."

Gabe's gut dropped and a quick sickness swirled inside him. Something happened to Bee? Again? Shit, that girl could not stay out of trouble. Sucking in a breath he worked to ease down his panic.

"Tell me," he said.

"She's been on Discipline." Charlie shrugged. "Two days at the table, no food, only water."

"Fuck," Gabe growled the word as his shoulders heaved. "But you saved her some of your portion, right? You've been feeding her?"

"No man." Charlie shook his head. "They barely give me enough calories as it is and she's not my responsibility."

Shooting up to standing, Gabe began pacing. Selfish asshole. She'd been two days without food while Charlie was eating full meals and Gabe was feasting on red meat down in breeding. He wanted to scream. He wanted someone to blame, and an ass to kick.

"Hey," Charlie continued speaking. "If I gave a portion of my meal to every captive on Discipline, I'd starve. I'm sorry, but six months ago you'd of just let her suffer like everyone else. I'm sure Val's been giving her something."

"Val's just as tiny as she is!" Gabe practically shouted the words as he whirled on his friend.

He knew he was being unreasonable. He knew it was unfair of him to ask Charlie to step in when Gabe was gone. But damn it, that didn't change how he felt.

"You've got to stop this," Charlie said quietly, unruffled by Gabe's outburst. "You taking care of that girl is only going to get her hurt. She can't be yours Gabe, in any sense of the word."

"She's not," Gabe spat as his chest tightened. "We're just friends. I'd take care of you the same way."

"Maybe so," Charlie reasoned. "But you can't pretend you don't want more. You've stopped screwing everything that walks, you spend every spare second you have with her, you haven't eaten with me in months. You're obsessed."

"I'm still going down to breeding," Gabe countered. "Don't get butt-hurt because I've made some new friends."

"Breeding is involuntary," Charlie lowered his voice. "And I see the look on your face when the assignment comes through. You don't want to go, not anymore."

"What are you trying to say?"

"I just want you to stop seeing her," Charlie ventured.

"That's total crap and you know it," Gabe hissed. "I'm doing nothing wrong."

"Yet." Charlie shook his head. "You haven't done anything wrong... yet. And you may think I'm just being a jealous dick, but I'm not. You're going to hate yourself when you ruin that girl."

"I'd never do that," Gabe spoke through gritted teeth.

Gripping the box of cereal, he shoved it back into his pocket and pushed out of their bedroom door.

Charlie didn't know what he was talking about. The guy just didn't understand. Bee was a friend, a really close friend, but nothing more. Charlie was just jealous of the time Gabe was spending with her and Val. That's what this was really all about.

At the end of the hall, Gabe eyed the scanner warily before depressing the call button on the elevator. Maybe for the first time in his life he was contemplating not using the thing. With a quick glance over his shoulder, he eyed the camera at the far end of the hall. The little red light was distant, but there.

Stepping to the side, he blocked the view of the scanner with his broad back and pretended to hold his forearm under it. There was *no beep because he wasn't close enough, but if anyone checked the footage they would see that he tried to comply. Sort of.*

When the elevator doors dinged open, Gabe stepped inside and pushed the button to go one floor up. The ride was quick and it had his heart thrumming. Charlie wasn't right. He just wasn't.

Another three seconds had the doors sliding open onto an absolutely silent hallway. No one was wandering around. No music played. No doors were propped open.

Stepping out onto the floor, Gabe stared at the far end of the hall and noted there was no camera there. Glancing up, he spied one camera in the corner just beside him. He knew from a prior visit to this hall (no it wasn't stalking, he'd just walked with her back from class) that Bee's room was the first door on his right. If he nudged the camera with his hand just the tiniest bit to the left, the angle would no longer record her door.

At his back, the elevator doors slid closed and Gabe was left standing there alone. Sucking in a short breath, he took two steps to the side and reached up. He was tall enough to grab the thing with the tips of his fingers and so he gave the camera that little nudge.

Before he could focus on the swirling nerves now exploding in his belly, Gabe stalked to Bee's door and tried the handle.

It wasn't locked, of course it wouldn't be. She shared a room with Val and the handle only locked from the outside. Pushing the door open, his heart beat painfully in his chest as he realized how crazy he was. At this moment he was walking into (unannounced and uninvited) the bedroom of not one, but two permanent placement females.

"Bee Bee," Gabe whispered as the door shut at his back. "You awake?"

His eyes darted between the two beds. Both girls were tucked in, their matching long brown hair cascading over their pillows. Patting at the cereal and chips in his pocket, Gabe sucked in a breath. No movement.

"Bee." Gabe cleared his throat and had both of them shifting in their twin beds.

"Gabe?" Bee's voice sounded drowsy as two pairs of emerald green eyes focused on him.

"Yeah." Gabe suppressed the smile that wanted to burst on his face. She was the one on his right and he crossed to her quickly. "You okay? You hungry?"

"Where've you been?" Bee's brow furrowed and she pushed herself up to sitting.

Kicking off his shoes, Gabe climbed up beside her and sat down. The mattress dipped with his weight as he settled in. He wasn't so close that he was touching her, but he was close enough to feel the warmth of sleep emanating from her body.

"I was sick," he lied.

He never talked about being in breeding, at least not with anyone other than Charlie, but this was the first time he outright denied it had happened. Inside, a single pang kicked off in his chest. He didn't want to lie to her, but still, he didn't want to admit where he'd been either. Maybe there really was some truth to what Charlie had said.

Swallowing hard, Gabe brushed the thoughts away.

"I haven't seen you for days," Bee complained, and had his heart hammering for more. She missed him. Oh, how he wanted her to miss him.

"I know, I'm sorry, but I brought you something."

Shifting around, Gabe reached into his pocket and drew out the small box of cereal and the bag of chips. Let her think they were from the infirmary, that was as good a place as any, and they did carry a few similar items there.

"Oh." The single sound of excitement coming from Bee's throat had Gabe grinning.

Snatching at the items, she tore into them without a second thought. There was the rip of the bag, the crunch of chips and then came her little moans of pleasure.

Gabe's whole body responded. What he wouldn't give for the opportunity to hear those sounds with her writhing underneath him.

But then Charlie's warning came back around to haunt him, and Gabe gritted his teeth. He would not be that guy. Bee was off limits and he wasn't going to screw her over, figuratively or literally.

Searching for a distraction, he focused his eyes across the room. Val was still lying in bed. Maybe he'd woken them both when he came in, but Bee's sister had promptly rolled away and snuggled deeper under her gray blanket. The steady rise and fall of her body signaled she'd already fallen back to sleep.

"Heard you were on Discipline," Gabe ventured, his eyes drifting back over to watch Bee's mouth in the dark.

There were no lights on in the room and no windows to the outside, but their door had a pane of glass in it. Light from the hallway trickled in so that he could see her face. It was dim, not pitch black. Come to think of it, no place in Cambric was pitch black, save for Isolation when they pulled a curtain down over the door.

"Yeah," Bee admitted, her hand going involuntarily to rub over her stomach.

"Why?" Gabe asked, and watched her move from the now empty chip bag to the box of cereal.

"I, um..." Bee huffed a laugh and looked sideways at him a minute.

"Tell me," Gabe demanded, frowning.

"I refused Ben," she admitted finally and shrugged.

"Bee Bee," he sighed.

Slinging an arm over her shoulders, Gabe pulled her body in close next to his. Surprisingly, she did not resist him, but instead kept chomping on the cereal. With his head tipped back against the wall, Gabe closed his eyes.

He should be telling her that refusing Ben was not okay. He should be convincing her to submit to her trainer, like Gabe himself had to do, and so many others had to do.

He should not be silently screaming victory in his head. He should not feel like flying up to the moon and pulling it back down with him. But the idea of Bee refusing to have sex with Ben had Gabe so keyed up, he was having a hard time giving her the advice he would give to a normal friend.

"I'll give you some of my meals," Gabe offered. "Whatever I can sneak out of the cafeteria."

"No, I don't want you to suffer, too." Bee polished off the cereal and then sighed. "I'll submit to Ben tomorrow. It'll be fine."

Biting at his lip, Gabe managed a stiff nod in the affirmative. He needed to encourage Bee to follow the rules. He needed her to get out of Discipline and get back to eating regular meals. But the idea of her stepping into that room with Ben so that the guy could...

Fuck. Shit. A flash of jealous rage wanted to rule him.

Agency rhetoric sounded in his head: unwarranted emotion of any kind is intolerable. There is no happy, no sad, no anger, no jealousy. There is only acceptance, fear, and respect.

Acceptance. He'd work hard on that one from now on.

"I better go," Gabe cautioned, though his arm refused to retract from her shoulders.

"Can you stay a little longer?" Bee whispered.

Exhaling a breath through his nostrils, Gabe worked hard to manage the war within him. Did he want to stay? Hell yes, he wanted to stay, but he also knew what would happen if they ever got caught. And the shitty truth was, Bee would be the one to suffer the most, not him.

"Go to sleep," Gabe said, forcing himself to let go. "I'll stay until you're out. Okay?"

"Okay." Bee gave him a sleepy smile before lying back down.

Shifting around on the mattress, Gabe leaned his body against the wall while Bee curled up on her side. He let his eyes absorb the sight of her so close to him, the flutter of her eyelashes as she watched him watch her.

"Thank you," she murmured. "You know... for the food."

"Of course." Gabe squeezed his eyes shut a moment. "What are friends for?"

CHAPTER 11

Val

STANDING STILL ON THE STAGE, LOOKING OUT OVER THE CROWD, Val kept an accepting soft smile on her lips. To her right, Jason was standing behind yet another podium, talking about economic policy, social programs and of course... freedom. The sun shining high overhead was relentless, causing sweat to drip slowly down her spine. They were in another Texas park today, with green grass stretching out in every direction.

Brushing her hands lightly down her conservative navy-blue dress, Val inhaled a slow breath and worked hard to hold down her panic. She still couldn't stand crowds, not after what they'd done to Jason so many years ago. Groups of people could turn on you in an instant.

Her hair was swept up and back from her face, her high heels tall but not too tall, her jewelry there but not audacious. They'd only been at this campaigning thing for a month or so, but every aspect of their lives now seemed to be about not offending potential voters. And when you were trying to get elected to the Senate, that goal was pretty much impossible.

On top of it all, the time spent away from Jace never failed to make her stomach sick. It didn't matter that it was only during the day. It didn't matter that he was safe in his new private school with a bodyguard following him everywhere he went. Val didn't like to be separated from her son.

She felt ill each moment her eyes weren't on him, like Cambric was going to come take him away, even though they'd lost the court case. It defied reason. It defied logic. But still, Val couldn't stop her underlying sense of dread.

And Jason was taking it easy on her, or so his campaign manager, Quentin Daniels, was always saying. The guy was short and wiry, with sandy hair, brown eyes and endless energy. With three successful elections under his belt, he was the best, or so everyone said.

For the most part, Jason went along with all of his suggestions, but there were some things her husband held firm on. One of them was the requirement that they remain local for these initial speeches. Quentin complained and even Val knew they'd have to start venturing further out soon, but for now, Jason wouldn't budge.

Whenever Quentin would hand him a new list of towns and events, Jason would bring out his black ball point pen and start crossing them off. Quentin would suck in a breath as he looked over Jason's shoulder but then her husband would glance back at the guy with that icy stare of his and even Quentin's mouth would slam shut.

I'm giving up everything, Jason would say. *For now, we focus local and work our way out later.*

What are you talking about? Quentin was incredulous. *You signed up for this. You want to be elected.*

Yeah, Jason would answer calmly, his eyes flicking up to Val. *I do.*

He didn't. Not really.

Jason hated politics. He hated the game, the glad-handing, the tempering of one's opinion to please others, the corruption. But he was doing it anyway. He had to.

They couldn't go back on the deal now. Not if they wanted a chance at freeing Gabe. And once you climbed into bed with the Constitutional Militia, there was pretty much no way to climb back out.

As her husband's speech wound to a close, Val felt Quentin stir just off to her left. Out of the corner of her eye, she watched him quietly approach her. Placing one hand on her back, he leaned in and whispered in her ear.

"Come with me," he said, and she gave him a slight nod.

Turning on her heel with a practiced air, Val kept her arms relaxed at her sides. Quentin led her off the stage and down a few steps where she felt her personal bodyguard join them.

The crowd all around them was thick, straining at the simple white ropes that had been set up to create a narrow walkway. It led to a large white tent that had been erected not one hundred yards away. To Val, it seemed too far.

The crowd had watched her come down from the stage and so people were leaning in now, sticking their arms out and calling for her as she passed.

Nodding her head at them, Val continued to force a smile and, as previously coached by Quentin, she waved. The people threw out questions as she walked by, snapping photos, and occasionally pushing their children at her under the rope.

Whenever this happened, Val couldn't seem to help herself. Coming to a halt, she would lean down as far as dignity and her dress would allow and talk to the kids. They were sometimes shy, twisting their hands behind their backs before telling her she was pretty, or their mommy or daddy was going to vote for Jason.

Val would smile comfortably at them, and think of her own son. Why was it so much easier to talk to these little people rather than their adult companions? She didn't know.

"Mrs. Riggs," her bodyguard's low voice held a warning as he looked down at her. "We need to keep moving."

"Alright." Val sighed.

Ducking her head, she helped the little boy she'd been talking to back under the rope where his parents were still busy taking videos with their phones. Val was under strict orders from Jason's security team to keep moving at all times and she knew lingering here, even because of children, was a no no. Unless security stopped her, she was supposed to continue walking, not running mind you... unless of course they were running.

Val wanted to roll her eyes, but she had been schooled enough as a D2 captive to contain the gesture. Every movement she made out here was catalogued. Every frown, every yawn, every itch, every blink. She had to look perfect and pleasant and supportive and happy at all times. These requirements were not hard for her, though. She could fake it all day long.

So with confident shoulders and a controlled inhale, Val made it into the large white tent. Its shade was immediately welcome, dropping the temperature by about ten degrees.

The humidity still clung in the air though, despite the protection from the sun.

"I pulled you a little early," Quentin was saying, as he guided her to an empty space beside one wall. "Because your greeting line is actually longer than Jason's."

"I don't understand." Brushing at the fabric of her dress, Val surveyed the orderly rows of people that wrapped around the tent like an amusement park line.

"Jason agreed to a VIP meet and greet with some of our more generous donors," Quentin went on. "We have a line over there for him, and this line is for people who want to meet you."

"Oh." Val sucked in a quick breath and suppressed her frown.

They had done this before on a few occasions, but Jason and she had always been standing together. He did most of the talking while Val would nod and smile and pose for pictures. This new arrangement made sense, though. And maybe it was necessary to handle the amount of people who had signed up.

Glancing around, Val noted there were far more people here today than in the past. In the background, she could hear Jason's speech over the loud speakers. He was at the part where he talked about the captive industry and the new legislation he promised to get passed if he were elected.

It was controversial and exciting and every time he got to this part, the applause and shouting of the crowd would force him to stop talking. What should take only three minutes to say would end up dragging on to fifteen. In her mind, Val could see her husband biting his lip a moment before giving them all one of his smiles.

Maybe he didn't want to be a Senator. Maybe he didn't want to give up his businesses and his privacy and his personal opinions. But that smile he would flash them, it was genuine. Jason believed in this legislation. He'd worked hard for it for almost half of his life. Val didn't know what would happen to them all, if it didn't pass.

"Mrs. Riggs, it is so good to meet you," a female voice intoned.

Holding out both hands, Val welcomed the strange woman now standing before her with a warm shake. The plump blonde was dressed up in a red, white and blue dress and behind her trailed five or six other women who matched.

"We want you all to know what big supporters we are of you," another woman said, and had the others nodding along.

"It's so exciting to see change like this," agreed another.

"Thank you," Val responded with a smile and shook each one of their hands. "My husband and I truly appreciate your support. We could not accomplish anything without you all helping."

The words were practiced and had been given to her by Quentin, but none of the women lining up beside her for a photo op seemed to notice. Val was good at delivering lines. Val was good at playing a part. As long as these people didn't probe too deeply in conversation, she felt she could handle them just fine.

Over the next twenty minutes or so, Val greeted and posed with a dozen more supporters. Some male, some female. Some old, some young. That was the thing about their voter base, it was widely varied. Quentin had tried to map it, but the people coming out to see Jason Riggs didn't fall along normal voting lines. There was something about him, even beyond the captive legislation, that seemed to draw in all kinds.

When another round of thunderous applause broke out, Val's eyes jumped to the next person in her line. She was an elderly woman, with perfectly styled silver-gray hair and twinkling eyes. As she made her way slowly forward with a cane in one hand and a bottle of water in the other, Val found herself wanting to close the distance between them.

Off to one side, Val's bodyguard put a finger to his earpiece and frowned. He was trying to listen to something, but the people cheering only grew louder. Jason must be exiting the stage now. They always went crazy when he left.

"Hello," Val was the first to speak this time and reached out to try to steady the woman.

"Thank you, dear." The old woman smiled before tipping forward suddenly.

Stepping in to brace her, Val clutched the lady in her arms and managed to keep her from falling completely. Then her bodyguard and Quentin were there, helping to right her as well.

It wasn't until the woman had stepped safely back that Val felt the cool wetness of her dress sticking to her own skin. Looking down, she saw that the poor thing had spilled the entire contents of her water all over Val.

"Oh my," the woman muttered, her face falling to worry. "I am so sorry."

"That's alright," Val soothed, then glanced at Quentin who looked stricken.

"Let's get Mrs. Riggs to the women's restroom immediately." Quentin stepped to Val's bodyguard who gave up trying to hear the voices over his earpiece and nodded.

Together, the three of them weaved quickly out of the tent and over to a public restroom situated near the center of the park. The security team had elected to block it off originally because they felt it was too close to the stage. They didn't want to have the crowd moving in and out of it during the speech.

While her bodyguard went in first to clear the space, Val waited in the sunlight with Quentin. She held her hand up to shade her eyes as he worried over his phone.

"Just stay in there and I'll have someone bring you a change of clothes," he explained. "It shouldn't take more than a few minutes."

"Okay," Val agreed.

"Jason needs me back at the tent, so I'll see you then." Quentin paused a moment and glanced up at her. "Sound good?"

"Sure." Val bobbed her head as her bodyguard made his way back outside and gave her a nod.

As she entered the concrete building, Val wrinkled her nose. It didn't smell exactly, but it wasn't the most pleasant place to hang out. Her heels tapped against the cracked cement flooring and as her eyes traveled over the worn porcelain sinks and slightly dirty mirrors, Val hugged herself.

Not a minute later, as promised, a woman walked into the bathroom with a fresh set of clothes folded neatly in her hands. Without a word, she offered them to Val before turning around and striding back out the way she'd come.

Cocking her head to one side, Val watched the young woman leave. Her wavy dark hair bounced against her slender shoulders as she disappeared back into the sunshine.

That's when Val felt it. The buzzing.

Startled, she nearly dropped the clean clothes onto the floor.

Fumbling around in the fabric, Val managed to set the bundle on the edge of a nearby sink before digging through them. All the while, a single black flip phone continued to vibrate.

With shaking hands, Val frowned at the device before sucking in a breath and flipping it open. Holding the phone up to her ear she bit at her lower lip.

"Hey Val," the voice on the other end said. "Remember me?"

CHAPTER 12

Jason

"WHERE IS MY *WIFE?*" JASON GROWLED THE WORDS THROUGH gritted teeth as his head of security, CT leaned in close to shadow him off the stage.

Keeping one hand in the air to wave, and a big fake smile on his face, Jason did his best to cover the absolute fury that was bursting inside his chest. Quentin Fucking Daniels had broken cardinal rule number one. Do not, under any circumstances, remove Val from Jason's sight.

He'd made that part perfectly clear, over and over and over again. And yet, the little power tripper had ushered her calmly away while Jason still had a good twenty minutes left on his speech.

Did the guy have any idea how hard it was to sound like a calm, intelligent human being when your wife is being stolen from you?

No. Of course not. Not many people do.

Because not many people have actually had their wife stolen from them. Like Val was literally ripped from his arms and sent straight into hell for *months*.

So, did Jason have a little control problem? You bet your sweet ass he did.

The only times he felt comfortable were when Val was in his line of sight, or when she was safe at home... behind a towering high security gate... with a team of private guards stalking the property.

Someone was going to pay. Someone was going to pay right now.

"Don't know boss," CT's low whisper came to huff against Jason's ear. The crowd was so damn loud, it was hard to hear anything.

Glancing at the big man over his shoulder, Jason fought the urge to bolt. He fought the flood of panic and the accompanying bile that now teased at the back of this throat. *They didn't know? CT didn't know?*

But as much as he wanted to drop his head and plow like a battering ram towards the large white tent, Jason knew he couldn't. People were crowding all around him, reaching their hands over the ropes to shake, or offering him things to sign.

Voters. Eyes. Cameras. Media. He was trapped here, making his slow and controlled way to the VIP meet and greet not a hundred yards away.

"Go find her right now," Jason hissed the words even as he smiled and accepted a blue ball cap to sign. "And bring her to me."

"Yes, boss." CT ducked his head and moved quickly past.

It was all Jason could do not to follow him. It was all he could do to casually move onto the next voter while two additional security guards took CT's place beside him. Val was okay, he coached himself. She was just inside the tent already. He was being paranoid, as usual.

Handing another signed hat back, Jason watched as the man placed it on his own head with a grin and held up his phone to take a selfie. Jason slid into the shot beside the man and flashed a smile. The crowd cheered. Jason wanted to scream.

~

Ten minutes.

It took ten long agonizing minutes for him to make his way through the horde of people and enter the shade of the tent. In all that time, Val and CT remained absent. Jason's heart was going to explode, he was sure of it.

"Quentin Daniels." Jason wrapped his palm around the back of the short man's neck and squeezed. "Just the man I wanted to see."

Lifting his gaze from his phone, Quentin's eyebrows raised in question as the pressure continued to increase on his neck. Leaning in close, Jason kept an easy smile on his face as he whispered in Quentin's ear.

"Where the fuck is my wife?" He hissed.

Giving the other man a little shake, Jason released him but did not step back. Anyone around them wouldn't think anything of it, although Jason couldn't prevent his own jaw from ticking.

"Using the restroom," Quentin responded warily. "She should be changed by now."

"Changed?" *What the hell?* They had absolutely not discussed an outfit change.

Frowning Jason was just about to open his mouth when Val and CT entered the tent at the far corner. Sure enough, she wasn't wearing her blue dress anymore. Her long legs were now mostly covered by a conservative cream-colored skirt while a soft red blouse fell gently about her shoulders.

She looked just as beautiful as she had before. He couldn't figure what the point was.

Crossing to her as casually as he could manage, Jason gathered Val against his body and held her tight. His hammering pulse was only now starting to slow. She was safe. She was right here.

"You okay?" He asked before inhaling the scent of her hair. She was like a drug to him and he was the addict.

"Yes, but-"

"But what?" Jason cut her off.

Pulling back slightly, his hand reached up to cup her jaw. His thumb stroked her cheek automatically as his eyes swept over her face. Something was off. But then she was plastering on her own fake smile and stepping back from him.

He hated that. He hated her fake smile, her Agency smile. It made him want to smash Shane and Cambric into tiny pieces.

"We'll talk later," she assured him quietly, as she nodded her head to the hundreds of onlookers in the tent.

He could do nothing but silently agree. And silently remind himself to keep moving forward with the plan.

The people in the tent began applauding, thinking they were nothing more than a loving couple. Their love story was yet another reason voters liked them, or so Quentin said. Too bad it was a fucking tragedy, not at all the fairy tale the media made it out to be.

True, they loved each other, they were still *in* love. They had money and power and nice things. But Val had suffered cruelly for years, and then Jason right along with her. Not to mention their son.

But then Quentin was leading Jason off to one side of the tent and sending Val to another. Jason wanted to protest. He wanted to combine the lines and tell Quentin to shove it. But there were too many people around, too many phones recording. He was powerless. It was the absolute worst feeling in the world.

Giving his head a shake, Jason tried to tamp down on his anger. At least Val was in his line of sight, but even so, his gut would not stop churning.

About one minute into the arrangement, he made CT go stand over by Val instead of shadowing Jason. The sight of CT's six and a half foot hulking frame hovering over his wife served to temper Jason's fear, but only a little. He needed therapy as much as Val did, but he didn't dare get it.

Several hours and way too many faces later, Jason found himself helping his wife into the back of an armored sedan. It had more space than a standard car but less than a limo and the driver was one of only two that Jason implicitly trusted.

CT always rode shotgun and so stood by the open door now, waiting for the moment Jason himself slipped inside. Over the years, the two of them had developed a pretty good routine, but after today, Jason figured he'd have to make some changes.

From now on, CT would be Val's personal bodyguard and Jason would find himself another. He wasn't going to go through this ever again. If Val wasn't with him, then she'd be with CT, end of story. Full stop. Quentin be damned.

When the little power tripper himself made to get into their car, Jason huffed a laugh and placed a palm flat on the guy's chest.

"You took my wife from me," Jason said quietly and watched Quentin's confusion twist into an exasperated stare.

"Her line was-"

"I. Don't. Care." Jason gritted his teeth a moment before going on. "You can take the chase car back to the house, but you aren't riding with me. We can discuss your continued employment in my office when you get there."

"But..."

Sliding quickly down into the air conditioning, Jason yanked the door closed. The truth was he didn't know if he could truly afford to fire Quentin, but it wouldn't hurt to scare the shit out of the guy for the next half an hour or so. Besides, he was just returning the favor. Hadn't Jason just suffered through about thirty minutes of anxiety himself?

"Hey," Jason spoke to Val as CT settled in the front seat, and the armored car began to pull away. "You alright? Everything okay?"

Gathering her close up against his side, Jason flung his arm around her shoulders and let his eyes travel over her body. Why had she changed? He was just about to ask when she reached into the pocket of her skirt and pulled out a black flip phone. Skirts have pockets?

"What's this?" Jason asked.

Accepting the phone in one hand, he flipped it open and eyed the unknown number that had most recently been dialed. There were no texts, it was old as dirt. He couldn't remember the last time he'd seen one like it.

"Ava called," Val whispered, her eyes looking worried.

"From the Militia?" He clarified as his chest squeezed tight.

He didn't want them bothering her. Clay had agreed to work solely through Jason. It was only one of a laundry list of stipulations that the two of them had hashed out. Turns out neither of the men took orders very well, and both had negotiated to within an inch of their lives. They were quite the match actually, all differences set aside.

"Yes, I told her a long time ago I wanted to work with the underground," Val continued. "She has some ideas about how I can still do that and I've been thinking of some things on my own."

"Val," Jason warned. "You shouldn't have to worry about this."

"But I want to help," Val pleaded. "I *need* to do this, Jason."

"*Need?*" His eyes darted over her face. "You think this will... help you?"

Nodding her head, Val's eyes drifted down to her lap. She was folding in on herself, like she did so often now.

Jason's heart kicked at him as he fought a swirling mix of anger and guilt. The Agency had done this to her, made her submissive and fearful again. It made him sick to think how they'd done it, and Val refused to say.

"Listen," he sighed, wanting with every fiber of his being to say no. "Does it involve you going out alone? Because I can't breathe when you're away from me, you know that. I won't survive if anything happens to you, not this time."

"I don't know exactly what she needs, but I can always take a bodyguard," Val offered as Jason's stomach sank. "And we can talk everything over beforehand. If you say no, then I won't go."

"But you want to go," Jason stated. "Doing this will help you, right? This is you asking for permission."

Pulling his wife onto his lap, Jason held her body against his chest and pressed his forehead into her neck. She was everything to him. She was everything to Jace. The idea of her being directly involved with the underground and the Militia scared the hell out of him.

At the same time, the idea that she was asking for permission had him split in half. His wife of the past five years would not have asked for his permission. She would have told him what she was going to do and he would have had to adapt, or she would have done it without telling him.

He wanted that woman back. He wanted to restore her somehow, the one that took birth control behind his back because it was a better choice for *her*. He missed that Val, even though she'd infuriated him at times.

"I've been thinking of some things," Val went on, her hand coming up to stroke through his hair. "Of ways maybe we can get Bee back on our side, and maybe help other captives at the same time."

"I don't want to agree to this," Jason admitted.

Shifting around, he pressed his lips to her neck before exhaling a long breath. How could he say no? If he truly wanted her back. If he truly wanted Val to break out of this Cambric induced servitude, then he needed to step up.

And when it all came down to it, Jason would give Val anything she wanted, all she'd ever had to do was tell him what it was.

"Alright." Jason sucked in a breath and worked to calm his beating heart. "Let's call Ava back. Let's hear what she has to say."

CHAPTER 13

Bee

BITING AT HER LOWER LIP, BEE SAT ON THE EDGE OF THE NARROW bed and looked up at her trainer. Ben was a handsome man somewhere in his 40s with dark hair, brown eyes and muscles to spare. He was fairly new to the position, having been a monthly subscription D2 captive for a long time himself.

But with a dwindling client list and a training job opening up, Cambric had elected to transfer him. Up until a few months ago, Bee hadn't taken much issue with the process. Now, though... she was struggling.

"I'm not going to force you to do anything, you know that," Ben was saying. "But I hate to see you go back on Discipline. You've lost enough weight as it is."

"I know," Bee answered solemnly, then glanced away.

The room was stark, with four blank white walls and no windows. A camera was fixed in the upper corner of the room and its red light was a constant steady stare. Beneath it, was a single metal sink and across from that was the bed. There was a chair, too, but Ben wasn't using it at the moment. He was pacing.

Running his large hands back through his tussle of black hair, he huffed a breath and eyed the camera over his shoulder. Bee watched him from the corner of her eye, knowing from experience that he was actually a very kind person. It's just that his job had certain requirements, and if she continued to refuse him, they were both headed for trouble.

"Have I done something to upset you?" He asked, causing her to lift her face and look at him.

"No." She gave her head a quick shake and frowned. It wasn't anything he'd done.

"I guess I'm just having a hard time figuring this out," Ben went on. Coming to a stop in front of her, he crouched down so they were eye level. "We've done this before. All you have to do is go through one more round of submissions and we're completely finished. We never have to have sex again after that."

"I know."

Bee ducked her head, but then Ben was reaching for her chin. Tipping it up to keep her eyes on his, he watched her for a few careful moments.

She felt her heart thudding in her chest, painfully so. She just didn't want to sleep with him anymore. Was that so hard to understand? It had been fun before, but now she didn't want it. Truthfully, she didn't want to be with anyone, except...

"I'm new to this," Ben whispered. "If I could fake these and pass you, then I would. But all of my sessions get audited for the first year. There's no way for me to save you."

"It's okay." Bee reached up to pat at his forearm.

With a sigh, he dropped his hand from her face and pushed away. Standing up, he backed a few steps then stopped.

"Maybe if you told me what was going on with you," Ben suggested. "Then I'd be able to find a work around."

"I don't know." Bee shrugged, not sure she was ready to admit to herself what the issue was.

"Do I smell?"

"No." Bee huffed a laugh as Ben grinned.

"Am I too ugly for you?" He continued. "Because you know you're way out of my league."

"Nice." Bee chuckled. "But we both know you're hot."

"Alright..." Ben resumed his pacing, but kept his teasing tone. "Is it not good for you? Because you're going to hurt my feelings if you say no."

Shaking her head, Bee held back another laugh. "Don't worry," she teased. "You're good at your job."

"Phew," Ben mocked. "You had me worried for a sec."

Eyeing her another long moment, Ben crossed to the bed and plunked heavily down beside her. In silence, they both stared at the wall.

"Is there someone else?" He asked quietly.

Bee's heart stopped beating as she held her breath. Was there? "I haven't been with anyone but you," she stammered.

"That's not what I'm asking," he whispered, leaning in close so only she could hear. "You're a permanent placement trainee, you aren't supposed to be with another man, but that doesn't mean you don't want someone else."

Swallowing hard, Bee straightened on the bed and crossed her legs. Did she want to be with someone else? Her stomach dipped as a nervous sweat broke out on her palms.

She wasn't allowed to want anyone. She wasn't allowed to choose. Her entire life she'd been preparing for this outcome. If she was lucky, she'd be purchased and used by only one owner, and hopefully he wouldn't be a demanding asshole.

"Alright," Ben exhaled slowly. "I can't say I understand your situation exactly, but there are times that I have to sleep with someone I don't want."

Frowning, Bee's eyes shot to his face. The idea that Ben didn't want to have sex with her either had never occurred to her. Was she that selfish never to think about how this was for him? Possibly, yes.

"I have a bit of advice," Ben continued. "If that's the case."

"I'm sorry," Bee bit out. "I never thought about how this was for you."

"Don't worry about it." Ben waved her off. "It's not an issue I have with you, but I have experienced it. That's all I'm saying."

"Okay." Bee nodded. "So how do you do it? When you don't want to?" That'd be a pretty difficult thing for a guy to fake, she figured.

"I think of someone else," he admitted. "I dream I'm with someone else, that's the secret."

"Wow." Bee pursed her lips before whispering. "Why does that make me so sad?"

"Look, it's not about being sad or not sad, okay?" Ben went on. "It's about surviving. It's about accepting and moving forward. Whenever I was down in breeding, I just did what I had to do to survive."

"Breeding?"

"Yeah." Ben cleared his throat. "They'd keep me there for two or three days sometimes. I just focused on the positive. I just pictured someone else."

Bee's stomach sank and she frowned. Breeding. Two or three days at a time. She knew someone who disappeared two or three days at a time. But Gabe had always said he was sick.

Now Bee was the one left feeling ill.

. . .

"Hey! Hey!" Camy was shouting over the blare of club music. "Don't quit on us yet. Drink your shot."

Squinting at her friend over the darkened table in their VIP booth, Bee snatched at the shot glass and tipped it into her mouth. With her head flipped back, she let the smooth tang of top-shelf Tequila slide seamlessly down her throat. She was no quitter. At least not at this.

"Good enough for you?" Bee shouted back as she slammed the empty glass down.

"That's about right," Camy countered, her eyebrows wiggling in the flash of lights.

All around them, the air seemed to pulse. They were on a balcony with music thumping from the floor below. Half-naked bodies smashed into each other, dancing and grinding as the DJ spun yet another song. They were at the most exclusive club in Austin, dropping thousands of dollars without so much as a thought.

"I have to admit..." Gino leaned in close to her ear. "I missed hanging with you Bee Bee Durand."

Nodding absently, Bee kept her eyes focused on the crowd. Gino was one of Camy's entourage, as they say. He was tall, with twinkling hazel eyes and short brown curls that hung down to cover his ears. Sitting beside her in the booth, Gino played with his beer bottle and absorbed the music.

They'd partied together in that brief time between freedom from Cambric and escape with Gabe. He'd always been super relaxed and friendly. Bee understood why Camy kept him around. He was the calm to her storm and big enough to protect her if her mouth got her into too much trouble. Which it oftentimes did.

Stacey, the third wheel to Camy's threesome, was currently dancing a few feet away. She was all hips and curves and thighs, making practically every head turn wherever she walked. With dark brown skin and raven black hair, her chocolate colored eyes were always sparkling.

When Camy needed someone to spice things up, Stacey obliged. When she needed someone to slow things down, Gino stepped in. It worked well. Bee had seen it.

"Social whore alert," Stacey tossed the words over her shoulder before sauntering back to their table.

Running a hand down her tight gold dress, she gave a quick jut of her chin towards the stairs. A bouncer in all black with massive shoulders was checking his tablet as a tall blonde waited beside him. After a beat, he gave the woman a nod and unclipped the red rope, letting her enter.

"Ugh, look away," Camy muttered.

Scooting closer to Gino, she made room as Stacey dropped into the booth on her other side. Bee reached for her champagne glass just in time to realize the thing was empty. Damn.

A quick glance at the bottle chilling beside their booth told her it was empty as well. Time to order another one… at $500 a pop.

Shrugging, Bee lifted a hand to signal the waitress. They were going to need it.

"Well, if it isn't the Evans and the Durands out to conquer the world yet again." The blonde stopped in front of their table with a smile.

"Leila," Gino intoned, as all the women around him remained silent. "How's it going?"

"It's perfect handsome," Leila purred. "Just divine."

"Out on your own tonight?" Gino asked as Camy shot him a glare.

"Why, yes." Leila brightened as if this wasn't entirely by design. "As it happens I am."

For the next thirty long seconds, everyone remained awkwardly silent. It wasn't Gino's place to invite her to hang with them and Camy couldn't stand her. Stacey was good either way, as usual, so that left the decision up to Bee, who was paying.

"Why don't you join us then?" Bee asked finally.

Camy swore under her breath and Stacey lifted a hand to hide her pretty smirk.

"Lovely." Leila beamed, ignoring them both.

Scooting to the side, Bee tucked herself up against Gino to make more room. As Leila slid down into the booth and fluffed at her already perfect hair, she reached for her ever present phone and held it up.

"Picture!" She announced and had Camy gritting her teeth.

That was the real reason why Camy didn't like her. If you partied with Leila, she made sure everyone knew it. For the rest of the night their debauchery would be well documented and uploaded to every social media outlet available.

For Camy, this was annoying at best. She had a free spirit and enjoyed life with a no strings attached attitude. Of course, that didn't prevent any number of her "sort of" boyfriends to call her up when they saw her out without them.

For Bee it was a sudden gift. Come tomorrow, Daddy would have no doubt that she wasn't isolating herself. Mission accomplished. Of course, every society blog in the region would know she was back on the scene, but hey, beggars can't be choosey and all that.

Leaning in, Bee placed an arm around Leila and gave the camera on the blonde's phone her very best Agency smile.

Flash.

The thing took the first of many, many pictures in an extra long night.

CHAPTER 14

Gabe

She was pissed at him. That was the only explanation. Staring at the back of Bee's head, Gabe sat in the cafeteria two tables away and ground his teeth together slowly. For the first time in half a year, she hadn't made room for him at her table.

And of course, he'd stood there, holding his red tray like an idiot, while Bee ignored him and Val blushed crimson. The other captives sitting with them had gone silent and for some reason it had taken Gabe way too long to realize she wasn't going to scoot over.

"What the hell?" He whispered the words now, even as his eyes refused to leave her pretty head.

"This is a good thing," Charlie reasoned. "Just let it go."

"But what the hell?" Gabe again, giving his head a shake.

At least his old friend had made room for him. At least Charlie had motioned him over and threatened the rest of his table into silence.

But for all of his kindness, Gabe found himself incapable of taking the guy's advice. Let it go? Fuck that fucking shit. Bee owed him an explanation. They were best friends after all, weren't they?

He gave her extra food when he could and walked her back from class. Hell, he even snuck into her room late at night and watched her fall asleep. They'd spend a good hour or two talking while she lay there blinking up in the dark. He'd memorized her lips, the smell of her blankets, the heat of her legs as they draped over his lap.

That was the trick, he always remained sitting up. He didn't dare lay down beside her, no matter how badly he craved it. Eventually, she would drift off and he'd sneak back out.

So what the hell had happened? He'd only been gone in breeding for two nights this time. He'd only missed two damn nights and she was already giving him the cold shoulder.

"Nope," Gabe spat the word out and made to stand up. No way was he letting this ride. No way.

Gripping him by the elbow, Charlie yanked him back down before hissing in Gabe's ear. "Where do you think you're going?"

"To talk to my..." Gabe finished the sentence in his mind. Girlfriend.

To talk to my girl. My girl. She's mine. The words kept repeating themselves inside of him. They felt so real. They felt so true, but he couldn't claim them. Gabe could never ever say that Bee was his, and the reality was... she wasn't. Not in the way that he wanted.

Raising his eyebrows, Charlie tilted his head to one side. "Your what?" He asked quietly.

"To my friend," *Gabe growled the correct answer, even though they both knew it was bull. "I need to talk to my friend."*

"Gabey." Charlie sighed. "Stop. Please, man. Just stop."

Bowing his head a moment, Gabe pushed his thumbs against his closed eyelids. "I can't," he whispered finally, his elbows propped up on the table. Defeat kept his head hanging low.

"She's your kryptonite," Charlie grumbled.

"Krypto-what?" Gabe raised his head, brow furrowed.

"Kryptonite," Charlie repeated. "Superman? Come on Gabe, even you can't flunk our pop culture class."

"Whatever." Gabe waved him off and let his eyes drift back to Bee.

She was standing from the table now, her empty tray clutched in both hands. Were her shoulders a little tense under her gray uniform? Could she feel his eyes on her? Then Val was getting up too and the both of them were walking off.

When Val shot him a pitying look over her shoulder, Gabe's whole body tensed. Maybe Bee wasn't speaking to him, but he'd be willing to bet his next three meals that Val would spill under little to no pressure.

"Nuh-uh," Charlie grunted.

Laying a heavy arm across Gabe's shoulders, Charlie held him fast. The captives all around them continued to eat. A few of the girls looked at him from beneath their lowered lashes before whispering to one another. It was about him, that much was obvious, but what exactly they said he absolutely did not care.

"This has never happened to you before," Charlie commented. "I get it."

"What?" Gabe's eyes shot to Charlie.

"Rejection," Charlie supplied and tried to hide the hint of a smile. "There's never been a girl who could walk away from you. It stings."

"Stings," Gabe mouthed the word and stared down at his still full plate.

Was that what this feeling was? This sick panic swirling through his veins? A sting? A bruised ego?

"Don't worry." Charlie gave Gabe's tray a quick nudge. "I can fix it."

"You can?"

"Yeah. Eat up, then we're hitting the gym. We're gonna work that girl right out of your system."

Nodding, Gabe plucked up his fork and swallowed hard. The scrambled eggs, sliced tomatoes and dry bread taking up space on his plate looked less than appetizing but it didn't matter. Maybe Charlie was right. Maybe this was just about him not getting what he wanted. It made sense right? Maybe this was him wanting what he couldn't have and all that.

Yeah. He shoved in a bite of egg.

Alright. He chewed the tasteless food.

Okay. He swallowed.

Reaching for his glass of water, he drank. Replacing it on the table, he began again. He ate until everything was gone. Then he stood with Charlie beside him and stalked off towards the gym.

All the while, his mind warred within him. What had he done? What had he said?

He tried to recall the last time they'd spoken. What had it been about? Had Bee been upset when he left? No, he would have noticed... wouldn't he?

Holding his right forearm out, he waited alongside Charlie as the gym guard scanned them in. The room wasn't huge, but it wasn't small either. A line of treadmills and elliptical machines faced a wall filled with windows. This room, along with the cafeteria was one of the few spaces in Cambric that had them.

Blue padded mats covered the floor with a variety of equipment positioned every so often. Men and women both sweated and jogged and grunted and lifted. Gabe's eyes tracked to one in particular and held.

Well... fuck him. If it wasn't Ben, Bee's esteemed trainer.

"Hey Chuck," Gabe spat.

In response, Charlie shot him a dubious look. He hated that nickname. When your name is the only thing you own, any unapproved variation in it tended to rub one the wrong way. But it was whatever right now. It was background noise to the energy filling him.

"Did Bee have any training time while I was gone?" Gabe continued.

His shoulders squared off, his lungs expanded. He felt high right now, so primed all of a sudden.

"Uh," Charlie let the word out before his gaze swiveled to follow Gabe's line of sight. "I think so."

Great. Good.

Here was the one guy who had everything that Gabe wanted. He was the only man who got to have Bee. The. Only. One. And now... well, now the guy was going to get the shit kicked out of him.

Did someone say sting?

Yeah, this was going to fucking sting.

"Get up," the male voice was gruff, breaking into Gabe's dreams.

On a groan, Gabe rolled onto his back and opened his eyes. He was back in Isolation, back in the present day. A Cambric guard was standing over him, after another second, he gave Gabe's thin mattress a kick.

"Now," the guy grunted, before turning away.

Rubbing one palm down his face, Gabe ignored the ache in his muscles and sat up. It had been this way for the past several weeks. The drugs they gave him every night had his mind swimming in vivid dreams... or memories. They were so real, it felt like he was living them.

Glancing to the glass partition, Gabe noted Charlie was still gone. They'd taken him out a few days previous and he hadn't been back. Gabe was hopeful that his old friend was back in the dorm tower. Gabe was hopeful that the fact Charlie was eating regular meals again meant his friend was returning to normal captive status. They would need that status to move forward with Gabe's plan.

"What do you want me to do?" Gabe asked.

Looking around, he noted his meal tray was absent. There was no water, no food, no little white pill that made him feel floaty and disconnected. Something was different about today, that much was obvious.

"Kneel," the guard instructed. "Forehead against the wall."

With a nod, Gabe complied. This part wasn't new. Cambric had been playing submission games with him for awhile now and though every bone in Gabe's body wanted to revolt, he knew he couldn't. He had to convince them he was compliant. He had to convince them he was broken.

So without any protest he pushed off his mattress and crossed to the wall the guard had indicated. Kneeling down, he scooted his body so that his forehead touched the wall. Hands drooping loosely at his sides, he waited. And he waited. And he waited some more.

It was hard to say how long he held himself there. His knees screamed at him. The toes of his bare feet strained to keep him balanced. His heart pounded and pounded with anger.

But it was an anger he had to let go. He couldn't let his desire to explode rule him. If he was going to get to his target, and complete his self-imposed mission, then he would have to be able to fake this for a long time.

Inhaling through his nose, Gabe closed his eyes and worked to ease his own tension. He could do this. He could beat them this way so long as he kept himself under control.

"Alright," the guard relented. "Up and to the showers."

Rocking back onto his feet, Gabe pushed up to standing on unsteady legs. The guard followed him out of his Isolation room and down the hallway. No one else was around. Stopping at the shower room, Gabe stepped inside, stripped and washed himself under the frigid cold spray.

When he was done, the guard tossed a clean uniform at him and Gabe got dressed in the pressed gray slacks and a white collared shirt. Well, almost all the way dressed, there were still no shoes. No shoes and no socks. He was barefoot and they would keep him that way for now.

"Outside," the guard instructed.

Stepping to one side, the guy let Gabe walk through first. At this point the guards always remained at Gabe's back. They never walked in front of him, they never gave him an opportunity to lash out.

The day that they stopped with the hyper-vigilance would be the day Gabe succeeded. At some point, a guard would lead him somewhere. At some point in the future, they'd feel like he was such a non-threat, that they'd allow him to walk along at their backs. That's when it was go time... not a second before.

Stopping at a wall scanner, Gabe held out his forearm and listened to the customary beep before pushing the door open and blinking into the sunshine. It was beautiful, but icy cold. Spring was close, but not here yet. Still, the sunlight held a special sort of warmth. He couldn't remember the last time he felt heat.

There were no blankets in Isolation. There was no hot water anywhere in Cambric. So this blessed glimpse of daylight had Gabe's heart swelling.

Suddenly he wanted to fucking cry. He thought he'd cherished every single day he had on the water in the Maldives. But now he realized he hadn't even come close to appreciating it.

"Over there," the guard said, pointing to the cafeteria door.

With a quick nod, Gabe followed the concrete pathway that cut through the expansive green lawn. Gooseflesh prickled along his exposed arms and neck. He felt every frigid footstep soak into the soles of his feet.

They were in a large courtyard, with extra high brick walls topped with barbed wire that connected various buildings. Ahead of him, the twin dormitory towers cast imposing shadows along the ground. He'd grown up here. He'd spent the first two decades of his life as a prisoner knowing only what Cambric showed him. Now that he knew better, this awful place made him sick.

Once inside the cafeteria, he was directed to the Discipline table. It was empty today, save for a red plastic tray that contained one barren plate and one vacant cup. There was even a plastic fork placed neatly off to one side, to remind you there was no food with which to use it.

"Kneel," the guard instructed.

Gabe swallowed hard. Normally, captives would just sit at the table and stare at the empty tray. This was a new level of submission, to be kneeling on the ground beside the table with hundreds of captive eyes on him and the smell of food permeating the air.

He. Hated. It.

Blowing out a controlled breath through his nostrils, Gabe shut his eyes and knelt down. He fought his impulse to scream. He fought his impulse to jump up and drill the Cambric guard in the nose. He fought his impulse to pick up the plastic tray and smash it into a million tiny pieces on the table before him. He fought.

But then a familiar voice was talking to him. The voice was chuckling and had Gabe opening his eyes. Shane. The object of Gabe's desire was now sitting lazily on the tabletop, his feet laced into expensive shoes, the bruising that surely must have marred his throat was gone.

"Kiss the floor, lover boy," Shane said. "Right now."

Lips parting a moment, Gabe blanched. Kiss the... what the fuck?

This *asshole*. Gabe sucked in a breath. This piece of absolute shit was in complete control of Gabe's life, and if Gabe wanted a real chance at him in the future... well, fuck.

All around them, the cafeteria was silent. Gabe couldn't tell if it was just that the amount of noise inside his own body was so loud he'd gone deaf, or if maybe everyone was watching. He thought probably the later.

Smirking, Shane lifted an eyebrow as the extra guards always lurking behind him stepped closer. Without another moment's hesitation, Gabe bent forward and did as he was told. He pressed his lips to the dusty, cold cement of the cafeteria floor... and he fought.

CHAPTER 15

Bee

Reaching onto her plate, Bee plucked up the lonely green apple and eyed it warily. It was perfect. Not too big, not too small. You could flush the core down the toilet when you were finished and no one would even know you'd snuck food out.

Nibbling at her lip, she glanced quickly over her shoulder. The hustle of the cafeteria went on all around her. No one was watching, well... except for Val.

"I don't know," Val whispered.

She was always like this. So timid. So accepting of her place. It was Val's exact reaction, that uncertain sort of fear, that made Bee's final decision for her.

Tucking the apple into her lap, Bee fumbled with the buttons of her dress. The gray uniform was form fitting, but there were two spots a pair of apples might be easily hidden. Like say... in one's bra.

"Give me yours," Bee hissed and of course, Val complied.

A few seconds later and the apples were safely tucked away. Bee *felt ridiculous, but only for a moment. All it took was one look at Gabe and guilt came crashing in to replace it.*

He was sitting at Discipline, staring down at his empty plate, the way he had been for the past two days. His beautiful golden hair was damp, his feet were bare. Before that, he'd spent an entire week in Isolation. And the thing of it was... it was all Bee's fault.

"How do I look?" Bee asked and Val frowned.

"You don't have to do this," she cautioned. She was always so cautious. "He wouldn't want you to."

"Yeah, well..." Bee sucked in a breath and stared down at her own meal. "I feel responsible."

"Responsible?" Val was incredulous. "He's the one who was fighting."

"I know." Bee glanced at her best friend. "But he fed me before, so I owe him."

"Are you sure that's all this is?" Val asked quietly, her fork poised over her chicken salad.

Heat rushed to Bee's cheeks and she gave her head a little shake. Was that all this was? A debt to be paid? Immediately her gut revolted. No. No, that's not what this was.

If she could have been honest right then and there, Bee would have confessed. If she wasn't surrounded by listening ears and gossiping mouths, then her words would have been easy. Instead of saying yes, she would have said no.

No, this wasn't just a debt to be paid. She wasn't going to sneak Gabe food to make them square. Nope, not even a little bit.

Truth be told, she was risking herself for the sole purpose of being close to him. Gabe had been gone for over a week now and his absence was eating away at her soul. She missed him.

She missed him sitting in her bed at night, she missed his dancing brown eyes and clever words. She missed his laugh and his smile, his broad shoulders and talk of freedom. The awful truth was... she missed that handsome, amazing, untouchable man like crazy.

And sure, she'd been hurt when she found out he'd been down in breeding, even more so when she realized he'd been lying about it for months. Every time he'd said he was sick, he was really down sleeping with someone else. And yes, she understood that it wasn't his choice. And she understood that they were nothing special to each other, they had no commitment, no relationship beyond being close friends.

But still... it burned so brightly inside of her. The jealousy. The absolute loathing. So yes, she'd snubbed him. She'd ignored Gabe in class. She'd avoided him in the halls and she hadn't made room for him at their table. That's right... their table. Because he'd been sitting next to her during every meal for months.

It couldn't be a coincidence that he'd gotten up from that very breakfast, walked to the gym with Charlie, and proceeded to slam a fist into Ben's face.

The rumors were flying, but on a few points everyone agreed. Ben gave as good as he got. Charlie and the Cambric guard stepped in before it got too bad. And both men were being punished over it because neither of them had snitched.

When Gabe was asked why the fight had happened, he said he didn't know. When Ben was asked why the fight had started, he said he didn't know. And so ended every captive fight ever. It was an unspoken rule, but a rule nonetheless. Captives. Don't. Rat.

Hard stop.

"Bee," Val began. "You haven't eaten anything."

"I know." Bee ducked her head and stared down at her salad.

Pushing her food around her plate, she sucked in a nervous breath. Somehow, someway, she had to get these apples to Gabe. If patterns held true, and he continued to behave, Cambric should release him back to his own dorm room tonight.

Flicking her eyes up and over, Bee watched the back of Gabe's shoulders. She watched him inhale, his ribs expanding ever so slightly beneath his white collared shirt. His arms remained loose at his sides, his spine straight, his face tilted down. There was a ring of dampness marring his collar where his golden curls dripped water onto his shirt.

He needed a haircut, she thought absently. Cambric had let the curls drift down around his ears. She couldn't decide if it made him even hotter than he already was.

As if he could hear her thoughts, Gabe turned his head ever so slightly and glanced at her over his shoulder. Freezing, Bee felt those dark eyes of his lock on hers. It was only a second before he righted himself. Only a second before he returned his gaze to his plate. He didn't want the guard to notice.

But just that tiny second had tingles exploding in her belly. Butterflies rushed through her system and had Bee clenching her thighs together.

Swallowing, she tried to work moisture into her throat, it was suddenly so dry.

"Eat." Val nudged her with an elbow.

Nodding, Bee stabbed at some lettuce with her fork and placed it in her mouth. She chewed, she swallowed and she tried hard to rid her body of this feeling. It wasn't an easy task.

By the time darkness had fallen and they were tucked up in bed, Bee had mastered herself. She was calm. She was in control. She could hardly remember that flood of strange excitement that had filled her.

Reaching beneath her mattress, she pulled out the twin apples and eyed them in the dark. They were smooth, their skin still perfect despite their travels throughout the day.

Looking over at the bed across from her, Bee watched the steady rise and fall of the gray blanket. Val was asleep.

Good little Val, always so compliant. She never got into trouble. And a part of Bee felt relief at that. She'd never had to watch Val be punished. The thought of it had her insides dropping. She would never want to see it. Watching her sister suffer through Discipline would be so much worse than enduring it herself.

Flinging the covers back, Bee slipped out on bare feet. She didn't need shoes for the short trip that was ahead of her. Out in the hall-way, it was quiet, as usual. No one wandered about late at night, not like on some of the other floors.

It was only a few steps to the elevator and then one flight down. Bee listened to the beep of the scanner as she exited her floor, then again as she entered Gabe's. She didn't think anything of it. This was all routine, all background. You beeped in and out of every place you went.

But as she stepped into the hall, her heart kicked up a few notches. There were captives everywhere. Men and women both, laughing, singing.

Bee's mouth dropped a fraction before she snapped it shut. It's not like she hadn't been down here before, but never in the middle of the night. It was a shock really, how rowdy it all was even though it was late.

"Hey Bee," a female voice greeted her. "What's up?"

"Amber." Bee exhaled in relief at the familiar face. "Um... I'm looking for Gabe's room."

"Are you?" Amber's eyebrows raised as a few other captives stopped to listen. "Well... it's that one down there."

"Thanks." Bee gave her a smile before making her way to the door indicated.

Stopping at the threshold, Bee looked inside. The door was propped open, with Charlie reclining on one bed reading and Gabe face down on the other. Neither of them noticed her. Clearing her throat, Bee stepped inside.

Charlie raised his head and after a beat, he swore.

"Nope," he announced. Snapping his book shut, he shoved off his bed and stormed out past her. "I'm not doing this."

"Um." Bee's brow furrowed a moment before her eyes skipped back to Gabe.

He was sitting up now, his mouth gaping open as he stared at her. Bee gave him a smile. Just the sight of him had every light in her body turning on. She felt filled with energy all of a sudden, with a nervous, excited sort of energy that had her cheeks flushing and her hands twisting together behind her.

"Are you hungry?" She asked.

Stepping further into his room, Bee reached into her bra and drew out the apples. She felt silly, having to carry them that way, but it's not like she had pockets... or pants. And he'd be happy to have the food, she figured. At least, when he'd snuck her some, it had been amazing.

"What are you doing here?" Gabe asked suddenly, a frown creasing his face.

"Bringing you food?" Bee's brow mirrored his. He wasn't happy?

"You can't be in here. Did you scan onto this floor?"

Shooting to his feet, Gabe crossed to her quickly and placed his hands on her shoulders. Bee's brain froze in place. The man was still talking. He was giving her a little shake and forcing her to walk backwards until she stood dumbly outside of his door, but she wasn't processing it.

He had no shirt on.

Gabe was naked from the waist up, his bronze skin rippling with muscles, his chest mere inches from her face. She could smell the freshness of his shower.

"You can't be here," Gabe was hissing. "The hall camera records my door."

"Wait... what?" Bee stuttered, her eyes darting all around as she realized he'd just kicked her out.

"Come on now, Gabe," Amber quipped. She was one of half a dozen other captives lingering in the hall. "Usually you give a girl what she comes for before showing her the door."

"That's not what this is," Gabe protested, before rolling his eyes and backing away.

"Wow." Bee huffed the word as a mix of humiliation and anger flooded her.

That's not what this is? And what had Amber said... Gabe usually gave girls what they wanted before kicking them out? Embarrassment crept up her face in the form of a crimson blush.

She was so stupid. Here she was, smuggling him food, feeling all these things for him, wanting... she didn't know what. And he was just kicking her out like some other chick he'd already had.

Except he hadn't even been with her. He hadn't even tried.

"You. Asshole." Bee's shoulders heaved as she said the words.

Cocking her arm back, she let the first apple fly. Gabe's face lit with surprise as it pegged him square in the chest. A chorus of laughter exploded all around them, followed by hoots of encouragement.

Putting his hands up in defense, Gabe retreated quickly into his room as Bee threw the next apple. The perfect, not too big, not too small, shiny piece of fruit she had carried so carefully with her all day, landed with a solid thump on his forehead before bouncing off to one side.

"Ow! Shit, Bee!" Gabe rubbed at the spot. "What the hell?"

Storming forward, Bee crossed back into his room and gave his chest a hard shove. He didn't even rock back a step. It was like she had no effect. She was weak. She was nothing to him, and it made her anger all that more bright.

"You. Asshole." Bee snarled the words again and made to push him harder.

Snatching at her wrists, Gabe held her fast and pulled her in close. "Are you crazy?" He hissed, his eyes darting over her face. "Why are you throwing shit at me?"

"You just kicked me out," Bee's voice cracked, she couldn't help it. "I'm trying to feed you and you just... like I'm just one of your other girls."

"Bee."

"No." Bee sucked in a ragged breath, wishing like hell she could stop this embarrassing flood of emotion. "I'm not one of your other girls."

"I know that."

"I'm not." Bee jerked her arms again, but he held them fast.

"Bee Bee." Gabe sighed.

"But why?" Bee looked up at him then, her eyes searching his suddenly for the answer. Her heart. It hurt. "Am I not pretty enough for you?"

"That's not-"

"You've never even tried," Bee whispered the words, her eyes dropping to linger on Gabe's lips. "What's wrong with me that you don't want me?"

"Don't want you?" Gabe's brows raised and his hands squeezed tighter on her wrists.

Before she knew what he was doing, Gabe was pushing her backwards. When her body slammed up against the wall, he kept right on coming. Her mouth dropped open and a squeak snuck out, but then that naked chest of his was pressed up against her breasts, pinning her in place.

Releasing her arms, Gabe's hands shot to her face as he crashed his mouth down on hers. It was electric, the contact.

Gabe's lips were demanding. He was kissing and nipping and groaning. When she finally parted her lips for him, his tongue dipped quickly inside her mouth and he began to taste.

She moaned into his mouth as her heart hammered against her ribcage. She couldn't help it. The aching sound left her body and went straight into his, where she felt a rumbling response in his chest.

His hips tipped into her belly then, keeping her pegged against the wall as his hands left her face. They slid down her sides, skimmed her breasts, her waist, her hips. He was everywhere all at once, making her want him. Making her want more, faster, further... until he was gone.

Shoving away from her, Gabe took a few stumbling steps back and ran his hands up through his tussle of golden hair. His shoulders were heaving and his eyes frantic.

Bee could only stare at him, feeling slightly dazed. A pool of want throbbed between her legs. She'd never craved a man this way before.

"Don't ever say that I don't want you," Gabe whispered finally. "But I can't have you, Bee Bee. I can't."

"So, what. You just want me to go?" Bee asked, her heart tripping painfully inside her chest.

"Yeah." Gabe covered his face with both hands as he said the words. "Just go."

CHAPTER 16

Gabe

SWEAT POURED DOWN GABE'S FACE, CAUSING A SALTY SORT OF STING *to fill his eyes. Blinking rapidly, he puffed through the irritation and kept going. The treadmill beneath his feet spun a fast pace. His thighs burned, his arms pumped and his lungs worked to suck in oxygen.*

Beside him, Charlie gave him a bit of side eye. The guy lived for this crap. He jogged along calmly, controlling his breathing, barely breaking a sweat. All the while, Gabe's body was revolting.

"You hanging in?" Charlie asked finally.

Exhaling out in hot puffs, Gabe gave his head a quick nod. No verbal answer. That was all the guy was getting.

Reaching over, Charlie turned the treadmill down a few notches. With a frown, Gabe smacked his friend's hand away and turned it back up.

Must. Run. Bee. Out. Of. System.

That was the goal. This was the way. He was committed, damn it.

"Look, you kicked her out, you did the right thing," Charlie reasoned. "She won't be back."

"Huh," Gabe grunted the word and shot Charlie a patronizing look.

If he thought that was the only problem, he simply had no idea what this was like. Yeah, Gabe had turned Bee away. And no, the girl of Gabe's dreams had not been back since. But that didn't mean the fight was over. No way. No how.

She was all he could think about. Bee filled his head during the day and haunted his thoughts at night. He'd had a taste. He'd had just the tiniest taste and it was like giving a single drop of water to a dying man in Isolation. Gabe wanted more. He needed more.

If he closed his eyes he could still feel the softness of her body beneath his hands. He could taste the sweetness of her mouth. Hell, he could hear her moan as he swallowed the sound into his own body.

"Faster," Gabe panted, and jabbed at the control panel. He had to turn his brain off. He had to turn this off somehow.

"Come on, man." Charlie frowned. "You're going to hurt yourself."

"Yup." Gabe smiled.

"Alright," Charlie hissed and slammed his palm down on the controls. "You want pain? Fine. Look over there."

"Huh?" Puffing, Gabe let his friend reduce his speed a final time and followed his line of sight.

The wall of windows in front of them made for a pretty broad view. On their left was a fenced off pool where some of the older kids took turns swimming. To the right was a small playground. A few toddlers cruised around on unsteady feet while their D1 nannies looked on.

"Call me crazy," Charlie whispered. "But that one with the curls looks a lot like you."

"Oh... shit..." Gabe's mouth dropped and he stumbled a bit.

Reaching out a hand, Charlie clutched at Gabe's arm to hold him upright. After a sharp inhale, Gabe managed to keep going. His feet slapped against the belt, and his arms somehow kept swinging, but inside, his mind was exploding.

He'd been sent to breeding early, he and Charlie both. Technically, Cambric wasn't supposed to make them have sex until they'd turned eighteen, but hey... The Agency didn't always play by the rules, that much was clear.

So Gabe had gone. Partly because he had to, and partly because he was a sixteen-year-old boy with a healthy desire to be with women. Lots and lots of women.

And that was what... four years ago now? Which would make his oldest kid three. Gabe swallowed hard and stared out the window. Up until this very moment he hadn't once considered the reality before him. He had kids.

Shit, he had lots and lots of kids. Kids he couldn't protect. Kids he couldn't provide for. Kids who would never know him.

Squeezing his eyes shut, Gabe stopped running. He let the treadmill spin him back, and right before he crashed, he stepped off. Lungs heaving, he threw his arms on top of his head and paced away. How many children had he fathered exactly? He'd never even bothered to ask.

Cambric brought him down there and he did his job and they sent him back up. Oftentimes, he was sent to the same woman but with large gaps between visits. Like a year long gap. But not once had he asked the most important question of all... Did you just have my baby?

What kind of prick did that? A young, naive one, but still, that was no excuse.

Pain.

He'd said he wanted it. Well... Charlie had delivered.

"Hey, man," Charlie lowered his voice. "You alright?"

"Yeah." Gabe gave his head a little shake to clear it. "I'm fine."

Beneath him that same old treadmill whirred. Sucking in oxygen, Gabe kept his feet slapping down and his arms pumping. They'd been back at this workout thing for a few months now and unlike in his youth, he no longer felt the need to manufacture pain. Pain was all around them. No need to go grabbing it out of the air.

Charlie had indeed been returned to general population. He was eating regular meals and looking like his old healthy self. Though it had taken a good deal longer, Gabe's now famous floor kissing display with psycho Shane had eventually earned him a trip back to general pop as well.

Sometimes eating crow, and stuffing it so deep down in your belly that it creates a black void, has benefits. Long term benefits. Benefits that Gabe was waiting with bated breath to collect.

"Room 115's on your schedule," Charlie commented.

"Yup." Gabe gave up a quick nod.

"That was Val's staging room." Charlie cleared his throat. "For the videos."

Gritting his teeth, Gabe stared out the wall of windows a moment. It was full on springtime now, with summer set to arrive any day. Off to the left, a group of boys were tearing around the pool. The sight of them made his gut drop. Some of them were his. More than likely, with those fucking golden curls he seemed to pass on at a moment's notice, a good handful of the rowdy kids out there belonged to him.

What sort of fate awaited them? What would their selection bring? Gabe could only pray they would turn out to be D1s. Domestic captives trained to mow lawns, chauffeur cars, clean houses, cook meals.

The odds weren't good though, he knew. Too many of them looked like him. Too many of them looked like their mothers. Too fucking pretty. What a damn curse. And he could do nothing but stare at them through glass and try not to cry.

Swallowing, Gabe pushed air out through his nose. Suddenly, he missed Jace. He missed that kid with the bright blue eyes and the quick laugh. He missed his nephew, the one who splashed him in the ocean and grinned so wide when he got to drive the boat.

Gabe missed the sound of Jace's little voice calling him uncle. He was the only kid Gabe would ever get a chance to mean something to. But now he was too far out of reach… and thank God for that.

"I wonder what they're going to do to you," Charlie said quietly. "They always have a plan."

"I don't know," Gabe huffed. "They switched out every guard, they have all new staff. Something has them on the run."

"Yeah." Charlie ducked his head. "I've been hearing rumors, actually."

"Like what?"

"Like I didn't want to say anything until I could verify."

"Chuck…" Gabe warned.

"I didn't want to mess with your head," Charlie explained. "Not until I knew it was true."

"Spit it out."

"It's Val."

Gabe stopped running.

Stepping off the machine, he threw a glance at his old friend before backing away. Val. The name was like a dagger straight to his heart. Had they found her body? How was Jason coping? And Jace? And… and Bee?

Bending forward, Gabe placed both hands on his knees and tried not to throw up. He fought the bile tickling at the back of his throat as his system flooded with guilt.

He should never have let her come back. It was all his fault. He should have gone to Cambric straight away. Then Jace would never have had to cry for his mommy and Jason would never have had to watch those videos of Ben with his wife. It made Gabe so sick.

"Hey." Charlie slapped at Gabe's back and shoved him forward. "Stand up. Walk on."

Stumbling forward, Gabe let Charlie prop him up. They paced around the room in silence, Gabe's arm slung across Charlie's shoulders.

For a minute, the new Cambric guard eyed them. He watched as Gabe sucked in air and Charlie rolled his eyes. Nothing to see here. Just a worn out captive and his trainer who knows better. After awhile, the guy relaxed and resumed his seat.

"She's alive," Charlie whispered, and had Gabe wanting to pass out all over again. "She escaped Gabey. Val fucking escaped."

CHAPTER 17

Bee

Wrapping her arms around his strong body, Bee closed her eyes and let out a long breath. This hug. This man. He'd helped her through some really difficult times and the flood of relief that it was finally all over was overwhelming.

Pulling back from her trainer, Bee looked up into Ben's face and smiled. A real, genuine, grateful smile.

"Thank you," she whispered and watched him duck his head in response.

"It's done," Ben replied and gave her another tight squeeze. "You did great, okay? Remember, you can do this. As long as you stay inside your own head, you can do this."

"I know." Bee exhaled before stepping back. "I appreciate your patience."

"I'd of done more if I could." With a quick swallow, Ben glanced away and rubbed at the scruff on his chin.

He'd cut every corner and made every exception that he possibly could for her. Bee wouldn't soon forget it. There'd been times over the past half a year when she'd refused him and he hadn't reported it. When Cambric caught him days later (because they always caught him) then he went without meals, too.

Still, even with an empty belly, Ben had never taken his punishments out on her. In the end, he went at Bee's pace. He'd played by her rules, so to speak, despite Cambric's apparent disapproval.

But now it was all over. She'd completed her final submissions as required and she wouldn't have to do them again. At least not until she was sold. But then it would be to a free person, and she figured she could deal with that fact as it came.

"Take care, okay?" Placing one hand on her lower back, Ben guided her towards the training room door, and pulled it open. "They don't like us hanging around too much with trainees so if you need anything then you'll have to come find me."

"I will," Bee answered automatically.

Stopping a moment on the open threshold of the door, she leaned up on her tip toes and placed a soft kiss on his cheek. Ben chuckled ruefully and gave his head a quick shake.

"You'll do fine," he assured her, or maybe he was telling himself. "Take care Bee. I mean that."

"You too, Ben." Bee pointed a teasing finger at his chest. "You take care, too."

Holding his hands up in mock surrender, Ben flashed her a bright smile and backed away. "Whatever you say lady," he teased and had her laughing right along with him.

He was probably just as relieved as she was, Bee thought. He was probably tired of being hungry and on Discipline at her expense.

When the door clicked shut, Bee passed her forearm beneath the scanner on the wall and listened absently to its beep. Turning, she started back down the crowded hallway. Her heels clicked against the flooring, her mussed hair swished at her back. She felt lighter somehow.

She was acing her classes now, eating full meals, and sticking close to Val. That thing between her and Gabe, whatever it was, was over. He'd kissed her like no one else had, then tossed her out of his room like it was nothing. Like she was nothing, and Bee had managed to avoid the jerk ever since.

Good riddance.

She could finally focus on reality. She could finally focus on being a D2 captive and earning her permanent placement status. She just had to suppress the fire inside of her. She just had to stomp out her need to make choices, her need to say no, to test, to decide.

Tucking a lock of hair behind one ear, Bee weaved her way down the hall. Although it was late in the day, there were still captives walking this way and that. It was crowded.

Lifting her chin, Bee glided through her fellow captives without really seeing them. Most of these people were heading to prep rooms to prepare for evening client meetings. At some point in the near future, she would be among them.

"Hey." The single word from the all too familiar voice had her nerves pumping.

Glancing to her left, it only took one look to confirm her body's instant reaction. Gabe. Damn him, why'd he have to be so hot?

Cambric had cut his hair recently, the golden curls were completely gone, replaced by a thick crop of short spikes. Then there was the heat from those dark brown eyes, the strong clean jaw and straight perfect nose.

Ugh. Why?

Purposefully, Bee refocused all of her attention on the hall before her. What did he want now? They hadn't spoken in weeks. Weeks.

Refusing to acknowledge him, Bee pursed her lips and kept right on walking. Even so, Gabe wouldn't take a hint. His hand came up to wrap around her elbow and the contact had her tingling. Tingling. Nothing Ben did had her buzzing quite like this.

"What do you want?" Bee hissed finally, tugging her arm from his grasp.

With a scowl, Gabe came up to walk next to her.

"You okay?" He asked, his eyes darting all over the side of her face. She could feel him looking. It was almost like a touch. "Did he hurt you?"

"What are you talking about?" Incredulous, Bee turned her head and locked eyes with Gabe.

"Ben," Gabe growled, his voice low. "Did he hurt you?"

With an exasperated sigh, Bee kept right on walking. "No. He's fine. Leave him alone. Leave me alone."

"Is that it then?" Gabe's brow dipped further. "I'm out. He's in. Just like that?"

"Are you listening to yourself?" Stopping short in the hall, Bee gaped. "He's my trainer and you're...you're..."

"I'm what?"

Glancing around, Bee threw up her hands before stomping forward. They couldn't be seen arguing here in the hall. There were cameras at either end and curious eyes watching. Besides, she didn't really know the answer. She didn't know what Gabe was to her.

"We used to be friends," Gabe whispered, as he continued walking just behind her now. "Best friends. I just want that again. Can't we be that again?"

Biting at her lip, Bee fought the flood of feelings Gabe brought on. Did she want to be friends? No. No, she did not. She wanted so much more than that.

She wanted him back in her bed at night, but not sitting up waiting for her to fall asleep. She wanted him back at her table for meals, but not just to trade food. She wanted him, like so many other female captives here had already had him. And the fact that that could never happen was simply too painful.

"Bee Bee." Gabe whispered that stupid nickname he had for her and her heart twisted inside her chest. "Come on Bee Bee. Talk to me."

"No," Bee choked out the word as her eyes got watery. "I don't want to be friends anymore."

Biting off a curse, Gabe grabbed her elbow and tugged her into a side corridor. It was dim and quiet as he pressed her back against the wall and stared. People kept walking past the end of the hall but no one glanced in at them. There was no camera here, only a few doors to empty prep rooms.

Bee swallowed hard and looked away.

"What do I have to do?" Gabe asked quietly. "What do I have to say?"

"I don't know." Bee's eyes came up to stare at his chest. His muscled, smooth, strong chest. The one she'd only been able to see naked once. Once had been enough, though.

Holding back a tiny groan, Bee felt heat pool between her thighs.

"You want me to tell you I'm in love with you?" Gabe asked, causing her eyes to shoot up to his. "Do you want to hear how I can't sleep? How I can barely eat without you there?"

Letting out an unsteady breath, Bee's heart began kicking against her ribs.

"You want to hear how watching you kiss Ben just now made me want to die?" Gabe shifted on his feet, his eyes boring into her. "How seeing you laugh with him makes me want to throw up? Or what about how they have to give me a blue pill down in breeding now, huh? I can't get it up, Bee. I'm so fucking consumed by you, I need drugs to get me hard."

"*Gabe…*"

"*I'm in love with you,*" he insisted.

Lowering his face, Gabe's eyes tracked to her mouth and held. "Every single piece of me wants every single piece of you. Each second you pretend like I don't exist has me drowning."

Squeezing her eyes shut, Bee held her breath. Her heart was going to explode, she was sure of it.

Tipping his forehead to rest lightly against hers, Gabe sighed. "Just let me be close to you, Bee Bee," he whispered. "Please."

Inhaling, Bee took in his scent. With her eyes closed, just the smell of him had her humming. He was in love with her? Was that what this was? A high so bright you can't stop smiling? A low so deep you can hardly breathe?

"*I'm in love with you, too,*" she whispered back.

Flicking her eyes open, Bee's breath caught in her throat as Gabe's mouth crashed down against hers. She felt his lips consuming, then his tongue dipping inside to taste her.

Moaning, she arched forward, pressing her chest into his, rubbing herself against him.

Breaking the kiss, Gabe's breath huffed out as his mouth dropped to her neck. His hands were braced on either side of the wall now, caging her in. She felt him hesitate a moment, his lips hovering just above her skin as his lungs heaved.

He was holding himself back, or he was trying to.

Bee's hands reached out to his hips, then skimmed up his sides. She'd never really touched him before, not like this. He was strong. She could feel his muscles bunched beneath his shirt as her fingers spread themselves over his abs then up to his chest.

Her eyes darted over to his and that's when he broke.

Suddenly, he was diving in. Licking and sucking and biting at the skin of her neck, down to her collar bone, then up under her chin. His hands left the wall to wrap in her hair where he tugged and tangled his fingers until she was gasping.

"Shit, Bee," he swore quietly as his hands traveled down to feel her breasts, then over her hips, where he gripped her hard and yanked her into him.

Picking her up, Gabe wrapped her legs around his waist and smashed her against the wall where he held her in place with his entire body. His chest pressed into her chest. His hips pressed between her legs.

The short gray dress she was wearing hitched up until the only thing separating them were her thin black panties and his gray slacks. She could feel him against her core, all of him.

As if sensing her thoughts, Gabe let loose a low chuckle and murmured against the sensitive skin just behind her ear. "Guess I don't need a little blue pill for you, huh?"

"Uh-uh." Bee's voice shook. Her entire body shook. She was trembling.

Shifting her hips, she ground herself against him, wanting more, closer, now. Her body was drawn up so tight, she felt she might explode.

Cursing under his breath, Gabe pinned her wriggling body in place. "You keep moving like that and I'm gonna to take you right here."

"Take me," Bee bit out, clutching at his heaving shoulders with her hands.

"Fuck, Bee Bee," Gabe hissed. "I can't do that to you."

"I want it." Bee's eyes locked on his. "I choose it. I choose you."

Groaning, Gabe's hand traveled down beneath her dress. His fingertips traced lightly over her soaked panties, back and forth until she was panting. She wanted to beg. She wanted to plead with him to keep going, to move the flimsy fabric to the side and finally touch her.

"Shit you're wet," he murmured. "Is all this for me?"

Nodding, Bee pressed her mouth to his neck and sucked. Her tongue snaked out to slide up beneath his jaw where she nipped at his smooth skin. She could feel the rumble that worked its way up his chest.

With a quick glance to the end of the corridor, Gabe wrapped his left arm firmly around her waist and stepped back. Shuffling a few steps to the side, he held his right forearm beneath a scanner and had one of the prep room doors swinging slowly open.

"Don't you scan. Keep your arm tucked in," he hissed, as he walked them quickly inside.

Lights flickered on, revealing an empty room lined with closets. Along the back wall, there was a lone countertop. Slapping at the switch on the wall, Gabe had the room plummeting into darkness once more. No red camera light shone. Cambric didn't have cameras in the prep rooms.

"We shouldn't do this," he said as he stumbled forward, still holding her up. "Tell me to stop."

"Don't stop," Bee pleaded, and felt him slam her butt down onto the counter.

Then his hands were everywhere. He was undoing the buttons of her dress, reaching in, cupping her breasts. Chasing his touch, Bee arched forward until she felt his mouth lock onto her nipple. She cried out.

Gabe's hand shot to cover her mouth, but he kept his tongue working. It flicked back and forth as he sucked and hummed against her skin. First one breast, then the other. Tipping her head back, Bee ran her hands through his hair.

Murmuring against her skin, Gabe removed his hand from her mouth and traced a slow path to her hips. When he got to her panties, she helped him slide them off, down and away. Then, reaching for him in the dark, Bee fumbled with the button of his pants, then the zipper.

Groaning, Gabe's hips jumped forward as he pushed himself into her hand. Bee tightened her grip around him. He hissed.

Running his fingers up the inside of her thighs, Gabe straightened and leaned his face in close to hers. When his hand reached her core, he kissed her lips, and let his fingers play between her thighs, testing, teasing, slipping inside.

Whimpering at the contact, Bee scooted to the edge of the counter and wrapped her legs around his waist. It felt too good. Better than anything she'd done with Ben and she didn't even know why.

Reaching down between them, she pushed Gabe's hand out of the way and lined herself up with him. Shifting her hips, she tightened her legs around his waist until he was gasping and pushing inside of her. This time she was the one to swallow his moans.

"I love you," Gabe panted the words as his mouth moved over hers.

Pulling out, he quickly slammed back in. Bee cried out, her hands gripping the back of his shirt in her fists as she held him against her. Tingles rushed around her core, building and pulsing and tensing each time he slid out and came back to her.

His hands clutched her body, squeezing and bruising. One at the back of her neck, one at her hip, holding her in place as he rocked against her, into her. Again. Then again.

Burying her face in his neck, Bee worked to muffle the moans that kept rippling up her own throat. So good. It was blinding. Her body was building and humming and heating.

"You feel too good," Gabe groaned. "I can't wait."

"Don't stop."

"Bee Bee," Gabe panted. "I'm gonna come."

"Me too."

With a cry, Bee felt herself tense all around him. Gabe's mouth sought hers as he moaned and released inside of her. She was pulsing and aching as he jerked and then stilled.

Drawing out slowly, he pushed back in once more. She groaned. Gabe's arms came to wrap around her body. His face buried itself in her neck. Everything still felt so good, the throbbing just wouldn't let up.

Panting, Bee blinked in the dark and worked to draw in air. This was nothing like the times she'd been with Ben. There was so much more to this. She had no idea that there was so much more.

Clutching her tighter, Gabe brushed his face against her neck, shaking his head slowly side to side. She could feel him shudder then, his shoulders tightening and his lungs heaving.

"I'm so sorry," he whispered. "I love you so much, and I am so fucking sorry."

CHAPTER 18

Gabe

Room 115 was not an unfamiliar one. Walking up to its tall door, Gabe held his right forearm beneath the scanner affixed to the wall and waited. First came the beep, then the click, and finally the door swung slowly inward.

Sucking in a breath, Gabe worked to steady himself. His mind was going in a million different directions. He wasn't sure what was waiting for him inside, but he knew it wouldn't be good.

Then there was the bomb Charlie had just dropped on him. Val. Alive. Free.

His heart wanted to erupt. He couldn't quite wrap his mind around how, but one thing was abundantly clear, Val had escaped Cambric.

Other captives were coming back from their recent client meetings with the news. Snippets here, pieces of gossip there. Some of it they'd heard over car radios, some seen in glimpses of magazines left carelessly in hotel rooms. Jason Riggs was running for Congress… with his lovely captive bride by his side.

"Lover boy," Shane's voice grated as he flashed Gabe a smile. "Right on time. Please, take a seat."

It took all of Gabe's willpower not to stiffen at the sound. He wanted to sneer. He wanted to pick Shane up by his neck, slam his face to the floor and make *him* lick it.

But a good captive would never do that. A submissive captive would keep a blank expression on his face and do exactly as he was told. So despite the hunger Gabe's fists felt for Shane's face, he walked three steps forward and took a seat on the single black stool in the center of the room.

Off to his right, a long-faced red-haired woman stood clutching a makeup kit. To his left, a metal rack held a small collection of men's clothing. Directly in front of him, two massive Cambric guards stood. Their thick arms were crossed in front of them, hands clasped, faces impassive.

With a roll of his shoulders, Gabe sat up straighter and worked to release the tightness in his own jaw. Shane was non-plussed, busy shuffling papers with his back to them now. Confident prick.

"You've been integrating well," Shane commented.

Turning, he held a single sheet of paper in one hand and leaned back against a long countertop. "No fighting. You're eating well. You're back to your prescribed weight."

Gabe didn't know what the fucker wanted him to say, so he just nodded. It was so damn hard to keep hate out of your eyes. So. Damn. Hard.

Tilting his head to one side, Shane watched him a moment. The paper crinkled softly in his hand as he tapped it against his thigh.

"There haven't been any problems with your submissions. That is… except for your little performance issue. But that's nothing new, and a blue pill should take care of that from now on, right?"

Gabe gritted his teeth. Yeah, kinda hard to get it up these days, seeing as he rather throw up in the toilet than follow through. But hey, he'd managed to work his way through everything else, despite seeing Bee's face everytime he closed his eyes.

That, and the fact his trainer had slipped him a few extra reds. He'd been high as fuck, but according to her, he'd still passed. Goody.

"When that last part gets sorted, then I think we'll be able to try another visit," Shane continued. His calculating eyes never left Gabe's. "Sharon was so insistent before, I went against my better judgment."

Gabe's eyes widened and his throat went dry. Sharon. Prison. Visit.

His heart was screaming at him, sending a sick sort of swirling panic through his veins. He had to remind himself that he had a plan. He had to remind himself that submitting now was a means to an end.

"You can't just send a captive who's been on the outside straight back to his mistress." Shane smirked now. "Intake has its purpose. I mean, look at you now."

The color drained from Gabe's face as Shane pushed himself off from the counter and walked forward. That look in his eye, Gabe knew what it meant. Playtime for psychos.

"Stand up," Shane instructed. "Strip."

Without hesitating, Gabe did as he was told. He'd come freshly showered, so his hair was damp. Pulling his gray polo shirt off over his head, he dropped it to the floor before reaching for the button on his slacks. His hands were shaking. That part he hadn't mastered yet, and when he glanced up, he saw Shane's eyes studying him.

Tugging his zipper down, Gabe kicked off his shoes first, then his gray slacks. When he was standing in just his boxers and socks, he sucked in a breath.

"All the way," Shane again, watching.

Swallowing, Gabe fought a shudder and complied. Before long, he was standing completely naked in a room full of people. This wasn't the first time. It wouldn't be the last.

"Kneel," Shane ordered.

And Gabe did.

He lowered himself to the floor, and kept staring straight ahead. Shane's pupils dilated ever so slightly as he stepped closer. This shit is what he lived for, and keeping Gabe in the dark about what was coming next was half the fun. Gabe knew these things about Shane implicitly. After all, he'd been just one of many victims over the years.

"On your belly," Shane again.

With a mix of humiliation and anger brewing in his blood, Gabe tipped forward and laid down on the ground. Turning his head to the side, he blinked at the wall. It was white, blank and lined with closets. There were clothes inside there, possibly even the dresses Val wore in those videos. If she could do this, Gabe thought, then he could do this.

Coming to stand over him, Shane stared down. Gabe could see him out of the corner of his eye, but he refused to turn his head. Slowly, deliberately, Shane placed his foot against Gabe's throat. Everyone in the room remained still.

Shane applied pressure.

The guards watched.

The woman in the corner watched.

Even Gabe remained where he was, fighting every impulse inside of him to jump up and break free. For a good thirty seconds, Gabe allowed his own airway to be smashed in on itself. He held his breath. No sense trying to suck in air, when there wasn't any to be had.

Finally, Shane smiled and stepped back. Gabe couldn't help but track the fucker with his eyes this time. His chest heaved in air and his throat throbbed from the contact.

Ignoring all of that, Gabe kept his body lying still and flat on the tile. He hadn't been given permission to get up, yet. He needed to wait for that permission, so he fought against every survival instinct he had, and remained on the ground.

"Good," Shane admitted. "Get up. Alicia will dress you and clean you up. You have a video to make."

Pushing up off the floor, Gabe swallowed painfully and barely stopped himself from clutching at his throat. It ached and although he didn't have access to a mirror, he figured it would definitely bruise. Hence the makeup.

While Shane once more turned his back and appeared busy, Alicia cautiously stepped up to the clothing rack.

Thumbing through the items, she selected a navy-colored business suit and silver-gray tie. Gabe stepped into his boxers first, then the pants. His legs were a bit unsteady. He had no idea where this was going.

Val's videos had been awful. Cambric had had so many men lined up for her, it had made half the nation sick. But that was because of her fame. Gabe didn't have that notoriety. He'd been a Federal witness at a high profile trial and nothing more. Even when he'd run off with Bee and the paparazzi had been hot on her trail, he'd managed to duck them. He was nothing and no one and he'd liked the anonymity. So what could this video possibly be about?

Shrugging into the long sleeve button-up shirt, he clutched the suit jacket in one hand and eased back to sitting on the stool. For the next twenty or so minutes, Alicia worked on him. She spread makeup over his neck and blended it up into his face. No one would see the damage. No one would know.

After styling his hair and gently winding the tie about his neck, Alicia held up a square mirror in front of him. Gabe stared at himself. For the first time in forever, he hated what he saw.

In the video he was about to shoot, he would look perfect. His curls dropped down just a bit onto his forehead, his square jaw was clean-shaven, his throat un-marred. But where everyone else would see a too-handsome fucker in his prime, Gabe saw a coward.

He stared into a coward's eyes. His eyes. Because what kind of man lays on his belly and lets his enemy step on his throat? If he had any balls at all, he'd of already laid waste to Shane, Cambric guards and long-term plans be damned.

"All set?" Shane directed the question at Alicia who ducked her head and backed away.

Bringing a camera over, Shane set it up on a black tripod, then began arranging a series of lights. When he was finished, he stepped up to Gabe and handed the piece of paper over.

"Read this word for word," Shane instructed. "Do not deviate. When you seem convincing enough, then you'll need to sign it in front of our attorney."

Gripping the paper in both hands, Gabe dropped his head and read, and read, and read.

"No." Gabe spat the word before tossing the paper to the ground. "No fucking way am I reading that."

"Is that so?" Shane raised an eyebrow as his eyes grew dark.

Gritting his teeth, Gabe hissed the next words quietly, "and there is *nothing* that you can do to make me."

CHAPTER 19

Jason

THE ENVELOPE WAS PLAIN WHITE AND SMOOTH. IT LOOKED LIKE any regular envelope. Running his thumb over the seal, Jason drew in a slow breath. He was back in Finn's office. Damn all the things that had happened in this office.

Glancing up, Jason caught the Federal Agent's eye. Surely, Finn already knew what the results were. There was no way he would simply run the DNA without checking it for himself.

Seeming to read his thoughts, the way he had so many times over the years, Finn shrugged.

"It's what you were expecting," he commented quietly. "I mean... why else would you have me run them?"

Heaving out a low groan, Jason's eyes flipped back down to the envelope. He slapped it absently against his palm and felt a creeping sort of pain spread itself across his chest.

Sure, he'd suspected a connection, especially after living

with Bee in the Maldives. But a suspicion and reality were two different things.

He was about to blow lives apart. Lives that meant something to him. Lives that meant something to his family.

"What are you going to do?" Finn asked finally, causing Jason to look up at him again. "This could stay between us. It could die right here in this room."

"No." Jason gave his head a stiff shake and frowned. "I won't lie to my wife."

"Open it then," Finn instructed. "Rip it off like a bandaid."

Sucking in air, Jason slid his finger beneath the flap of the envelope and listened to the ripping sound. It tore open easily enough and before he knew it, the DNA results comparing Val Riggs to Veronica "Bee" Durand sat before him.

They were a partial match. Half-siblings. Val and Bee were biological sisters.

And since the original test they'd performed all those years ago comparing Val to Lillian Durand had come back negative, that only left one conclusion. The girls shared the same father, but not the same mother.

"Shit," Jason spat the word before rubbing at his face.

"I'm guessing Bernard Durand has a secret or two," Finn commented. His fingers drummed against the desk as he leaned back in his chair.

"Have you looked into it?" Jason's eyes shot up to Finn who shook his head.

"This is off the books remember?" He said. "I mean, I could if you want me to."

"No, that's alright," Jason grumbled, his gaze dropping once more to the paper clutched in his hands. "He's been married to his wife for over thirty years. Both the girls are younger than that, so no matter which way you swing it… he cheated."

"You gonna go all guy code on him?" Finn asked. "Rich boys stick together and all that?"

"Hell no." Jason's lips twisted as a sour taste filled his mouth. "I could give a shit about him. It's just that… his wife is my mom's best friend. This is going to destroy her. Plus, Bee's struggling. I don't know what this will do to her sobriety. I mean she's passing drug tests, but the alcohol's got her hard."

"Yeah, I've seen some headlines," Finn acknowledged, ducking his head.

"You keeping tabs?" Jason studied the man who used to be his close friend. His confidante. The one he trusted above all else.

"Not exactly," Finn admitted before looking up to the ceiling. "But it's hard to miss the evening news. She doesn't keep a low profile."

"Huh," Jason huffed in agreement, didn't he know it.

Quirking a half smile, he glanced away. His campaign manager was still fuming over Bee's latest antics. More table dancing in exclusive clubs, thousands of dollars in bar tabs, men and women both hanging all over her.

The spectacle itself wasn't illegal, but when you're running for Congress and your wife looks exactly like a certain perpetually drunk heiress… things can get hairy. More than once the media had tried to say Val was the one out partying, not Bee, and that Jason was scrambling to try to cover things up.

Folding the paper quietly, Jason placed it back in the torn envelope and slid the entire mess into his jacket pocket. Good ole' Quentin Daniels was really going to freak out now, given that Val and Bee were actually biological sisters. This thing had salacious scandal written all over it.

Pushing up to standing, Jason smoothed at his suit. Over Finn's shoulder, that same solitary window looked out onto the street below. How many times had he stood at that window while his and Val's lives were being blown apart? Too many.

"This room is cursed," Jason announced and this time Finn was the one to smile.

"I kinda like it," Finn countered. "I've got a thing for the truth."

"Truth and justice and all that, right?" Jason repeated sarcastically. "I remember."

Standing across from him, Finn leaned forward over his desk. Both of his hands fisted on the tabletop while his eyes locked on Jason.

"I'm sorry," he said. "About handing Val over to those fuckers and not being completely honest with you and Gabe. I'll never stop being sorry."

Jason bobbed his head automatically and ground his teeth together inside his head. The memory of Gabe right before he'd handed him over would never, ever leave him. He'd taken a free man, a good man, and because of his own desperation, he'd traded him back to Cambric like cattle.

It made him sick.

So sick, in fact, that he was giving up everything in an attempt to fix it.

"There were... *are*... so many other things at play here," Finn added. "Things you can't know about. And the Militia..."

"Has you by the balls," Jason supplied as Finn's eyes darkened. "I know. Any word from them by the way?"

Snapping his mouth shut a moment, Finn fought his own immediate response. Jason waited, watching his former friend battle himself.

"Your poll numbers are good," Finn said finally. "They wish you'd take a firmer stance on the second amendment though."

"A firmer stance?" Jason scoffed. "I'm carrying right now. I'm armed everywhere I go. There is no firmer stance."

"Still."

"Well, you can tell Clay to go fuck himself," Jason spat. "I'm going to win this Senate seat *my* way, and then I'll do what we all agreed on. That's it."

"If you think that's all Clay wants, then you're beyond naive."

"If he thinks I'm just going to roll over, then that makes two of us."

Raising his eyebrows at that, Finn straightened his spine and extended his hand. As usual the gesture hung in the air between them for several seconds.

Everytime Jason saw Finn's hand waiting for a shake he flashed to that night. He felt the knee in his back, the sidewalk kissing his cheek and then he watched Finn perp walk his wife down a dark New York alleyway. Away from him, away from freedom, away from safety, as Jason screamed himself hoarse.

"Somethings in life you just can't get over," Jason murmured quietly and backed away. He just couldn't do it today. He just couldn't shake this man's hand.

"I know." Finn cleared his throat as his arm dropped to his side. "I know."

CHAPTER 20

Bee

The music was pumping as strobe lights flashed all around them. Bee moved her body in time to the beat, the deep base seemed to dictate the thump of her heart. The hot guy in front of her reached for her hips, and teasingly, she brushed him away.

He was at least six three, with glittering blue eyes and a broad chest. Despite wagging her finger at him, he grinned. At least, that's what she figured his mouth was doing. Kind of hard to tell exactly as her vision blurred.

Spinning around, Bee increased the dizziness. She needed another glass of champagne, or maybe something harder. The two bottles she'd already consumed just weren't cutting it anymore and the truth was, she didn't want to be here. She wanted to escape, to blackout.

"Veronica, right?" Hot Guy was saying something in her ear, pulling her back against his chest.

Why couldn't she feel anything for him? He was definitely

good looking and seemed nice enough. He was probably a good time.

With a frown, Bee glanced back to the VIP table. Gino's brown curls swayed as he bobbed his head to the rhythm. Damn those curls, she thought. Wrong color, but damn them anyway.

Camy was leaning forward over the table, her red hair draping like a curtain as she inhaled a thin line of white powder. Throwing her head back, Camy ran a hand beneath her nose and laughed.

Blinking slowly, Bee watched as Gino's hazel eyes swung away from Camy and over to her. He went from casual cool, to shoving out of the booth in like two seconds flat. *Shit.*

Turning in Hot Guy's arms, Bee peered up into his face.

"Time for you to go," she said, and had him laughing.

"What?" He smiled again, revealing nice straight white teeth. "But we just got started."

"Nope." Gino's hand slapped heavily down on Hot Guy's shoulder. "You're out."

"Who the hell are you?" Shrugging him off, Hot Guy turned on Gino and stared him down. They were about the same height actually. "Her boyfriend?"

"Nah, man." Gino stepped closer. "But you aren't either. And unless she's smiling, you're out."

"You need to back off."

"I don't think so."

As the two men continued to escalate, Bee's vision of them blurred in and out. Gino took his watchdog duties very seriously, so this little display was nothing new. In about ten seconds, a few bouncers would magically appear out of nowhere and the almost-fight would end the same way a dozen others had.

Gino stayed.

Hot Guys went.

That was what money could do for you. That, and it could get you drunk and high which would inevitably lead to passing out. So it was all worth it, in the end.

Swaying slightly, Bee turned away from them and tottered back to the booth. Camy was blinking into the strobe lights and giggling to herself. Bee slid down beside her and eyed the white residue spread all over the table. She wanted some. There was no doubt about that, but Daddy was still giving her weekly drug tests so it was still a hard no for her.

She took the tests. Daddy funded her bank account. She earned another week of freedom in her hotel suite.

"You know…" Camy leaned in to "whisper" conspiratorially. "You could do Gino if you wanted. He's actually really good in bed."

"Yeah, I'll pass," Bee murmured.

Flicking her eyes up, she narrowed her vision on the VIP bar. It was much smaller than the main bar, but still it was packed tonight.

"Do you have the buzzer thingy?" Bee asked, her eyes dropping to the table in search of the little electronic call button that summoned their waitress.

"I pushed it like half a dozen times," Camy offered. "They're extra busy. We'll get you another bottle soon."

Sliding down into the booth beside her, Gino pushed his curls off of his forehead and sighed. Bee knew from experience he wouldn't be mentioning Hot Guy. His duties included silence and that seemed in line with his personality anyway. He stopped things from spreading.

Alternatively, Stacey started them. Glaring impatiently at the empty bottles littering their table, Bee bit back an impatient huff. Somewhere else in the club, Stacey was making heads turn. If she were here right now, Bee would be willing to bet a hundred dollars the waitress would be, too.

Taking out his phone, Gino swiped his thumb absently across the screen. They were just killing time now. They were always just killing time.

"Hey, um…" Gino let loose a low whistle. "You check your phone lately?"

"Me?" Bee's eyebrows raised as he gave her a quick nod. "No need."

"Yeah." Gino's gaze jumped from Bee to Camy. "I think there's a need."

Scrambling for their purses, Bee and Camy searched for their phones at the same time. When she got to hers, Bee had to work hard to steady her vision as she swiped and entered a code. The screen unlocked and revealed the usual.

About fifty unanswered texts, and six or so missed calls. Jason. Val. Daddy. Mommy. Same same.

With a shrug, Bee chucked her phone down in the booth beside her. She didn't need to read what those people had to say. At least not right now.

Camy's eyes shot up to Gino and she swallowed. "Should we go?" She asked.

"I'm thinking it's too late," Gino commented.

Tipping his chin towards the VIP section entrance, he eased back to lean against the booth. The bouncer was face to face with three men in suits. One was tapping his finger against the bouncer's tablet, while the other two scanned the room.

Sliding his own phone over to hover in front of Bee's face, Gino gave her a nod. Read it, he seemed to say. Bee's eyes narrowed.

On the screen, a series of texts were displayed. They were entirely one-sided. Bee's gut dropped.

10:15pm Jason: I know you're partying with her G. She better not be high right now.

10:20pm Jason: You need to answer my calls. I've got to talk to her tonight.

10:22pm Jason: Pick up your phone.

11:03pm Jason: I can't exactly be seen where you are. Pick up your damn phone G, for old times.

1:16am Jason: Fine. Looks like I'm coming to you.

"Shit," Bee hissed and slapped the phone down onto the table.

"Shit is right," Gino agreed, his eyes still trained on the VIP bouncer.

Following his line of sight, Bee swallowed hard. Jason Riggs' entrance was like a ripple in a still pond, and he hadn't even shown his face yet.

The first wave affected the club's staff. All of a sudden, the bar was being cleared. Guests were being handed drinks and ushered down the stairs. Crowd or no crowd, the only thing that trumped money… was power.

"Should we move?" Bee asked, her words slurred slightly as the music continued to pump all around them.

"There's nowhere to go," Camy pointed out.

Beneath the table, Gino's hand reached to clasp Bee's in his own. He gave her a quick squeeze, as if trying to reassure her, but her head was spinning. The lights were still strobing all around them and as people were leaving, their phones were being wiped.

That's right, the men in suits were waiting at the exit, plucking up phones and much to the party goers dismay, they were clearing them. That was the second ripple in the pond. Jason made waves, even when he was nowhere in sight.

Squeezing her eyes shut, Bee covered her face in her hands and groaned. She didn't want to see him. She didn't want to talk to him. The last time they'd been in the same room, it'd been with Gabe. The two men had been trying to explain themselves, to explain why Gabe needed to trade himself back for Val, to explain why they couldn't just wait for the outcome of the damn trial.

She hated him.

She hated them both for that, for the choices they got to make, and the ones that she didn't.

"You don't have anything on you, right?" Camy whispered.

Opening her eyes, Bee watched Gino give his head a shake. They were worried about their stash. They were worried about being caught carrying. But then back behind the VIP bar, there was movement.

Gritting her teeth, Bee felt the betrayal ring hard in her blood before she even caught sight of him. But then there he was. The final ripple in the pond.

Future Senator Jason Riggs, clad in simple dark jeans and a black hoodie. His perfectly styled brown hair and brighter than bright blue eyes shone at her like a beacon. He must have been escorted inside using an employee entrance.

Then just behind him, came Val, also in skinny blue jeans

and a dark hoodie. Her brown hair was swept up in a ponytail.

Bee's gut sank all the way to her toes. Val.

God. Bee loved her, and missed her, and hated her, too.

No, Val hadn't made the deal the guys had. And yes, she'd deserved to get out of Cambric. It wasn't that. But how Bee felt wasn't entirely logical, the feelings were there just the same.

Exhaling a ragged breath, Bee felt her lungs burning. Val reminded her so much of Gabe, so much of their shared past and wrecked future.

Walking towards them through the haze of lights and thrum of music, Bee couldn't help but stare. Val and Jason were flanked by two massive men in suits. It was so cliche, she was only surprised the bodyguards weren't wearing sunglasses.

When the group of four stopped at their table, Bee managed to rip her eyes off of Val and settle back on the man himself.

Jason glared.

Not at her, but at Gino.

"Tell me this white shit all over the table isn't up her nose," he demanded, pointing a finger at Bee.

Putting his palms up in surrender, Gino shrugged. "I don't know what you're talking about Riggs. It was like that when we got here."

"Bull. Shit." Jason's eyes traveled to Camy. "You forget who you're talking to. I've played this game, remember?"

"And we haven't breathed a word of it." Camy raised an eyebrow at him. "Even when the reporters came snooping, so just back off."

"You have nothing to tell," Jason countered, his eyes growing dark.

"So stop being a prick," Gino put in. "Bee's clean."

"She doesn't look clean." Jason's eyes came back to rest on her. "I need to know what she's taken."

"How. Dare. You." Bee snapped. Pushing shakily up from the table, she came to her knees in the booth and leaned forward. "Get the hell out of here. I never want to see your face again."

"Bee." Val stepped closer, her eyes sad and pleading.

"And take your perfect Senator's wife with you," Bee spat. "Go live your perfect lives with your marriage and your son and your career and leave me the hell alone."

"I can't do that," Jason lowered his voice. "It's time for you to come home, Bee. It's time for you to stop this."

"No!" Bee yelled the word in his face but he didn't flinch. "You took everything from me! I'm not going anywhere with you, not ever."

"Please, Bee. Please." Val reached out, but then Jason was stepping in front of her.

He was stroking his wife's hair, shielding her body with his own. Even so, Bee could practically feel the tears leaking from Val's eyes. After all, they'd grown up together. This was killing Val, Bee knew. Her heart was breaking, but that made two of them. And it wasn't the first time, was it?

"Come on." Bee tipped her chin at Camy. "We're leaving."

"Oh no." Jason whirled around and planted his feet. "They're staying. This club is filling back up. This night will go on like nothing happened. Only thing to change will be you, Bee. You're coming home with us."

"I said *no*," Bee gritted out the words as Gino tensed beside her. "Or don't you understand that word anymore?"

"I understand you're drunk," Jason countered. "Or high… maybe both. I get that you hate me. I get that you hate the world right now, but what about Val? What about Jace? They need you, Bee. It's time for you to come home."

"Go away." Bee suppressed a sob as her eyes darted to Val. "Don't use my nephew against me."

"You want Gabe back, right?" Jason asked.

Bee's heart skipped and stuttered in her chest. How could he ask that? How could he use Gabe against her, too? The selfish fucking…

"We're going to get him out, Bee," Jason continued quietly. "But we need your help for that."

Bee's hand slapped over her mouth as tears burst from her eyes. Suddenly she could hardly breathe. Her lungs were heaving but she wasn't gaining any air.

"Come home to us, Bee Bee," Val whispered. "We've got so much to tell you."

CHAPTER 21

Gabe

"YOU'RE THE MOST BEAUTIFUL WOMAN IN THE WHOLE WORLD," GABE whispered the words in Bee's ear before inhaling her scent. Her dark hair was falling down all around him, tickling his face and his neck. And he didn't dare brush it away. She was lying on top of him, her naked body was pressed against his. He couldn't hope for anything more.

They were tucked into her bed together, a place Gabe had managed to sneak in as often as he could during the past eight weeks. With the single gray blanket pulled up over their heads and Val snoozing quietly in the bed across the room. It was the middle of the night and time was running out.

Gabe had to sneak back to his own room before the morning guards did their rounds. On second thought, he could hope for something more... he could hope for freedom.

"Someday," he began, as Bee giggled and ground her hips down on him. "We'll both get out of here, Bee Bee."

"Shhh." Shushing him with her lips, Bee pressed her bare breasts against his chest. "Focus, Gabey. Just one more time."

Smiling into the dark, Gabe inhaled a deep breath. This woman was insatiable. She acted like he hadn't satisfied her already... twice. Flipping her onto her back, Gabe reached between her legs and secured a few moments of silence from her.

"We're going to be free someday," he continued, listening to her panting beneath him. "Maybe we'll be really old by then, but I'm telling you... we can be together."

"Uh-huh," Bee gasped as he continued to work his fingers over her, then inside of her. She shifted her hips against him, and he felt his own body stir once more.

"I'm going to take you to an island somewhere far away." Gabe lowered his mouth until his words exhaled all over the skin of her neck, then her breasts. "We're going to live there together, Bee Bee. You and me. Free. Sound good?"

"Mmmm, sounds good," Bee repeated the words, her hips chasing his hand as he pulled away.

"Patience my greedy girl," Gabe teased.

With a frown he could feel, Bee reached between them, wrapping her fingers around him, stroking him. He bit back a groan. To this day Cambric still had to give him pills to get hard. He took them before they made him go down to breeding, and he took them when they sent him to his trainer.

But with Bee... he didn't need them at all. With Bee, he was ready to go whenever she gave him that look... or touch... sometimes multiple times. Like tonight.

Three times in the span of a few hours. Three. Times.

He was going to need water. Lots and lots of water.

. . .

"Thirsty?" The question banged around in his mind, waking Gabe from his dreams... or memories.

Cracking his swollen eyes, Gabe winced at the pain that exploded in his brain. He hurt. Why did he hurt?

"We could just tube you again," the voice continued. "Like last time."

Oh yeah. Lowering his lids, Gabe rolled to his back on the thin mattress and groaned. He was back in Cambric, except this time... he didn't have Bee. He'd left her on the outside, where she was safe, where she belonged. Thank God.

Uhhh, it was like he was in some screwed up time machine. He just wanted to get back to Bee's bed. He just wanted to get there, where his heart beat against her heart, and his body slipped inside her body.

But no. He'd jumped forward in time, so that thing he was just living, it was only a memory.

There was no going back there, not for real. In this time, where he had to live now, there was Shane and there was the video. There was the letter they'd wanted him to read... and sign.

No.

Not no, but fuck no. He would never do it.

So... they'd beat the shit out of him. Maybe more times than he cared to recall.

"Tube it is then," the voice again.

There was shuffling in the room, boots on concrete, muffled voices. Gabe's eyes flew open, or they tried to, but everything he saw was blurry. He felt hands on him, holding him down as he writhed and bucked on the mattress.

Then a needle was pricking at his skin and cuffs were slapping over his wrists and he was floating. Floating. His jaw went slack and the last thing he recalled was the thick plastic tube being pushed down his throat. It hurt. He hurt. Why did he hurt?

CHAPTER 22

Bee

"DADDY," BEE PLEADED. "SAY SOMETHING."

Blinking up at her father, Bee sucked in a breath. She was sitting in Jason's living room, shaking and sweating and holding back the vomit collecting in her throat. Detox. Sobriety. It was way harder than a hangover, that's for sure.

Beside her, sat Val. They were wedged right next to one another. Long legs touching, hands clasped, twin breaths puffing out. Across the room, their father paced. Their. Father.

His hands kept running roughly through his short chestnut hair. It was their same color of brown, only just recently having been sprinkled with strands of gray. Occasionally, he glanced over at the two of them with this look on his face.

He'd open his mouth, his eyes darting from Bee to Val and back before his jaw would snap shut and he'd continue wearing tracks on Jason's marble floor.

Leaning back against one wall, Jason watched him, too. His arms were folded over his chest, his jaw clenched tight. Just beside him, a beautiful oil painting of vineyards was hanging on the wall. All around the room, light poured in from large windows.

Summer House was especially gorgeous this time of year, hence the name. But the blazing heat from outside didn't touch the air conditioned room. Even so, Bee continued sweating.

Her slick palm clutched onto Val's. A slight tremor worked its way through her body. She was crashing. Jason and Val had taken her home from the club and they were forcing her to sober up. They'd hit her with the news about their shared DNA and mentioned a plan to free Gabe. If she wanted in, she had to get straight and stay that way.

And duh. She wanted in.

"Yes. Please, Mr. Durand," Jason intoned. "Say something."

Stopping in the middle of the room, Bee's father looked up at them again. His face had drained of color, his emerald green eyes appeared just a touch glazed.

"I'm sorry," he said suddenly, his eyes bouncing from Jason to the girls. "I'm just shocked."

"Shocked?" Jason shoved up from the wall. "It can't really be all that surprising, can it?"

"It was a long time ago, Jason," Bernard spat, his shoulders tensing. "I was a very young man."

"If you're about to ask me if I ran the DNA twice," Jason began. "Don't."

Frowning, Bernard pressed his fingers to the bridge of his nose.

Gripping Val tighter, Bee drew her sister's hand into her lap. Sister. Like for real this time.

Val leaned her shoulder against Bee's side and held her breath. It was true all along. It really was. They'd been sisters by blood, just like they'd thought. That meant Jace was her biological nephew and Jason was her brother-in-law.

A part of Bee leapt for joy, another part plummeted to her toes. How the hell did this happen? How did Bernard Durand lose two daughters to Cambric?

"Daddy," Bee tried again, drawing his eyes back to her on the couch. "Please just… tell us, okay?"

Running his fingers back through his hair, Bernard looked pained.

"Like I said, I was very young. Your mother and I married at the urging of our families. I was nineteen, she was eighteen."

"Why?" Val asked. "Why so young?"

"That's the way it was done back then." Bernard's face softened as he looked at Val, like he was actually taking her in for the first time. "She was a Russel and I was a Durand. The families had wanted a connection for decades and we were it."

"But…" Bee bit at her trembling lip, willing her emotions to stay in check. "You love Mom. Don't you?"

"Yes." Bernard ducked his head and blew out a breath. "I do. Very much. But it took time to grow."

Stepping closer, Jason shoved his hands in his pockets and cocked his head to one side.

"How did you meet Val's mother?" He interjected. "Who was she? Do you know her name?"

"I don't remember her name," Bernard admitted, his eyes zeroing in on Val. "I'm sorry."

"You don't *remember?*" Jason's eyebrows raised.

With a shake of his head, Bernard crossed to the two women still seated on the couch and dropped to sit on the coffee table in front of them. His hands clasped together between his knees and his chest puffed in and out for a moment.

"I swear to you," Bernard spoke quietly. "I didn't know about you. If I'd have known…"

"Daddy," Bee cut him off, feeling Val squeezing her tighter. Now Bee wasn't the only one shaking. "What did she look like? Is there anyway we can find her?"

Leaning back, Bernard ran a hand down over his face. Glancing skyward, he pursed his lips a moment before dropping his head back to face them. Something flashed in his eyes, guilt, regret? It was gone in a second, replaced by sadness.

Pure and simple. Bee knew that look. She wore it as well.

"Did your mother ever tell you about her pregnancies?" Bernard began, his eyes locking on Bee.

"No." Bee shook her head, frowning.

"Well, she had three miscarriages before you," he supplied. "One right after the other and her body was wrecked. We were both wrecked."

Sucking in a breath, he tried for a tentative smile. "But then there was you. She kept you longer than the others, but she was sick. She was so sick, Veronica."

"I didn't know."

"It was never our intention to burden you." Bernard shrugged. "We were just thrilled when you finally came, healthy and alive. We could stop trying after that. You were all we needed."

"I don't understand," Val's voice quaked, drawing her father's eyes over to her. He ducked his head.

"Lillian was on bedrest, and had been that way for about six months," Bernard supplied. "It was draining on everyone. I just had to get a break for a weekend, just some time with my friends. That was all it was supposed to be."

"But…" Jason crept forward, his brow furrowed as his eyes danced over Val. He was worried about her.

"But things were done differently back then," Bernard put in, glancing at Jason over his shoulder. "I was at a friend's house in the Adirondacks. He ordered some company."

"What kind of company?" Jason growled.

Circling around the couch, he came to a stop standing directly behind the women. Leaning forward, Jason's right hand came to rest on Val's shoulder, while his left settled on Bee's. He was bracing them, trying to protect them from the truth, whatever it was.

"Captives," Bernard admitted. "D2 captives."

"Like me." The words were out of Bee's mouth before she even realized it. "Like Val. You ordered captives just like your daughters."

"And that fact has haunted me for years, Veronica," Bernard pleaded, his panicked eyes jumping between the women seated across from him. "I was twenty-five years old and scared out of my mind. I'd lost three children that I'd never know and I swore God was about to steal my fourth one and my wife right along with her."

Drawing in a ragged breath, Bernard's eyes glistened as he spoke. "I know that isn't a good excuse, but you're not the only one with an alcohol problem. Maybe that's why I let it go on with you, Veronica. Because in a way, I get it. We don't deal with stress well."

"You..." Bee's mouth dropped.

She'd never seen her father drink. Not a drop, actually.

Glancing over to Val, Bee watched the tears streak down her sister's pretty face. A face that was eerily similar to the one staring back at them from the coffee table. They both looked like their father. So very much like him. Why had she never *seen* it before?

"Your mother..." Bernard cleared his throat as he addressed Val. His hands clasped and unclasped as he braced them over his bent knees. "Was a beautiful, kind woman. I remember her smile and I remember that she liked to dance. She made me forget how badly I was hurting and then she left. It was only for one night.

And no, I don't remember her name, only that she had sandy-blonde hair. I don't even remember the color of her eyes. God, Val, can you ever forgive me? I swear I didn't know she got pregnant. I never saw her again, and Cambric never contacted me."

"I... I..." Val stuttered and stammered before clutching at her chest.

Jason was on her in an instant.

Letting go of Bee, he tucked his arms around his wife's body and pulled her up and over the back of the couch. Stumbling a few steps, he wrapped his arms around her body and rocked her. His lips whispered quietly against her hair. She began to cry.

The sound was muffled, but Val's shoulders shook, and the pain she felt seemed to echo up on Jason's face. His eyes were stormy. He stared hard at Bernard.

Bee let her gaze follow Jason's line of sight until she too was looking at her father. He wasn't a bad person, she thought, not really. Try as she might, she couldn't muster any real anger for him. He was just a human being, like the rest of them, trying to get by.

"I will help in anyway that I can," Bernard began, his words halting as his eyes pleaded with Jason. "I can give you the timeframe I was there and the name of my friend. It's been decades now, but maybe we can find something about her."

"I'll handle it," Jason cut him off. "Maybe you should just go."

"Okay." Bernard ducked his head and cleared his throat.

Pushing up from the coffee table, he wiped a few of his own silent tears from his cheeks before chancing a look down at Bee. She was just like him, wasn't she? They acted out when they were hurt. They drank and carried on. They were the life of the party, until it wasn't a party anymore.

Springing to her feet, Bee took the first step forward into his arms. Her father coughed and clung to her, burying his face in her hair.

"I love you," he whispered. "I love your mother."

"I know," she answered, because she did.

"Maybe..." he sniffed again before continuing. "Maybe when all this clears up, Val will be willing to see me."

Bee's heart ached for him, and she found herself giving him a quick nod.

"Maybe I could spend time with both of you," he went on quietly. "And Jace, too."

Jace. Bee squeezed her eyes shut. That was his grandson, too. And after what Gabe had told her in the Maldives, it would likely be his only one.

"Will you tell Mom?" Bee asked instead, drawing back to study her father.

"Yes," he managed, as the color drained from his face. "I'll tell her. I promise."

CHAPTER 23

Gabe

"Hey, don't go," Bee's voice came out whisper quiet.

Her body was pressed against his side, one arm thrown over his chest as they lay tangled together.

"Mmmm," Gabe hummed, his eyes closed, his thoughts thick. "But I need to go, Bee Bee."

Exhaling on a sigh, Gabe pulled her in even closer. It felt so good just to lie here, her legs wrapped up with his, her hair draping over his shoulder and chest. He was on his back in her dorm bed, completely drained and completely happy.

"Not yet," she protested, then nuzzled her lips into his neck.

It felt right. They felt right. But he really should go now, it was getting late. Somewhere in the back of his mind, Gabe knew it had to be pretty late.

"I need to go," Gabe murmured again. His chest was getting heavier with each breath. Sleeping beside her would feel sooooo good.

"Just five more minutes," she murmured.

"Alright," he relented. "Five more minutes."

They were words Gabe would never forget.

~

The first thing he heard was shouting. It was loud and undeniably male, causing adrenaline to release in Gabe's system. Before he could even open his eyes, there were hands on him. More than one set of hands, grabbing and yanking and pulling.

A split second later, his naked body was impacting the floor and Gabe's eyes finally came into focus.

Shit.

Holy shit.

He was still in Bee's bedroom and it was morning. There were Cambric guards all over him, two... no, maybe three. And Bee was screaming from somewhere behind him.

Val was sitting not an arm's length away. She was motionless. Her legs were drawn up in her bed, her knees pulled to her chest. Her mouth gaped open and her eyes were wide. She was looking at the other side of the room. She was looking at Bee.

Twisting on the ground, Gabe fought to turn his head. He fought to look back at Bee, but the guards were sitting on him, laying on him. All the air in his lungs expelled in a rush and a sick sort of panic took over.

"Bee!" Gabe screamed her name. "Get off me! Get the fuck off me!"

But the guards only grunted in response as they used their combined weight to hold him in place.

That's when he saw her.

Bee entered his line of sight just in time for him to watch her struggling. A guard had her by the hair. She was naked and scream-ing. Her fingernails were scratching at the guy, but he was twice her size, literally twice her size. She had no chance, Gabe thought. None.

"Bee!" Gabe screamed again, his throat was aching, his heart burning a whole in his chest. "She didn't do anything! Leave her alone!"

"Gabe!" Bee screeched his name, but by that time the guard had had enough.

Cocking back one of his meaty fists, he popped her square in the face and knocked her out.

Boom. Done.

Her eyes rolled back in her head, and her body was crumpling.

The sound of the hit was sickening. A crunching. Flesh meeting flesh. Gabe would never, ever forget it.

Nope. The memory of Bee getting knocked out would haunt him for years. In his dreams, he'd hear her call his name, followed by the hit. It would echo in his mind long after she was gone, waking him in the night, sending him to the toilet to throw up.

But these were things he wouldn't understand until later. At the time it actually happened, he simply lost it.

Gabe felt the impact of Bee's limp body hit the floor just beside him. It ripped him apart at the seams.

In an instant, he was writhing and rolling and throwing punches. His elbows hit something, his shins hit something. He couldn't tell if he was landing his fists against the guards or the surrounding furniture. He couldn't see anything, in fact, he was blind.

All he saw was a curtain of red. All he felt was blood rushing through his veins, then his vision narrowed. It was like he was staring down a tunnel, with only a tiny circle at the far end.

There was the floor. Then a guard's boot. Then the leg of a chair.

His ears picked up the sound of shoes running. The skin on his arm registered a sharp pinch.

Then came the slowness.

Darkness.

Sadness.

Defeat.

His body betrayed him. It gave up the fight long before he was ready. Gabe slipped into the black without the slightest hesitation. It was like giving up on Bee wasn't any trouble at all.

When he swam back towards consciousness, it was just as slowly as he'd left it. There was a thin mattress beneath his left shoulder. His body ached, like he'd been resting in one position for too long. Biting back a groan, Gabe rolled onto his back and brought his hands to his face.

Inhaling sharply, he drug his palms from his forehead to his chin. He'd had a nightmare, he thought absently. Like the worst nightmare ever.

Clearing his throat, Gabe dropped his hands and let his head flop to one side. When he opened his eyes, he blinked blearily at what he saw.

"Bee Bee?" He asked.

His voice was scratchy, his throat felt so raw. "Hey, you okay? What... the..."

Shooting up to sitting, Gabe glanced wildly around him. He was in Isolation.

Shit. Shit. Shit.

But Bee Bee was just there on the other side of the glass partition. She was sitting by herself, shaking and afraid.

His nightmare had been real. Cambric had caught him in her bedroom. Naked. In her bed.

Shoving up to standing, Gabe weaved and stumbled his way to the glass. He slapped both palms flat on the partition before reality finally... finally caught up with him.

"Val?" He asked quietly, as the cowering woman sitting before him came into focus. They looked so damn alike, at first glance, he'd thought she was Bee. "You okay, Val? Where is she, honey? Have you seen her? Where's Bee Bee, Val?"

Tipping his forehead to rest against the glass, Gabe let the tears flood his eyes and roll unchecked down his cheeks. What had he done? What had he fucking done?

From her seat on the floor, Val looked up into his face and shook her head. She was trembling, her whole body would not stop shaking. She was dressed up in that stupid short gray dress all the girls had to wear and there were no blankets in Isolation.

They kept the rooms pretty cold. Even so, Gabe knew she wasn't shaking from the temperature.

Biting at her lip, Val drew her knees up to her chest and laid her head down on them. Quietly, she began to rock. Back and forth. Back and forth.

She was too afraid to say anything out loud. Val'd never been here before, Gabe recalled. She'd only been at the Discipline table once, and she'd never been to Isolation.

"I'll get her back," Gabe croaked. "I swear to you, Val. We'll get her back, okay?"

Lifting her head, Val ran her forearm beneath her nose and sniffed. "How?" She whispered finally. "She's gone, Gabey. She's gone."

"She's somewhere," he insisted.

They wouldn't kill her, would they? That asshole had hit her pretty hard, but still. She was alive. She had to be alive.

That guard was a dead man, Gabe thought suddenly, and sucked in a breath. If Gabe ever got the chance, that guy was dead... and everyone else was, too. Shit. Fuck. Bee Bee.

Before his throat closed up on him, Gabe spoke again, "I'm going to stop eating. I'm going to stop taking that stupid pill. No more breeding, no more trainer. They'll bring her back, Val. I swear to you, I will fix this."

He spat out the words, but Val just stared at him. Blinking. No response.

Promises. Gabe ducked his head. He just kept making promises.

He'd promised he would stay friends with Bee, only friends. It'd taken him six months to break that one. Then he'd promised not to fuck Bee over. Not literally, not figuratively. Four weeks later... boom, that promise was shot all to hell, too.

Then he'd promised to keep her safe. He'd promised to keep them a secret, to always sneak out of her room, to never risk her being caught.

Shoving back from the glass, Gabe stumbled his way to the lone door of his cell and pounded his fists against it.

"Do you hear that?!" He screamed. "Bring her back! She didn't do anything! We never did anything!"

His voice echoed in the empty room, bouncing against the stark walls and concrete floor. They didn't believe him. No one believed him.

Cambric didn't believe he hadn't had sex with Bee. Val didn't believe he could get her back. Hell, at this point Gabe didn't even believe it himself.

Promises.

He fucking sucked at keeping promises. Clutching at his stomach, Gabe braced one hand against the wall and sucked in air. He was going to be sick. He was going to vomit all over the floor.

That's what happens when you hate yourself.

That's what happens when you have no one else to blame.

Gabe's self-loathing was only further solidified over the next two weeks.

That first promise he'd made? To stop eating?

Well, he'd tried that... but then they'd starved Val, too. Promise broken. He ate.

Then came the next promise. He refused to take that little blue pill. Without it, he couldn't get it up. He was useless in breeding, useless to sell as a D2, useless for his trainer. He figured he had Cambric beat that time.

Then they'd sent that son-of-a-bitch Ben to Val's room.

Surprisingly, Gabe had made it through the first session. He'd curled up in a ball beneath his mattress and plugged his fingers in his ears. But the second time around, he was unable to turn a blind eye.

It was the middle of the night and the lights had popped on. The door to Val's cell opened and shut with a slam.

Gabe blinked against the light and groaned. Pushing up to sitting, he'd just managed to get his bearings when Val had whimpered. Fucking whimpered.

Ben was being rough. He had her bent over by the glass partition with her face pressed against it so Gabe could get a really good look at her. Then he was shoving her dress up over her hips and yanking down on her panties and he was threading his fingers through her hair and jerking her head back. She bit her lip and whimpered again.

Gabe came undone.

His vision kept interchanging Val's face with Bee's. Ben had trained them both, after all. He'd had them both. Is this how he did it? Is this how the fucker had always gone about it? Gabe's mind exploded.

What happened next wasn't even planned, it just happened.

Within two seconds, he was slamming his forehead into the glass. Over and over and over.

Cue the bloody nose, split eyebrow, and swollen hands from smashing into that fucking partition. When his head started swimming he switched it for his shoulder. He kept ramming into the glass, rattling it until the guards rushed in and tackled him.

He went down screaming. Screaming and spitting blood and crying like a little bitch.

Boom. Promise broken.

Not a day later, Gabe was swallowing that little blue pill. He willingly popped the damn thing into his mouth right before dinner, and everything he ever cared about disappeared.

There was no more Bee.

There was no more Val.

And there was no one more to blame than Gabe. At least that's how he felt.

He hated himself. More than any of them, he hated him. Because without Gabe, Bee would be just fine. Without him falling so hard for her, Bee would be safe. She'd be a permanent placement D2 on her way to another life.

So, Gabe's insides hollowed out and he turned into a dead man walking. Walking. Always walking.

How can a dead man put one foot in front of the other? Gabe didn't know, but somehow, he did.

CHAPTER 24

Bee

Running her hands against the buttery smooth leather, Bee let out a breath. Outside the passenger side window, fields of wheat flashed by. Field after field after field, golden soft in the bright light of day.

"Where are we again?" Bee asked finally. Throwing a glance to her left, she eyed Val. "Arkansas? Ohio?"

Huffing a laugh, Val rolled her eyes. "Oklahoma," she corrected, not for the first time.

"And you think this is going to work?" Bee gestured around the luxury SUV, with its double enforced tinted windows and bullet proof everything. "She's going to talk to us like this?"

"I don't know," Val admitted, her eyes darting up to their driver and the hulking security sitting shotgun. "But Jason wouldn't let us go otherwise."

"And we for sure have the right address?" Bee pressed.

"Ava thinks so," Val repeated. "She's rarely wrong."

"But she's not always right," Bee countered. "Right?"

"Bee Bee." Reaching across the backseat, Val placed her hand on top of Bee's. "We've been at this for months now, but these sort of things take time. The worst she can say is no."

"That's not the worst thing she could do, though," Bee countered. "She could tell."

"If she's anything like Charlie said," Val reasoned. "She won't tell."

Blowing out a breath, Bee gave up a small nod and let her gaze drift back out the window. Val didn't release her hand. In silence, they sat there together, side by side, soaking up another day as sisters, another day as spies.

Okay, so maybe spy was a strong word, but what they were doing was covert, and important. What they were trying to accomplish was maybe the best thing Bee had ever done in her life.

For the past several months, Bee had managed to stay sober. She'd moved in with Val and Jason and she'd begun her work for the underground. They were stealing captives right out from under their agency's noses.

They weren't waiting for Jason to get elected, although that seemed imminent now. They were being proactive, contributing and succeeding everywhere except for at Cambric. That fortress remained impenetrable. Perhaps until now.

"This is the place," CT murmured.

He was the hunk of beef riding shotgun, and the most trusted of Jason's security team. By now Bee had gotten used to his constant presence, though he was still somewhat of an anomaly.

He lived alone in the guest house on Jason's property but

he rarely spoke. No friends visited him, no girlfriends or wife or children. He took no personal calls that Bee had ever witnessed and almost no time off.

He was getting rich with every passing day on Jason's payroll for sure, but what was the point of money if you never did anything with it? Eyeing him now, Bee watched him point a thick finger out to their right, and the driver slowed.

"Here?" Bee asked, scrunching her nose. "It looks like a farm."

"It is," Val confirmed and withdrew her hand. "Charlie said they were rural. He loved it here."

"Hmm," Bee's response was non-committal.

Glancing down at her phone, she swiped through the information they had on Charlie's wife. Five-foot-two, auburn hair, brown eyes. Her driver's license photo revealed a smattering of freckles across the bridge of her nose and high up on both cheeks.

She was pretty, with pearly white teeth that were straight on top and a bit crooked on the bottom. Cute.

Swiping right, Bee's brow furrowed as she read. Alana Carol Gandel. Married. No children. Her maiden name was Watts, but she'd kept her married name.

Bee bit at her lip.

This woman had kept Charlie's name, even after all these years without him. That said something about her. That said something about them together.

Bee kept reading, kept swiping. The farm was inherited, and struggling. Since Charlie left, it had faltered, but Alana still owned it, and all accounts said she still worked it herself. Payroll records had her hiring a series of farmhands, but none of them stuck.

Sort of like Charlie, they breezed on and off the farm in under a year. Though Alana wouldn't know him as Charlie. He was Paul Gandel to her, or he had been, once upon a time.

Looking up, Bee's eyes narrowed on the two story house in the distance. It was white, with a wide porch wrapping around the entire thing. The shutters on the windows were a deep green, although as they approached, Bee noted the paint was chipping.

Slowly, the SUV bumped them down the long dirt driveway. There was an empty field on one side of the car and rows of corn on the other. Behind them, another SUV bumped along as well. That one was filled with additional security. Talk about overkill.

Both Val and Bee had tried to talk Jason out of the extra detail but he simply would not budge. He didn't care if their transportation screamed government. He didn't care if it screamed money, and begged locals to take a second glance. All he cared about was having enough protection swirling around his girls so that he could sleep at night (his words).

So here they were, parking in this lady's gravel driveway, looking every bit like outsiders coming with bad intentions. Great first impression. Great way to earn some trust.

Bee spared Val a quick glance and was rewarded with another eye roll. Baby sister had grown a pair, Bee thought, somewhere along the way.

Shoving out of the vehicle, Bee huffed an impatient breath when CT managed to get out first. Blocking her path, he pressed a single finger to the side of his ear and spoke quietly. Then there were car doors slamming and men in suits stalking around. Gravel crunched beneath feet as two men went around back and one more crested the creaking porch steps.

"You're making this way harder than it has to be," Bee hissed at CT's back.

Tilting his head just the tiniest bit, he threw her a quick look before turning back to the porch and rolling his shoulders. That was all she would get, Bee knew. The damn giant of stone thought she was an annoying gnat. Message received, loud and clear.

"Can I help you gentleman?" The woman's voice was high up, causing them all to tip their heads back.

There, perched on the open windowsill of a second story room, sat Alana Gandel. Dressed in blue jeans and a button down plaid shirt, her auburn hair was pulled back into a messy pony tail. With a shotgun gripped loosely in one hand and one foot dangling out the window, she made for quite the picture.

CT's hand went instinctively to the gun at his back, but he didn't pull it. After all, Alana's shotgun wasn't pointed at anyone. It was just there as a sort of warning. And Alana was a woman alone in her own home, with five grown men crawling around her property. Bee couldn't help but grin.

Spunky. Good job Charlie boy. Good job indeed.

"We're looking for Alana Gandel," Val spoke out, holding one hand up to shade her eyes.

"Ain't never heard of her," Alana countered.

A taunting sort of smile played along her lips as her twisted twang curled down to their ears. Bee's grin broadened. Val frowned.

All the while, Alana's booted foot bounced just a little as it dangled lazily in the autumn breeze.

"Really?" Val tried again as she glanced down at her phone. "Is this 17311 Old Creek Road?"

"Sure is," Alana confirmed, bobbing her head. "Whoever ya'll lookin' for don't live here though."

"That's too bad," Bee piped up, causing Val to shoot her a questioning look. "We wanted to talk to her about a man she once knew. Maybe you've heard of him? He went by the name Paul."

Immediately, Alana's face fell. What once was taunting and bright became storm clouds in a split second. Cursing under her breath, Alana drew her leg back through the window and slammed the glass shut.

Bee could here her stomping boots descend through the thin walls of the old house. CT tensed just ahead of her and the driver, who had been standing in front of Val, made to push her back into the vehicle altogether.

But then the front door was swinging open and there was no shotgun in sight. Alana stood on the threshold, folded her empty arms over her chest, and glared.

"Don't tell me ya'll was married to him, too," she declared, and had Bee laughing out loud.

Giving CT a shove (though he barely moved an inch) Bee pushed her way to the porch steps. Dressed in designer blue jeans and a plain sweater, she and Val had both tried to down play their lifestyle. It didn't work.

Alana's intelligent eyes swept over Bee in an instant before darting to Val. She cocked an eyebrow and waited.

"I was never married to him," Bee announced, then felt Val come to stand just beside her. "Val, were you?"

"No, I wasn't." Val cleared her throat nervously. "We grew up together, the three of us."

"That so?" Alana didn't budge, and she didn't uncross those stubborn arms of hers either.

"Just so we're clear," Val continued. "Is this your Paul?"

Bringing her phone up to her face once more, Val swiped quickly through it. When she got to a recent picture of Charlie, she offered it out for Alana to see. They'd gotten the photo off of Cambric's website a few months ago, when The Agency had finally placed him back for sale.

He was monthly membership again, so that was a good sign. It meant he was eating. It meant he was okay.

Staring at the photo, Alana's arms dropped limply to her sides. It was like Bee could feel her hurting. Those sassy eyes went glassy a moment, and then she was coughing into a closed fist and glancing away.

"What'd he do now?" Alana asked quietly. "Why're y'all here?"

"May we come in?" Val ventured, and Alana huffed.

"No you may not," she said, and the fierceness was back. "I haven't seen him in years and I don't know where he's at. So whatever it is you're hoping to find here..."

"His name isn't Paul Gandel," Bee cut in, and drew Alana's words to a stop. "He was born Charlie, just one name. Like I was known as Bee and she was born Val."

Narrowing her eyes, Alana's gaze jumped from Bee to Val. A recognition flickered. It was just there at the back of her mind, smoldering a moment before the knowledge took flame.

"Wait... are you..."

"I'm Val Riggs and I was born a captive," Val said, and stuck out her hand for a shake. "This is my sister Bee."

"Also raised as a captive," Bee put in.

"Val Riggs... as in..." Alana's words were slow as her mind clicked through the implications. "So that would make Paul..."

"Charlie," Bee corrected. "That would make Charlie a captive as well."

"Oh my God." Alana's hands shot to her face and then she was sinking to the floor.

Crouching, with her head between her knees, Alana sucked in air. Bee shot a look at Val, whose own face was crumpling. They'd had a thing, Charlie and Val. A special sort of friendship that was more, but wasn't. Val had told her about it, confessed those sins that were so common to captive life.

It wasn't something she could tell Jason. It was something Val was afraid he wouldn't quite understand. And Bee had agreed. There were things that happened to you as a captive, relationships that formed, bonds that were forged because you had no other choice. It wasn't like being free, and getting to choose when to stop.

Gabe's face jumped to the forefront of her mind. Was he finding comfort at Cambric? In all the heartbreak and chaos and demands of being a D2, was Gabe's heart splitting? Like Val's had? Like Charlie's and so many others?

Bee's heart plummeted to her toes. It hurt so badly, she wanted a drink. She wanted to escape the pain. But instead of running this time, Bee chose to fight. She shoved the thoughts of Gabe from her mind and focused on what she could control.

Convincing this woman to help them was priority number one. If they were going to get eyes back inside Cambric, then Alana Gandel was the key to getting it done.

Bee caught Val's eye and lifted her chin towards Alana. Val bobbed her head.

Cresting the remaining steps, Val knelt down beside the broken woman and laid a tentative hand on her back. Bee cleared her throat and listened to her sister's words.

"Charlie didn't leave you because he stopped loving you," she murmured. "He left because he'd escaped Cambric and they were hunting for him. He didn't want to get you in trouble. He didn't want them to ever know about you."

"Oh my God," Alana repeated. "Paul."

Lowering her hands, Alana pressed her palms to the old wooden slats of the porch and bowed her head. Bee watched a few tear drops stain the dry planks. It wasn't long before they stopped coming though, and Alana sucked in a ragged breath.

Seeming to pull herself together, she raised her head and eyed the both of them.

"Y'all still want to come in?" She asked before shoving up to standing.

Wiping her hands together, Alana sniffed once and eyed the array of men in suits lingering on her patchy lawn. "I've got plenty of sweet tea and biscuits, if y'all are hungry."

CHAPTER 25

Gabe

"Good morning, lover boy. How are we today?" Shane's voice grated like nails on a chalkboard down the inside of Gabe's skull.

Cracking open one eye, Gabe glared. From his position on his narrow mattress, Gabe counted two Cambric guards standing off to one side of his cell. Then there was that fucker Shane.

"Your face is looking good again," Shane went on, kicking off from his position against the closed door. "Body's all healed up. You ready to try this thing again?"

Lifting both arms slowly, Gabe brought them out in front of him and extended his middle fingers. With a grin, he forced a dull chuckle.

"Funny guy, huh?" Shane shook his head like he didn't care, but Gabe knew better. "Maybe you'll think twice this time."

Giving a quick nod towards the glass partition, Shane

waited for Gabe to look through to the other room. Gabe refused.

Not only did he not give a rats ass what poor sap was in there this time, but he also knew his refusal pissed Shane off. And that was all Gabe lived for anymore, the chance to piss Shane the fuck off.

They'd been playing this cat and mouse game for forever now it seemed. Gabe had lost track of time. He'd lost track of meals skipped. He'd lost track of the beatings. And at this point he didn't care who was in the Isolation room next door. Truly.

They'd already put Charlie in there, and when that didn't work, they starved Gabe's former trainer for awhile.

Then came the parade of girls from breeding that he'd been with, and after them came the other girls from his past at Cambric. None of them made an impact.

Sure, Gabe felt guilty. He was sorry when they missed meals. He was sorry when they occasionally got slapped around. But nothing… nothing, was going to convince him to make that video, or sign that form. Nothing.

"You're not even curious?" Shane took a step closer, his voice dropping. "You don't care who your next victim is?"

Looking Shane dead in the eye, Gabe grinned.

"You've taken everyone that I care about away from me," he said, a twisted sort of laughter bubbled at the back of his throat. "I have no one left. There is no one here that I give a shit about, so whoever you've got stashed over there won't change anything."

"Is that so?" Shane again, creeping closer. "Are you sure about that?"

"Yeah," Gabe scoffed and folded his arms casually behind his head. "That's so."

"Hmmmm," Shane tisked quietly as a silky smile spread across his face. "Better take a look first. Don't you think?"

For a minute, maybe more, Gabe stared at Shane. The room fell to silence, where the only sounds were Gabe's own breathing and the steady thump of his cold dark heart.

He wasn't going to look.

He wasn't going to give Shane the pleasure.

But then he heard a sound, and before he could stop himself, Gabe turned his head. In an instant, everything changed. The color drained from his face and his mouth hung slightly ajar.

Holy. God. *No.*

Gabe

Wiping his damp palms along his thighs, Gabe blew out a shaky breath. He knew the moisture would probably leave a stain on his expensive gray slacks, but he did not care.

Lifting his head, he eyed the front of the courthouse. How long had it been since he'd walked through there a free man? Judging by the shift in weather, it had been almost a year, though he didn't actually know what month it was.

Clearing his throat, Gabe tried to dislodge the uncomfortable feeling that seemed permanently wedged there. Beside him, a Cambric guard reached for a bottle of water and handed it over. They were in the backseat of a dark sedan, waiting at the curb.

Shane was sitting shotgun, with all of his attention centered on his phone. He never sat in the back anymore. Not with Gabe there, at least.

With a quick shake of his head, Gabe declined the offered drink. Surprisingly, the guard said nothing before stuffing the bottle into the pocket of the seat-back in front of him. If it had been anyone else, the bottle would've already been opened and shoved down Gabe's throat. Maybe some people still had a conscience, way down deep in there somewhere.

Rubbing a hand across his tightening chest, Gabe continued to stare. People walked up and down the stone steps, the crisp fall wind tugging at their clothes. They were business people, free people, in their suits and their skirts with their ties and their heels. It was nothing like before. It was nothing like arriving here with Jason, prepared to do battle, prepared to enter that courtroom and trade himself back for Val.

There were no media people swarming. No cameras and microphones. No pushing crowds and gawking passersby. It was just a normal day. None of these people knew what was about to happen. And if they did, maybe none of them would care.

"They're ready for us," Shane announced, before twisting around in his seat to eye him. "Time to put all that training to use. You need to be convincing."

Bobbing his head, Gabe let his eyes fall to the floor. He could hardly stand to look at the man, let alone do his bidding. But here he was, about to destroy everything.

As the car doors all around him popped open, Gabe found his own hand reaching for his handle. He stalled out for a second as his fingers wrapped around the cream-colored plastic. It was his left hand that caught his eye, hanging there as if it was owned by someone else. And as Gabe stared hard at his own skin, that empty ring finger taunted him.

Another choice left unmade. Another experience he would never have.

Why the hell had he let that one slide?

Now he'd never get the chance to get down on one knee and ask. He'd never feel the rush of relief when Bee said yes. He'd never be the one to feel her ring on his finger, and he'd never get to slip his ring on hers.

Nope. Some other lucky bastard would someday get that pleasure. It would never be Gabe. Some other guy, who wasn't such an idiot, would make Bee his wife and Gabe would never hold that claim over her. She'd never be *his* in that way.

At the realization, a sick sort of tremor went through him. Biting hard at his lip, Gabe held back the angry bile that collected at the back of his throat. What the hell had he been waiting for? Why wasn't that the first thing he did when they'd hit the Maldives?

He couldn't fucking remember.

"Hey," Shane's voice was muffled by the still closed door as he rapped an impatient knuckle on the window glass. "Get out, lover boy. We don't have all day."

Swallowing down his hatred, Gabe yanked at the handle and had it opening with a pop. They'd disengaged the child locks for this little trip. They knew he wasn't going anywhere.

When he stepped out into the air, Gabe found it was brisk and cool. A shiver ran through him. Reaching for the button on his suit coat, he fastened it as they walked, then automatically, he smoothed at his tie.

This part was all training. It was all muscle memory and years of repetition. Although his insides felt like a raging storm, his outside appeared calm and nonplussed. He would do as he was told. He would perform as he was directed.

Together, they crested the stone steps, appearing like any other group of businessmen or lawyers. Albeit the two

Cambric guards were pretty large. They both got an additional screening when moving through security. It surprised Gabe to note that neither of them were carrying a gun.

Once inside, they navigated a series of elevators and corridors. Their expensive shoes squeaked against the worn linoleum floor until they finally stepped onto faded Burgundy carpeting. Inhaling sharply, Gabe took in the scent of stale air, old furniture and poor ventilation. A drip of sweat trickled down his spine. He tugged at the knot of his tie.

Glancing back at him, Shane frowned.

"You better get this right," he hissed. "You know what's waiting for you at Cambric if you don't."

"I will," Gabe answered, his voice surprisingly even.

Seemingly convinced, Shane turned back to face forward just in time to stop at a receptionist desk. The young woman sitting behind an old computer monitor clicked and hummed to herself. It wasn't until all four of them were looming over her, that she pushed at her glasses and looked up.

"Can I help you?" She asked, blinking, undisturbed.

"We have a meeting with Judge Harbertson in his chambers," Shane responded and offered her one of his cold smiles. "We're from the Cambric Agency."

"Oh, of course." Frowning, the woman attempted to shake off the bastard's icy stare and tapped on her keyboard. "Yes, please go right in."

"Thank you," Gabe added and stared right at her.

With a slight smile twisting his lips, he looked deep into those unremarkable blue eyes of hers. He looked until her cheeks were dusting pink and she was tucking an errant brown hair behind one ear. Nodding her head, she gave him a half smile in return.

"You're welcome," she breathed the words out as her eyes dropped to Gabe's lips.

Shane gave a little huff before leading them to the large double doors. Turning to follow him, Gabe kept his face easy and shoved one hand casually in the pocket of his slacks. This was all training, too. This was many months worth of reconditioning.

It didn't matter that inside his head, Gabe was screaming. It didn't matter that he'd wanted to pick up that computer and smash it against the wall.

He couldn't. He couldn't fight this. He couldn't do what he wanted, say what he wanted, be who he wanted. Not today, not tomorrow, not ever again.

They had him.

They fucking had him now, and there would never be a day when they didn't.

So every woman was now a mark. And for that matter, every man was a mark, too. The old Gabe was back on display. The life of the party. The shameless flirt.

Unlike Shane, who couldn't hide his inner monster, Gabe's eyes would appear genuine. His smile would be, too. Hell, even his laughter would sound real.

He was just that good. It didn't matter that he was a living, breathing, lie.

And in the end it was that very ability to pretend that saved him... or rather, it saved *them*. The ones still back at Cambric, whose lives depended on his performance.

Because no one had warned Gabe what would be waiting for him on the other side of those courtroom doors. No one had told him that he would be walking into a judge's chambers where his former mistress, Sharon Baine, sat with her team of attorneys and waited.

So when Gabe walked into the room and glanced casually around, no one knew that fear was shooting itself into every extremity he had. When Sharon smiled up at him, and the judge watched carefully, and Shane glanced back over his shoulder, Gabe merely ducked his head and looked properly contrite.

Because that's what a man is supposed to look like when he's about to make a confession. He should look apologetic. He should look reserved and sheepish, a little embarrassed even.

So that's how Gabe looked.

When he took the seat that was offered to him, and recited the lines that Shane made him memorize, he looked the part. Hell, he sounded the part, he acted the part, he *was* the part. And Gabe knew from that moment on, that's all he would ever deserve to be… a part.

CHAPTER 27

Bee

SMOOTHING AT HER PERFECT BOB OF DARK HAIR, BEE straightened her shoulders and glanced around. The room wasn't small, but even so, the space felt crowded.

Running a hand over the creamy leather of the long couch, Bee crossed her slender legs and kept an easy expression on her face. This was it. Election night.

Beside her, Jace wiggled and squirmed and rolled his lovely blue eyes. Bee bit at her bottom lip and suppressed a smile. Her nephew was stuffed into a formal suit, just like his daddy, and his grandfather, and his Uncle Jeremy.

The entire Riggs family was present, dressed to impress in dignified skirts, dresses and suits. But like any other seven-year-old boy, Jace was all energy.

He wanted to roll around on the floor. He wanted to jump up and down on the couch. He wanted to yell and howl and run.

But for the media cameras that were currently rolling in

the room, he had to sit still. The press ate this stuff up. They wanted live footage of the perfect family, waiting for the final verdict on election night.

"Want to play a game on my phone?" Bee asked, wiggling her eyebrows as her nephew's face brightened.

"Yeah!" Jace nodded his head and snatched at the phone as soon as Bee produced it.

Within ten seconds, the little guy had his head bowed, eyes focused, and was statue still. Bee exhaled in relief just as her mother and Elaine Riggs shot her disapproving frowns.

Jace wasn't supposed to be seen using too much technology. It didn't show well in the opinion polls. Bee grinned. Screw the opinion polls, it was better than the kid melting into a whiny puddle on the floor of the hotel suite.

Out of the corner of her eye, Bee watched Val and Jason finish off yet another interview. Their campaign manager had arranged for certain members of the press to spend the day with the Riggs family while voters took to the ballot box. So for the past five hours, they'd all been holed up in this suite with an ever increasing crowd of supporters and campaign workers crowding one of the ballrooms on the floors below.

When this was all said and done, Jason would have to go down and make another speech. Either he would be announcing his victory, or admitting defeat.

A large flat screen television hanging on one wall blared out the latest news while the rest of the family perched on the surrounding couches and chairs. The press wanted to catch Jason's expression the moment he discovered whether he would be a Senator or not.

"I'm glad that part's over," Val murmured, as she slid down next to Bee on the couch. "I don't know how he does it."

"He was born for it," Bee countered as she wove her hand in her sister's. "Whether he likes it or not, he'll make a good politician."

"Ugh," Val grunted the word under her breath but stopped short of wrinkling her nose. The cameras were still rolling, after all.

"I see you gave in to the phone," Val commented, her eyes shifting past Bee to rest on her son. "You held out longer than I would have."

At that comment, Bee laughed. "Mommy Dearest and your esteemed mother-in-law were not happy. But with the cameras here, they couldn't exactly say anything. Guess the media does have its benefits."

"Hmm." Val shifted around in her navy-blue dress and sighed. "Maybe I should hire them to follow Elaine around from now on."

"Maybe." Bee smirked at the thought.

"How is your mom doing?" Val ventured quietly, her emerald green eyes coming to rest on Bee's face. "You know, with everything."

Dipping her head, Bee swallowed before answering. Things weren't so great, actually. Their father had followed through and confessed his infidelity. Lillian hadn't taken it so well. It was sort of hard to process a decades old affair and an illegitimate daughter, especially after the information had been leaked to the press.

As a result, the Durands were no longer living together. Lillian couldn't stand to be in the same building with Bernard, let alone the same room. That was why Bee's mother was here tonight, while her father was not. He hadn't been invited.

And that part was hard. Bee found that she really missed

her father, and from Val's round-about comments, she knew that her sister was curious about him, too. Val wanted to see him again, and Bee wanted more than anything to arrange it. But if she did, and her mother got wind of it, then more hearts would be broken.

"It's fine," Bee lied finally. "She's fine."

Settling into a brief silence, Bee let her eyes cruise around the room. The television was droning on incessantly, alternating between local updates about the voting in Texas and national headlines. Jason was standing beside his brother now, their heads bent together, discussing something quietly.

It was probably about Jason's old businesses, Bee figured. Jeremy had taken over completely so that Jason could run for Congress without any suspicion of corruption. Word was, little brother was doing a bang up job. Guess success just ran in the family, Bee thought.

In the opposite corner, the tv crews adjusted their equipment and chatted calmly amongst themselves. Voting would continue for another three hours so they still had plenty of time on the job. Biting at her lip, Bee held back a small frown.

It was hard not to think of them as the enemy. But as Bee observed them sipping water and laughing together at some private joke, she realized they were just people, too. They had a job to do, and they did it. Even though mostly that job involved crucifying someone Bee loved.

Standing just behind them, CT leaned back against one wall. He was one of three bodyguards lingering in the room, but among them, he stood out. His broad shoulders seemed to stretch the material of the expensive black suit he wore and the overhead lights glinted off of his clean-shaven head. He was massive.

And despite his size, the serious, silent giant was trying to fade into the background. *Yeah, right. Nothing that big can fade.*

Bee pursed her lips. To look at him here you'd never know what a softy he was. The guy had been all *pleases* and *thank yous* at Alana Gandel's house. Guess the way to a man's heart really was with a little sweet tea and biscuits.

Speaking of which, Bee needed to follow up with her. The next phase of their plan was coming up soon and she wanted to make sure Alana was ready. It would bring Bee one step closer to freeing Gabe, which was all she could focus on these days.

She woke up in the morning and didn't take a drink, because she had to free Gabe.

She worked for the underground and kept herself busy, because she had to free Gabe.

She lived with her sister and helped with the campaign, because she had to free Gabe.

She played nice with the press and stayed away from the bar, because she had to free Gabe.

She had to free Gabe. *They* had to free him. There was simply no other alternative.

When CT caught Bee staring at him, he arched a slow eyebrow, but at the same time he absolutely refused to smile. Rolling her eyes, Bee quickly stuck her tongue out at him and watched as the corner of his mouth twitched. Ha, she thought, so there *is* a funny bone in there somewhere.

"Oh God," Val breathed the words next to her, and clutched hard at Bee's hand.

Whirling towards her sister, Bee's brow furrowed and she was just about to speak when a sound from the flat screen television caught her attention. Following Val's line of sight,

Bee's mouth dropped open in shock as every other voice in the room fell silent.

Gabe.

It was Gabe there on the national news. He was giving an interview, or rather, telling a story. Bee's heart leapt in her chest at the sight of him. He looked so good, so healthy and handsome, same as ever.

They'd let his hair grow just a bit, until you could see the golden ends curl on his forehead. He was dressed in a gray suit, with a white button-up collared shirt and navy-blue tie wound perfectly around his neck. As he talked, Bee's eyes darted over the contours of his face. His strong jaw, his playful brown eyes and endearing smile.

She. Missed. Him.

God, if she'd thought she was heartbroken before, seeing him now only made her realize how much more she still had to suffer.

"No, Gabey," Val whispered the words, or rather whimpered them as she squeezed Bee's hand tighter.

Frowning, Bee forced herself to tune in. She had to work to clear the whooshing in her head so that she could actually listen to what Gabe was saying.

"Why did it take you so long to come out with this?" The interviewer asked, shoving a microphone closer to Gabe's contrite face.

"Well…" Gabe paused a moment and looked straight at the camera. "I was under the control of some very powerful people. It wasn't until I returned to my home that I felt safe enough to tell the truth."

"And by home, you mean the Cambric Agency?" The interviewer prompted.

"Yes." Gabe nodded his head easily. "I'm so thankful to have made it back. I feel relieved."

Bee's stomach sank as her eyes dipped to read the ticker-tape headline rolling along the bottom of the screen.

Sharon Baine to be released from prison. Star witness recants testimony. Judge grants appeal.

For the next several minutes the room remained eerily silent as they all watched Gabe talk. He accused the FBI of coercing him into giving false testimony against Sharon. He accused Jason of paying him off to get it done.

Bee's vision narrowed until all she could see was Gabe's face. The words he spoke were measured. His voice alternating between remorseful and apologetic. The expression on his face appeared earnest.

Overall, his story was believable, at least to anyone who didn't know the truth. But Bee knew the truth. Just like Val knew it. And Jason knew it.

Suddenly, Bee's legs felt like jelly. Stumbling forward off the couch, she tipped and tripped towards the television on the wall. Once she got there, she braced her hands lightly on the screen on either side of Gabe's face.

All around her, the room swirled. People were shuffling now, phones were ringing, there were a few shouts.

But all Bee saw was Gabe. All she heard was Gabe. And in her mind she wondered what he must have endured to bring him to this point. What had they done to him, to get him to lie in this way? What horrors had he experienced in the past year that finally made him break?

"Gabey," Bee whispered to the tv as tears streaked down her cheeks. "What did they do to you, Gabey?"

But then the screen before her was changing. Gabe's face was no longer there. Instead, it was a picture of her... of Bee... leaning up against a large television... in a lavish hotel suite... crying.

Sucking in a breath, Bee took a step back and glanced over her shoulder. Chaos. The room had devolved into chaos, with bodyguards yanking people out the far door, and Jason pressing a phone up against his ear, and a single camera zeroed in on Bee's face.

"Don't you see?" Bee stammered, speaking directly into the lens as the final media holdout recorded her. "They're making him do this."

The cameraman took a single step back, widening the shot. Just over his shoulder, Bee watched CT toss a reporter out the door before turning back. Bee's eyes darted over to the camera again, it was still rolling.

"They've had him for almost a year," she continued, pleading. "He's probably been starved and beaten. Other captives have probably been starved too, all so that he would do this."

Swallowing, Bee felt her heart splintering as it pounded in her chest. Images flashed through her mind, of her own punishments, and of others she had seen. Gabe. Oh God, poor Gabe.

"This is what Cambric wanted all along," Bee's voice cracked. "Can't you see that he's lying? Can't you understand why?"

Then CT was descending. He was grabbing the reporter by the collar of his shirt, yanking him up into the air. The camera tumbled to the carpeted flooring and rolled to a stop.

Glancing over her shoulder, Bee watched the live shot continue playing on the flat screen mounted to the wall. She listened, like so many other millions of viewers were probably listening, to the reporter scream about assault charges and civil rights.

And in the background, Jace was crying. Val was rocking him on her lap and Jason was hovering over them, growling into his phone. Lillian was gasping and Elaine was dashing to the camera on the floor and switching it off.

CHAPTER 28

Jason

THE COOL METAL SLIDING AGAINST THE PAD OF HIS THUMB WAS soothing. Keeping his hands resting easily at his sides, Jason spun his silver wedding band around and around on his ring finger. It was a subconscious habit, one that helped to keep him from crossing his arms over his chest.

As his brother droned on about alternative energy and the need to invest in new land out of state, Jason kept one eye on the cameras in the corner of the suite. He had just finished his last mandatory interview before the polls closed, but they had another three hours yet and the crews would be camping out the entire time.

With a glance to his young son, Jason instantly regretted the commitment. He should've made Quentin give them a break. He should've arranged for the press to leave and come back later in the evening. Then Jace could've run around for a bit without being judged for being a rowdy little boy.

Hell, who was he kidding? Then they could *all* relax for just a short while.

"I was kind of hoping you wouldn't get elected," Jeremy chuckled ruefully a moment before rubbing at his chin. "Then you could come back to the company."

"Huh?" Half-listening, Jason eyed his younger brother.

When had Jeremy grown up? All of sudden the high school baseball prodigy was a twenty-something executive with a bum shoulder and too much responsibility. Man did that fact make Jason feel old.

"Your numbers are good," Jeremy elaborated. "They say there's no way you can lose. Is it so bad that a part of me wanted you to?"

"No." Jason gave his head a quick shake before slapping a hand down on Jeremy's good shoulder. "I get it. This wasn't what you had in mind for your life. Believe me, I understand."

"But I mean, I *do* want you to win, too," Jeremy rushed on. "It's what you want, and it's the right thing. No one else has come this close to freeing captives."

"Yeah." Jason ducked his head and bit at his lip.

It's what you want. Right.

That's what his family thought. He hadn't told them about the Militia. He hadn't wanted to involve them, for their own safety.

With a sigh, Jason dropped his hand to his collar and tugged at his tie. The television on the wall was spitting out statistics about the Texas race right now. And it was just like Jeremy had said, they all thought he would win... like by a landslide.

But then the program was cut short with a flurry of important sounding music and *Breaking News* graphics. When the screen cleared, and Gabe's face came into focus, Jason couldn't hide his shock.

His hand shot from his tie to cover his gaping mouth as the entire room went silent. And as Gabe proceeded to make his "confession" on the national news, Jason's mouth slowly closed and his arms fell limply to his sides.

The things Gabe was saying. Holy. Shit.

He'd recanted his testimony. Sharon Baine was being released from prison. Her sentence was overturned. As if that wasn't enough, Gabe was accusing the FBI of coercing him into testifying in the first place. And on top of that, he was accusing Jason of paying him off.

That meant Gabe was officially tainted. Any evidence against Sharon that he had provided (the computer records, the financial statements, the incriminating emails) were considered fruit of the poisoned tree. The Attorney General couldn't use any of it.

It didn't matter that the records were true. It didn't matter that the FBI had later obtained a warrant and that Bee's DNA test had come back positive (along with that of over thirty other captive girls). It didn't matter that the FBI had uncovered Sharon's personal emails.

The ones that proved she was the mastermind behind the kidnapping scheme. The ones that tied her to more than one major drug cartel. The ones that discussed not only human trafficking, but drug trafficking as well.

In Jason's pocket, his phone began to ring.

Well... both of his phones actually. There was the smart phone that everyone used to contact him, and then there was that little black disposable flip phone. The one that only one person ever used.

Flipping it open, Jason didn't need to glance at the archaic display to know who it was before grunting, "Hey."

"You seeing what I'm seeing?" Agent Finn's voice was tight on the other end of the line.

"Sure am," Jason hissed. "A heads up would've been nice."

"We had no idea," Finn countered quickly. "Looks like you're not the only asshole who can bribe a federal judge."

"I'm going to pretend like I didn't hear that," Jason growled, then flicked his eyes to the media people holed up in the corner of the room.

At first they'd been just as dumb struck as everyone else, but now they were on the move. Not good.

Snapping the phone shut, Jason shoved the thing into his pocket and strode forward to head one of the crews off. CT was awaiting Jason's signal in the corner. Bee was tottering past him, getting out of the way.

The female interviewer… her name was Rachel… or maybe Rebecca… patted her sleek updo of blonde hair before stepping close to Jason and shoving a microphone in his face. The cameraman behind her shifted around for a good shot. Jason sucked in a long breath as his heart began to pound heavily against his ribcage.

"Stunning new developments in the Cambric Agency Kidnapping Case," Rachel/Rebecca began. "We're here with Jason Riggs for an exclusive first response. Mr. Riggs, what do you have to say?"

"Many years ago, when I first met Gabe, he was under the control of very powerful people, and they weren't the FBI and myself," Jason replied. He couldn't believe how steady his voice was sounding. "Sharon Baine and the Cambric Agency controlled him then, and they control him once again. I am very sorry to hear that he has recanted his testimony, but what Gabe is saying now is simply not true. The FBI never coerced him and I absolutely did not bribe him."

"But what about the five million dollar payout?" Rachel/Rebecca asked. "You've admitted to that in the past."

"Gabe himself demanded that money in order to buy his own freedom," Jason countered. "It's also been documented that he paid it back to me while he remained free. Every cent."

"But…"

"I think it's more important," Jason cut her off. "To focus on what Gabe has said and done while he was free, rather than what he has been forced to do as a captive."

"But isn't he an investor in several of your companies?" Rachel/Rebecca rushed on. "Aren't you still tied to him financially?"

"I am no longer involved in any of those companies," Jason countered. "I separated from them in order to run for Congress."

"That's right." Rachel/Rebecca bobbed her head. "How do you think this will affect the election tonight? Will the citizens of Texas still be willing to elect a leader who seems to always be at the heart of corruption?"

Frowning, Jason pursed his lips and ground his teeth slowly together. She was accusing him of corruption? So that's the way they were spinning it?

All of a sudden it seemed like fifty phones were ringing. Their mix of high-pitched tones and steady vibrations permeated the air. All over the room, his security guards were shifting nervously while the other film crews were shoving roughly by them.

His father and mother were giving their own interviews

now a few feet away, while Val was holding Jace in her arms. He was beginning to cry.

Jason felt a fresh flood of anger hit his blood stream and he had to work to contain it. His son shouldn't have to see this, all these adults rushing around acting crazy. In the far corner, CT tipped his head up and caught Jason's eye.

Yeah. Jason gave him a slight nod in the affirmative. Time to get the cameras out of here. CT shoved off the wall, followed by two other members of his team.

With a quick glance over his shoulder, Jason saw Bee sobbing against the television screen while a camera hovered not two feet away from her face. Didn't these people have any compassion?

Returning his attention to the woman in front of him, Jason went on, "I think the timing of this latest stunt will be obvious to Texas voters, don't you? It makes sense that The Agency would release Gabe's interview on election night. They're afraid of what will happen if I win. If you're looking for scandal and corruption… start with Sharon Baine."

Before Rachel/Rebecca had a chance to respond, she was being hauled away. Her black heels flashed in the overhead lights as she kicked and yelled.

Her cameraman shifted around to record her and chaos erupted. Everyone with a press badge was being escorted out. Quentin Daniels was at the door to the suite, trying to get in. The whole spectacle was being filmed live for the world to see.

Shoving his hand back into his pocket, Jason pulled that same old black flip phone out and pressed the thing to his ear. It had been vibrating the entire time.

"He's going to want to see you," Finn's voice was the only

quiet thing in the room. "To discuss Plan B if you don't get elected."

Moving to stand over his wife and son, Jason squeezed the phone as hard as he possibly could as he growled his response, "*That* is a last resort."

"Well..."

"Fuck, Finn," Jason's voice dropped as he hissed into the phone. "You don't really want it to go that way... do you?"

"No," Finn admitted quietly. "No, I don't."

CHAPTER 29

Gabe

DROPPING HIS HEAD, GABE STARED DOWN AT THE PLATE SITTING before him. It had clean, white edges and was perfectly square. In the center, sat a giant ribeye steak, medium-rare, with a heaping baked potato wedged neatly beside it. Just like before, the potato overflowed with sour cream, chives and little bits of bacon, his favorite.

Off to the left side was a crisp green Caesar salad. On the right, was a frosty glass of beer. It was probably a Stone IPA, because he'd favored those when he'd lived here before.

Swallowing thickly, Gabe fought the fresh flood of bile that rose up in the back of his throat. If he had any choice at all, he would be racing to the bathroom right now so that he could throw up.

But that was the kicker, wasn't it?

He had no choice. None at all.

So instead, he fought his natural impulses, and reached quietly for his silver fork.

Gripping the expensive utensil hard in one hand, Gabe blinked down at the spot next to his plate where a knife should have been placed. Nope. No such luck there. The staff knew not to trust him with anything pointier than a dinner fork, even though he hadn't so much as complained since this whole thing began.

The stakes were too high now. It wasn't just about Gabe's own suffering. The Agency had his kids... *his kids*. It was one thing to let a fellow captive starve, it was another thing entirely to do it to your own children. Even if before that day in Isolation, the five boys standing in the adjoining room had never seen him before.

Well, they knew who he was now, and he wasn't going to let anything happen to them. At least, he would do whatever he could. He would do whatever The Agency wanted, whatever Sharon wanted.

"Aren't you going to eat?" Sharon asked from across the table. "We can get you something else, if you'd rather not have steak."

Unable to keep his jaw from clenching, Gabe glanced up at her quickly before returning his gaze to his steak. The day after Sharon was released from prison she'd sent for him. Shane had come to his cell in Isolation holding a pair of beige slacks and a pale-green button down shirt. Gabe had known instantly what was in store.

But even knowing what was coming, he'd gone along anyway. He'd stepped into those pants and tucked in that shirt like it was just another day. Then he'd boarded the private jet with two hulking Cambric guards sitting just behind him.

When they'd touched down in California, the assholes had

loaded him into a black town car and delivered him personally to Sharon's Santa Barbara estate.

If he bothered to lift his head now, Gabe would see those very same guards leaning casually back against the far wall. They'd traveled with him here that day, and had followed him from room to room ever since, silent, watchful.

Gabe wasn't sure if they were here to prevent him from hurting himself or Sharon. At this point, either option would be welcome.

"The steak looks good," Gabe managed finally, his voice still a bit unsteady. "I'm just not sure how I'm supposed to eat it without a knife."

"Oh! Of course." Sharon clapped her hands together and gave a light chuckle. "We'll have Arnie come cut it for you."

Brushing her auburn hair behind one ear, Sharon flicked a wrist in the air absently. At the far end of the room, a slightly built man in his late-sixties pushed open a door and crossed quickly to Gabe's side of the long marble table.

Even in the dim lighting, Gabe's eyes tracked the flash of a steak knife held carefully in the man's hand. He was a D1 captive, a servant of the household that Gabe knew from when he'd lived here before.

Back then things had been different, though. Back then he'd been allowed to cut his own food, and watch tv, and use the internet. Back then, if he wasn't sleeping in Sharon's bed, he could retreat to his own private bedroom, one with a door that wasn't constantly locked.

Scooting back his chair now, Gabe watched silently as Arnie cut up the steak on his plate. Across the way, Sharon leaned closer and pushed her tits at him. The sight of her flashing that red lipstick smile and batting her false eyelashes made him absolutely ill.

She still wanted him. She still gave him the red pills to make him high and the blue pills to get him hard. She still took him to her bedroom at night, not seeming to care how awkward it was with the two security guards watching them the entire time.

Gabe couldn't figure out if she was actually in love with him, or if she was just a controlling psychopath, or maybe she was just plain delusional. When you're on your knees in front of someone you hate, the reasons why you're there just don't matter much after awhile. It becomes background noise. You stop trying to make sense of everything... or anything.

Anyway, nothing in his life made sense anymore. Just like now, Sharon was saying things. She was speaking words that Gabe should probably be listening to, but he just couldn't fucking focus.

All he could see was that damn knife.

All he could think about was what it would feel like to hold it in his hand.

Could he wrestle it away from Arnie? Without a doubt. But then what? Would he have enough time to jump the table and get to Sharon? Maybe.

But then the guards would be on him. How many swings of that knife would he get? Would it be enough to kill her? Because he couldn't risk just injuring her, he'd have to make sure she was dead.

And even if he did actually kill her, Shane would still have his children back at Cambric. What would that sadistic fucker do to them, if Gabe managed to murder his boss?

Licking his lips, Gabe watched the knife flick back and

forth across the plate not eighteen inches from his chest. At his sides, his hands curled themselves into fists, then loosened. He felt a rush of tingles race through his body. He should do it. He should just grab the thing.

Glancing up, he caught the flash of Sharon's pale-blue eyes. She was watching him. She knew, or maybe she suspected, what he wanted to do.

Sucking in a breath, Gabe's eyes darted back down to his own plate. There was really only one way to make this nightmare end. There was really only one way to save his kids.

If Sharon didn't have Gabe, then there would be no reason to torture his children. If Gabe was dead, then his kids would be safe. The logic clicked like a slow clock ticking down time inside his head.

Gabe's heart was hammering now, so much so that it hurt. He swore every person in the room could probably hear it.

Swiping one sweaty palm down his thigh, Gabe reached out. His hand cruised towards the edge of the table...

But just then, Arnie straightened up his spine and stepped back. The steak was cut. His job was done.

Gabe gaped, like his mouth actually fell open and hung there.

While he continued to look dumbly on, the D1 captive tucked the knife safely back at his side and strode away down the length of the table. Then he was gone. Just like that. In a matter of seconds, the door was open and shut once more.

Sharon was still talking, Gabe realized, as he slowly shut his mouth.

"There you can have a bite now," she was saying. "Tell me how you like it."

"What?" Gabe's eyes drifted back over to her.

He was still trying to come to grips with what had just happened. The near miss. The cost of his own hesitation. His whole body was reeling from it. He felt short of breath.

"The steak, the steak," Sharon repeated, gesturing at him with her fork. "Tell me how you like it."

"Oh." Gabe's gaze fell once more to his plate and the juicy bits of meat staring back at him. He shook his head. "It looks great."

He was a coward. He was a world-class self-preserving coward.

Swiping one hand beneath his nose, Gabe moved to scoot his chair closer to the table. His fork was lying beside his plate at an off angle where he'd dropped it when Arnie had walked in.

Clearing his throat, Gabe's brow furrowed a moment as he concentrated all of his attention on his dinner. Deliberately, he picked up his fork. It was a miracle his hand wasn't shaking. Sucking in a quick breath, he speared a piece of steak and then shoved it sloppily into his mouth.

It was the most disgusting thing he'd ever tasted.

It was like ash on his tongue. It tasted of submission and hatred and defeat and fear.

"It's delicious," Gabe murmured quietly as the meat landed with a thud down low in his belly. "The best I've ever had."

CHAPTER 30

Charlie

HE WAS WEARING TIGHT BLUE JEANS AND CLEAN BROWN COWBOY boots. He couldn't remember the last time he'd worn anything like it. Well, scratch that… he didn't *want* to remember the last time he'd worn anything like it.

Staring at the floor of the elevator, Charlie listened to the whirl and hum as he rode up to the twenty-fifth floor of some high rise hotel. He'd never owned a pair of boots this new before. The ones he'd had in his free life were always well-used and caked in cow shit. It was all he could afford back then.

Slowly, Charlie's mouth twisted into a slight smile at the memory. He still preferred the ones he'd bought with his own money over these fancy new things. To him, the dirty hand-me-downs were priceless.

But this brand new outfit is what the client had requested he wear, so this is what The Agency had put him in. Standing beside him now, a Cambric guard was whistling quietly. It was a tune Charlie didn't recognize, but regardless, the habit was annoying.

Blowing out a frustrated breath, Charlie glanced up at his own reflection in the shiny metal doors. He was going to visit a brand new client today. He hadn't had a new client in forever… not since before Val.

And after she'd gone "missing" had come the food strike, and after that, came Gabe. Charlie's old friend had materialized in the cell beside him, and just like old times, he was back to running the show. Gabe made demands, made plans, talked revenge.

So Charlie had complied, because that was what Charlie always did. He stopped starving himself. He started working out again.

And by the time Charlie had fully recovered, the first thing Cambric did was send him back to his former monthly clients. He'd hoped to get information out of the deal, but no. They'd missed him, were worried about him, indulged him as best they could.

Even so, they were nervous. The Agency had instituted new rules, and the handful of women who he saw regularly were too afraid not to abide by them. So there was no more internet access, no phone access and no live television. Charlie now lived a life in the dark, so to speak, and he'd grown used to it, after a time. Even if his busy brain was turning to mush.

Before Val had escaped, one of his clients used to let him take online classes while he was staying with her. Another one used to bring him books to read. Now though, Charlie had been reduced to a sort of masseuse companion that also provided happy endings. He cuddled, he cooked dinner, he rubbed… wherever.

The whole arrangement wouldn't be such a hard pill to swallow if he actually swallowed the pills The Agency gave him. But drug use damaged your body. It destroyed your muscles and internal organs. It made it harder to run. Harder to breathe. Harder to sleep. It also damaged your brain, and so Charlie always opted out.

Of course that was when Gabe's plan for revenge seemed plausible. Now though, the guy was gone. Another one bites the dust and all that.

Still… it's not like Charlie couldn't pull it off himself. He knew what Gabe had wanted to do and really all he needed was another captive to help a little. One who was big and strong. Maybe Ben would be willing to do it?

Giving his head a slight shake, Charlie ran a hand back through his short crop of blonde hair. They'd buzzed his head while he was starving himself, but it had grown back in, no problem.

In front of him now, the elevator doors dinged open. The Cambric guard went first and Charlie followed behind.

The hotel was nice, with its wide well-lit hallway and ornately carved doors. Whoever this new client was, she had money. Or maybe her husband had money and she had secrets and time. It didn't really matter to him.

Rolling his shoulders, Charlie worked to ease out a bit of tension that had crept up on him. He was nervous. Why the hell was he nervous?

"This one," the guard mumbled as he glanced down at his phone. "Room 25-233."

Ducking his head, Charlie came to a stop beside the guard

and swallowed. *Breathe in. This is just another day. Breathe out. Don't let your mind rule you.*

There, he thought, cool as a cucumber.

Right as rain.

Lifting his gaze, he read the silver numbers that adorned the fancy door. Whoever this lady was, he figured he could always press her back against a window and stare out while he did his thing. They were in New York somewhere so maybe the windows had a nice view.

He liked windows. He liked looking out.

But then the guard was knocking at the door and the thing was swinging inward. At the sight on the other side, all manner of thought fled him.

His wife.

His fucking wife was standing on the other side, that sassy red hair tumbling around her face, those intelligent brown eyes flashing recognition at him.

Charlie's mouth dropped and he stumbled back a step as if someone had hit him. Shit. It felt like someone had hit him. It felt like a heavyweight boxer had punched him square in the chest.

Stifling a short grunt, he clutched at his chest with one hand. All the air whooshed out of his lungs. Thankfully, the guard didn't seem to notice. The guy had been standing just in front of Charlie when the door had opened and he was already walking inside.

Apparently he was as enamored by Alana Gandel as Charlie was shocked. Typically the women paying for a D2 companion didn't exactly look like her, and the guard was chuckling and talking all low.

No... wait. Actually, the guard was flirting with her.

Flirting.

The realization had Charlie's whole body tensing. This asshole was grinning and holding out his tablet for Alana to sign. And she was just smiling right back at him, telling him her name was Frankie, or some crap while the guy reached out to touch her arm.

Snapping his jaw shut, Charlie stalked into the room and leaned back against a nearby wall. Purposefully, he unclenched his fists, and instead folded his arms carefully across his chest. His heart was hammering so hard right now, he was seeing stars.

"Now if you have any issues whatsoever," the guard was saying. "I'll be waiting just outside the door. You can call out for me, and I'll come in. Alright?"

"Why, thank you," Alana drawled as she handed the man an extra keycard to the room. "But I'm sure there won't be a problem. Charlie here came highly recommended."

The sound of his real name on those lips of hers gutted him. Charlie. She called him *Charlie.* What the hell was she doing here? How had she found him?

"Of course," the guard bobbed his head as he slipped the keycard into his back pocket.

It was standard procedure with first time clients, but even so, the fact that the overly friendly guard now had a key to Alana's room had heat working up Charlie's neck. This wasn't safe for her. She was too close to The Agency. Too fucking close.

She'd harbored a captive, committed multiple felonies without even knowing it. He couldn't decide if he was straight up pissed, or scared out of his damn mind. Even so, he couldn't rip his eyes off of her. She was nodding her pretty head and walking the guard to the door.

After it clicked closed, she twisted the deadbolt lock and latched the chain. All the while, her back remained to him. His eyes roamed the curve of her slender shoulders, down the length of the flowery dress she had on and landed on the sweep of her creamy thighs. She was petite and fiery and so unbelievably beautiful.

Then she was turning to face him. She tucked both hands behind her back and leaned against the closed door. Tears rimmed her eyes and she exhaled a shaky breath. For several seconds, Charlie just stared at her face. It was like he was trying to absorb her, like if he looked long enough, he could commit every freckle that dusted the bridge of her pixie nose to memory.

"Paul…" she gasped the name, then cleared her throat. "Or, Charlie. Do you prefer Charlie?"

His eyes widened just a touch as her words sank in. Cambric had never known his stolen identity. What would happen if they found out? Could the guard hear her? He was standing just on the other side of the door.

Shoving off the wall, Charlie crossed to her in three giant strides. Fear and anger collided inside of him as he grabbed her by the arm and yanked her off the door. He heard her little cry of surprise, but the rushing in his head drowned most everything else out.

She had to leave. She had to get the hell out of here. She had to get the hell out of New York.

"What in the…?" Alana hissed at him and wriggled in his grasp.

Charlie just kept dragging her along behind him. Glancing frantically around the hotel suite, he felt a flood of panic unleash itself inside him. Where could he hide her? Where could he keep her safe?

When his eyes lit on the bathroom door, he all but jogged to it and shoved her inside. Letting go of her arm, Charlie's breath heaved in and out of him at he braced himself in the doorway. Alana's furious eyes bored into him and that smart mouth of hers began to run.

"Just where do you get off thinkin' you can toss me around like a sack of damn corn, Paul Gandel?" She demanded. Her fists rested on her hips and she cocked her head to one side.

"You shouldn't be here, Alana," Charlie accused, trying to keep his voice low. "You need to get out of here right now."

"Bullshit," Alana spat. "I ain't goin' nowhere."

"Oh yes you are," Charlie dropped his arms to his sides and took a step closer.

Alana did not take a step back.

Tipping her chin up, she looked straight down her nose at him... or well, straight up her nose at him, seeing as he had about eight inches on her. Damn she was pretty. Even more so when she was fighting mad like this.

Stretching out his right hand, Charlie swore he could still feel the softness of her skin beneath his palm. Squeezing his hand shut again, he reminded himself why he couldn't risk touching her. Him touching her was what got her into this mess in the first place. She'd been too good for him back when she'd stopped her car on the side of that two-lane high-way, and she was definitely too good for him now.

"Come on, baby," Alana mocked. "Make me go."

Running a rough hand over his face, Charlie groaned. Fuck this tiny woman got to him. He wanted to make her do something, alright. Standing so close to her had his entire body humming, and she had to know it. She had to.

Inhaling sharply, he could smell the lilacs of her shampoo and the lavender of her body wash. He swore every bottle in their shower at home had been purple. It had so many memories assaulting him. Suddenly, he just wanted to cry.

Biting hard at his lip, Charlie bore down and removed the hand from his face. She was still standing there, daring him to put his hands on her again. She was all bravado and smartness. She made him so weak.

"It's not safe here," he pleaded.

Try as he might Charlie couldn't keep the tremor from his voice. That's all it took to have his wife softening. Crossing to him, she wrapped those impossibly delicate, impossibly strong arms of hers around his body. He held his breath, fought the urge to grab her back, fought the urge to gather her to him and never, ever let go.

"God I've missed you," Alana spoke quietly into his chest.

That's when he broke.

Sweeping her up, Charlie kicked the bathroom door closed and turned to press her back up against it. He felt her wrap her legs around his waist and then he was kissing her. His mouth found her lips and he was licking and nipping and groaning as she kissed him right back.

"I love you so damn much," Charlie confessed. Breaking their kiss he ran one hand through her hair and stared into her eyes. "How the hell did you find me? You seriously can't be here, Alana. You could go to prison."

"You think I'm worried about Biff the security guard outside?" Alana huffed indignantly as a cocky smile flitted over her lips. "I've got backup. No one's puttin' me in jail, so you can just relax."

"Backup?" Charlie's brow furrowed but he didn't release her. He wasn't sure he'd ever be able to let go of her again. "What the hell is going on?"

"It's a long story," Alana amended.

"I've got some time," Charlie countered, then shifted his hips against her.

Not a whole lot of time, he thought, but there was no way he was moving from this spot until he knew she was safe. Pursing her lips, Alana exhaled through her nostrils a moment.

Charlie raised an eyebrow. Brushing his fingertips over her cheek, he held his breath. So fucking beautiful. How was he allowed to touch this?

"Let's just say an old friend of yours sent me," Alana admitted finally. "And a few more of her friends might be staying in the room next door. They make Biff outside look like a Kindergartner with a water gun."

"Alana," Charlie warned as he tapped a single finger on her chin. "Tell me straight, or I've got to kick you out now. In fact, *I* should've left already and told the guard the visit was off."

"Fine." Alana pouted a moment before dropping her voice. "Val sent me."

"What?" Charlie's arms came loose and he barely caught his wife on her way down to the ground.

Staggering back a step, Charlie watched Alana smooth at her dress and sigh.

"Val showed up at the farm," she explained. "She told me where you were and asked for my help. How could I say no? If I got to see you again, it'd all be worth it."

"Val." Charlie felt the color draining from his face. "Wait… what kind of help does she need?"

Twisting her hands in front of her body, Alana proceeded to look at everything in the bathroom but him. She only stopped when he reached out to brace both of her arms.

"Tell me, Alana," he said quietly. "What's going on?"

"There's this group… goes by the name, Constitutional Militia," Alana whispered. "You heard of 'em?"

"No." Charlie shook his head.

"Well, they been smugglin' captives out of agencies and such. They got Val out."

Charlie's heart picked up the pace. He couldn't let himself think it. He couldn't let himself hope.

"And?" He prompted.

"And they got kicked out of Cambric, they can't get a team back in," she rushed, her eyes darting over his face. "At least not yet."

"Alright."

"But if they had someone on the inside," Alana explained. "Someone who could pass them information…"

"Someone like me," Charlie finished for her.

Disappointment flooded him. They weren't here to get him out. They were here to keep him in. Fuuuuuck.

"They promised me…" Alana stepped closer and gripped his hands tight in her own. "That as soon as they can, they'll get you out. Okay? They *promised* me."

Closing his eyes, Charlie held back the wetness that gathered in his eyelashes. They weren't tears if he didn't let them fall, right?

After taking one steadying breath, he reached blindly for his wife only to find her already stepping into him. Wrapping his arms tightly around her waist, he gathered her soft body up close against his.

Damn it.

Damn this life.

Laying his chin on the top of her head, he bit down on the inside of his cheek and held his breath.

A few seconds passed with them like that. Quiet. Still.

Alana ran her hands along his back, soothing him. She was so strong that way. So much stronger than he was, with so much more hope. Truth was, Charlie was fresh out of hope these days.

"Okay, Alana," he murmured finally. "What do your new friends need to know?"

CHAPTER 31

Bee

From the backseat of the SUV, Bee could barely make out the gates of Summer House. It was another cold January day, but with the sun blinking out from behind a cover of shifting clouds, it shouldn't be this hard to see the entrance to her home.

Even still... between the crowd of protestors and the throng of supporters, the tall black wrought-iron fencing faded into the background.

"They're all vultures," her driver grumbled under his breath as his hands tightened on the steering wheel.

As the car slowed to a crawl, Bee felt each bump and rumble of cobblestones beneath the tires. Carefully, they rolled past the media vans, the camera crews, and members of the public. Everyone was just milling around in their heavy winter jackets, waiting.

And it was like this every single day now.

It was like the entire country was on the verge of some-thing. Everyone was simply waiting for it to happen.

Letting loose an impatient huff, Bee tapped her perfectly manicured nails against the inside of the tinted window. She really didn't have time for this crap today, but ever since the election in November, their affluent Texas neighborhood had been inundated.

And yes, Jason had doubled his private security force, but even as a newly elected Senator, there wasn't much he could do about the lingering crowd.

That's right. He won the election, although by a much narrower margin than had been anticipated.

The timing of the scandal that released Sharon Baine from prison had had its effect. The voters remained uncertain. Could they trust Jason Riggs? Or should they believe Gabe's latest testimony?

It had Bee feeling nervous. The point of Jason getting elected was to get more power, right? More control, more influence, that had been the goal. But here it seemed to have had the oppo-site effect. He couldn't even keep his own front lawn clear.

Coming to a stop at a small guard shack, the driver rolled down his window and held up his credentials. One of the guards dressed in a pressed uniform stepped over to them. Dipping his head down, he eyed Bee sitting in the backseat.

Pursing her lips, she smoothed at her cream-colored wool coat and forced a half smile. It was actually really hard trying not to look like a bitch on a mission these days, especially since that's exactly what she was.

With a tight nod, the guard stepped back and motioned with his hand. Past the hood of the black SUV, Bee watched the gates slowly part. Quickly, she glanced back over her shoulder at the throng of reporters. Not one of their cameras was pointing her way.

Hmmm. Only a few short weeks ago, they'd of been pounding on the windows and screaming their ridiculous questions. After her emotional display on election night, they'd been relentless.

Would you go back to Cambric if you could be with Gabe?

Do you regret being a free person?

Is it true Cambric owns your love-child?

Will you ever forgive Gabe for moving on?

The media chose to paint Bee as the jilted woman in a love-gone-wrong story. And the nation just ate it up. Head-lines about her heartbreak and Gabe's betrayal had dominated the mainstream media for well over a month now. It was awful.

"Here we are, Mademoiselle," the driver announced.

Shifting the SUV into park, he popped open his door and proceeded to walk around to her side. Bee's eyes traveled over the clinging ivy that wove its way up the stone face of the estate. Beneath the arched front door, Yvette was already waiting.

Ducking her head, Bee tucked a lock of her hair uselessly behind one ear as the driver opened her door. Instantly, the winter air swirled around her body. Gathering her long coat more closely around her, Bee stepped first one tall leather boot onto the ground, and then the other.

Back to Summer House.

Back home with news.

Cresting the steps quickly, Bee passed through the open

front door and was soon standing in the marble foyer, shrugging off her coat. Warmth flooded the house.

"Is he home?" Bee asked as she handed her coat to Yvette.

The older woman gave her a simple nod and gestured off to the right. "He's in his office."

"Thank you." Bee ducked her head before adding, "and my sister?"

"She's at the barn," Yvette supplied. "I'll let her know you're here."

"Thank you, Yvette." Bee grabbed for the woman's forearm and gave her a quick squeeze. "You make this place feel like a home."

With a small smile, Yvette nodded quietly and moved away. In the Maldives, Gabe had refused to keep a staff, and at the time that had been fine with Bee. She'd liked their privacy, she'd enjoyed their mornings alone. It had just been the two of them so they hadn't needed much, but Bee couldn't help but wonder.

What if things had turned out differently? What if they'd had a house filled with children, maybe a little help would've been just right. Yvette felt like family, after all.

Blinking back the same old bitter tears that wanted to fall, Bee strode through the house with a singular purpose. Gabe had fixed it so they would never be able to have a child together. He'd done it without asking, he'd done it without telling her, even. Maybe his reasons had been good, and maybe he was just plain selfish. But either way, what was done was done.

Towards the rear of the house, just down a hall from the massive kitchen, Bee stopped at the closed door to Jason's home office. Lifting her hand, she rapped quickly on the wooden surface and waited. On the other side, she could hear a glass clink and a drawer slide open.

"Just a minute," Jason called and had Bee rolling her eyes.

No doubt he was expecting her, Yvette had likely texted him the second she pulled in, not to mention the security check at the gate. With a twist of the knob, Bee pushed inside.

"What the hell, Bee?" Jason accused as he fumbled with a crystal decanter filled with whiskey. "I said just a minute. In polite society that means you wait outside."

"You don't have to hide that from me." Bee folded her arms across her chest and tipped back against a nearby wall. "I can see alcohol and not dissolve into a needy puddle."

"We said this would be a dry house." Jason glanced up at her as he shoved the bottle into a drawer in his desk and slammed it closed. "And we meant it."

"Fine," she grumbled and glanced around. "You all good Senator? Just taking the edge off?"

With a groan Jason flopped down into his oversized leather office chair and ran a hand back through his brown hair. He'd just returned from DC the day before and already the job was wearing on him. At least that was what Val had said.

Speaking of which, Bee's sister glided into the office just then on bare feet. The second she appeared in the doorway with those dusty blue jeans and form-fitting white top, Jason's eyes lit. He tracked his wife's movements as she made her way over to Bee for a quick side hug and then down to one of the chairs sitting opposite his desk.

Sticking her tongue in her cheek, Bee was almost jealous. *Almost.* Mostly… she just missed Gabe.

After a beat, Bee swung the office door shut and followed Val's lead, taking the seat just beside her sister.

"I'd like to start off by reminding you how much I hate you leaving with no security," Jason began, tugging on his already loose blue striped tie.

"You said yourself, the less people directly involved the better," Bee reasoned. "Plus the driver is your guy from France, right? He can handle himself. He's fine."

"Yeah, I trust him, but…" Jason's brow furrowed, and he glanced at his phone sitting neatly on his wide desk. "These people are dangerous, Bee."

"It's only Ava," Bee reminded him. "She's my contact, not some six-foot-six Militia recruit."

Picking up his phone, Jason's thumbs flew across the screen as he answered some text or email. Bee huffed a breath and shot Val a scowl. Her sister blinked innocently before flashing her a knowing grin.

"Jason." Bee snapped her fingers at him. "Did you hear me?"

"Huh?" Jason lifted his head and blinked at her.

"I said you're the only one with six-foot-six goons stalking around intimidating everyone. If I was the Militia, I'd be more worried about Ava coming here, than me going there."

"Well, she can't come here," Jason spat. "None of them can."

"I know that," Bee sighed. "I was only using it as an example."

Raising one eyebrow Jason stared hard at Bee a moment until Val cleared her throat. Behind them, there was one quick knock at the door before it opened.

Turning in her seat, Bee couldn't help but huff in exasperation at the sight of CT stepping into the room. Jason's massive head of security kept a passive look on his face as he shut the door softly behind him and leaned up against a wall.

Six-foot-six yes, but the man was anything but a goon. He was smart. Wicked smart. And thereby in on everything.

"So, what did Ava have to say?" Val asked finally, drawing everyone's attention to her.

"Well, Alana's meeting with Charlie worked, and he's getting us information," Bee confirmed. "Cambric used Gabe's children as leverage to get him to recant his testimony. That's why he made the confession in the first place, and that's why he keeps giving out interviews and making public appearances."

"Good God." Jason covered his face with one hand and blew out a slow breath. "Do they have any movement on that? Any way to get his kids out?"

"That's the thing." Bee licked at her bottom lip and leaned forward. "They can't get to the five boys Shane is holding, but all the other kids seem to be off The Agency's radar. Ava was thinking we could run an adoption scam to start buying the rest of them, but it will take a lot of money."

"Like how much money?" Jason asked, his brow furrowing deeper. "How's it work?"

"The underground is running the same scam on a few of the other agencies right now," Bee explained. "They get couples to pose as parents looking to adopt. If they're lucky, they can get two or sometimes even three siblings out at a time. But they have to pay the couples, buy the kids, keep an in-house attorney, get fake identities, find real families for the kids to land in eventually…"

"Okay, I get it," Jason cut in. "It's costly. And I hate to break this to everyone, but I'm fresh out of disposable income. My businesses are tied up, and everyone is watching every penny I spend."

Bee's heart sank. She'd known it would be a long shot for Jason to afford all this.

"Hey." Val reached out and brushed at Bee's hand. "What about... um... your dad. I mean, what about *our* dad? Would he be willing to help?"

Looking her sister square in the eye Bee bit at her now trembling lip. "I'll talk to him. Or maybe we could both talk to him together."

"Yes." Val nodded. "Let's both talk to him."

"Okay." Bee swallowed hard before continuing. "If we can get Daddy to fund us, then it will still take a few months. If we're really careful, I think that we could probably buy most of Gabe's kids out of Cambric. The thing is, we would need to buy other kids too, so as not to draw too much attention and Charlie will feed us their names. Of course, he wants us to get as many of his own kids out that we can as well."

Chancing a quick glance at Val, Bee saw her sister pale slightly. Even the mention of Charlie still had her clamming up. Guilt was a hard thing to shake.

"That still leaves five of Gabe's boys there," Jason pointed out. "And they're all Sharon needs to keep him right where she wants him. What about my idea? What does Ava think about a Militia raid?"

"She says her brother won't risk breaking into Cambric, and the underground isn't trained for that," Bee rushed.

"Clay Montgomery is *such* an asshole," Jason spat and rocked back in his chair.

When he threw a questioning look at CT, the big guy simply shook his head.

"It would be extremely high risk," CT spoke quietly. "Cambric is a brick and iron fortress. It's easily defended and the guard staff is well armed. We could probably pull it off, but not without casualties."

"Shit," Jason swore. "If we were linked to the break-in, then it would sink the legislation. We're going to have to wait."

"But all this time, Gabe's suffering," Bee protested. Leaning forward she squeezed the arms of her chair in both hands. "And his sons are, too. Can't we do anything?"

"We can pass the legislation," Jason countered. "I'll see if I can get something just for captive children put together by itself. Maybe then, even if the full bill doesn't pass, we can get all the kids out. It'd be a start."

"But how long will that take?" Bee glanced at the tight faces all around the room. "Do you think you have the votes?"

"I'm not sure yet," Jason explained, spreading one hand out on his desk. "We were all just sworn in, so now we're sort of feeling each other out. I think I'm close though. I know I've got Senator Higgins in with me, so he can help introduce me around."

"Wait." Val frowned. "Peter Higgins?"

"Yeah, you've met him." Jason nodded. "You carried his card around all those years ago. His wife is Tawny Higgins. She's a House Representative now and he's a Senator."

"No." Val pursed her lips and gave her head a quick shake. "No, that's not right. He's not anti-captivity. He switched sides."

Jason blew out a breath and cocked his head.

"He and his wife are very anti-captivity. His wife voted to pass the legislation when it was in the House last year. They want to abolish the industry as badly as we do."

"They aren't married anymore," Val reasoned. "She left him."

"What? Tawny has *not* left him. I just spent the past two weeks with these people." Jason's brow furrowed and he leaned forward over his desk. "Val? Where is all of this coming from? What aren't you telling me?"

"I... I uh..." Val's eyes flicked in desperation towards Bee whose stomach dropped.

That look on Val's face, she knew it all too well. Secrets.

"Val," Jason's voice dropped low. "Baby. Tell me what makes you think Peter Higgins is pro-captivity."

"Because he told me so," Val spit out.

"You talked to Peter Higgins?" Jason asked. "When?"

"When I..." Val glanced again to Bee who reached out to steady her sister's shoulder. "When he..."

"Just say it," Bee whispered. "Whatever it is, just tell us."

"He was a client," Val admitted. "The last time I was at Cambric."

"He was..." Jason sucked in a breath as the information sunk into his brain. "You weren't allowed to have any clients. We got the injunction before..."

"He was the first one," Val cut in. "He ordered me in the red dress, and I was brought to this hotel and..."

Val's voice drifted into nothingness. Her sentence hung in the air, unfinished.

In silence, Bee watched all of the color drain from Jason's face. It was like he was picturing it. Peter Higgins. His wife. The red dress from the videos. The hotel.

Shooting to his feet, Jason stumbled back from his desk. His office chair slammed against the low wall behind him, making the single wide window in the room rattle. Val jumped in her chair at the sound, and even Bee flinched.

CT, however, remained unmoved.

"He's a dead man," Jason spat as he looked to CT. "He's a fucking dead man."

"But we didn't…" Val began to protest.

"You keep them here." Jason ignored her, still speaking directly to CT. "Neither one of them leaves this house until I return. Got it?"

"Yes, boss." CT nodded as Jason blew past him and ripped open the office door.

"But, Jason!" Val called, as she shoved up from her chair. "Please, he didn't…"

Stepping into her path, CT's wide body filled the door frame. Bee rose from her seat too, but the two women were no match for that much man. CT simply held up one arm while he pulled the door closed with the other.

"Sorry ladies," CT murmured. "Orders are orders."

"This is bullshit," Bee growled and beside her Val began to cry.

"You can't let him go, CT," Val pleaded. "You have to stop him!"

"You want me to stop a man from going to kill his wife's rapist?" CT cocked a rare eyebrow. "I don't think so."

"Peter Higgins did not rape me." Val sucked in a ragged breath and threaded trembling fingers through her hair. "We never had sex, okay? We were interrupted. He left the hotel and I passed out."

"He left the hotel," CT repeated. "Was that before or after you passed out?"

"Before," Val answered quickly. "I swear it was right before."

"Fine," CT bit out the word, then held up one finger. "But the two of you are to stay in this office until I return. Swear to me."

"We swear it." Val held up both hands in surrender and looked to Bee.

"We swear." Bee nodded. "We'll stay right here."

CHAPTER 32

Gabe

THE SOUND OF GLASSES CLINKING AND PEOPLE MURMURING filled the garden. In the far corner, Sharon threw back her head and laughed. Tugging on the front of his light jacket, Gabe kept an easy smile fixed to his miserable face.

Beside him, a young blonde woman in a jade-green cocktail dress sipped at her champagne.

"This is amazing." The woman exhaled a breath and gestured around. "I can see why you wanted to come back."

"Yes," Gabe lied through his pearly white teeth and nodded his head.

The woman was a reporter. Some up and coming hot shot from one of the big three news stations. She'd covered the recent election and was now doing a focus piece on the captive industry. Of course, the piece was entirely biased and funded by Sharon herself, but once it was released on the evening news, no one would know the difference.

"Was it just the lifestyle you missed or was it Sharon herself?" The woman asked.

Her name was Heidi Lincoln and even though the cameras weren't currently shoved in Gabe's face, he knew she was likely still recording him. Everything was on the record with this woman. Well… almost everything.

"Surely Veronica Durand would've been able to give you something like this as well," she continued.

Ducking his head, Gabe had to fight hard to hide the sucker punch to his gut. Veronica Durand. Bee Bee. They were always bringing her up now, and for some reason it wasn't getting any easier to hear her damn name.

"I was under the control of some very powerful people," Gabe repeated the line he had delivered a million times already. "I had to get away from them somehow and fix the wrongs I did to Sharon. I couldn't let an innocent woman rot in prison."

With a half smile, Heidi reached out and ran her palm down Gabe's forearm. She was painting him as a hero in her story, that much was obvious. Gabe just wasn't sure if she actually believed it or not. But as long as she kept making those faces at him and twisting the ends of her hair, he figured he had her.

Sharon would be sending Gabe to the reporter's bed in a matter of days no doubt. His *mistress* wouldn't want to waste this opportunity for some extra leverage. Nothing like a little blackmail to make sure the story went in the direction she wanted.

Lifting his head now, Gabe made eye contact with the very woman he hated most in the entire world. About thirty people milled about between them, but Sharon was still watching him out of the corner of her eye. When he focused on her, she met his gaze and gave him a quick wink.

Not yet darling. He could hear her silky words echo inside his own head, almost as if she were whispering them in his ear. *She's not desperate enough.*

With a subtle nod, Gabe glanced down at Heidi and extracted his arm from under her hand.

"Please excuse me," he said quietly, and moved away through the crowd.

Nothing makes a woman want you more than walking away from her when she's not ready. The art of D2 work was too fucking easy.

Pushing through one of the patio doors, Gabe stepped back inside the Santa Barbara mansion. The door swung closed with a snick at his back, and instantly the sounds of the party dimmed. In the background now, he could just hear the constant crashing of ocean waves. They were right on the beach here, with the garden overlooking the water.

"Fellas," Gabe acknowledged his twin shadows as they entered the space. "You both gonna watch me take a piss?"

"We watch everything else," one of the guards said with a grunt. "Just get on with it."

Making his way across the dark hardwood flooring, Gabe left the living room and entered a long hall. Paintings adorned the walls, but he didn't bother looking at any of them. He could give a shit what was around him. If it couldn't be used as a weapon, then it was meaningless.

Once at the bathroom door, he hesitated, his hand resting a moment on the brass knob. Would he ever have a moment alone again? He fell asleep with one of them sitting in his room. When he woke up, the other one was there, watching.

Occasionally, they showed him pictures of his boys. If Gabe was behaving himself, then his kids seemed fine. They'd even smiled in some of the photos. But if he wasn't behaving... well, the last time he'd talked back to Sharon, his oldest boy had gotten a black eye.

Fuck. It made him so heated just thinking about it.

"Seriously guys." Gabe turned and eyed the both of them. "This is getting ridiculous. What the hell do you think I'm going to do in there?"

"Escape," one offered.

"Drown yourself in the tub," the other supplied.

"Shit," Gabe hissed. "Can't I hold onto my dick in peace for once?"

Glancing between them, the guards shared a long look. Finally, one of them shrugged his massive shoulders.

"Leave the door open," the other one said.

Gabe sighed.

Twisting the knob, he pushed into the bathroom and shoved the door hard against the wall. In here, he didn't have to suppress the angry scowl that now pushed itself onto his face. He loved the sound of violence, the slamming of doors, the rattling walls. He hoped one of *her* priceless pieces of art dropped to the floor and shattered into a million pieces.

Stalking to the white porcelain toilet, Gabe flipped up the lid with a loud pop and unzipped his pants. While he stood there, peeing for the entire hallway to hear, he looked around.

Same vanity with nothing but useless soap inside.

Same fancy sink and designer cupboard (the thing only held toilet paper and extra hand towels. He knew, he'd checked before.)

Same white-tile shower that no one ever used.

Damn it all to hell. There was nothing in here that could be used as a weapon.

Well... he could maybe smash the mirror into pieces with his fist, but there wasn't enough time for that. The guards would be in here holding him back in less than five seconds. There was never enough time.

Zipping up, Gabe reached for the handle of the toilet, but then hesitated. Why should he flush? Fuck it, let someone else flush the damn thing. He hoped one of the guards had to look at his piss before they pulled the handle.

Retracting his hand, Gabe's eyes slid along the tank of the toilet. Wasn't there something long and metal just inside there? The mechanism that makes the whole thing work, it should have a metal arm attached to the handle. He'd replaced one in the Maldives once.

Suddenly Gabe's hand was reaching forward. His heart picked up the pace, kicking angrily inside his chest while fresh air refused to pass through his lungs. He could do it. He could rip the lid off the tank and yank the metal piece out...

And then what?

He could stab the guards. But there were two of them, not to mention a couple dozen more people just outside. He'd need to kill Sharon dead if this was going to be worth it.

Or... well, he could just do what needed to be done to protect his kids. He could use the metal thing on himself.

Shit.

That would take some serious doing. It wasn't like a knife or anything.

"Hey!" One of the guards called from the hall. "Flush that thing already or I'm coming in."

Squeezing his eyes shut, Gabe felt his heart sink so deep in his chest he could hardly feel it anymore. He'd hesitated. Again.

Coward.

Weakling.

Shifting his fingers to the handle of the toilet, Gabe bit hard at his lip as he did as he was told. He flushed.

CHAPTER 33

Jason

HE FELT THE RAGE IN EVERY INCH OF HIS BODY. HIS SKIN WAS hot and tight. He was itchy in fact, so fucking itchy. He wanted to hit something, smash something, kill something. Well. More like *someone*.

Looking out the fifth story window, Jason kept his hands shoved deep into the pockets of his expensive black slacks. Down in the street, a bunch of cars drove by unawares. A few more were stopped at a red light, while an old lady with a walker shuffled slowly along the crosswalk. Her long winter coat tangled around her legs in the crisp breeze.

Just behind him, Agent Finn shifted uncomfortably.

"So did he, or didn't he?" Finn asked cautiously. He was such a stickler for details.

Refusing to face him, Jason felt his own jaw twitch. It was like he was a high schooler all of a sudden, picking apart a buddy's tall tale. *But did you go all the way, man? Or just... part of the way...*

"The man ordered my wife on a silver fucking platter, Finn," Jason intoned. They'd been through this. "Just because he didn't get to complete his transaction, doesn't make it any less heinous."

"I'm not saying that," Finn protested. Jason could hear him tapping his stupid blue ball point pen on the desk. "I just need to know whether I should be talking you out of this, or into it. You're both sitting Senators for God's sake."

"Alright." Turning to face him, Jason leaned his back against the closed window and folded his arms over his chest. "The guy kissed Val, repeatedly. He put his hands all over her, under her damn clothes, but that was as far as he got."

The words tasted like bile on his tongue. When CT had caught Jason in the driveway the day before, he'd been ready to burn Peter Higgins to the ground. But after staying up all night with Val, finally getting her full story, he'd crumpled like a damn leaf.

He was so fucking drained after all that, but he was grateful, too. She'd finally been honest with him. His wife had finally told him everything that had happened to her, and everything that hadn't.

"Okay," Finn was measured. "So you're *not* going to have him murdered."

"As good as that sounds, no, I'm not." Jason dropped his arms to his sides and buried them in his pockets once more.

"So, you want me to tell Clay…"

"That I plan on blackmailing Peter Higgins into voting for our legislation," Jason supplied. "If he doesn't vote our way, then I'll tell his wife everything she needs to know about his little visit with Val. It will either be his marriage *and* political career down the drain, or…"

"Just his financial backers pulling the plug after years of funding," Finn supplied. "How do you know they won't threaten to tell the wife as well? I'm sure they're keeping tabs on him."

"If he votes our way and they come after him, then I'll promise to have Val deny that it ever happened," Jason spat.

He hated having his wife do that, but she'd agreed to, in order to get their legislation passed. "But I still need to know who else the Militia has in their pocket. I've got to count the actual Senate votes, and I need names from Clay."

"I'm not sure Clay can give you those names." Finn frowned.

"I've got to have them," Jason demanded as he shoved off the wall and took a few steps forward. "The actual vote is in another few months and I have to know who I need to be targeting right now, and who I can leave the hell alone. I'm not going to approach them if I don't have to, so Clay has nothing to worry about."

"You have no idea what you're getting yourself into here." Finn leaned back in his chair and stared up at Jason's face. "This is the big leagues. You don't even know half of the real players."

"Oh, and you do?" Jason accused.

Finn's face clouded over and he glanced away.

Taking a step closer to his former friend, Jason's brow furrowed. What the hell kind of secrets did good ole' Finn have in that head of his?

"Come on Agent," Jason's voice was low. "It's do or die time. How badly do you want to free these people? Women. Children. From a *lifetime* of slavery, Finn."

"There's another organization," Finn admitted finally and

sucked in a quick breath. "Clay knows about it, but he does *not* control it. I can send some feelers out and get back to you, but you've got to trust what I can give you and not push it past that, okay?"

Jason rolled his eyes.

"Do not ask around about these people, Jason. I am serious. They'll kill you and Val and not blink an eye to protect themselves."

"You seem to know an awful lot about this other organization, *Agent*." Jason cocked his head to one side. "Anything else I should know about you?"

"You know everything about me that matters, *Senator*." Agent Finn pushed up to standing and extended his hand for a shake. "And this time... I'll be the one to contact you."

Blinking down at the hand hanging between them, Jason's jaw clenched involuntarily. The asshole did this every single time. It was like he kept pushing for some sort of absolution. After everything that had gone down between them, Finn was still seeking his forgiveness.

Sucking in a breath, Jason reached out and slammed his palm roughly against Finn's. They squeezed hard once and shook before letting go.

"Whatever you say." Jason stepped back and buttoned his coat. "Until next time."

"Yeah. Until next time," Finn echoed.

CHAPTER 34

Bee

"OH GOD, I'M SO NERVOUS." BEE EXHALED THE WORDS AS SHE rubbed her hands together.

"Don't be." Stepping up beside her, Bernard Durand threw an arm around his daughter's shoulders and drew her in tight against his side. "Everything is going to be just fine. I promise."

Together, they looked out the wide front windows of his Texas estate. Bernard in his beige slacks and button down shirt, Bee in her stylish ocean blue dress. She'd wanted to look nice for this occasion, but not over-the-top. With a pair of low heels, a simple silver necklace and matching dangling earrings, she figured she'd hit the mark.

Although her French manicure was impossibly chipped now due to the fact that she couldn't keep the damn things out of her mouth. Biting your nails was a nervous habit. One that would absolutely not be tolerated within the walls of Cambric.

Bee's lips curved into a rueful smile. Screw. Those. Ass... *A-holes*, she corrected.

Language.

She had to watch her language now.

Outside, it was springtime. A cool breeze swirled the air, but still, it was warm. Perfect in fact. March in Texas was mild.

Bee swallowed once and tried to shake the tingling from her fingers. Her father had a thing for Italian architecture so his impossibly big home was made of cream-colored stone, complete with a red-tile roof, overflowing green gardens and a small vineyard.

It was a lovely home, with eleven bedrooms and nine bathrooms. But would *they* think so? Their car should be pulling down the driveway any minute.

Fumbling for her phone, Bee glanced at the time... again. It was one-thirty in the afternoon and their flight should have touched down at noon. *Their* as in they... as in there were two of them.

"This is all happening so fast," Bee protested. "It's only been two months, I expected it to take longer."

"Well..." Bernard gave her a little squeeze before glancing over his shoulder. "That's why your mother and I are both here to support you. We're a team, remember?"

Turning her head, Bee managed to give her mother a tentative smile. Lillian Durand nodded firmly before smoothing at her updo and striding to her daughter's other side. When Mommy Dearest took her hand, Bee felt some of her nerves float away.

"That's right." Lillian looked out the front window as well.

"You are going to make the best mother, my love, I just know it."

"I don't want to push that word on them." Bee blew out a breath.

Her eyes tracked the slope of the hill, the far off neighboring homes, the breeze tickling the nearby trees. Anything to keep her mind occupied. Anything to keep her heart in check.

"Guardian then," Lillian offered, and on Bee's other side her father nodded his head.

Her parents weren't living together, but now they were speaking, at least. When Bee and Val had come to their father with the adoption idea, he hadn't hesitated to climb on board. When Lillian had found out, she'd been the next in line. There were no tears, no guilt, no holding back. Nothing that Bee had expected.

Nope. Lillian Durand had simply gathered her daughter into her arms, kissed her cheek, and asked when they could get started.

So, both of her parents had come together once more to support her, and Bee couldn't deny that she really needed them. This covert, sneaky stuff was no joke.

And the plan was working. Thanks to the Durand's massive cash infusion, Ava and the underground had been able to set up an adoption scam successfully targeting Cambric. Charlie was feeding them the names of children, and the first two of Gabe's own daughters had been purchased/adopted out of the captive system yesterday morning.

It usually took longer, Ava had cautioned them, but with

the vote on Jason's captive legislation mere weeks away, the entire country's economy was wavering.

Captive prices were falling, especially on long term dependents like children who had little to no value until adulthood. Cambric was looking to offload a few of them, although they weren't dumping their inventory like some other agencies. It was more like they were hedging their investment.

And free people everywhere were growing more nervous. So many industries depended on captive labor to survive. Auto manufacturing, food processing, farming, mining. Prices were dipping in places and sky rocketing in others.

As the Senate vote neared, protests and rallies were growing in size and fervor. A few riots had broken out in some of the inner cities.

But none of that mattered today. Not when Gabe's girls were almost safe, almost free.

In the silence, Bernard's phone beeped plaintively. Drawing it out of his pocket, he held the thing up to his ear and glanced at Bee.

"Yes, Taylor." Bernard gave his daughter an encouraging smile. "Let them in."

Sucking in a breath, Bee squeezed her eyes shut and fought the sudden pounding in her chest. What did she know about them? What details could she focus on?

The girls shared the same father (Gabe), but were from different mothers (who were still in Cambric). They were ages six and seven. Their names were *Annalise* and *Robin*. Why did their names make Bee want to cry?

She didn't know the answer, but when Bee had first read them, she'd thought of Gabe so intensely. She'd been alone in her room when the email had come through. Then all at once, she could see his smile, hear his laugh, almost feel his fingers slip along her bare shoulder. She'd sucked in a breath, bit at her lip and fought the urge to sob like a damn baby.

It was a fight that she lost on that particular night. That night, and many nights after that. But come morning, Bee was ready for more.

More adoptions, more freedom, more everything.

And Ava kept forwarding the purchase information to Bee as it came in, and in turn Bee gave it over to her father. Because Gabe's children weren't the only ones they were saving, they were just the most personal to Bee.

In order to manage it all, Bernard had set up a foundation through which to funnel the financial transactions. With a legal staff that could rival a baseball team, he ran everything through a series of shell corporations. Bee's father may have been born rich, but he hadn't spent a day wasting it.

In fact, he was crazy smart, and that had been news to Bee. It was amazing what you could learn about a person by working with them. He'd managed to take a pipe dream project of saving Gabe's kids and expand it.

The goal was still to get as many children out of Cambric that they could first, then pray the legislation passed, and proceed to contact the birth mothers once they were freed. If the legislation didn't pass, however, then the next phase was to try to purchase the mothers as well.

Of course, that might prove to be more difficult. It would certainly take longer, anyway. Maybe years.

Until then, Bee insisted that all of Gabe's biological children live with her. Though she'd agreed to move back to her parent's estate initially, she knew in the back of her mind what she needed to do, where she needed to go.

She needed to move all of Gabe's children out of the country.

She needed to get them all safely to the Maldives.

No extradition. No captive law. No agencies. She was taking no chances.

"Here they come," Lillian murmured.

Bee's eyes shot open wide.

The silver Bentley cruised down the driveway and slowly navigated the final circle around a central fountain before coming to a stop in front of the estate's heavy double front doors. Bee's mouth went dry as she continued to stare out the window. Then the driver was popping his door open and unfolding his tall frame from the car.

Bee's heart thumped. She watched him striding around to the rear…

Leaving Bee's side suddenly, Bernard crossed the dark wood of the foyer before opening the front door and standing on its threshold. When Bee glanced quickly to him, he smiled and held out his hand.

"They'll be more comfortable," he said. "If they see a woman first. Don't you think?"

"Of course," the words slipped from Bee's lips in a whisper. Her mother nudged her side.

"Think of Jace," her mother said. "What would he need from you right now, if he were here?"

"A smile." Bee ducked her head and felt suddenly steadier. "And ice cream."

"That's my girl." Lillian bobbed her head knowingly.

And that was all it took. Bee was crossing to the open door and the girls were coming up the stone steps and it was like deja vu. They looked so, so much like their father. Golden curls framed their faces, with high cheekbones and *his* pink lips and two pairs of wary brown eyes staring up at her.

On the one hand, it was like looking at Gabe, but on the other, it was like looking at herself and Val. They were nervous, but kept their faces plain. Their tiny hands were clasped between them, the taller one holding on maybe a touch harder than the shorter. It melted Bee. It melted away her nerves and her doubts and her insecurities.

Kneeling on the stone landing before them, Bee placed her palms flat on her thighs and flashed a smile.

"Hi girls." Bee let her eyes absorb them. "My name is Bee and I was a captive once, too. Just like you."

"You were?" The taller one's brow furrowed, a bit unbelieving while the shorter one simply stared.

"Yup." Bee bobbed her head and gave an exaggerated sigh. "So I know for a fact that you've never had ice cream before. And it just so happens I have a ton of the stuff."

"Ice cream?" The taller, and apparently bolder one… *Annalise?* spoke again. Had to be Annalise, she was the elder.

"It's a special treat." Bee wiggled her eyebrows now. "My nephew Jace loves the stuff. He's seven, too."

"Is he here?" Annalise asked, her eyes darting around.

"Not right now," Bee amended. "But he lives pretty close. Would you want to play with him sometime?"

"Um…" Annalise's eyes locked back on Bee, but before she could make up her mind, the shorter one piped up.

"He's seven?" Robin's smile lit up her cherub face. "I'm six."

"Hmmm." Bee quirked a smile. "That still makes you old enough for ice cream. I'm sure of it."

"It does?" Robin's eyebrows lifted and she looked for confirmation to her sister.

Beside her, Annalise tilted her head thoughtfully at Robin before returning her gaze to Bee. She was wary, not sure if she could trust everything coming out of Bee's mouth. If anyone understood that sort of uncertainty, it was Bee. So she waited.

After a few long seconds, Annalise ducked her head.

"Let's try it," Annalise said and released her sister's hand so that Bee could take it.

All at once, Bee's heart swelled a few sizes bigger. Suddenly her chest was too tight to fit all of the love exploding there.

Rising to her feet, she turned with Robin's little palm held gently in her own.

When Annalise had said *let's try it*, what she'd really meant was *let's give this crazy lady a chance*. And as a former captive, Bee knew what this chance was worth. These girls were giving her one shot at gaining their trust, and she was not going to blow it.

Even if it meant ice cream sundaes and ponies and dolls and dresses and straight out bribery. Bee would keep Gabe's girls safe. They would come to trust her, and she would never let anyone hurt them. But better than that, better than all those things, Bee would make them both *free*.

CHAPTER 35

Gabe

The room was dimly lit.

Lifting his face from the mattress, Gabe tried to focus on the rectangle of light that pushed itself around the drawn shades in the bedroom. Despite narrowing his eyes, the whole world seemed to tip and sway. It was like he was on a boat out at sea, although he knew for a fact that he was still on dry land, locked up tight inside Sharon's Santa Barbara mansion.

Rolling onto his back, Gabe ran a hand down his face and blew out a hot breath. He was so fucking high right now. So high and so drunk and so...

Blinking, he lifted his head and stared down at his own naked body. He was hard. He was still wearing a condom and he was still hard... because the pills always did that to him.

Letting his head crash back down onto the mattress, Gabe turned his face to one side and eye-balled the curvy brunette passed out beside him. She wasn't the reporter... Hilga...

Heidi? which was surprising. She was some random chick from Sharon's party last night, and her name eluded him.

Around two in the morning, his *mistress* had simply pointed to the woman in the tight black dress and told Gabe to go. So he went. He went for like four hours, judging by the dawn light peeking into the room.

With a groan now, Gabe pushed up to sitting and cradled his head in both hands. His skull was throbbing. Between the booze and the pills, his brain was getting fried. Sucking in a ragged breath, he winced. His lungs felt like they were on fire.

He. Hated. This.

Flinging his legs over the side of the bed, Gabe tottered his way to the ensuite bathroom. After shutting the door, he twisted on the water in the sink and stuck his entire face beneath the cool flow. It felt so fucking amazing.

For a solid minute, maybe more, he let the water soak and slide and slip down his skin. Then he was sucking at the water, lapping and licking it from the air like a dog. He was so thirsty. So unbelievably thirsty.

The sound of the door opening at his right side did not surprise him. In fact, he didn't need to open his eyes to guess who it was.

"Time to go," Junior, one of Gabe's guards, whispered.

Keeping his face beneath the water, Gabe did not open his eyes. Nope. He just kept right on drinking, and maybe swaying, as his hands clutched loosely on the marble counter.

"Jeez, she pumps you with too much shit," Junior grumbled, before twisting the water off. "Flush the condom and step into your pants man, I don't wanna have to haul your naked ass down the hall."

Giving his head a slight shake, Gabe remained bent over at

the sink, which was a mistake. Everything around him swirled at the movement, causing his knees to buckle beneath him. So dizzy. He was so unstoppably dizzy.

"Shit," Junior spat the word quietly and huffed a breath. Gabe felt a pair of large hands grip him under his arms. "She's lucky you sealed the deal. Video footage came through clear as day."

Nodding, Gabe allowed himself to be drag/walked to the bed. With the anonymous woman still sleeping on the far side, Gabe plopped down on the edge and blinked. He watched in slow motion as Junior helped him into his clothes. He was like a small child, lifting one leg like a good boy, then the other.

When he was sloppily dressed, Junior hoisted him up once more and shuffled him from the room. The long corridor was cool and dark. The wood beneath his bare feet felt smooth and clean. Gabe didn't know where exactly he was being led to. It could be his own little prison of a room, which was one floor up, or it could be to Sharon's bed, which was on the level above that.

"Dude." His second guard, Chavez, met them at the bottom of the stairs. "This looks like a bottle of Jack and two pills too many."

"Sounds about right," Junior grunted in reply. "But this lady was the important one, so she had to make sure he followed through."

"Still." Chavez reached out a hand and gripped Gabe's shoulder. "His pupils are blown. You're not gonna be sick are you?" Leaning closer to Gabe, he peered warily into his face.

"Let's just get him back to Sharon," Junior grumbled. "Your turn to watch that shit show."

"Fuck. No." Chavez straightened quickly and jerked his

hand away. Gabe felt his body twist in on itself. "It's definitely your turn, Junior."

"Nah, nah, nah." Junior shook his head. "You lost that last bet. You're taking double duty."

As the two massive guards argued over who was going to babysit Gabe's own special brand of torture, the room proceeded to spin. Stooping, Gabe braced both hands against his knees and kept his eyes wide, watching as the room went around and around and around.

Then suddenly, everything stopped.

"Whoa." Gabe managed to utter the single word before proceeding to throw up.

Bending forward, his body heaved violently as his stomach pushed up into his throat. He heard the contents (that would be one small bottle of *Gin*, thank you very much, and five beers) splash out all over the wood.

Jumping back, both of his guards groaned as Gabe let everything go. He threw up on their shoes. He threw up all over himself.

Dropping to his hands and knees on the floor, Gabe felt his elbows shake and his stomach convulse. He had no control, he couldn't stop this shit show if he wanted to. The part of his brain that was able to still recognize that fact, didn't fucking care.

If he hadn't been in so much damn pain, he might've started to laugh. Truth be told though, all he was able to do was silently cry. Tears rolled out of his eyes and dripped straight onto the floor, they blurred his surroundings.

"What should we do with him?" Chavez asked.

"Hospital?" Junior's voice was hushed.

"Not an option," Chavez again. "They'd only pump his stomach and he's doing plenty of that all by himself."

"Better ask *her* then," Junior intoned.

Both Chavez and Gabe groaned, but for different reasons. Then he was being lifted. They were clutching his arms and he felt his lower body thump, thump, thump up each and every step as they ascended to the second story.

At some point, Gabe must have blacked out, because the next thing he knew a spray of cold water was raining down on his body. Gasping, he shot upright in the large porcelain tub and opened his eyes. He was still fully clothed, and completely soaking wet.

The shower head high above him poured down water. Gabe winced and turned his face to one side. *Breathe in through your nose, out through your mouth. Something like that.* Helped when your nostrils didn't feel like flames were shooting out of them.

"He wasn't like this with her, was he?" Sharon's voice echoed in the bathroom, causing Gabe's stomach to twist even more violently.

"No, Ma'am," Chavez answered. "He was fine. He just crashed right after."

"And she enjoyed herself," Sharon prompted. "You can tell from the video that she wanted him, right?"

"Yes, definitely," Chavez again, sounding slightly uncomfortable as he cleared his throat.

"I'll need to see the footage right away." Sharon's heels clicked closer, and Gabe shrank in on himself, squeezing his eyes shut tight. "But I'm trusting that it's what you say it is. You're sure you can tell that it's her? You can see her face?"

"Absolutely," Chavez assured her. "There's no question that it's her."

"Hmmm," Sharon hummed to herself as her heels stopped their clicking just beside the tub.

Gabe could feel her crouch down beside him, even though he kept his eyes shut. Trembling, he gripped his own arms with his hands and fought the sickness that swirled inside of him. Her perfume drifted beneath his nose, her soft sigh filled his ears.

"You did good, darling." Sharon reached out a hand and stroked at his upper arm with her fingers.

The water continued to fall. Gabe was going to puke, or his head was going to explode, or his lungs were going to melt, he was sure of it.

"Your little Senator friend thinks that he's the only one who can play the blackmail game," Sharon continued quietly, tracing her nails up and down Gabe's arm all the while. "He forgets who invented the game, darling. He forgets who's the best at it."

Gabe's eyes popped open and he shifted in the tub. *Senator? Who did he know that was a Senator? No one.*

Sharon's full red lips curled into a Cheshire Cat grin. Her cheeks flushed with excitement. Her eyes danced. This is what really turned her on. This game. This twisted, fucked up, life destroying, game.

"I know I've been keeping things from you, dearest," Sharon intoned, batting her lashes deliberately as she cocked her head to the side. "It would be almost more fun to tell you."

Her right hand and wrist were wet from the spray of the shower. Gabe could see the drops beading on her pale skin and rolling off. He shuddered.

Keeping things from him? Shit, that was an understatement. He was in a total black hole.

No television. No internet. No news.

Even at Sharon's lavish parties, the attendees seemed to have been warned. They did not discuss things around him, not anything of significance anyway. And all those tv interviews he'd done? Sharon had been present, in the background, monitoring everything.

Gabe knew nothing. He felt nothing. He was nothing.

"Let's just say…" Sharon chuckled a moment and withdrew her hand. "That your friend's sorry attempt to pass this legislation will make absolutely no difference in the end."

"Legislation?" Gabe forced the word from his mouth, but it came out slurred and disjointed. Even so, Sharon nodded, like she understood everything perfectly.

"There will be no freed captives." Sharon tisked to herself and shook her head slightly. "The legislation has to make it past the President's desk before it can become law."

Gabe's brow furrowed, he wasn't quite following…

"The President has to sign it," Sharon explained. "Which will be so hard for him to do now… especially when his very religious, very married daughter has just had some very good sex with a very captive man."

Gabe blinked. Slowly. His heart thumped once, hard.

"On video," Sharon added finally before shoving back from the tub and walking away.

CHAPTER 36

Jason

THE SET OF GOLD CUFF LINKS HAD TWIN *R*'S ENGRAVED ON them. Jason rubbed his thumb soothingly over one initial as he stared out the hotel window. His father had owned these cuff links, and his father before him. Now it was Jason's turn to wear them at his wrists. For luck, Senior had said.

Glancing over his shoulder, Jason eyed the door to the ensuite bath. His wife had left it slightly ajar. He could hear her humming to herself as she applied makeup in the giant mirror over the double sink. She was happy.

After everything she'd been through, she was finally happy. And Jason liked to think it was in part because of him. He'd done all of this for her, after all. For her and their son.

Turning his attention back to the window, Jason smoothed at his black tuxedo jacket and frowned. He felt... such a strange mix of triumph and despair. He'd done things in the past year that he was absolutely not proud of, but they were things that had to be done.

With a shake of his head, he dismissed the guilt.

Outside, night had fallen. It was dark, with no moon, but even so, the White House shone like a beautiful candle in the distance. What would it be like to live there? In that fishbowl filled with immense success and abysmal failure, good and evil?

He didn't envy the poor bastard. Not after Jason's last year spent in the political arena. It had been hell. But that hell was all about to pay off.

Inhaling, Jason filled his lungs until they couldn't take in anymore air. Then slowly, he blew out his breath. They'd won. The final vote was yesterday, and the damn legislation had passed the Senate, 52 to 48.

Holy.

Shit.

All captives were about to become completely and irrevocably free. It was done. The only thing left was for the President to sign the damn thing into law, and then Gabe would have his walking papers.

Along with millions of other people.

It was going to be a cluster-fuck of epic proportions.

Ducking his head, Jason rubbed at the back of his neck. The entire country was rumbling. It was like standing at the bottom of a snow capped mountain, listening to the crack and groan of an avalanche looming.

Where would all these captives go? What would they do to survive? Could the businesses that formerly owned them afford to hire them back as free people?

There were so many questions and admittedly not enough answers. But in Jason's experience, the cost of doing the right thing was always high. He figured now it was just time for everyone to pay up.

And besides, they had another week, maybe two, before the President finished reading everything and stamped his approval.

"Hey," Val's voice sounded from behind him and he turned to look at her. "You ready?"

Sucking in a breath, Jason felt his heart give one giant thump in his chest before it stuttered to a stop. She did this to him. Dressed in a floor-length red satin gown, with her dark hair swept up in a twist, Val knocked him completely out.

It had been like this from the second he'd set eyes on her in that glass box in New York. He'd known right then. Something inside of him had just felt it. She belonged with him, and he with her. That was it.

"You look..." Jason searched for the right words to say to her, but they all seemed so cliche. *Beautiful. Sexy. Unreal. Why are you mine? I'm so relieved you're mine.* "Amazing."

Val chuckled before giving him that sultry smile she had on speed dial. It lit him up like a Christmas tree, but as always, he fought the heady rush she brought on.

Cocking his head to one side, Jason shoved one hand in his pocket and held the other out to her. Without hesitation, she crossed the room and placed her delicate palm in his.

Warmth shot up his arm as he gathered her body close and proceeded to bury his face in her neck. When she giggled and squirmed in his grasp, he smiled against the soft sweep of her skin, pressing his lips down to kiss and nibble and nip and tease.

Would he ever not feel like a greedy bastard when it came to her? Would there be a time in his life, maybe when they were old and gray, where he didn't feel the need to mark her as his? He wasn't sure. And anyway, there wasn't enough time right now to do what he *really* wanted to do to her, and they both knew it.

"We're going to be late," she chided, and reluctantly Jason released her.

"The party is at Senator Bourey's estate," he countered. "We can't technically be late."

Arching a knowing brow at him, Val played with the ropes of diamonds draping her neck. She *knew* he wouldn't follow through, especially since this celebration was supposed to be overflowing with DC's finest... and filthiest, but that was beside the point. He had to go.

He'd made several backroom deals in order to get the anti-captivity legislation through Congress. He couldn't go back to being a normal businessman. Maybe not ever.

Letting loose an audible sigh, Jason patted his pockets. Wallet. Phone. Then adjusted the shoulder holster hidden beneath his insanely overpriced jacket. Colt 1911 nestled semi-comfortably under his left armpit... *Check.*

Watching him, Val's brows drew together in concern. She wasn't entirely comfortable with the whole concealed carry thing, but Jason wasn't about to let CT and his security team do all the heavy lifting. Call him a control freak, but worst case scenario always ended with you being alone with the threat.

Better to have a weapon and know how to use it, then lose your life... or worse, your wife. That little nightmare was never going to happen again. Ever. *Fucking Finn.*

Forcing a smile and shoving away the memories, Jason offered her his arm. When Val slid her hand into the crook of his elbow, he felt some of his tension ease. He was overreacting, like Val always said.

"Did you talk to my mom?" Jason asked, as they left their room and stepped into the hallway.

CT and his brother (who knew the guy had like four brothers?) Owen, shoved off the wall and came to attention. Their broad shoulders stretched the fabric of their dark suits, making their dangling ties look pencil thin.

Jason eyed them both. He had to tip his head back to look at their six-foot-five frames, and it's not like he was a short guy himself.

Of course, that's where the brother's similarities came to an end. Where CT's head was shaved clean, Owen's boasted a thick crop of jet-black hair. Where CT's eyes were a steady chocolate brown, Owen's were a color-changing hazel. Where CT was quiet, reserved, and definitely not funny, Owen couldn't stop himself from cracking bad jokes.

And of course, Jason couldn't stop himself from laughing at them. Even when it was completely inappropriate. Even when a room full of Congressman were staring at him.

But since CT was now assigned to guard Val, as well as head up the entire team, Jason was sort of stuck with Owen. Which he didn't entirely mind, the guy was good at what he did. Almost as good as CT. Almost.

With a quick nod, Jason kept on moving towards the elevator. His guards followed. Tucked into his side, Val kept pace.

The sound of her high heels were muffled against the plush carpet, but she didn't miss a beat. She never did, at least not at this sort of thing.

"Yes." Val ducked her head before quirking a small smile.

The elevator doors dinged open and they stepped inside. "Jace is having a movie marathon with your dad. He yelled good-night at me from across the room."

"Mom didn't make him stop and talk to you?" Jason lifted an eyebrow. If so, the woman was certainly losing her touch.

"Oh, I didn't want to interrupt," Val rushed. "He's having a good time and I heard his voice so that's enough."

The elevator doors slid closed. CT leaned forward and depressed the Lobby button. The box jerked slightly, then began its whirring descent.

"Good." Jason rolled his shoulders and stroked his wife's hand. Progress. Jace was several states away and she wasn't hyperventilating. "And Bee?"

"She's busy." Val used her other hand to fan herself with her clutch purse. The elevator was hot. "But seventeen kids, three nannies, a full kitchen staff and a maid would keep anyone busy."

"Seventeen now?" Jason's eyebrows raised. "That's... that's..."

"Amazing right?" Val prompted.

Not the word he was going to use, but okaayyy. The elevator came to a stop and CT moved his body in front of Val. As the doors slid open, he peeked his giant head out and then proceeded to walk forward.

All clear.

Limo should already be at the curb.

"They're all in Male?" Jason asked, though he already knew the answer.

He just wanted to keep talking to his wife. It helped to distract her, and if he was being honest, it helped to distract him, too. To say he'd had a fair amount of death threats would be an understatement.

"Yes." Val nodded easily. "The private island was too isolating for the kids, so she bought a house in the city. You know, there's a grocery store and an arcade and a school…"

"A private school?" Jason kept the questions coming, even as his eyes darted all around.

The Lobby was quiet, and the hotel staff, too. No one was rushing to warn them of an impending crowd outside. CT seemed unruffled as he pressed a single finger to his earpiece and gave a slight nod. All is well. That's what that meant.

"No, they're going to public school," Val answered, and it had Jason breaking into a wide grin.

Veronica "Bee" Durand was really something else. Seventeen kids, none of which were biologically hers, rich as a fucking skunk, and sending every one of them to a public school in the Maldives.

Her parents must be having a heart attack.

Well, at least the pair of them were on speaking terms now. And Bernard was making all the right overtures towards Val. He wanted a relationship when she did. He wasn't being pushy, and Val seemed receptive, so Jason was okay with it.

On the other hand, the elephant in the room was proving to be a bit harder to deal with. But Jason had his best investigator on it, and if it was possible to locate Val's mom, then he would. He absolutely would.

"Limo's just through the doors," CT commented quietly. "I'll exit first."

"Good." Jason pulled Val to a stop a few feet from the glass doors with Owen lingering at his back.

As the hotel doorman pushed one door wide, CT strode

through quickly and ducked off to the right. A few seconds later and Jason watched him cross back to the left before coming to a stop. When he lifted his hand and motioned them forward, Jason squeezed his wife's palm and together, they left the hotel.

The air outside was cool. He almost sighed in relief.

Some might say Jason was being paranoid, having all of this private security, taking all of these unnecessary precautions. Some might say he was a self-important power tripper who thought too much of himself. Jason could give two shits what *some* might say.

Where had they been when he'd been beaten by a mob on the streets of New York? Where had they been when the rear window of his Aston Martin was smashed to pieces with a brick? They were quarterbacking from their living room couches, that's where they'd been.

Frowning, Jason felt his whole body filling with tension. Was tonight going to go smoothly? Or was it going to be a repeat of past events?

All of these thoughts swirled through his head in the brief time it took CT to climb into the rear of the limo. Jason watched the thing sag with the guy's weight before he helped Val to slide in next. Then Jason was ducking his own head into the dark space, and after him came Owen.

The limo dipped even lower, rocking a bit as the two big men on either end tried to settle themselves. Their long legs took up too much space, their knees pressed up close to their chests, their heads touched the ceiling.

"Bit of a tight fit," Owen commented as the driver slammed the passenger door shut. "But I'm a tight fit *every-*

where..." he paused for effect and shot Val a filthy grin. "I'm proportional, in case you were wondering."

Winding the fingers of his left hand through his wife's, Jason suppressed an eye roll and tried to get comfortable himself. Did he mention the bad jokes? More like dirty jokes, but still.

"Now, now, big boy," Val countered, arching an eyebrow and crossing her long legs seductively despite her tight dress. She was the only one that came close to fitting in the limo. "Remember, I've been trained to do things that would make even you blush. You can't get to me."

Owen's mouth dropped and Jason barked out a laugh.

Hell yes, buddy. This was the exact reason Jason kept Owen around. The guy diffused the tension. Always. And not only that, but his humor brought the old Val back into play. She teased and taunted and snuggled closer to Jason and it made his heart feel oh so good.

On the far side of the limo CT shot his brother a glare and shook his head slowly. Owen's grin grew even wider.

"What?" He asked, shrugging and holding up both wide palms in question.

"You're so embarrassing," CT muttered quietly and the limo rolled forward. It was the most the silent giant would say on the subject.

Not fifteen minutes later they were pulling to a stop in front of a Georgetown mansion. The thing was all red brick and white columns and old money. The good humor that had dominated Owen's face faded into nothing as he opened the passenger door and exited the limo.

Jason blinked out at their surroundings through the purple tint of limo glass. It was nighttime, but the house was lit up with its dozens of windows shining and its front courtyard on full display.

People milled about. A few reporters snapped lazy photos as several couples dressed in black tie approached the entrance. The double doors were thrown wide, and the noise from inside filtered out onto the street.

"I know the guy running Bourey's security," CT offered. "He's good."

"I'm cleared to carry inside?" Jason asked, eyeing the pair of guards doing a quick pat down at the front door.

"Absolutely," CT confirmed.

Nodding his head, Jason glanced at Val and tried for a reassuring smile. He could ask CT if he'd spoken to the guy personally. He could grill him on the size of the house and the difficulties of managing this sort of party, but he didn't need to. CT had that covered.

That's why he cleared three-hundred fifty thousand a year… *plus* expenses, not including the rest of his team. At this rate, Jason was going to need to start taking the bribes being offered to him. You could only live on static investments for so long.

"All good," Owen's voice sounded from outside.

Leaning in close, Jason gave Val a lingering kiss on the cheek.

"Ready?" He asked and she plastered on that big fake smile that could fool anyone. Well, anyone but him.

"Let's go." Val ducked her head, and they went.

~

Inside the house, the crowd was thick. Even with all of the windows thrown wide to let in the evening air, it was stuffy and warm. Reaching for the button of his jacket, Jason undid it and glanced to his left at Val. She fanned herself with her clutch.

Snagging a cold glass of champagne from a passing tray, Jason handed it off to his wife and glanced around. He would be drinking water tonight, though most people here would assume it was Gin on the rocks.

Never can be too careful. He preferred being alert to being relaxed.

As Jason and Val made their way through the wide foyer and into the expansive living room, CT and Owen faded back against opposite walls. There was hardly enough room for the guests to mingle, let alone their array of guards.

The room swirled with a mix of Congressman, support staff, lobbyists, philanthropists and high ranking business-man. Leaning back against the floor to ceiling book shelves, stood a variety of security. Some were private and some were secret service, which meant there must be a foreign dignitary or two in attendance.

Jason knew for a fact that neither the President nor the Vice President were expected to be here tonight.

"Oh my God," Val exhaled the words just beside him and gripped his left hand tight. The champagne glass in her other hand swayed and Jason reached quickly to steady it.

"What?" He hissed, his brow furrowing as he jerked his head around to follow her gaze.

"It's him," she gasped, her eyes locking onto a familiar figure. "I can't believe it's him."

"Gabe," Jason mouthed the name as he straightened, his heart hammering suddenly in his chest.

And sure enough, there he stood, clad in a perfectly pressed tuxedo, a demon with auburn hair and thick curves hanging onto his side.

Sharon Baine.

The nerve of that fucking woman. What the hell was she doing here at a party to celebrate the end of captivity? With a captive on her arm, no less.

Jason could practically feel his blood boiling, and the moment Gabe lifted those brown eyes of his and caught sight of Val, Jason swore time stopped. His old friend blanched. The color drained quickly from his face and his mouth hung down a fraction.

It was quite the contrast to a second before, when Gabe had been all charming smiles and broad shoulders and twinkling eyes.

He thought she was Bee, Jason realized, and glanced down at his wife. Of course, they looked just alike. Gabe thought that Bee was standing there in the flesh, staring at him from not twenty feet away.

Lifting his face, Jason caught Gabe's eye and gave his head a slight shake. *No buddy. Wrong one, this one's mine.*

Ducking his head, Gabe worked to compose himself. Jason watched the guy's jaw clench and then just as quickly as he'd shown them the truth, he covered it up again. When Gabe lifted his face, he was oozing nonchalance. He even managed a light chuckle.

Fuck. It was like watching Val on those videos. It made Jason want to smash his fist through something.

"What's *she* doing here?" Val rasped. "And why is she smiling? He'll be free in a matter of days, right? Right?"

"That's right." Jason rubbed a rough hand over his mouth before muttering, "I'll send CT in after him if I have to. She won't get to keep him."

Just then the *she* in question caught sight of them. Her ruby red lips twisted up in a triumphant smile as she raised a delicate hand in the air and waved. *Waved.*

Before he had a chance to think, Jason was crossing the living room towards them. He tugged Val along at his side and used his right shoulder to push people out of the way. He couldn't help himself. Challenge fucking accepted.

Coming to an abrupt stop right in front of Sharon and Gabe, Jason's jaw ticked. She'd lost. *Lost.*

As in businesses gone. Captives gone. Gabe gone. Poof, it was all going to dissolve on her in less than two weeks.

"Sharon," Jason managed quietly, as the crowd around them hushed.

"Senator Riggs, darling." Sharon smiled broadly as her eyes did a slow crawl up his chest. "So good to see you, and your lovely wife, of course."

Beside him, Val's glass of champagne slid through her fingertips and crashed noisily to the marble floor. Turning slightly towards her, Jason stared down at the shattered glass and swirl of liquid. He was distracted. And so was everyone else.

Later, he would wonder if things would have gone down differently. If Val hadn't dropped her glass, if everyone's eyes hadn't been focused on the floor, would Jason have seen it coming?

That's the thing about hindsight though, it's always clear as day. In the moment, things are murky… cloudy… too fast.

So when Gabe took that step into him, Jason hardly felt it. It was so quick, less than a heartbeat really, he didn't register the loss of his gun.

It wasn't until the 1911 was firing a single round not twelve inches from his head, that Jason's brain reported the lightness in the holster beneath his left armpit. But by then, it was too late.

Boom.

The shot echoed in the room.

Thump.

Sharon's body hit the floor.

Then everyone was screaming and scrambling. The crowd was frantic, trying to get away. Men in suits were charging forward off the walls, drawing their weapons, shouting.

The room emptied faster than Jason could have imagined, leaving him standing in the middle of it all, with Val blinking just beside him and about twenty guns pointed their way.

Facing them, eyes wide, stood Gabe. He was holding the gun up to his own temple now. His chest was heaving. He was panting, his finger twitching uncertainly against the trigger.

"No!" Jason shouted, holding his hands out in front of him. "Nobody shoot!"

There were a few answering grumbles from the men in suits surrounding them, but thankfully everyone was frozen in place. No one had a clear shot at Gabe, not while Val and Jason were standing there, unarmed.

Over Gabe's shoulder, Jason watched Owen hold his gun

steadily out in front of him. That meant CT was likely somewhere at Jason's rear.

"Gabey," Val's broken voice was the only one filling the room now. "Why did you do that? You were going to be free."

"I was never going to be free," Gabe hissed, his wild eyes darting from her face to Jason's and back again. "And she has my *kids*, Val. My boys. Shane's hurting them."

"I know," Val jumped in, wiping at the tears streaming down her cheeks.

"I've got to make it stop." Gabe pressed the gun a bit harder against his own temple. "There's no point in hurting them, if… if…"

"Don't do it," Val cut him off. "Don't pull that trigger. Bee has your kids, Gabey. She's got them safe in the Maldives."

"What?" Gabe's eyes drifted from her face to Jason for confirmation.

Bobbing his head in agreement, Jason swiped quickly at the sweat beading on his own brow.

"We've got them all now," he lied. "Your boys are safe. No need to kill yourself. Put the gun down."

When Jason stretched his hands back out towards Gabe, one of them was covered in blood. That wasn't sweat collecting on his brow, it was little bits of Sharon's head. Holy shit.

Gabe had blown Sharon Baine's head off in a room full of people.

Time slowed. Gabe's eyes danced away from Val to settle on Jason and then back over to Val. It was like he was trying to make up his mind. It was like he was building the courage to do it.

His finger pulsed against the trigger, almost imperceptibly. Over Gabe's shoulder, Owen made his move.

"Drop it!" Jason shouted, but Gabe was a few seconds too late.

Owen's massive arms wrapped Gabe's shoulders. The gun pitched forward. Val screamed.

Boom.

Another shot rang out, and Jason stumbled back.

Staggering, he took a few steps before he felt his knees give way. The ceiling flashed above him and his back impacted the floor. His breath came out in a whoosh.

Then Val was on top of him, pressing her hands to his body, screaming. Then CT was rushing up behind her and another man in a suit along with him. They were shouting, and there was the sound of people running.

Jason blinked up at them dully before trying to sit up and shove them off, but then he looked down. He saw all of the blood soaking his shirt and he stopped.

He'd been shot.

It was him bleeding.

Then his mind shut off. Jason felt his brain slow to a crawl. His eyes rolled back in his head, and he was gone.

CHAPTER 37

Gabe

HIS CHEEKBONE EXPLODED WITH PAIN AS IT IMPACTED THE COLD marble flooring. Blinking, Gabe opened his mouth to gasp for breath, but he couldn't get any air into his lungs. There was a three hundred pound whirlwind on his back, and the sound of a gun ringing in his ears.

In front of him, not six inches from his face, was Sharon. Her dead eyes stared into his living ones. Gabe's mouth gaped open and closed, open and closed… like a fish on dry land.

He'd killed her. She was dead.

He hadn't hesitated this time, not when the chance had presented itself. Jason's jacket had that slight bulge in it that was once so familiar, and Gabe took a chance. Sure enough, Jason had that same gun in that same holster that Gabe had seen a thousand times before. They'd practiced with it in the Maldives, back when Gabe was a free man.

And Gabe hadn't thought twice. It wasn't like the million

other times when he'd imagined how to make himself a weapon. Nope. This weapon was real and ready to go.

In an instant, Gabe's eyes had tracked to that spot just under Jason's left arm. He didn't even blink. He'd just stepped close to his old friend and pulled the gun free in one easy motion. Turning, he'd flipped the safety off, held the thing up to the side of Sharon's head, and pulled the trigger.

Boom. Point blank.

Sharon.

She'd dragged him to this party, dressed him up, paraded him around in some rich guy's house. He didn't know what state he was in, let alone why he was here. After months... *years?* of torture, he really didn't care.

Besides, he'd known his part. Smile. Act charming. Look good. Answer simple questions in a way that made Sharon seem like a saint.

If he complied, then his boys would be fed. If he failed, then he'd receive another photo of his kid sporting a black eye, or maybe some bruising on his child's bare back, or a red hand print on a pair of too thin thighs.

Squeezing his eyes shut, Gabe fought the flood of memories. The pictures were so fucking haunting.

In the background now, sirens wailed. They sounded so very far away, but then again everything was dull compared to the pounding in his head.

The gun had gone off a second time. He hadn't meant to squeeze the trigger, but then something had hit him from behind and his hand had jerked and...

Had he shot himself in the head? Was he about to die?

Twisting on the hard floor, Gabe sucked in a bit of air as

he turned his head to the other side. That's when everything came into focus.

Val was screaming.

Her back was to Gabe as she climbed on top of someone who was lying on the floor. It was a man in a tux, and he was trying to shove her off. *Jason?*

But then a massive guy in a suit was flinging himself down on top of them both and Jason's body flopped back to the ground. His feet and legs went limp. He stopped struggling.

There was blood everywhere.

"Call an ambulance!" Someone shouted, as Gabe's awareness returned full force. He'd shot Jason.

"Get her out of here," another person called.

"No one touches her!" The giant man straddling Jason yelled. He had both of his arms locked straight as he applied pressure to Jason's upper body. "She doesn't leave my sight!"

Then people were scrambling and feet were shuffling. Men in suits were getting in the way and Gabe craned his neck in an attempt to see. Words formed on his lips, but his mind was blank.

No.

Fucking no. Not Jason.

"CT." The man lying flush on Gabe's back barked out the name and had the suit sitting on top of Jason glancing up. Gabe recognized his face, then. CT, the bodyguard.

"Tell the cops he needs suicide watch," CT called. "Don't leave him until they make you."

"Roger," the giant on his back responded before pushing up to standing and yanking Gabe up along with him.

Gabe stared down at his friends. He couldn't rip his eyes away if he tried. There was blood spatter all over Jason's clothes and face, then a crimson puddle oozing out from somewhere beneath his back.

Val was leaning over him, cradling Jason's face in both of her hands while CT continued to apply pressure to Jason's shoulder.

"Open your eyes, baby," Val crooned, her voice shaking as she stroked her fingertips down her husband's cheek. "Come on back to me. There you go. It's not time to sleep right now, okay?"

As Gabe watched, Jason's eyelids fluttered. Groaning, the guy's face scrunched in pain and he sucked in a sharp breath. Gabe felt his heart re-start then. He hadn't known the thing had stopped beating until that moment.

"It's a shoulder wound," CT commented, his eyes locking on Val's face. "He'll be fine."

"You hear that?" Val stuttered. Leaning closer she pressed her lips to Jason's. Gabe could almost feel the guy sigh. "You can't leave me and I won't leave you, okay?"

"Gabe?" Jason rasped the question and had Gabe's gut dropping.

"He's fine," Val rushed, and glanced up to lock eyes with him.

What Gabe saw in those emerald green depths blew him away. She wasn't angry with him. Why the hell wasn't she fucking furious? He'd just shot Jason. Shot him. Could have killed him.

"He's *not* going to say anything to the police," Val continued, staring hard at Gabe. "He's going to wait patently for our lawyer, and he's absolutely *not* going to try to kill himself *ever* again."

Clenching his jaw, Gabe fought the stinging in his eyes and

the tightness in his chest. His face was throbbing and Jason was moaning and the sirens were screaming so loud now, it was like a hundred police cars had pulled to a stop outside.

At his back, the big bastard that had ahold of Gabe's arms gave him a little shake. Gabe swallowed hard and finally dropped his head in acceptance. He would do what Val asked of him. He had no right to refuse.

His eyes drifted to the sleek handgun that lay discarded on the swirling white marble floor. The giant behind him seemed to track his gaze.

"Just keep your mouth shut," he growled into Gabe's ear. "Live to fight another day."

Tilting his head up, Gabe stared at the vaulted ceiling. The pounding of boots sounded in the foyer. Dozens of cops flooded the room. There was some shouting. Hands were raised.

Gabe closed his eyes as they grabbed him. He heard the snap of cuffs, felt the bite of metal dig into his wrists. After that, it was all a blur.

As the giant behind him struggled to keep control of the situation, Gabe glanced back at Val over his shoulder. She wasn't looking at him anymore, she was looking down at Jason. Her blood stained hands were stroking his face.

An ambulance crew came rushing past, and Gabe watched dully. Jason would be okay. That's what CT had said.

At his side now, the giant tasked with watching him continued to bargain and cajole and keep pace with the officers as they led Gabe out of the house. He flashed some credentials, mentioned some past military service and name dropped his way into the front seat while Gabe was shoved unceremoniously into the back of a nearby police car.

Even the ride to jail wasn't long. At least it didn't seem that way to Gabe.

One moment he was leaning his head back against the stiff plastic seat, his arms bound awkwardly behind him, and the next thing he knew the car was shifting into park. Owen Beckett, because that was the giant's name, exited the shotgun seat, but waited casually for the police officer to come around and open the rear door.

Gabe blinked up at them both. Everything seemed too slow all of a sudden.

"You should get his face looked at," Owen commented as the officer reached in to grab Gabe's arm. "It's swelling pretty bad. His cheek could be broken."

"We have a nurse," the officer responded, nonplussed. "This is where we part ways, by the way."

Gabe scooted to the edge and struggled to stand up. The officer kept a tight grip on him even as he slammed the door closed and started walking.

"I was hoping to tag along," Owen countered, keeping pace as the officer led Gabe towards a giant red brick building.

"And I was hoping assholes would stop killing women, but here we are just the same." The officer squeezed Gabe's upper arm tighter and jerked him to a stop in front of the entrance to the jail.

Through the glass doors, Gabe could see a long desk with several men and women in blue uniforms standing behind it. Beside him, Owen's brow furrowed and he let loose a low sigh.

"Look, innocent until proven guilty right? You could have the wrong guy in custody right now. You weren't there."

The officer rolled his eyes and Gabe swallowed, letting his focus shift to his feet.

"All I know is, he's a suicide risk," Owen continued. "*And he's got very powerful people coming for him, a US Senator being one of them. You wouldn't want to be on the wrong side of that when it happens, right?*"

Silence settled between the two men and Gabe kept his eyes on his shoes. The shiny black tops were covered in dried blood. The streaks coated his feet and they didn't stop there. No, the cast-off spray stained his pants as well, though being black, the dark red of blood was more difficult to see.

Sharon's or Jason's? Sharon's or Jason's? He didn't know. Both, maybe.

"Fine." The officer heaved a tired breath. "Suicide watch. We'll take care of him, but you aren't coming in."

"Okay," Owen relented. Gabe watched the guy's wide hands come up, placating. "Alright."

Jerking open the glass door, the officer shoved Gabe through it and followed close behind.

Immediately, Gabe was assaulted with noise. The sounds of men talking, shoes skidding along linoleum, a tv blaring in the distance, metal doors slamming.

His vision narrowed into a tunnel and he felt suddenly short of breath. The reality of what he'd just done was finally sinking in. He'd been a prisoner his entire life. He'd been born into Cambric, with its guard staff and rules and high brick walls. He'd grown up there, lived there, for the vast majority of his life.

Then for a brief beautiful moment, he'd been free. His dreams had come true. All he'd ever hoped for, he'd gotten. Bee. Safety. Anonymity. Their island.

And even when he'd returned to Cambric, he hadn't quite given up hope. Hope that someday… somehow… he'd be free again. But now…

Now, he'd murdered someone, and not just anyone. Gabe was a captive, and he had murdered a free person.

Glancing around, he took in the sterile white walls, the security monitoring systems, the officer shoving him towards the desk. Inside here it was just like at Cambric. Here was just another form of captivity.

Maybe it had another name… jail.

Maybe it was run by another system… the government.

But here Gabe was just the same. And this time… *this* time, he would never, ever escape it.

CHAPTER 38

Bee

The hallway was narrow and it had no windows. Swiping her sweaty palms down her thighs, Bee took short, quick steps. Her black pencil skirt restricted her strides, but it was professional and conservative and expensive, so she'd put it on.

Smoothing at the white fabric of her button-down shirt, Bee fought the urge swirling inside of her. She could really use a drink right about now, just a tiny sip to take the edge off. But the answer was no, she reminded herself. No matter what happened, she was a mom now. She couldn't slip back into old habits.

Glancing quickly over her shoulder, Bee eyed the army of people following her down the corridor. The clicking of high heels and squeak of men's oxfords mixed with the heavy thud of guard's boots.

There were three prison guards bringing up the rear, and two walking up ahead of her. It took that many people to manage a group of their size. Five lawyers, two private security, a television crew, an annoyingly persistent journalist…

Overhead, a single tube of fluorescent lighting flickered as they passed. This place was so similar to Cambric, it had Bee's insides balling up.

Beside her, Bernard Durand cleared his throat. Catching her hand in his, her father gave a little tug and caught her eye. He was going to make this okay. That's what he'd said the second her plane had landed back in the States. *I'll take care of this Veronica. I promise.*

With a nod, Bee kept her hand laced with her father's and sucked in a breath. He was here, managing the chaos for Bee, while Lillian had flown to the Maldives to manage the kids. Thank God they were working together on this. Thank God they were willing to support her.

Not three days ago, when Bee'd gotten the call, it had been heart stopping. Without a second thought, she'd started packing. Jason had been shot. Sharon Baine was dead. Gabe was in jail. She'd wanted to fall apart right then, but she couldn't.

She'd had her children's eyes on her at the time (that's right *her* children, because they didn't have anyone else, now did they?) and so she'd done her best to hide her shaking hands. *I have to go on a little trip,* she'd explained. *I'll be back before you know it.*

There was some whining, some scoffing, some silence, and even some tears, depending on the kid. But the one thing they all had in common was the wariness lingering in their eyes. They were building trust… but slowly.

"Here." One of the guards came to a stop just ahead of them and jerked a thumb at a heavy metal door.

Bee took a steadying breath and dropped her father's

hand. Gabe was sitting behind that door. The guards had already pulled him from his cell, but the prison staff had really dragged their feet about the whole thing. It was late in the day now. There wouldn't be much time to speak with him before visiting hours came to an end and they were all kicked out.

"Maybe we should let Alan go in first." Bernard turned to his daughter and placed his hands on her arms. He was talking about his lead attorney, who was now officially *Gabe's* lead attorney. "Let him assess the situation. Last we heard, Gabe was detoxing from something."

"No." Bee was firm even as she hugged herself. "I want to see him first."

Bernard's head whipped up then, and he glared at someone over his daughter's shoulder. "Hey. You're not authorized to record this. Nothing until I say so."

Bee glanced back at the slim blonde reporter and her cameraman, both lingering a few steps away. Heidi Lincoln. The woman had some serious connections, which had gotten her a phone call with Alan, and then Bernard, and finally with Bee.

"We aren't filming," Heidi assured them and motioned for her camera guy to lower his lens. "And you can trust me. You've seen all the footage I have so far, I'm on your side."

"You're on your side," Bernard countered, his brow furrowing. "The side of ratings."

"I'm on the side of truth," Heidi corrected, then directed her gaze at Bee. "I just need an interview from him. Just ten minutes, I swear. You've seen everything I have."

Ducking her head, Bee acknowledged that statement. She'd seen it. When you couldn't sleep at night, you sat up for hours watching video footage sent to you by your father's high-powered attorney. And so far, it seemed Heidi Lincoln had evidence to spare.

An audio recording of Sharon promising to have Gabe delivered to Heidi's bed.

Video footage of two men shoving a collection of unknown pills into Gabe's mouth, then later dragging an unconscious Gabe up a flight of stairs.

Interviews from several women admitting to sleeping with Gabe, only to be blackmailed about it later. They were still so afraid that their names were redacted, their faces kept in shadow, and their voices distorted.

If she was to be believed, Heidi Lincoln was the last true investigative journalist with any sort of pull in the industry. She swore she had a prime time release slot lined up on one of the three major networks.

After months of work, she was ready to hit play.

The only thing that she *didn't* have was an honest interview from Gabe. And she wanted it… said she needed it for her piece, which she was calling: *The Captive Rising, The truth about the Cambric Agency and the legal sex trade.*

"Me first," Bee said, her eyes boring into Heidi's. "And if he agrees to it, then you can interview him."

"Alright." Heidi bobbed her head and glanced at her cameraman. "Okay, we'll wait here."

Sucking in a deep breath, Bee shook the nerves from her fingertips. She hadn't seen Gabe in over a year. At least, not in person. The last time had been on their dock in the Maldives, with him climbing into his sleek white powerboat, shoving designer sunglasses on his face and backing away.

Now here he was, just on the other side of the door.

Words floated through her mind. So many words.

Some from their attorney: he's detoxing, they don't have his blood work back yet, they don't know what he's on.

Some from Heidi: he's a rape victim, a sexual assault survivor, he exhibits all the classic signs of a battered spouse.

Some from Jason (while still lying grumpily in his hospital bed): he tried to kill himself, be careful what you say to him, we told him you have all of his kids.

Some from Val: he loves you, he's always been the strong one, help him to stay strong.

"Okay." Bee nodded to the guard. "Let me in."

Clasping her hands in front of her, Bee watched as the guard rapped his knuckles on the door before producing a set of keys and twisting them in the lock. Yanking on the handle, he pulled the door wide and Bee stepped in.

The first thing she noticed was that there was a window in the room. Her eyes darted instinctively up to it, such was a habit she'd picked up back at Cambric. The square of glass was fairly small and it had thick black bars running across it, but still, it was there.

In the corner just beside it, stood another prison guard. He was tall and thin, with a grayish-blue uniform and grim expression.

Her eyes flitted from him to a single wooden table positioned in the center of the concrete flooring. It had two matching chairs on opposite sides. In one chair, sat a man clothed in an orange jumpsuit. His head was tipped down, his hands folded together on the flat service, as if he were in prayer.

Around his wrists, a pair of shiny metal handcuffs were attached to a length of chain. From what she could tell, the chain ran from his wrists through a metal loop in the table and down off the side. Unable to blink, she tracked its path to where it cinched around the man's waist, then fell to the floor where it bound his ankles to yet another metal ring sunk into the concrete.

"Gabe," Bee breathed the word out into the air.

The man at the table did not look up.

His golden hair had been buzzed short, making it appear almost blonde. The skin of his neck was sallow and damp with perspiration.

The thing was, it wasn't hot in the room. No, it was quite cool actually. After a few more seconds of staring, she noticed him shivering. Detox. She knew it all too well.

"You can release him," she said, tipping her face up to eye the guard. "And then you can leave."

"Can't do that," the guard countered, rocking forward on his toes. "He's on suicide watch."

"I. Don't. Care." Bee gritted the words out, feeling a flood of frustration overtake her. "Go ask your superior, or I will."

With a smirk, the guard crossed the room and pushed open the door. After a few murmured sentences, he ducked his head back in and smiled at her.

"Can't release him, but I'll step outside," he said, and then walked out.

The sound of the metal door closing on the small empty space echoed sharply. The walls were concrete, the flooring too. It was so very similar to Isolation back at Cambric, except there was no glass partition in the wall, no mattress in the corner, no viewing window in the metal door.

"Gabe," Bee tried again, and still he did not stir. "Gabey. Please. Please look at me."

His shoulders hunched beneath the orange jumpsuit and

his hands clenched into fists on the tabletop. The chain running from his handcuffs scratched dully against the wood. Bee's insides somersaulted. Was he angry? Was he...

Taking a few steps forward, she heard the snap of her own high heels echoing against the flooring, but when he finally lifted his head, she froze.

Shifting to lean back in his chair, Gabe did as she asked of him. He looked at her.

Bee's throat closed in on itself. She couldn't swallow or speak, let alone breathe.

His face was broken. His right cheek was covered in purplish bruising, his left eye was black, both of his lips were split and swollen. Those chocolate brown eyes of his were glazed over, even as he kept his gaze averted.

Bee bit back a gasp. Gabe flinched.

After another long beat, he ducked his head, and cleared his throat.

"Bee Bee," he managed finally, before squeezing his eyes shut, and pressing his mouth into a firm line. "You should go."

"Wha- what?" Bee frowned.

"You. Should. Go." Gabe repeated the words slowly before he swallowed hard and turned his face towards the window.

As his fists clenched and unclenched, the metal chain on the table shifted, scratching on the wooden surface once more before clinking against his cuffs. He was trapped there. The most he could do was turn away.

"No," Bee whispered. "I choose to stay."

The muscles in Gabe's jaw ticked as she made her way over to him. He closed his eyes, but she knew he couldn't keep out the sound of her approach. Could he hear her heart beating for him? Could he hear it pounding furiously inside of her chest?

"Stop," he said, just before she reached out to touch him. "You don't know where I've been."

"Oh, Gabey." Bee's heart splintered as tears pricked at the backs of her eyes. "I know exactly where you've been, because I've been there, too. Remember?"

Climbing on top of Gabe's lap, Bee wrapped her arms around his shaking shoulders. It was awkward. With his bound hands wedged between them, the chain attaching him to the table dug into her side and the tabletop pushed into the middle of her back, but it also felt exactly right. Being this close to Gabe was *home*.

And by the way he buried his face in her neck and gripped the front of her blouse in his hands, she knew he felt it, too. They belonged together. They fit.

"I love you," she soothed, stroking both hands over his newly shaved head, then down his neck, and over his shoulders. "I should have come with you when you left the island. I should have spent every second with you that I could. I'm sorry."

"No," Gabe croaked the word, fighting against the silent tears that were dripping down between them. Shaking his head slowly side to side, he murmured against the skin of her neck. "I'm no good for you. You deserve so much better, Bee Bee. You always have. That's why you have to leave."

"Gabey..." Bee pressed her lips softly to his forehead, relishing in the way he leaned into her kiss. "I may have to leave you tonight, but I'm *always* going to come back. I'm taking a page from Jason's book. I'm not giving up. Not ever. We will get you out of this."

"There is no way out of this." Gabe yanked on her blouse before leaning his head back to stare into her eyes. "I've killed a free woman, in a room full of witnesses. This is it for me."

"Don't ever repeat that," Bee hissed. "Daddy has the best lawyers money can buy, and Heidi has made some good points. You may be able to claim self-defense. You exhibit all the classic signs of a battered spouse…"

"Wait," Gabe cut her off, as he worked to focus his eyes. "Heidi?"

"She's a reporter."

"No." Gabe shook his head almost violently, then cringed at his own rush of movement. "She's on Sharon's payroll. You can't trust her."

"I've seen the footage she's put together so far," Bee explained. "If she actually took money from Sharon, then she backstabbed her big time. The piece is all about abuse in the captive industry, specifically abuse of you. She has video evidence, audio recordings, witnesses. What they did to you, Gabey. It's all there for the world to see."

"Bee." Gabe sucked in a breath and let loose a long shudder. His skin was clammy beneath her fingers, but she stayed put. "My kids…"

"I have them." Bee nodded, then gulped at the half-truth. She just couldn't lie to him. Not with him raw and exposed like this. Not with him giving her his trust. "But not all of them."

"What?" Gabe's eyes widened, fear contorting his features.

"I have seventeen of your beautiful, healthy kids safe in the Maldives," Bee explained. "But the rest are still at Cambric."

"My boys?" Gabe's voice pitched as his hands began to shake between them. "Shane has… Shane will…"

"We've filed complaints with Child Protective Services, but at this point there's nothing more we can do," Bee rushed on. "The President is expected to sign the anti-captivity bill next week. When they're released, we'll be waiting for them. I swear it."

"That's never going to happen."

"Yes, it…"

"No." Gabe's body jerked as he attempted to shove backwards in his chair and failed. Apparently it was bolted to the floor. "That law's never going to get signed."

"But…"

"I'm telling you," Gabe cut her off. "Sharon made me… I mean I had to… *Shit.* Fuck. Bee Bee, I slept with the President's daughter. Sharon taped it and is using it to blackmail him. That law is never going to pass. My kids are never going to be free, and neither is anyone else."

Bee's mouth fell open a moment as the information washed over her. Blinking, she gave her head a little shake.

"No," she said. "That can't be right."

Squeezing his eyes shut, Gabe tipped his forehead to rest against hers. His hands spread themselves out over her belly. The chain connecting his cuffs to the table bit into her left side even further, but the discomfort was worth the closeness.

"I'm sorry," he whispered. "I've done things…" Trailing off, Gabe bit at his lower lip and sniffed. "A part of me really did want to die."

"Gabe."

"It would be better," he continued. "My boys would be safe right now. You could find someone who deserves you."

"Gabe." Bee gripped his shoulders and shook him until his

eyes popped back open and locked on hers. "Stop this right now. We can fight this."

Huffing a breath, Gabe went to look away but Bee stopped him. Placing her palms gently on both of his cheeks she forced him to stay still.

"We can get the truth out there," she said, feeling every bit of her words settle deeply in her soul. "We can tell the whole world what the President is going to do. We can put his corruption out there for the nation to see."

Gabe's eyes narrowed and he sucked in a breath.

"Can you do that, Gabey?" Bee asked quietly, her eyes darting back and forth across his face. "Can you tell Heidi the truth? Can you tell it to the world?"

CHAPTER 39

Charlie

IT WAS NEARING DUSK BY THE TIME THE DRIVER PULLED THE
dark sedan into Cambric's massive garage. Charlie sat stiffly
in the back. His spine was straight, his broad shoulders barely
kissing the leather of the seat.

Tension. He felt it in every inch of his being. The tightness
stretched itself along each muscle, working its way into his
very bones, it seemed.

"What a mess," the driver grumbled.

Beside him, a Cambric guard merely grunted. About a
hundred protestors had been blocking the wide iron gates.
They were holding signs, chanting and making a general
spectacle of themselves. But that was nothing new, they'd
been doing it for weeks now.

After a few blaring honks of the horn and an engine rev or
two, they'd separated just enough for the car to squeeze by.

"Just park already," the guard sighed. "Shane wants them
all in before the final meal."

Charlie's stomach clenched and his fists followed suit. *Shane*. That name alone had him burning.

You'd think the guy would ease up after the anti-captivity legislation had passed Congress and Sharon had lost her head… literally. But nope. The guy's grip on power had only tightened.

Of course, Charlie only knew these things because of Alana. His weekly visits with her were the only thing that made life worth living. Seeing her in that hotel room for a handful of precious hours was like walking all day through the desert and finally arriving at a pool of cool water.

Like a dying man, Charlie would dip his head down to her and drink, and drink, and drink. But when he came up for air, Alana would give him more news, and inevitably send him back on his way. Back to Cambric. Back to captivity. Back to hell.

And for Gabe… and his kids… and Val and Bee, Charlie returned meekly to his guard. Each and every time. Even though it made his insides scream. Even though he felt like flying all apart at any moment.

And it'd been going on like this for months now. But today…

Today had been something different.

Today, Alana had shown him a video on her phone. It was of Gabe. His face was a smashed up mess. His eyes were bloodshot. His words rasping, but clear. Oh, so fucking clear.

The Captive Rising. Rising from what, Charlie couldn't say. From the ashes? From the dirt and filth Sharon had immersed Gabe in?

No matter.

It was a national phenomena. Gabe was a phenomena. He

was now a viral video. An overnight sensation, complete with hashtags (whatever the fuck those were) and millions of shares and likes and blah blah blah.

Alana had been so excited about the video. She'd been so hopeful. *Change is coming. Can't you see, baby? You'll be out of this soon enough.*

God, she was so naive. And Charlie hadn't had the heart to dissuade her. He'd simply wrapped his arms around his wife, his woman, and held her closer to him. Because despite the viral video and the impending investigation into the President's "alleged" corruption, the anti-captivity legislation had fallen by the wayside.

The law was stalled out. It was sitting on the President's desk, where it would continue to sit, for God knew how long, until all of the accusations about his potential veto power were worked out.

So... no freedom for captives. Not now, anyway.

And that's when Gabe's final words on that video were hammered like stone into Charlie's mind.

They will never let you be free, Gabe had said, staring directly into the camera.

Shit, it was like he'd been speaking right to Charlie in that moment. *If you want freedom, then you're going to have to take it.*

Pressing his lips into a thin line, Charlie blinked away the memories and watched as the guard got out of the car and came around to pop open his door. The child locks were on. The rear doors didn't open from the inside.

"You good?" The guard asked, giving him a once over.

Charlie merely nodded and crawled out into the stale air of the garage. It was late spring in upstate, which meant the air during the day was warming up and lingering in the large metal building. It was muggy and uncomfortable. But that was life as a captive, muggy and uncomfortable.

Following behind the single guard, Charlie weaved his way through rows of cars, vans and limousines. In the far corner, a line of captives was filing through the single exit door. As they drew closer, Charlie could hear the incessant beep that signaled each captive's acceptance back into custody.

Beep.

The line would take a step forward.

Beep.

The next captive would file through.

Soon it was Charlie's turn. And like an obedient little sheep, he held his right forearm beneath the scanner affixed to the wall and listened to the sharp beep once more. Only this time, it struck like a lightning bolt straight to his soul.

He didn't want to do this anymore.

Suddenly, he was looking at the years he had left on his life, and he was seeing them stretch on and on and on into oblivion. He had decades left. *Decades*.

And they would all be lived right here within the walls of Cambric. Not with Alana. Not on their farm. Because Gabe was right. That law was never going to pass. And Charlie was never going to be free.

Sure, they'd keep trying. People like Jason Riggs would keep pushing, but the opposition would just keep moving the line. The goal was unattainable. Because one side was playing fair, and the other side was playing dirty.

So the people controlling Alana would tell her to wait. And in turn, Alana would tell him to be patient. And the carrot would keep dangling on a string in front of Charlie's face, and like an ass, he would keep plodding along towards it. But...

Fuck it.

Maybe it was time to even the score.

Striding into the courtyard, Charlie left his guard back in the garage. The guy was off the clock now and it was up to Charlie to see himself to dinner, or to the gym, or to shower, or to bed.

He didn't need an escort because he was considered a low-risk captive. He'd only ever made waves because of Val, and that little mess had since been trained out of him, or so Shane thought.

Lifting his eyes, Charlie took in the gray streaks reaching across a cloudless sky. He was scheduled for the last meal tonight due to his appointment with Alana. Sucking in a breath, Charlie let a small smirk cross his face. You know who else had last meal? Ben. Ben did. All the trainers did.

Moving quickly, Charlie directed his steps towards the cafeteria. He cut across the wide green lawn, feeling the spring beneath his shoes. His fingers itched and curled at his sides. Was he really going to do this?

Gabe's plan had seemed crazy to him before, but he'd always humored the guy. Back then, Charlie had just wanted Gabe to keep going. He'd just wanted his friend back. But now?

Now it seemed pretty fucking plausible.

And he'd tossed the idea around with Ben a time or two since Gabe had left. Ben was big and strong, and he had this buzz about him. It was like he was living on borrowed time, too. After having a taste of freedom, he'd never been able to ease completely back into captive life, same as Charlie.

Beeping his way through the double doors of the cafeteria, Charlie was assaulted with noise. Hundreds of captives were eating and talking under the bright fluorescent bulbs that populated the ceiling. Casually, Charlie selected a red plastic tray and slid into line.

As his eyes scanned the room, a white ceramic plate was placed on his tray. Yellow corn, not on the cob. A baked potato, no toppings. A small green salad, with tomatoes… yay. Chicken breast, no skin.

Years as a captive had him cataloging all of these tiny details. But for the first time in a long time, Charlie actually did not care. There, in the center of the room, hovering over some poor schmuck at the Discipline table, stood Shane. He had two guards with him, both of which looked bored out of their minds.

Charlie's fingers curled around his tray reflexively, and he felt his heart give a little extra tap against his ribcage.

Now for the missing puzzle piece.

Moving easily with the crowd, Charlie scrutinized each and every picnic table. When he found Ben, his eyes lit. *There's my boy.*

Settling down beside him, Charlie set his tray on the picnic table with a tap and closed his eyes. He wasn't even hungry. He'd lost his appetite the second that video of Gabe had played on Alana's phone.

"Are you a praying man now?" Ben asked quietly. His plastic fork stabbed at something on his plate, Charlie could hear it.

Huffing a breath, Charlie slowly opened his eyes. "Maybe I should be," he commented wryly before shooting Ben a wicked grin.

Ben's brow furrowed as he shoved the bite of chicken into

his mouth and proceeded to chew. "Something I should know?" He murmured, after he'd swallowed.

"Little message from Gabe," Charlie acknowledged, and felt everyone around them fall to silence.

"Oh yeah?" Ben's eyes darted all around before he placed both of his elbows on the table and pretended to care about his food.

"The law isn't going to pass," Charlie said quietly. "He says we're never going to be given freedom. He says we'll have to take it."

A ripple went around their table after his announcement. Captives bent their heads closer to one another, murmuring and grumbling. Ben cleared his throat and shifted uncomfortably on the bench seat.

"I thought that was supposed to be a sure bet," he hissed.

"No such thing," Charlie countered.

Placing a wide palm flat on the tabletop, Charlie leaned back slightly and tapped his pointer finger on the plastic surface for several moments. The cafeteria was buzzing still, but the energy in the air was changing.

News was getting around fast, but to the Cambric staff it all still sounded the same. Captives eating. Captives talking.

"I don't know what to say," Ben admitted finally. He gave his head a little shake and pressed his lips into a thin line.

Turning to look at him, Charlie watched Ben's jaw tick as his teeth ground together inside of his head.

"I'm done," Charlie said. "I'm ready to be done."

Whipping his head up, Ben met Charlie's gaze. When the two of them had discussed Gabe's plan a few months ago, it'd been hypothetical. They'd worked through scenarios, sharing whispered words in the workout room. It had been a fantasy really. A far reaching fantasy.

"You aren't…"

"I am," Charlie cut him off and bobbed his head. "Are you willing to run interference? I'm not sure how much shit you'll be in."

"Fuck," Ben spat the word out and looked down at his hands.

Charlie stared down at the guy's hands, too. They were resting on his lap, palms up. They were smooth and free of the sort of calluses they'd once earned.

Ben had told Charlie about the orchard. About his year away. Turns out they had more than a few things in common. Farming and rural life being one of them.

All around them now the buzzing continued. In that moment though, it seemed like they were all alone. Ben rolled his wrists, cracking the joints before heaving out a long sigh. His shoulders slumped briefly before his spine snapped straight.

Then, without a word, he shoved up from the table, grabbed Charlie's full tray of food and walked away.

This is happening.

Charlie's eyebrows lifted in momentary shock before his body caught up with his mind. Then he was getting up, too. His heart was thundering against his ribcage, his breath was hot in his lungs.

Cruising empty-handed between the rows of tables, Charlie's eye tracked Ben's progress. He was just one body among many. A big body… but still, Shane's guards didn't even look his way.

Clenching his hands into fists, Charlie blinked purposefully, trying to sharpen his focus. He had to hang back in the crowd for a bit, lingering maybe ten feet from the Discipline table while Ben cut across the open space.

Shane had his back to them. He was sneering down on the poor captive hunched at the Discipline table. It was a woman. She was thin, her black hair dripping wet, her feet bare. Charlie swallowed.

He didn't recognize her from behind, not in her uniform, but he knew her in the same way that he knew himself. She was hungry. She was thirsty. She was sore and tired and broken.

The way they all were. The way he himself was. But no more.

He couldn't stomach it for a single breath more.

Lifting his chin, Charlie stared at Ben's back. His old friend did not turn around. He just continued to cross the space, passing Shane casually and moving directly in front of the guards.

Charlie froze. Every muscle in his body tingled. His lungs expanded as he held his breath.

Then Ben was tripping. He was falling forward suddenly, and the full tray of food he clutched in both hands exploded all over one of the guards.

"Oh," Ben exclaimed loudly, as his knees hit the hard ground. "I'm so sorry."

"What the hell," the guard spoke the words with more annoyance than anything else, as he looked down at his food-covered clothes.

The second guard standing beside him laughed. *Laughed.*

Then Shane was looking up, resting his fists on his hips and shaking his head slowly side to side. All of his awareness was facing the guards. He didn't even feel Charlie lingering at his back.

Bingo.

This was it. And all it took was five strides. He was so close. This was so much easier than he'd imagined.

Without hesitation, Charlie closed the distance between them until his chest bumped into Shane's back. Then he did what he'd seen in those videos on the internet. When Alana had been passed out in their hotel bed and Charlie had hours left on his time with her, he'd taken her phone and done a little research.

So it was easy really.

Charlie wrapped his right hand around Shane's chin and braced his left on the back of the guy's head. Then he twisted as fast and hard as he could, making sure to bring the asshole's chin up at an angle towards the ceiling while he pushed the back of the guy's head down to the floor.

And fuuuuccckk. He *felt* the snap. It took more force than he thought, but it was quick.

Stepping back, Charlie stared dumbly as Shane's lifeless body collapsed to the floor. His own mouth parted slightly, as if mimicking the death he saw there.

In front of him, the captive at the Discipline table began to scream.

Then the guards were on him. He was being slammed to the ground.

His back took the hit against the concrete. His breath exploded out of his lungs.

"Code five! Code five!" One of the guards was shouting, as the other one rolled Charlie onto his belly. "We need a medic! We need..."

"Shane's dead!" The female captive climbed up onto the Discipline table and started yelling. "Don't just stand there! There's five hundred of us and five of them!"

Charlie blinked up at her, his face turned to the side as the guard on his back zip-tied his wrists together. That's when he heard it. The rumble of the floor beneath his ear was explosive. A thousand feet were moving at once.

Pandemonium.

In an instant, the weight on his back disappeared. The guard shoved away from him and was gone. There were shouts. Tables screeched and shifted across the floor. The sound of breaking glass popped in the distance.

In front of his face, Charlie could see feet criss-crossing, then he was being yanked upright.

"We've gotta get you out of these," Ben's voice sounded against the back of his neck. "The kitchen should have knives."

Nodding, Charlie picked up his feet. Together, he and Ben ran into the crowd. They pushed through the flow of bodies, all trying to make it out of the cafeteria. He and Ben were pushing up stream, heading past the food distribution line and into the now unguarded doors to the kitchen.

On the threshold, Charlie stopped and stared.

"Holy. Shit." Ben exhaled the words just behind him.

They weren't the first to get here. Captives were dashing through the space, knives clutched in their hands.

Every burner on every stove was set to high, and that was a lot of stoves. Flames were licking at the air. A captive darted by, tossing dish towels on the burners. Smoke began rolling.

"Find a knife," Ben bit out shakily. "I'll pull the fire alarm. They're going to burn the building down."

Without a word, Charlie ducked into the space. His hands

were bound at his back, but he crossed to a set of drawers and turned around. Awkwardly, he began yanking drawers open and glancing over his shoulder to see what was inside.

It was getting hotter, smokier. Perspiration beaded on his brow. He started coughing.

Then the fire alarm went off. A bright flash of white light strobed the room and a siren let loose in a series of bursts. Every locked door in the building automatically swung open. It was the law, after all.

And even though they'd never had a fire drill at Cambric, the building was inspected by the government once a year. The stairwells that were kept locked and off limits to captives, were now flung open. All the doors, too. They were expected to file peacefully into the courtyard, and line up, even though they'd never actually done it.

Charlie's hands closed on the black handle of a knife. His lips curled into a sneer. They were expected to do a lot of things, now weren't they?

"Thank fuck." Ben returned to his side, hacking and wheezing into his shirt. The smoke was thick as it curled against the ceiling.

Taking the knife from Charlie, he sawed quickly back and forth. After a few seconds, the zip ties sprang apart. Charlie rubbed at his wrists and darted for the door. Ben pocketed the knife and chased after him.

When they entered the cafeteria, it was nearly deserted. A few stragglers were leaping through shattered windows out onto the grass. The fire alarm continued to blare. There were no guards, no staff and next to no captives. It was almost peaceful.

Charlie inhaled deeply and glanced at Ben.

Then the gunshots rang out.

Pop, pop, pop, pop, pop. A rapid succession sounded somewhere out in the courtyard. Screams that had been dull background noise a moment before, now rose in pitch and frequency. Charlie swore as he and Ben both started running.

Glass crunched beneath their feet as they jumped through a partially shattered window and out onto the lawn. It was dark outside, with thousands of bodies swirling together in the courtyard.

All around them, the high brick walls of the perimeter loomed. Across the way, the doors leading to Isolation and the front office stood open. To their right, the doors to both dormitory towers were also open. Out of them poured a steady stream of bodies. Captive bodies.

"Get back!" A male voice was screaming. "Stay back!"

Then the gunshots came again. Pop. Pop.

Pop, pop, pop, pop.

Charlie's eyes shifted towards the sound as bodies started dropping indiscriminately. There was a guard standing on the far wall over by the iron gates. He was screaming as captives slipped through the bars.

"Break the gates!" Charlie shouted. Then he was running.

Ben followed, echoing him, "Break the gates! Push them open!"

The crowd was resistant at first as Charlie and Ben pushed and shoved their way across the courtyard. But then all at once Charlie felt the tide change. They were all moving in the same direction, now. They were all heading towards the same goal.

When they neared the black iron, the guard standing atop

the brick wall continued to fire. All around them, bodies fell. People screamed and shoved and panicked.

"Push!" Charlie shouted. "Help me push!"

He wrapped his hands around the cold iron and shoved forward. Ben did the same. Then another captive, then another. Beside him, Charlie watched smaller captives continue to wriggle through the bars and flee into the waiting crowd of protestors.

On the far side, the protestors were screaming. Some held up their phones, recording everything.

Bullets rained down.

People continued to stack up on either side of Charlie until there wasn't any room left. Then more began to press into his back. The weight of their bodies made it so he could hardly breathe.

He was being crushed against the gates. He was too big to squeeze through the bars.

Sucking in a shallow breath, Charlie gasped for air. Then his vision was blurring, and his body was screaming, and the noise all around him began to fade away.

Seemingly at a distance, he heard another barrage of bullets.

Then felt the release.

The gate collapsed, sending him flying forward. He landed in a heap on top of the bars. His lungs expanded of their own accord, demanding the air they had so recently been denied. His mouth hung open, his extremities tingled.

All around him, people were running. He felt their shoes hit his back, his legs and arms. Captives were fleeing, pouring out of the gates, stomping all over him.

"Stop!" A voice was screaming. "You're going to kill them!"

And for the second time in less than an hour, Ben was yanking Charlie back to his feet. Once they were both upright, there was no fighting the tide. They tripped and stumbled and ran together until they were free of the gates.

Looking back over his shoulder, Charlie watched his fellow captives flowing like a river out of Cambric. The gunshots had ceased. The guard on top of the wall was gone.

"Let's go," Ben hissed, gripping Charlie's upper arm tight in his hand. "Don't look back."

Returning his focus forward, Charlie's eyes zeroed in on the tree line just across the paved road. He picked up his feet, charging towards it, with hundreds of other captives at his side.

He was free.

He was out.

And *this* time, he was never going back.

Jason

"It's getting messy out there," Owen commented.

Jason tipped his head up from his seat on the edge of the hotel bed and eyed his personal bodyguard. The guy's massive shoulders filled the far window. The golden-hued drapes were pulled slightly to one side as he stood there, looking down at the surrounding DC streets.

Darkness framed him. It was the middle of the night, but they were both fully dressed and on edge.

"You don't have to stay," Jason forced the words to pass his lips even as his right shoulder throbbed.

Damn bullet wound was a through and through they'd said. He was lucky it hadn't hit bone or blown all apart inside of him. But still… it fucking *hurt*. He'd been released from the hospital over a week ago, and yet the pain lingered.

At the window, Owen merely shrugged. He wasn't going anywhere.

With CT escorting Val and Jace back to France, they both

knew how false Jason's offer to leave actually was. The streets were crawling with rioters. Police sirens echoed constantly, followed quickly by fire trucks. A revolution was happening and before too long, the city was going to burn. Jason needed Owen's protection.

"You locked and loaded?" Owen asked.

"Yeah." Jason dipped his head as his eyes traveled to the gun lying on the mattress beside him.

It was one of CT's. He'd given it to Jason before he'd boarded a private jet two days previous. Val and Jace were with him, along with Jason's mother, both of his sisters and their families. His father and brother left the following day. They were all in France now and that was a good thing. Jason had wanted them out of the country, even if he himself was unable to go.

The writing on the wall was pretty clear now. The anti-captivity bill wasn't going to pass legally and so shit was hitting the fan, so to speak. After Gabe's video went viral, people were taking to the streets. Things were getting violent.

"Any reason this couldn't be done in a safe house with a White House backdrop?" Owen grumbled.

"No time," Jason offered.

But that wasn't the real reason. Nope. This had been a stipulation from Clay Montgomery himself. Jason had to make a video in person, in front of the White House, no exceptions.

The Constitutional Militia required this final thing from him, and if Jason didn't uphold his part of the bargain, then they wouldn't uphold theirs. Which would make the past year and a half of Jason's life pointless.

On the bed, lying beside the black handgun, Jason's cell

phone lit up. An incoming call from a blocked number flashed across the screen. This could be the one he'd been waiting for.

Reaching for his cell, he swiped his thumb quickly to accept the call and held the phone up to his ear. A familiar voice rumbled on the other end; for once, it had his nerves settling.

"Cambric burned to the ground last night," Agent Finn began. He was so fucking casual, like it hadn't made headline news.

"Body count?" Jason cut to the chase. His shoulder ached.

"Thirty-seven," Finn stated.

"Women and children?" Jason bit his lip.

"A few," Finn admitted. "But they were gunshot victims."

Jason squeezed his eyes shut. One of the guards on site had flipped out and sprayed the crowd with bullets. A group of protestors had been outside the gates at the time and recorded the entire thing with their phones.

And Jason had seen the videos. He'd heard the screaming, as had every other person in the world with access to a television or phone. It was all over the news, all over social media. It was sickening.

"Anyone we know?" Jason inhaled sharply through his nose.

"One." Finn cleared his throat.

Don't be Gabe's kid. Don't be Gabe's kid. The words ran like ticker tape through Jason's mind.

"Shane Hayes," Finn announced, and Jason could practically see the serious FBI Agent grinning. "His body is pretty badly burned, but they're 99% sure that it's him. Autopsy is scheduled for tomorrow."

Jason's mouth twisted into a small smile as his chest lifted. "Looks like neither one of us got a chance at him then."

"Yeah." Finn blew out a breath. They'd both wanted to kill the bastard. "Looks that way."

"So…" Jason's eyes flipped up to lock on Owen's back. The burly guard was still standing at the window, still staring out into the night. "I'm right where our buddy wants me. I'm right in the middle of the shit."

"What about your family?" Finn asked.

"They already landed in France," Jason offered, though he was almost positive Finn knew this. "Everyone but Bee. Her dad's freaking out."

"We have her," Finn confirmed what Jason had already suspected. "She's safe. She wouldn't leave without him."

"Figured as much." Jason exhaled and went to lift his arm to the back of his neck before remembering his wound. Wincing, he gritted his teeth and returned his right hand to his lap. "Everything's exploding, Agent. Our buddy has the chaos he wanted. When can I finish my part?"

"You can shoot the video tonight," Finn instructed. "Make sure the White House is in the background, all lit up and pretty. When it's done, send the video on to Clay directly. He'll use it when the time is right, maybe over the next few days."

"And how will I know you've done your part?" Jason asked, gripping the fabric of his slacks in his hand.

The timing of this production was not lost on him. He'd played this game for long enough now. The country was filled with tension and uncertainty. If Clay wanted to make his move for power, now was the time. When the public was questioning its own government. When the country's citizens were consumed by fear.

All of the captive agencies were currently on lockdown. Across the country, there were multiple reports of internal riots, violence and destruction on a massive scale.

Somehow, the captives on the inside of the agencies had gotten information about Gabe and *The Captive Rising* video. They knew the anti-captivity law was stalled out on the President's desk. They were revolting.

People were taking to the streets now, captive and free alike. Protesting, burning businesses, looting. It was widespread chaos. It was an uprising.

Agency owners were calling for the President to intervene. They wanted him to send in the national guard. The thing was, half of the military was made up of G1s, Government Captives.

Would the President send captives to put down a captive uprising? Would the G1s shoot their own?

"Once I get the confirmation from Clay that he received your video, I get my walking papers," Finn announced.

On the other end of the line, Jason listened to the snap of a gun loading. It made his heart jump.

"You're going in there yourself?" Jason ventured, he was almost jealous.

"I'm heading a small team," Finn confirmed. "So get to it, *Senator*."

Jason huffed a breath and felt a familiar warmth flood him. "Finn," he said quietly, closing his eyes.

"Yeah?"

"Stay safe, friend."

"You too," Finn echoed just as quietly. "I told you I was sorry."

"Yeah." Jason cleared his throat. "Just keep our boy safe, and we're even."

"Roger, that," Finn responded, then the call cut out.

CHAPTER 41

Gabe

Lying on his back, with his hands folded over his stomach, Gabe stared up at the ceiling. It was made of concrete. Surprise, surprise, his favorite thing ever. There were cracks splintering in a thousand directions. He traced them with his eyes.

Beneath him, the mattress was lumpy and thin, but despite all that, he looked at the positive. At least he was up off the floor, *and* there was no other bunk looming above him. One of the perks of being on suicide watch was no jail buddy to share a cell with.

The steel frame of his bed was shoved up against the length of one wall and there was even a small wooden desk complete with a chair situated on the opposite side. In the back corner, there was a silver metal toilet (that didn't have any water in it) and a tiny metal sink.

That particular item *did,* in fact, drip a steady bit of water.

Over and over and over again, Gabe listened to a solitary drop hit the sink.

Maybe it would have driven someone else insane, but Gabe sort of liked the water. It was a different kind of company. Not like the waves lapping at the shoreline in the Maldives, but still.

Somewhere off in the distance, a door slammed. It wasn't an unusual sound here. Doors were always slamming. Sometimes the sound was accompanied by yelling and the echo of voices.

Because the door to Gabe's cell was solid, he could never quite make out the words, if there were any words being said at all. It could just be someone screaming. That was a definite possibility.

Exhaling a long breath, Gabe continued to scrutinize the ceiling. It was pretty high, actually. He could only touch it when he stood on his desk, which was bolted to the floor. There were a few names scratched into the surface. Either it was done with someone's fingernail or maybe this cell wasn't always the suicide cell.

Maybe *Dave* and *Ricky* and *Zero* had been given pens. Sure looked like it.

Closing his eyes, Gabe let his face fall to one side. His cheek still throbbed, and the twin splits to both of his lips had scabbed over. But the general swelling to his face was going down and he no longer felt like he was going to throw up every second of the damned day.

The process of detox was chugging right along. He was unsure how many days he'd been in here altogether, but at least he'd gotten to see Bee that one time.

His heart pinched in on itself at the memory of her. She

was so unbelievably beautiful. And he was so unforgivably wretched.

The things he had done… they haunted him. Made him feel tainted and dirty. If he'd had access to a shower, he would have scrubbed and scrubbed at his skin. But he didn't. They'd sprayed him with a hose once and tossed powdered soap on him, but that was it.

Another door slammed. Gabe rolled onto his side.

Raising a finger, he traced the spiderweb of cracks that populated the wall. Here too, were many names. Names and hash marks and little doodles. Mostly of dicks. Why the hell would you sit here and draw a damn dick on the wall? Of all the things you could draw…

Gabe sighed.

A door slammed again. Closer this time. Gabe lifted his head slightly and frowned.

Boots squeaked on linoleum. Many boots. There was shouting in the distance, and then an alarm went off.

Pushing up on one hand, Gabe angled his body so he could look at his door. It had a single pane of square glass near the top, but it was covered from the outside with a white flap of some sort. The flap was thicker than paper, but beyond that Gabe couldn't tell. Vinyl, maybe? Cloth?

As part of Gabe's life here, a guard would come to his door once every hour, lift the flap and tap on the glass. If Gabe didn't want trouble, he would have to wave at the door in response. That way the guard had confirmation that Gabe hadn't managed to off himself. Lowering the flap, the guard would move away.

Rinse. Repeat. Time and time and time again.

Even throughout the night, a guard would come. Gabe

never got to sleep for more than an hour at a time. It sort of made him miss the pills, if he was being honest.

So even with the alarm sounding loudly in his ears, Gabe watched for the lift of the flap. He'd learned to anticipate it, to expect it. So this time when it finally came, he had his wave ready.

Gabe rocked up to sitting, raised his right hand above his head and stopped short.

A pair of dark eyes assessed him. He knew that fucking twinkle.

"Get back!" The voice shouted, and the flap dropped back into place.

What the…

Boom.

The blast from the door had him scrambling. Gabe backpedaled off the bed, landing hard on his tailbone. Smoke rolled into the room, then a flood of bodies. Four military bodies, all clothed in black from head to toe, with ski masks pulled over their heads and shiny rifles clutched in their gloved hands came to stand over him.

"Well if it isn't our very own *captive rising*," one of the men said.

Sauntering over to the corner, with the solid door hanging open behind him, came the familiar soldier. It was like a damn movie. Gabe blinked slowly as the man crouched and gave him a once over.

"Hello, Gabriel," the soldier said quietly. "Maybe next time you'll listen to me when I tell you not to do something, yeah?"

"Finn?" Gabe's mouth dropped as the soldier nodded.

"Ready to blow this popsicle stand?" Finn asked. Rising to his feet, he offered Gabe a hand. "I know I am."

CHAPTER 42

Bee

Examining her reflection in the mirror, Bee tucked her short chestnut hair behind her ears. No. That wasn't quite right. Shifting on her bare feet, Bee brushed her fingers through her hair again and brought it forward. Better.

Blowing out a breath, she stepped back and smoothed her palms down the front of her soft cotton dress. It was a cream color with pale green pinstripes running its short length.

Ugh. Too cliche? A dress? But it brought out the emerald in her eyes, and she wanted to look good.

Stomping out of the small bath, Bee paced to the window of her second story bedroom and looked out. The valley that unfurled itself in front of her was lush and green. Bee's eyes traced the winding path of the dirt road that ran from the front of the farmhouse, skirted a wide cow pasture, then disappeared into the distance.

It faded from view far too quickly in a thick stand of trees.

A mix of pines and hickory and maple populated the whole area, crawling up the steep mountains that surrounded the farm on all sides. They were remote, to say the least.

She was in the heart of the Constitutional Militia now, but even so she felt completely safe. Ava had sent her here after Bee had called from DC. Gabe's video had gone viral and people were taking to the streets. There were riots and looting.

Daddy was frantically trying to ship her out of the country (despite her resistance) and Jason was, too. Between the both of them, Bee knew she didn't stand a chance. So when Val and Jace had both boarded their private jet, Bee made yet another choice.

She chose to disappear.

Yes, she knew she should be leaving the country, too. It was the smart move after all. But try as she might, she just couldn't bring herself to escape this crumbling world without *him*. So Ava had sent a car for her, and that was that.

A rap on her bedroom door sounded out, causing Bee to glance over her shoulder.

"Come in," she called and listened to the creak of the door opening.

"He'll be here in five minutes," Ava said, balancing her little dark-haired daughter on her hip. "Just stay up here okay? He's a bit unsteady, so we'll bring him to you."

"Unsteady?" Bee's brow furrowed and she nibbled at her bottom lip.

"He's in one piece," Ava assured her. "It's just a lot to take in. You understand."

"Yeah." Bee ducked her head. "Okay."

Returning her gaze forward, Bee studied Ava's reflection

in the window pane. The petite blonde was lingering, staring intently at Bee's back. She was pretty, with delicate features that she'd obviously gifted to her young daughter. On her hip, the child babbled and giggled and yanked on Ava's blouse.

"We'll find the rest of his kids," Ava said finally. "This mess will settle down, and we'll be able to track them. I'm sure they're fine."

"Thank you," Bee whispered the words before exhaling a shaky breath.

"Look, Charlie made it back to Alana, right?" Ava went on, even as her daughter's giggling turned into protesting screeches. "Gabe's making it back to you. We'll get the kids, too. That's all I'm saying."

"Of course." Bee swallowed hard and fought the pin prick of tears threatening to fall. She didn't want to fail him. She didn't want to fail any of them. "Thank you for all you've done, Ava. Seriously."

"You helped too, you know." Ava shifted the child to her other hip and began to bounce her. "Just a little."

Huffing out a quick laugh, Bee dipped head in acceptance. Seemingly satisfied, Ava pulled the door closed and padded off down the hallway.

Leaning her hands on the wooden ledge of the windowsill, Bee resumed her vigil. It was mid-afternoon maybe, with the sun having already started its slow descent towards its destination in the west. The air outside was warm and fresh. The air inside, too.

Before too long, an old pickup truck broke through the far tree line. Bee's eyes snapped to it as her heart picked up the pace. Gabe was in there, right? He was in there and he was in one piece... just unsteady.

God, what did that even mean?

Shoving away from the window, Bee started for the door before remembering Ava's words. They wanted her to stay put. They would bring him up to her. Slapping her hands against her thighs, Bee bit back a growl and returned to the window.

Stay put. Stay put. When had she ever agreed to such a thing in her life?

But then the truck was stopping in front of the house and a man was shoving out of the driver's seat. He was dressed in simple blue jeans and a black t-shirt. Bee couldn't make out his face beneath his ball cap, but then Ava was rushing out to greet him and he was wrapping her and the baby up in his arms.

The little girl squealed and Bee's heart felt like it was going to explode. That wasn't her Gabe. He was familiar somehow, in a way she couldn't quite place, but he was definitely not *her* man.

That's when the passenger side door opened with a pop and another man climbed out. He too was wearing blue jeans and a black t-shirt. A navy-blue ball cap was pulled low on his head, but unlike the first man, he glanced up at the house.

It was like he could sense her. It was like he knew she was there, staring at him, because his eyes locked immediately onto hers through the window and her breath hitched.

"Gabe," Bee gasped the word before slamming one palm flat against the glass.

"Go on," the driver called out to him, causing Gabe to break eye contact and glance at him over his shoulder. "Up the stairs, second door on your right."

In an instant, Gabe was gone. Bee watched him jog up the porch steps, duck under the overhang, and disappear.

Shoving back from the window, she turned on her heel and ran to her door. Her breath was coming quick now as nervous tingles exploded in her body. Gabe was here. He was all right. He wasn't chained to a table or flashing that fake smile at a camera.

Wrapping her hand around the brass knob, Bee yanked the door open. A heavy set of footsteps pounded their way towards her up the wooden stairs. Bee stepped out into the hall, one hand clutching instinctively at her throat. She could feel her pulse jumping beneath her fingers.

Then Gabe was cresting the stairs.

"Bee Bee," he called, his long legs eating the distance between them.

"I'm here," she answered before he slammed into her.

Wrapping his arms around her body, Gabe picked her up and backed them both into her bedroom. With a kick, he swung the door shut behind them and clutched her tighter. Every inch of his body was pressed hard against every inch of hers. So much so, that she could feel him shaking.

"Bee Bee," he repeated, burying his face in her neck. "Oh my God, Bee. Oh my God."

"Hey," she soothed. Reaching up to the back of his neck, she stroked at his skin. "It's alright. It's all gonna be alright, now."

"I love you so much," he croaked, squeezing her. "Did I ever tell you that? I'm so fucking crazy about you."

"You did." She nodded as tears poured from her eyes. "So many times you told me. And I'm crazy over you too, remember? I'm in love with you too, Gabey."

"Fuck. *Why?*" Pulling back, Gabe let go of her abruptly and ran a frustrated hand along the back of his neck. "I'm so bad for you, Bee Bee. I've always been beneath you, and now... and now after I..."

"Stop this," Bee whispered.

Reaching up, she pressed her palms gently to his cheeks. Her thumbs brushed slowly over the stubble that had grown there. "You've done nothing wrong."

Squeezing his eyes shut, he turned his face away with a grimace. "Every inch of my skin *itches*. I wish I could scrub it all off. I wish I scrub *them* off of me."

"Hey." Bee frowned. "It's over now, okay? It's all over."

"I killed someone," he bit out, his eyes popping open to settle back on hers. "And I can't stop thinking about it. I can't stop seeing it... seeing *her*."

"Come here." Tugging Gabe towards her Bee backed up to her bed and sat. "Let's give you something else to think about okay? You want to see your kids? I've got so many pictures of them now."

"You do?" Gabe remained standing, hesitating as she patted the mattress beside her.

Giving him a reassuring smile, Bee reached for her phone on the nightstand and began pulling up photos. After flashing the first one at him, Gabe caved. Plopping down heavily beside her, he tipped his head against hers and watched.

Bee scrolled and scrolled and scrolled. She offered comments on each and every photo. Annalise playing by the sand. Robin making silly faces in the kitchen. Evan getting tangled in his fishing line. Reed with his arm wrapped around Declan's shoulders, the two of them grinning at the camera.

About halfway through, Gabe began to soften. His shoulders eased, he flung his arm around Bee's waist, she could hear him sigh.

When they were finished looking, Bee set the camera aside and crawled up into bed. Gabe kicked off his shoes, flung the covers aside and tucked himself in beside her.

With his arms wrapped around her body, his chest pressed to her back, Bee blinked into the darkening room and listened as Gabe drifted off to sleep. They were still fully clothed. Him in his blue jeans and shirt, her in her dress, but that was alright. She didn't care.

She was just happy to be near him, to have him safe and beside her. They would figure out everything else as it came.

Sometime in the middle of the night, Bee awoke. She wasn't sure what did it. Her eyes just popped open and she stared into the dark. Moonlight poured through the bedroom windows, casting shadows along the floor.

At her back, she could feel an emptiness. Gabe. He was gone.

Sitting up swiftly, Bee cast the covers aside and glanced about the room. That's when she heard it. The running water. The spray of the shower. Eyes narrowing, she noticed the light filtering out beneath the closed door of the ensuite bathroom.

"Gabe?" She called. Her voice was raspy with sleep, so she cleared her throat. "Gabe?"

He didn't answer.

Shoving out of bed, Bee walked in bare feet over to the door and twisted the knob. It was locked.

"Gabe?" Bee tried again, louder. It was hard to keep the panic out of her voice. "Are you alright? If you don't answer me, I'm coming in."

No answer. The water continued to pour down. That was the only sound.

Reaching up on her tip toes, Bee ran her fingers along the ridge of the door frame. An old time push key fell to the floor where she bent to clutch it in her trembling hands.

He was okay, she told herself. He was just showering. In the middle of the night. Without warning. For no reason.

Pushing the key into the tiny hole in the knob, Bee heard the lock pop and quickly she pushed the door wide.

"Gabe?" She asked again, more tentative this time.

Steam filled the space. It was hot and sticky and humid. Stepping into the room, she held her breath before pulling aside the flowery shower curtain.

"Oh Gabey," Bee exhaled sadly. "What are you doing?"

He was sitting on the floor of the shower, his knees bent, his arms wrapped loosely around them. His shaved head was hanging down as water poured all over him.

At her words, he did not look up. He was naked. His skin bright red from the scalding hot spray.

Crouching down, Bee braced one hand on the edge of the tub and tilted her head to one side. How long had he been in there?

Narrowing her eyes, she noted the rawness of his skin. It wasn't just the hot water that had him red. He was covered in rough scratches.

"What's all this?" She asked, extending a finger to trace lightly down his arm.

"Just trying to get clean," he murmured, lifting his head to eye her. "Just trying to get them off me."

Pursing her lips, Bee fought the overwhelming sadness that flooded her.

"You've hurt yourself," she noted carefully.

"They're still all over me." He sniffed and looked away, still sitting in the bottom of the tub, still letting the hot water bounce off of him. "I can't get clean."

"Gabey," she whispered. "You can't hurt yourself like this. I won't let you."

"I have to get clean," he said, his eyes shooting back up to hers. "For you. For my kids. But I can't get them off of me."

"Okay." Bee ducked her head. "Alright, Gabey. I know how to get you clean."

"You do?" His brow furrowed.

"We're going to wash each other," she supplied before pushing up to standing and stepping into the shower with him. "I was just like you, remember? Everything you've had to do, I've had to do it, too. So if you're dirty, then so am I."

Shaking his head abruptly, Gabe huffed out a short breath. "No, you're not," he argued. "You…"

"Yes…" Bee cut him off. "We're just the same and we're going to get clean right now, together."

Tipping his head up, Gabe's dark eyes tracked over her dress as water poured down to soak it. He frowned.

Standing up straighter, Bee pulled the straps off of her shoulders, then reached behind her back to undo the zipper. It fell heavily down around her ankles, where she bent to pick it up and fling it out of the shower. Her panties came next. She hadn't bothered with a bra.

The faucet was pelting her head and back now. It was so

insanely hot. Her hair was drenched and her skin stinging. Even so, she endured the spray.

Gabe's gaze crawled up to her neck, lingering there before settling on her mouth. She swallowed and held perfectly still, letting him take his time, letting him look. His stare burned into her flesh for several seconds before it traveled back down the length of her body.

His eyes absorbed the swell of her chest, the dip in her waist, the flare of her hips, the flesh of her thighs. He licked his lips. They weren't swollen anymore, but the split in both the top and bottom were scabbed over.

"It's too hot for you," he commented.

Pushing up to standing, Gabe took a step forward until the entire length of his naked body was hovering inches from hers. Bee had to tip her head back to look into his face. His lips were pressed in a firm line, his brow still furrowed as he reached around her to adjust the water.

She wanted to kiss his mouth softly. She wanted to take away his pain. But she held herself back.

"It's all over now," she said quietly and grabbed the bar of soap off the corner shelf. "They can't touch you anymore. They can't hurt you."

Gabe sucked in a ragged breath. His hands clenched into fists as he straightened and stared down at her.

Glancing away, Bee busied herself with other things. She rubbed the bar of soap between her hands, creating suds before replacing it calmly on the shelf.

Reaching first for Gabe's right hand, she brought it between them and gently smoothed at his fingers. He opened his hand for her and let her wash it. In silence, he stood there while she worked the suds up his arm, then switched to the other side.

"No more scrubbing yourself raw," she murmured, her eyes flicking up to his and then back down. He was watching her intently. His brown eyes tracking her hands as they soothed his skin. "If you keep doing this to yourself, then I will, too."

"Bee Bee," Gabe rumbled her name, but she only shook her head.

Continuing on casually, she took her time. Occasionally, she would pick up the bar and make more suds. Her hands traveled over his shoulders, across his muscled chest and down his toned abs.

She stopped short of the V leading to his hips. She didn't want to force her touch on him. She wasn't sure where his head was at.

"I don't blame you," he spoke quietly. "If I were you, I wouldn't touch me there, either."

"What?" Bee's brow furrowed as she peered up into Gabe's face. "You think I don't want you?"

"I told you," Gabe hissed. "You don't know where I've been. I'm tainted."

"And I told *you*," Bee countered. "I know exactly where you've been, because I've been to the same horrible place. Did it make you love me any less?"

"Of course not."

"Then why would it be any different for me?" Bee raised her eyebrows as the water continued to pour down around them. "Can I wash you there? I just want your permission."

Staring down at her, Gabe shifted on his feet before grunting out his answer. "Yes," he said.

Keeping her eyes on his face, Bee worked more suds between her palms before reaching between them and taking him in her hand.

As she worked the soap along his length, Gabe tipped his head back and let out a low groan. His left hand reached out to brace against the yellow tiles of the shower wall. His right hand wrapped around the back of her neck.

"Do you want me to stop?" She asked.

"No." He shook his head. "Don't stop."

So she didn't.

Gripping him tighter, she continued working her hand along his length, listening to him groan, watching his abs tense and ripple.

Between her legs, she felt herself tingling, aching, yearning. It had been so long since they'd been together. She missed him. She missed every single part of him.

"On second thought," Gabe rasped as his head snapped forward and his eyes settled on her face. "You're going to need to stop."

"What?" Bee's brow furrowed, but before she knew what was happening Gabe was picking her up.

Turning to the side, he pressed her back against the wall and slammed his mouth down on hers. She wrapped her legs around his waist and held on as he kissed and licked and nipped at her lips.

"Oh God, I missed you," he whispered, before his tongue danced down to her neck and behind her ear.

Bee moaned, rubbing her breasts against his chest until he was shifting his hips in response. His hand snaked down between them, and his fingers rubbed her in all the right places. If she thought she'd been aching for him before, it was nothing compared to the hot demand now throbbing between her thighs.

"I love you so much," Gabe whispered. His mouth had returned to hers as he lined himself up.

"I love you, too," Bee rushed her response, grinding herself against him.

"Bee Bee," he hissed between kisses, his tongue darting across her lower lip. "Don't ever leave me."

"I won't ever leave you," Bee's response turned into a lingering moan.

In one swift motion, he pushed inside of her. Sensation exploded everywhere. Pleasure rippled and pulsed and hummed all over her body.

It came from down there, where Gabe pulled out, then pushed himself back in. It came from her mouth, where his lips consumed hers. It came from her chest, where his heart hammered for her, just as hers hammered for him. It came from everywhere, lighting her up.

Letting loose another moan, Bee worked her hips against him, asking him for more, faster. Gabe gasped into her mouth as he complied. His eyes scrunched shut as his arms squeezed tighter on either side of her body.

His chest was holding her against the wall. Her breaths were coming in short and tight. All the while he kept working himself inside of her, building pressure. More, then more.

"I'm going to come," Bee panted.

"Me, too," Gabe groaned.

With a jerk, he slammed himself against her. She cried out, pulsing around him as they both found their release.

Gabe's lungs sucked in air, as his face fell to her neck. He murmured quietly against her skin, keeping his hips in place, unwilling to let her go.

"I love you, Gabey," Bee sighed again, running her hands over his back and up into his hair.

"I love you too, Bee Bee," he answered. "We're never going to be apart ever again. Not even for a day."

CHAPTER 43

Gabe

THE COOL BROWN LEATHER OF THE COUCH ENVELOPED HIM. Leaning back into the wide sofa, Gabe flung his arm across Bee's shoulders and pulled her in closer. Her leg ran the length of his leg, her hip settled against his hip, her body tucked into his side. But still… she just wasn't close enough.

Twisting to the side, Gabe wrapped his arms around her waist and yanked her up onto his lap. Burying his face in the smooth skin between her shoulder blades, he inhaled. She was like a drug to him. He needed his hit.

Without missing a beat, Bee swatted at his hands, now pressed against her belly, and kept chatting away to Ava. The petite blonde was sitting on a nearby recliner while a pint-sized toddler tipped and weaved her way across the living room floor.

The baby girl, Nina was her name, stomped her chubby legs over to Finn, who was lying flat on his back, making faces at her. When she came to a stop, towering over him, she gave him a wicked grin before diving head first onto his belly. The serious FBI Agent pretended to groan in pain as his daughter squealed her delight.

"It's going to be bedtime soon," Ava commented dryly.

"Yeah, I know." Finn huffed, hoisting his girl up above his body so she could fly like superman.

"Well, you're riling her up," Ava complained. "It's time to quiet down. Plus, I've got to call Mason, and check how he's doing."

A flatscreen television blared out news on the far wall. Laughter echoed from the nearby kitchen where several Militia members were lingering over their dinner. On the floor, Finn continued to make faces at Nina, who kept her arms spread wide and shrieked.

Brushing a few strands of chestnut hair from Bee's neck, Gabe pressed his lips to her skin. She was casual, wearing a little white tank top and skinny jeans. Screw casual, he thought, she was edible.

"Marry me," he breathed the question out against her back and had her giggling.

"I already said yes," she scolded, looking back over her shoulder at him. "You can't keep asking me."

"I can," Gabe countered and frowned.

Reaching for her left hand, he rubbed his thumb over the spot where a real ring should be sitting. They were stuck at the farmhouse, and it had only been a week since his jail break. His face was still all bruised up (which he did *not* want his kids to see) and catching a flight out of the States was a little sketchy these days, especially if you were a wanted criminal.

So all kidding aside, Gabe hadn't exactly had time to ring

shop. Hell, he hadn't even known he'd get this opportunity to be with Bee again, let alone make her his wife. His. Wife.

His.

He fucking loved the sound of it.

Thankfully, a certain resourceful Federal Agent had provided him with a black permanent marker. When Gabe had drawn a ring around that damn left finger of Bee's, it was the best feeling in the entire world. Even better than when she'd drawn one teasingly on *his* ring finger, and that, admittedly, was a close second.

"Alright baby girl," Finn announced. "Queen Mommy has spoken. Time for bed."

"Noooooooo," Nina wailed as Finn rolled to the side and set her flailing body beside him on the ground.

Shoving up to standing, Finn plucked his daughter up and attempted to cradle her in his arms. She arched and twisted and screamed impressively. Ava sighed and drug a hand down her face.

"Awesome," she mumbled.

"Hey," Finn whispered conspiratorially to his daughter. "I'll sneak you a treat if you're good."

"Tweeet?" Nina's tears dried up instantly and she clung to her father's t-shirt.

"Seriously?" Ava tried to hide her smile.

"Well, Mommy has to call big brother, right?" Finn's dark eyes danced. "It's a win-win."

Frowning, Gabe glanced between them. "You have a son?" He asked.

"Um..." Finn blinked down at Gabe a moment before tipping his chin at Ava.

"It's complicated," Ava offered. "His dad is..."

"Don't even go there," Finn cut her off.

Lifting Nina up over his head, he had her squealing again before striding out of the room and up the stairs. Ava blew out a breath and flopped back into her recliner.

"It's alright." Gabe squeezed Bee tighter, pressing another quick peck to her back. "We get it."

"Speaking of sons..." Bee stroked his arm. "Do you have any news?"

Holding his breath, Gabe shut his eyes. A little over a week ago, Cambric had burned to the ground. Shortly after the release of *The Captive Rising* video, a riot had started in the cafeteria. It spread from there to the courtyard where people were massacred while trying to escape.

The idea that his kids had been in the middle of all that, without anyone to protect them, made Gabe absolutely ill. Two days later, Charlie had managed to get in touch with Ava's underground organization. They, in turn, hooked him back up with Alana, but by that time, the entire state of New York was burning.

There were riots in the streets, shootings, protests on a massive scale. Businesses were boarded up. No one could get groceries or gas.

The last they'd heard of Charlie, he was making his way out of the area on foot. And unfortunately, he didn't have any information about Gabe's kids.

In fact, no one had tabs on Gabe's kids. And how could they? Captives were slipping away, walking out of private residences, businesses, government housing. It was a revolution.

On the video, Gabe had told his fellow captives to take

their freedom if they truly wanted it. Well, the entire country was doing just that. And it was incredibly violent.

"Actually, we think we may have found one." Ava drummed her fingers on her knee. "The underground has him in a safe house where we're keeping a bunch of captive kids until this blows over. We're just not sure if he's yours and there's no way to get DNA done right now…"

"Do you have a picture?" Gabe's eyes flew open and his heart raced in his chest. "I could tell you if he's one of the five Shane had picked out. I'd know their faces anywhere."

"Well, we'd still need to confirm with DNA," Ava trailed off, her brow creasing.

"I don't care about that," Gabe cut in. "Those boys suffered for me. They were beaten and starved because Shane thought they were mine. That *makes* them my children, blood or no blood. Is there anyone else who wants him? A mom, maybe? We'll take her too, if she's willing."

"No." Ava shook her head. "It's just him. I'll get you a picture."

"Thank you." Gabe exhaled a breath and leaned back in the sofa.

Bee tilted back with him, letting her back rest against his chest. He closed his eyes and inhaled her scent. The smell of her calmed him. The weight of her calmed him. Even so, it took several minutes for his pulse to level out.

He had to remind himself it had only been a week or so. They would find the rest of his kids. He only prayed that when they did, they would all be okay.

On the wall, the tv continued to drone. Pictures flashed across the screen as reporters offered commentary. Havana Agency had burned down too, with well over a hundred casualties, most of them children. Free people were screaming their heads off about that one.

The following day, the owners of Sion Hill fled the country. After they left, the staff just opened the doors and let all the captives walk out. Thousands of people were wandering the streets, no place to sleep, nothing to eat, with just the clothes on their backs.

As a result, a few major highways between states had been shut down by the National Guard. The government was trying to control who came and went, but it was only resulting in further conflict.

And now the Constitutional Militia was making its presence known. They'd recently shown up at Ramsey House, which had been taken over by its captives and was currently surrounded by the National Guard. No shots had been fired yet, but the stand off was tense.

Half of the G1s were captives themselves, and with some encouragement from the Militia they'd defected to the other side. The government was losing trained members of its military to the Constitutional Militia every single minute of every single day. And even when the order to shoot defectors on sight was given, not one single shot had been fired.

The free National Guardsmen had been trained and housed for years alongside their captive counterparts. Not one man was willing to shoot his brother in the back for wanting to be free.

As more images flashed across the television screen, Gabe blew out a slow breath.

Downtown Atlanta was on lockdown, with people running through the darkened streets, tossing Malatov cocktails through shattered storefront windows. Then Chicago appeared, where an angry crowd was standing toe to toe with a line of police in full riot gear. Rocks sailed through the air. Then the streets of DC came to life, and it was like looking at the same city, over and over.

Ava grabbed the remote and turned up the volume. The screen went dark a moment before a familiar face flickered into view.

"Jason?" Bee hissed, as she sat up straight on Gabe's lap.

Following suit, Gabe pushed forward and scooted to the edge of the couch, still balancing Bee on his knee.

Jason was standing on top of a building, dressed in a black suit. His right hand was tucked into the pocket of his slacks. Beneath his jacket, his white dress shirt was unbuttoned at the collar. His face looked grim.

Judging by the darkness that surrounded him, it was late into the night. He stood there all alone, save for whoever was shooting the video. It looked like it was being recorded by a cell phone. At his back, the White House could be seen all lit up like a candle.

"Good evening," Jason began. "Some of you may not know me. For those of you that don't, my name is Jason Riggs and I am a Senator from the state of Texas."

Just then, a siren pierced the air. Jason clamped his jaw shut and glanced over his shoulder. Down below him, somewhere the camera couldn't see, a police car or fire truck or ambulance was probably screaming by. He waited for the sound to leave before continuing.

"I, like you, find myself standing in the middle of a country that I no longer recognize," he said. His arctic blue eyes zeroed in on the camera as the person filming took a step closer. "All of a sudden, our homeland has become a scary place. It's hard to know who you can trust. It's hard to know who is a friend and who is an enemy."

Gabe shot a look at Ava, who nodded her head in agreement at the television. She didn't look surprised by Jason's sudden appearance. As she bit at her bottom lip and tapped her fingers on her thigh, she looked more eager than anything else.

"Behind me, a President accused of corruption sits protected in his home," Jason went on. "He has a bill sitting on his desk, waiting for his signature. That bill was passed by politicians that *you*, the people, elected. It passed the House. It passed the Senate."

Pausing, Jason let another siren scream by. He glanced at the ground, then back up into the camera.

"That bill, when signed into law, is going to end all of the chaos and violence you now see around you," he stated. "When the President signs his approval, and all captives, government and otherwise, are officially made free, then the rioting and protesting and looting and murdering *will* stop.

You have nothing to fear from captives. You have nothing to fear from your fellow man. Transitions like these can sometimes be scary, but I assure you that our country remains strong. The Constitutional Militia have stepped up to help us. This organization is one that I promise you, you can trust."

Bee glanced over her shoulder at Gabe and lifted her eyebrows. You hearing this? She seemed to say. Gabe cinched his arms around her waist and drew her closer to him.

"As soon as we can," he murmured against her skin. "We're getting the hell out of here."

Returning her gaze to the television, Bee nodded her head.

It wasn't that Gabe didn't trust Ava or Finn. It wasn't that he didn't owe his life to the Militia, he did.

It was just that this game was deeper and more widespread then he'd imagined. It was a game of power and influence and control. He just needed to get away from it. He needed to take Bee and his kids and get far, far away.

"So I come to you tonight," Jason's voice raised slightly. "Demanding that our President sign the anti-captivity bill that now sits on his desk. Let him put an end to this madness and work together with the Constitutional Militia to bring stability back to our country."

Another siren pierced the air.

Jason gave a slight nod.

And the video cut out.

CHAPTER 44

Val

Six months later - Christmas Holiday in the Maldives

DANGLING HER FEET IN THE CERULEAN BLUE WATER, VAL watched a dozen children splash in the pool. The sun was high overhead, warming her skin and making her sigh. Jace bounced in the shallow end, laughing with a golden haired boy just his same age. He was one of Gabe's. He was one of thirty-two.

Val smiled. Bee was out of her damn mind.

Lifting her face, she leaned back, her hands braced on the edge of the deck. The pool was set over the ocean. The lapping of waves sounded against the nearby shore.

"Who wants a hot dog?!" Gabe called.

Stomping across the deck with a silver platter clutched in his hands, Gabe's eyes traveled over a mere fraction of his brood. Some of the kids were inside the house, watching tv, playing video games, or even reading. A few of the older boys were out on the far end of the dock, their fishing poles sunk in the water, sipping sodas.

"Me! Me! Me!" A chorus of voices exploded.

Scrambling out of the water, six or seven kids made a run at Gabe, who quickly lowered the tray to a nearby table and took a step back.

"No running!" He shouted, then shot Val a wicked grin. "There's plenty more to go around. Just give me a few minutes."

"You asked for this," Val called to him and had Gabe chuckling ruefully.

"I sure did," he admitted, before heading back to his grill to start another round.

"No hot dog for you?" Bee asked, bumping her shoulder playfully against Val's.

They were sitting side by side, enjoying the tropical air. A pair of virgin Pina Coladas rested between them. Val shook her head.

"I think I'll pass," she sighed. "Jason promised to take me out when he gets off this conference call."

"Oooo a date," Bee teased, dipping her head. "Must be nice."

"Sure is," Val agreed. "You guys still good to watch Jace?"

"Absolutely." Bee reached for her drink and sipped it before adding, "What's one more?"

Huffing out a laugh, Val kicked her feet in the water and shook her head. What's one more? That little sentence is what had gotten Bee and Gabe into this mess in the first place.

Kids, upon kids, upon kids. But truth be told, she'd never seen either of them more happy.

"So," Bee ventured. "Everything seems to have calmed down back in the States. Captives are integrating into free life pretty well, all things considered."

"Yeah," Val nodded. "The President stepped down and the Vice President is working closely with the Militia for now. Seems like everything is going alright."

"Is Jason going to move you and Jace back anytime soon?" Bee asked.

"I'm not sure." Val's brow furrowed. "I hate to keep switching schools, and we just settled back into our place in France."

Bobbing her head, Bee pursed her lips and looked out over the water. After a beat she reached for Val's hand and clutched it in her own. Squeezing tight, the two of them held on and enjoyed the peels of laughter and screams of dismay. Kids. So many kids.

"I love you, sister," Bee whispered finally.

"Hey." Val tugged on her hand. "I love you, too."

Behind them, the French doors to the house hung open. Music drifted out as Gabe cruised back and forth, adding more hot dogs to the grill. Jason stepped out beside him and slapped him hard on the shoulder. Gabe turned around and gave him a playful shove.

"You owe me," Jason accused.

"Not a chance rich boy," Gabe countered. "You actually owe me."

"Whatever." Jason brushed him off as his eyes narrowed on his wife.

Val's insides summersaulted, as they always did when Jason looked at her that way. Like he would consume her if he could. Smoothing both hands down the sides of his blue board shorts, Jason crossed to Val and took a seat beside her on the deck.

His legs dangled in the pool and his shoulder bumped hers. For several long moments, the three of them gazed out over the ocean. Bee on her left side, Jason on her right. It was so beautiful here, with the ocean stretching out as far as the eye could see.

"I have news for you," Jason began quietly.

"Oh?" Val glanced to the side and watched his face.

Jason's jaw ticked, and he kept his eyes directed over the water. When Bee made to get up, he cleared his throat and shook his head.

"I sort of think you should stay," Jason explained, and had the two women glancing at one another.

"Alright." Bee ducked her head and sat back down.

"Val…" Jason sucked in a breath and then turned to look at her. "I found your mother."

"What?"

Instinctively, Val reached again for Bee's hand. Finding it, the sisters held on. Jason nodded quickly, his eyes darting over her face.

"I got the DNA results back yesterday, and she's a match," he supplied.

"She's alive?" Val's mouth parted slightly, her heart dipping and soaring all at the same time.

"Yeah, she is." Jason gave her a small smile. "Her name is Evelyn. She's in her late fifties and lives in Canada."

"But… how…"

"After she had you, she was sold to Havana Agency where

she was trained to work as a secretary." Jason explained. "They then sold her as a permanent employee to a small business located in Canada that manufactures linens."

"Linens," Val repeated the last word Jason had said, her brain was reeling from the flood of information.

"Yes, and the owner of that business became quite taken with her." Jason reached for Val's thigh and ran his palm down it. "He signed papers making her legally free, then hired her back full time."

"So…" Val frowned. "My mother. Evelyn…"

"Evelyn," Jason confirmed.

"Is free," Val finished.

"Yes." Jason nodded. "And she would be very interested in meeting you. If you'd let her."

"Oh my God," Val gasped the words as her hand shot up to cover her mouth. Tears formed in her eyes and beside her she could hear Bee crying, too. "I have a mother."

"You do." Jason cleared his throat and nodded his head.

"And I can meet her."

"You can." Jason laughed this time. "Do you want to, baby? I don't want to do anything that you don't want to do."

Pursing her lips, Val nodded her head. Her heart was pounding and the kids were laughing and the music was playing and Gabe was cooking. All around her there was family and love and freedom and life.

"I want to," Val said finally, smiling through her tears. "I want to meet my mom."

"Then you will," Jason said.

Leaning in, he pressed his lips to hers and filled her whole heart with light.

A word from the author:
Book hangover much? I've got the solution.
Have you read about Agent Finn yet???? Come on… he's
worth it. VANISH ME

Want another completed series? Start here—> OUTLASTING
AFTER

Join my ARC Team!
Click on the link: ARC TEAM - LK MAGILL

Sign up for my newsletter…
LK MAGILL NEWSLETTER

Reviews, pretty please…
Each and **every positive review makes a huge difference.** Be
it Amazon, Kobo, iBooks, Barnes and Noble; no matter the
retailer, I read and appreciate them all.

Websites:
Like me on Facebook:
https://fb.me/LKMagill1
Follow me on Instagram:
https://www.instagram.com/lk.magill.author
Check out my Amazon page:
http://amazon.com/author/lkmagill

ALSO BY LK MAGILL

VANISH ME

The Captive Series:

THE CAPTIVE BORN - Book One
THE CAPTIVE MISSING - Book Two
THE CAPTIVE RISING - Book Three

Outlasting Series:
A Post Apocalyptic Romance (*trust me... you'll freaking love it*)

OUTLASTING AFTER - Book One
CHASING TRUTH - Book Two
SURVIVING THE WALL - Book Three
BREAKING BEFORE - Book Four (Coming Spring 2020)